The Edge

Also by Catherine Coulter in Large Print:

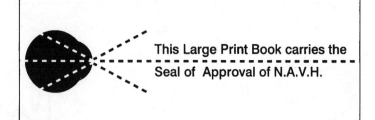

This Large Print Book carries the Seal of Approval of N.A.V.H.

The Edge

Catherine Coulter

Thorndike Press • Thorndike, Maine

Published in 1999 by arrangement with G. P. Putnam's Sons, a member of Penguin Putnam Inc.

This is a work of fiction. The events and characters portrayed are imaginary. Their resemblance, if any, to real-life counterparts is entirely coincidental.

Thorndike Large Print ® Basic Series.

The tree indicium is a trademark of Thorndike Press.

The text of this Large Print edition is unabridged.
Other aspects of the book may vary from the original edition.

Set in 16 pt. Plantin.

Printed in the United States on permanent paper.

Library of Congress Cataloging-in-Publication Data

Coulter, Catherine.
   The edge / Catherine Coulter.
      p. cm.
    ISBN 0-7862-2240-9 (lg. print : hc : alk. paper)
    ISBN 0-7862-2241-7 (lg. print : sc : alk. paper)
    1. Large type books. I. Title.
  PS3553.O843 E33   1999b
   813'.54 21—dc21   99-046182

TO CURRY ECKELHOFF

Incredible competence aside,
you're a wonderful friend,
you've got a great sense of humor,
you're generous to a fault,
and you're a blonde.
    Here's to all of us hanging out in the
Pink Palace.

— *C.C.*

Prologue.

Edgerton, Oregon

The night was black and calm, silent except for the mellow whine of the newly tuned Porsche engine, yet she heard the soft, sobbing voice pleading with her again, whispering low and deep. It never left her alone now.

No one else was near, it was just Jilly driving alone on the coast highway. The ocean stirred beside her, but with no moon out, it looked like an empty, black expanse. The Porsche, sensitive to the slightest touch of her fingers, gently swerved left, toward the cliff, toward the endless expanse of black water beyond. Jilly jerked the car back to the center line.

Laura's voice began sobbing in her brain, then grew louder, filling her, until Jilly wanted to burst.

"Shut up!" Jilly's scream filled the car

for a brief moment. Her voice sounded harsh and ugly. It was nothing like Laura's had been, like a small child's sobbing, lost and inconsolable. Only death would bring peace. Jilly felt that voice, Laura's voice, build inside her again. She gripped the steering wheel and stared straight ahead, praying to herself, chanting for it to stop, for Laura to go away.

"Please," she whispered. "Please stop. Leave me alone. *Please.*"

But Laura didn't stop. She was no longer a child, speaking in a sweet, terrified voice. She was herself again, angry now, and this time foul words frothed from her mouth, spewing rage and saliva that Jilly tasted in the back of her throat. She banged her fists on the steering wheel, hard, harder still, rhythmically, to make the malevolent voice go away. She opened the window, pressed it all the way down and leaned out, letting the wind tear her hair back, and her eyes sting and water. She shouted into the night, "Make it stop!"

It stopped. Suddenly.

Jilly drew a deep breath and pulled her head back into the car. The wind whooshed through the car and she sucked in mouthfuls of the cold air. It tasted wonderful. It was over. Thank God, finally it had stopped. She raised her head, looking around, wondering where she was. She'd been driving for hours, it seemed, yet the dashboard clock read only midnight. She'd been gone from home for a half hour.

Her life had become whispers and screams until she couldn't bear it. Now there was silence, deep and complete silence.

Jilly began counting. *One, two, three* — no curses, no whispers, no small child's pleading, nothing, just her own breathing, the soft hum of her car. She threw back her head and closed her eyes a moment, relishing the silence. She began counting again. *Four, five, six* — still blessed silence.

Seven, eight — soft, very soft, like a faraway rustling of leaves, coming closer, closer. Not rustling, no, whispering. Laura was whispering again, begging not to die, begging and pleading and swearing she'd never meant to sleep with him, but it had just happened, he'd made it happen. But Jilly hadn't believed her.

"Please, stop, stop, stop," Jilly chanted over that feathery voice. Laura began screaming that Jilly was a pathetic bitch, a fool who couldn't see what she was. Jilly stomped down on the gas pedal. The Porsche lurched forward, hitting seventy, eighty, eighty-five. The coast road swerved.

She kept the car directly in the center of the road. She began singing. Laura screamed louder, and Jilly sang louder. Ninety. Ninety-five.

"Go away. *Damn you, go away!*" Jilly's knuckles were white on the steering wheel, her head low, her forehead nearly touching the rim. The engine's vibrations made Laura's screaming voice convulse with power.

One hundred.

Jilly saw the sharp turn, but Laura yelled that they would be together soon now, very soon. She couldn't wait to get Jilly, and then they'd see who would win.

Jilly screamed, whether at Laura or at the sight of the cliff dropping some forty feet to the heaped and tumbled black rocks below. The Porsche plunged through the railing, thick wood and steel, picking up speed, and shot out to the vast empty blackness beyond.

One more scream rent the silence before the Porsche sliced nose first through the still, black water. There was scarcely a sound, just the fast downward plunge, the sharp, clean impact, then the quick shifting and closing over, the calm water returning to what it had been just a second before.

Then there was only the black night. And calm and silence.

1

Bethesda Naval Hospital Maryland

I jerked upright in bed, clutched at my neck, and doubled over as a god-awful pain ripped through me. I'd heard a man yell, just beside me, nearly right in my ear. I couldn't draw a breath, I was suffocating. And a guy who wasn't even there was yelling at me and I was dying. I finally managed to heave inward and suck in a huge breath.

I'd felt a mountain of frigid water crash down on me like the whale had closed down over Jonah. But I wasn't drowning. I knew what drowning was, remembered it as clearly as if it had happened yesterday. I was seven years old, swimming with my older brother, Kevin, who was flirting with some young girls. I'd gotten tangled up in some underwater branches. It had been Jilly who'd jerked me out, smacked my back hard as I'd gagged and choked, until water gushed out of my mouth.

The dream wasn't like that. It was as if I'd been hit by that water just a moment before there was, quite simply, nothing. Nothing at all. Just stillness, no pain, no questions, no fear, just an utter blank.

I swung my legs over the bed and stamped them hard on the ancient linoleum, savoring the sluice of pain that rumbled through my shoulder, my ribs, my collarbone, my right thigh, and other parts of me that were healing well enough so that gradually I'd dropped them out of my inventory. That delicious sharp pain brought me fully into my favorite hospital room, planted me firmly in the here and now, out from under water in a nightmare that had left me being nothing at all.

Still, when my feet hit the linoleum, the shock of the impact punched me back, and I nearly fell. I grabbed the bed railing at the head of the bed, took a deep breath, and looked around. My feet were still on the floor, flat on off-white linoleum that I'd come to hate in the past two weeks as much as those pastel green and tan walls. Leave it to the military to pick those colors. But you couldn't hate when you were dead, so I was glad there was something there to prove to me that I was alive.

I'd been lucky, they'd told me. The blast hadn't zeroed in on my heart or my head or anything vital. It was like I'd gotten hit by a two-by-four all over — a bit smashed here, a bone broken there, a muscle twisted out down lower. My feet and my back had escaped, with just faint bruises marching up my spine. The explosion missed my groin too, for which I was profoundly grateful.

I just stood there by my bed, breathing and savoring all the air that was here, all of it mine.

I looked down at my messed-up bed. I wasn't about to fall back into that bed because I knew the dream still hovered, just beyond in the ether, much too close, waiting for me to sleep again. I wasn't about to. I stretched, slowly and carefully. Still, every move brought a jab of pain from somewhere in my body. I breathed in deeply and walked slowly to the window of my hospital room. I was in the newer hospital, built in 1980, a massive building attached to the original hospital, built sometime in the 1930s. Everyone there complained about having to walk miles to get anywhere. I wished I could walk even a part of a mile, and complain with them.

I saw a few starburst dots of light from the five-level open parking building across the way. The parking building as well as half a dozen support buildings were connected to the hospital by long corridors. I couldn't see more than a dozen parked cars from where I stood. Lights spiked up from lamps set at close intervals throughout the landscaped grounds. There were lights even in among the trees. My law enforcement instincts told me there were no places for a mugger to hide — too many lights.

There hadn't been any lights at all in the dream, just darkness, wet darkness. I walked slowly to the small bathroom, leaned over very carefully, cupped my hands under the water tap at the sink, and drank deeply. As I straightened, water ran down my chin and dripped onto my chest. I had dreamed I was drowning and yet my throat felt drier than that wool-parched, blistering air in Tunisia. It made no sense.

Unless I hadn't been the one drowning. Suddenly, deep down, I knew. I hadn't been the one to drown, but I'd been there, right there.

I looked around expecting someone to be there, close to me, right behind me, ready to tap me on the shoulder. For over two weeks since I'd been pounded into the desert sand by the bomb blast, there was always someone there just beside me, speaking quietly to me, jabbing me with needles, endless numbers of needles. My arms ached from all the shots and my butt was still numb in places.

I drank more water, then slowly raised my head, careful as always not to move too quickly. I stared at the man in the mirror above the sink. I looked like oatmeal, gray and collapsed, like I wasn't really alive. I was used to seeing a big guy, but the person staring back at me wasn't at all substantial. He looked like a lot of big bones strung together. I grinned at him. At least I still had my teeth, and they were still straight. I felt lucky my teeth hadn't been blown out when that bomb exploded and hurled me like a bag of feathers some fifteen feet across desert sand.

When my friend Dillon Savich, another FBI agent, saw me in the gym, he'd probably just shake his head and ask me where I'd stashed my coffin. I knew it would take a good six months before I could go toe-to-toe with Savich again and have a slim prayer of holding my own with him at the gym.

I took a deep breath, drank more water,

and switched off the bathroom light. The figure in the mirror was shadowy now. He looked a lot better that way. I stepped back into the bedroom, to the stark outline of the single bed and the huge red digital numbers on the clock some friends had brought me, wrapped with a bright crimson ribbon. I looked at the clock. It was just seven minutes after three A.M. I remembered Savich's wife, Sherlock, also an FBI agent, telling me when I was floating between pain and the oblivion of morphine that every minute that clicked by on the clock meant I was that much closer to getting out of this place and back to work where I belonged.

I walked back to the bed and slowly lowered myself down on my back. I pulled up the single sheet and thin blanket with my left hand. I tried to relax, to settle and ease my muscles. I wasn't about to go to sleep again. I closed my eyes and tried to think logically and clearly about the dream. Yes, I'd felt water, but not really drowning, just a shock of water pouring into me. Just a taste of water. Then nothing at all.

I raised my left hand and rubbed my fist over my chest. At least my heart had calmed down. I pulled in more deep breaths and told myself to stop the drama crap and think. Think cold, that was the rule at the Academy. I had to stop the panic and think cold.

It took me another couple of minutes to wonder whether it hadn't been a dream at all, but something else. As clearly as I saw the face of the digital clock on the utility stand beside my bed, I remembered seeing Jilly's face.

I didn't like that at all. That was nuts, plain nuts. A strange dream where I was drowning, only not really, and for some reason Jilly was back there somewhere in my brain. I'd last seen Jilly at Kevin's home in Chevy Chase, Maryland, at the end of February. She'd acted a little strange, no other way to put it, but I hadn't really paid all that much attention, just tucked it away. Too much other stuff going on in my life, like going to Tunisia.

I remembered talking to Kevin about Jilly the day after she had flown in from Oregon. Kevin, my older brother, had just shaken his head. Living on the West Coast was making Jilly a little eccentric, and don't worry about it. Nothing more than that. Kevin was career army, had four boys and not a whole lot of time to be thinking about the oddities of his three siblings. It had been just the four of us for eight years now, since our parents died in a car accident, hit by a drunk driver.

I remembered Jilly droning on about all sorts of things — her new Porsche, her dress that she'd bought at Langdon's in Portland, some girl called Cal Tarcher she didn't seem to like, and the girl's brother, Cotter, who Jilly had thought was a vicious bully. She'd even gone on and on about how good sex was with Paul, her husband of eight years. There didn't seem to be any particular point to any of it as far as I could see. Now what she'd said seemed more than just simply eccentric.

Was Jilly drowning in my dream?

I didn't want to let that thought dig itself into my brain, but it had weaseled in with that dream, and it wouldn't leave now. I was tired, but not quite as tired as just the day before or the day before that. I was mending. The doctors would nod their heads and smile at each other, then at me, patting my unbruised right shoulder. They had talked about letting me go home next week. I decided I would make it sooner.

I knew I wasn't going back to sleep, not with that dream waiting for me, and I knew it was waiting, certain of it. I knew it was waiting because it didn't really feel like

18

a dream, it was something else. I had to deal with this.

I decided then and there that I'd give my right nut for a beer. I didn't think it through, just pushed the call buzzer. In four minutes, according to my digital clock with its big red numbers, Midge Hardaway, my night nurse, stuck her head in the door.

"Mac? You okay? It's really late. You should be asleep. What's the problem?"

Midge was somewhere in her thirties, tall, with short honey-colored hair and a sharp chin. She was smart, reliable; you could count on her in a crunch. Whenever I'd drifted back to consciousness at the beginning of my stay here, she'd be right beside me, talking quietly to me, her fingers lightly stroking my arm.

I smiled at her with what I hoped was my best boyish smile, filled with irresistible charm. I wasn't sure she could even see it because the room was very dim, the only light coming from the corridor at her back. But I hoped she could at least hear all the effort I was putting into my voice. "Midge, save me. I'm in bad shape here. I just can't stand it any longer. Please, you've gotta help me. You're my only hope."

The corridor light framed a smile that

was at once sympathetic and filled with laughter that she didn't bother to hide quite enough. Then she cleared her throat. "Mac, listen to me now. You've been out of commission for over two weeks. I guess since you're feeling better, this could become more and more of a problem. But hey, hon, I'm married. What would Doug think? He's got this temper, you know?"

Forget boyish charm. I tried for pathetic. "Why would Doug care? He isn't here. He wouldn't even have to know if you think it would upset him, which I can't begin to imagine that it would."

"Now, Mac, if I weren't married, I'd be truly tempted, even though you're not even close to batting a thousand yet in the health department. Hey, I'm flattered. You're good-looking, at least you were in that photo they used of you in the newspaper, and you've got the use of both hands now. But the way things stand, Mac, I just can't do it."

"I'm really dying here, Midge. I'm not lying to you. Just this one time and I won't beg again — well, at least not until tomorrow night. Just one, Midge. I'll go slow. I've already got drool pooling in my mouth."

She stood there just shaking her head

back and forth, her hands on her hips, very nice hips I'd noticed nine days ago when I finally wasn't so dulled from painkillers. I sighed. "All right, if it's really against your ethics, or Doug's ethics. But I'll tell you, Midge, I just don't see why it's such a big deal. And why your husband would care is beyond me. He'd probably be begging just like I am if he was in my bed. Hey, maybe you could call Mrs. Luther. She's tough, but maybe she'll give in. I think she likes me, just maybe —"

"Mac, are you nuts? Mrs. Luther is sixty-five years old. For God's sake, you can't be all that desperate. Ellen Luther? She'd probably bite you."

"Why would she do that? What are you talking about?"

"Mac," she said with great patience, "you're horny after two weeks of celibacy. I can understand that. But Mrs. Luther?"

"I think you've got the wrong idea here, Midge. I don't want Mrs. Luther. I want you in that way, but you're married, so I only think about that in passing, like any other guy would, you know, maybe once every five minutes or so during the day, maybe more the better I feel. No, what I'm dying for, what I want more than anything in the world, is a beer."

"A beer?" She stared at me for the longest time, then she started laughing. That laughter of hers grew until she had to come into the room and close the door so she wouldn't disturb other patients. She was doubled over with laughter, holding her sides. "You want a beer? That's what all this is about? A damned beer? And you'll go real slow?"

I gave her my innocent look.

She paused a moment in the open doorway, shaking her head and still laughing. Said over her shoulder, "You want a Bud Light?"

"I'd kill for a Bud Light."

The Bud can was so cold I thought my fingers would stick to it. There couldn't be anything better than this, I thought, as the beer slid down my throat. I wondered which nurse was hoarding the Bud in the nurses' refrigerator. I drank half the can in one long slug. Midge was standing beside the bed, just looking down at me. "I hope mixing the beer with your meds doesn't make you puke. Hey, slow down. You promised you'd make it last. Men, you really can't believe them, not when it comes to beer."

"It's been a long time," I said, licking beer foam off my mouth. "I just couldn't help myself. The edge is off now." I heaved a thankful sigh and took a smaller drink, realizing that she wasn't likely to get me another beer. At least the terror of that nightmare was deep below the surface again, not sitting right there on my shoulder, waiting to whisper in my ear again. I had about a quarter of a can left. I rested it on my stomach.

Midge had moved next to me and now she was taking my pulse.

"My neighbor, Mr. Kowalski, waters my plants when I'm out of town or in the hospital, like now. He also keeps things dusted. He's a retired plumber, older than the paint on my great-aunt Silvia's house, and real sharp. James Quinlan — he's an FBI agent — he sings to his African violets. Healthiest critters you've ever seen. His wife wonders when she'll wake up some morning to find some plants cozying up to her in bed. Oh shit, Midge, I want to go home."

She lightly cupped my face against her palm. "I know, Mac. Soon now. Your pulse is just fine. Now, let me take your blood pressure." She didn't tell me what it was, but she hummed under her breath, something from Verdi, I think, and that meant it was good. "You need to go back to sleep,

Mac. Is your stomach happy with the beer? No nausea?"

I took the last pull of beer, kept the burp in my throat, and gave her a big smile. "I'm fine. I owe you, Midge, big time."

"I'll collect sometime, don't you worry. Your plants sound great. Hey, how about I get Mrs. Luther for you?"

I whimpered, and she left me alone, grinning and waving at me from the doorway. In the next instant, Jilly's face slammed back into my mind.

"You've got to face it, Mac," I said very quietly to myself in the still night, looking toward the window that gave onto the nearly empty parking lot. "All right. Let's just say it out loud. Was that a dream or some kind of prophecy? Is Jilly in some sort of trouble?"

No, that was bullshit. I knew bullshit.

I didn't go back to sleep. Truth was I was too scared. I wished I had another beer. Midge dropped by at four A.M., frowned at me, and shoved a sleeping pill down my throat.

At least I didn't dream for the three hours they gave me before the guy with the blood cart came by, shook my bruised shoulder to wake me up, and shoved a needle in my vein, all the while telling me that just before the turn of the millennium, when all the computers are going to implode, he is going to move to Montana and buy a generator and a gun. He never paused in his talk, slapped down a Band-Aid hard over the hole in my arm, and whistled as he pushed his torture cart out of my room. His name was Ted and he was, I thought, what the shrinks call a situational sadist.

At ten o'clock that morning, I simply couldn't wait any longer. I had to know. I dialed Jilly's number in Edgerton, Oregon. Her husband, Paul, answered the phone on the second ring.

"Jilly," I said, and knew my voice wasn't steady. "Paul, how's Jilly?"

Silence.

"Paul?"

I heard a shuddering breath, then, "She's in a coma, Mac."

I felt an odd settling deep inside me, the slow unfolding of the package whose contents I already knew. I hadn't wanted this, but it hadn't really surprised me at all. I prayed as I asked, "Will she live?"

I could hear Paul fiddling with the phone cord, probably twisting it over and over his hand. Finally he said in a dead voice, "Nobody wants to even take a guess,

Mac. The doctors did a CAT scan and an MRI. They say there's hardly any damage to her brain, just some tiny hemorrhages and some swelling, but nothing to account for the coma. They just don't know. They hope she'll come out of it really soon. Bottom line, we have to wait and see. First you getting blown up in some godforsaken place, and now Jilly in this ridiculous accident."

"What happened?" But I knew, yeah, I knew.

"Her car went over a cliff on the coast road last night, just after midnight. She was driving the new Porsche that I gave her for Christmas. She'd be dead if a highway patrolman hadn't been passing by. He saw the whole thing, said she just seemed to let the car drift, then speeded up through the railing. He said the Porsche made a perfect nosedive into the water. The water isn't more than fifteen to twenty feet where she went over. The Porsche headlights were still on, thank God, and the driver's side window was open. He got her out on his first try, a pure miracle, he said. No one can believe he managed it, that she's still alive. I'll call you as soon as something changes — either way. I'm sorry, Mac, real sorry. Are you feeling better?"

"Yes, much better," I said. "Thank you, Paul. I'll be in touch." I laid the receiver gently back into its cradle. Paul had evidently been too upset even to wonder why I'd called him specifically about Jilly, at seven o'clock in the morning, West Coast time, the very morning after the accident. I wondered when Paul would think of it, wondered when he'd call me, asking about it.

At that moment, I didn't have a clue what I'd tell him.

2

"Mac, for God's sake, what are you doing out of bed? No way the doctors said you could leave. Just look at you. You don't look so hot. Your face is as gray as dingy old curtains."

Lacy Savich, known to everyone in the Bureau as "Sherlock," began shoving my chest lightly, pushing me back toward the bed. I'd managed to get my legs into a pair of jeans and had been in the middle of fighting with a long-sleeved shirt when she came in.

"Back into bed, Mac. You're not going anywhere. How'd you get those jeans on?" Sherlock tucked herself under my armpit, trying to turn me around, trying to force me down on that damned bed.

I stopped and she couldn't move me. "Listen, I'm all right, Sherlock. Let me go.

I don't want you under my bare arm. I haven't had a shower yet."

"You're not that ripe. I'm not moving until you at least sit down and tell me what's going on."

"Okay, I'll sit," I said, and truth be told, it was a good thing I planned to sit quickly, though not on that bed. "Oh, all right. If you insist, Sherlock." I smiled down at her. She was a small woman with a head of thick, curly red hair, confined this morning at the back of her neck with a gold clip. She had the whitest skin and the prettiest smile that was warm and sweet unless she was in her mean mode, when she could chew metal if it came right down to it. We'd come into the Bureau at the same time, all of two years ago now.

She managed a surprising amount of my weight, walking lock-step, veering sideways so she could push me down onto a hospital chair. Once I was seated I grinned up at her, remembering the two of us going up the ropes in our final physical exam at the Academy. I hadn't known if she'd be able to do it or not, and I hadn't been about to leave her. I'd hung beside her, encouraging her, calling her names, insulting her at a fine clip until she finally made it all the way up the rope with those skinny arms of hers. Sherlock didn't have a lot of upper-body strength, but she had something a whole lot better — guts and heart. She was more fond of me than I probably deserved.

"You're going to talk to me. The doctors are shaking their heads. They've already called your boss and I'll betcha they'll be here ready to roll you into the floor if you take so much as one step toward that door. Here's reinforcements. Dillon, come here and help me figure out what's eating Mac. Look, he's even got his pants on."

Dillon Savich raised a dark brow at that, his expression saying quite clearly to me, *The shit better have his pants on.*

I settled back in the chair. What difference did five minutes make? I'd still be out of here soon enough. Besides, it was best that some of my friends knew what was going on.

"Look, guys, I've got to go home and pack. I've got to fly out to Oregon. My sister was in an accident last night. She's in a coma. I can't stay here."

Sherlock knelt beside the chair and took one of my big hands between hers. "Jilly? She's in a coma? What happened?"

I closed my eyes against immediate memories of that demented dream, or whatever it had been. "I called Oregon early this morning," I said. "Her husband Paul told me."

Sherlock cocked her head to one side and studied me for a moment. Then she asked, "Why'd you call her?"

Sherlock not only had heart and guts, she had this brain that could accelerate electrons.

Savich was still standing by the open doorway, looking fit and big and tough. His eyes were on his wife, Sherlock, who was just looking up at me, waiting for me to strip open my guts for her, which I was about to do. No contest.

"Just sit back and close your eyes, Mac, that's right. I won't let anyone bother you. I wish I had some of Dillon's private reserve whiskey from Kentucky. It would mellow you out quicker than Sean can get Dillon up with his best yell."

"That didn't make a whole lot of sense, Sherlock, but let me tell you that Midge brought me a beer last night," I said. "I didn't puke. It tasted really good." An understatement. I couldn't imagine sex being better than that one Bud Light.

"I'm so happy for you," Sherlock said, and patted my cheek. And waited. I watched her look over at her husband, standing there just inside the hospital room, all calm and relaxed, his arms crossed over his chest. It was a pity that there weren't more like him at the Bureau, instead of the clone bureaucrats who were too afraid to do anything that hadn't been sanctioned for at least a decade. I hated it when I saw it, prayed I wouldn't turn out to be like that in the years to come. Maybe I had a chance not to be, in the Counter-Terrorism section. The bureaucrats did their thing in Washington, but in the field the rules fell away. You were on your own, or at least you were if you were on the ground with a terrorist group in Tunisia.

"A dream," I said finally. "It started with a dream last night. I dreamed about drowning, or about someone drowning. I think it was Jilly." I told them everything I could remember, which was nearly all of it. I shrugged and said, "That's why I called so early this morning. I found out the dream, or whatever it was, had happened. She's in a coma." What is that going to mean? I wondered yet again. Will she live but be a vegetable? Will we have to decide whether or not to unplug her?

"I'm scared," I said, looking at Sherlock. "More scared than I've ever been in my life. Facing those terrorists with only a

.450 Magnum Express wasn't even in the same ballpark. Getting blown into the air in that car explosion didn't come close to this, trust me."

"You wasted two of them, Mac," Savich said, "including the leader, and you would have been blown into a thousand pieces if it hadn't been for a bit of luck — the angle of the blast was sharper than they intended — and a well-placed sand dune."

I paused a moment, then nodded. "That I understand, but I don't understand this dream; it's just plain scary. I felt her hit the water. I felt pain, then nothing, like I was dead.

"I was with her, or I was her, or something. It's crazy, but I can't pretend it didn't happen. I've got to go to Oregon. Not next week or even in two days. I've got to go today."

Because Sherlock was right here with me, because I was so scared I wanted to howl and cry at the same time, I leaned over and pulled Sherlock up against my good side. One skinny little arm came around my neck. I felt tears clog my throat, but I wasn't about to let them out. I'd never live that one down, even if neither of them told a single soul. No, I just held her close, felt that soft hair of hers tease my nose. I looked over at Savich. The two of them had been married a year and a half. I'd been Sherlock's Man of Honor at their wedding. Savich was well known and well liked in the Bureau. Both Savich and Sherlock were in the CAU, the Criminal Apprehension Unit, headed by Savich, who'd created the unit some three years before. I managed to get myself together and said, "You've got a good one here, Savich."

"Yeah, on top of everything else, she gave me the neatest little kid in all of Washington. You haven't seen Sean since he was a month old, Mac. It's time you did. He's pushing five months."

"I'll get over as soon as I can."

"See that you do. Hey, Sherlock, you okay? Don't worry about Mac. He'll go to Oregon and see what the hell's going on. We'll be here if he needs backup, not more than a five-hour plane ride away.

"Mac, are you sure you're ready to climb back onto your horse? You still look a bit on the weedy side. How about coming to stay with us for a couple of days before you take off? We'll put you next to the baby's room. Too bad you can't breast-feed. That would make up for us having to take care of you."

As it turned out, I ended up staying at the hospital for another day and a half until, frankly, I couldn't stand it anymore. I spoke to Paul twice a day. There was no change in Jilly's condition. The doctors were still saying there was nothing they could do but just wait and see. Kevin and his boys were in Germany, and my sister Gwen, a buyer for Macy's, was in Florida. I told them I'd keep them posted as often as I could.

I flew west that Friday, on an early morning flight from Washington Dulles. I rented a light blue Ford Taurus at the Portland International Airport without much hassle, which was always a pleasant surprise in my experience.

It was a beautiful day, not a hint of humidity, no rain clouds, a mild seventy degrees with a light breeze. I'd always liked the West Coast, especially Oregon with its raw, wild mountains and deep-cut gorges with rapids roaring through them. And the ocean, sweeping against the coast for some three hundred miles, all of it savage and magnificent.

I took my time, knowing my physical limits, not wanting to feel like I was going to fall down in a dead heap. I stopped at a

Wendy's in Tufton, a little town near the coast. I saw the sign to Edgerton off Highway 101 an hour and a half later. There was only a spur west, 101W, a narrow paved road that ran four miles to the ocean. Unlike the scores of towns that were bisected by the coast highway, Edgerton was luckily situated west when they'd decided to take the highway more inland to the east. There were a few signs advertising three bed and breakfasts. The BUTTERCUP B&B sign was the biggest, shaped like a psychedelic flower and painted purple and yellow, announcing that it was right on the edge of the cliff, and showed a gothic structure that looked bleak and menacing on the billboard. If I remembered correctly, Paul had told me once that the folk here in Edgerton called it the Psycho B&B. There was another sign for a small diner called The Edwardian, claiming to have the best British cuisine, something I thought must be an oxymoron, based on my culinary experience during my year at the London School of Economics.

I remembered there had once been a small hotel on the narrow strip of beach at Edgerton, but it had been washed away during a winter storm in 1974. I tried to imagine such a thing and couldn't. I remembered the movie where a tsunami at least a million feet high had taken out Manhattan, and grinned. I remembered wondering if the Indians would be interested in buying back the island after that. I stuck my head out the window and smelled the ocean, tart and clean and salty. I loved the smell, felt something expand inside me anytime I was close to the sea. I sucked in that wonderful sticky, salty air. That really deep breath hurt me just a bit, nothing close to what it would have done if I'd tried it a week ago.

I slowed the Ford down to navigate a deep pothole. My brother-in-law, Paul Bartlett, Jilly's husband, was a man I didn't know all that well even though he and Jilly had been married for eight years now. They'd wed right after she'd gotten her master's degree in pharmacology. Paul had finished his Ph.D. the year before. He'd grown up in Edgerton, gone back east to Harvard. He'd always seemed to me a bit standoffish, a bit of a cold fish, but who really knew what another person was like? I remembered Jilly telling me how great sex with him was. No cold fish I knew of was into that.

I'd been surprised when six months

before, Jilly had called to tell me that she and Paul were moving back to Edgerton, leaving Philadelphia and the pharmaceutical firm — VioTech — where both of them had spent the past six years of their professional lives. "Paul isn't happy here," she'd said. "They won't let him continue with his research. He's really into it, Mac." But what about you? I'd asked her. There'd been a brief pause, then she'd said, "My clock is running out, Mac. We want a child. I'm going to lie low for a while and we're going to try to get me pregnant. We've discussed this thoroughly and we're sure. We're going back to The Edge." I smiled a bit, thinking of that name. She'd told me a long time ago, before she and Paul were married, that Edgerton had been discovered by an English naval lieutenant, Davies Edgerton, way back toward the end of the eighteenth century. The name had been corrupted over the years by the locals to the point that most of its denizens now just called it The Edge.

I was nearly there. The four-mile drive to the ocean was rough, and that was why the engineers had swung the highway to the east. There were deep ravines and hillocks, a wide gully with a bridge over it, some stunted pine and oak trees, and at least a dozen potholes that looked like they hadn't seen maintenance since World War II. There was little greenery yet, too early in the spring. A sign said EDGERTON — FIFTY FEET ABOVE SEA LEVEL AND 602 RESIDENTS. My favorite resident was in the Tallshon Community Hospital, some ten miles north of Edgerton, in a coma.

Jilly, I thought, my fingers tightening on the steering wheel, did you go off that damned road on purpose? If you did, why?

3

I was deep inside myself and it was comforting. When I first realized I wasn't dead, I was shocked. How could I have survived? I'd whipped the Porsche right off the cliff, hanging, hanging, before it plunged clean as a stabbing knife through that black, still water.

Then I didn't remember anything at all.

I couldn't feel my body and perhaps that was a good thing. I knew there were people around me, whispering as people do around those badly hurt, but I couldn't make out their words. It was odd, but they weren't really there, just hovering, insubstantial shadows. Like the shadows, I was here too, but not really. If only I could have heard and understood what they were saying. Now that would have been delicious.

At last I was alone. Completely alone. Laura wasn't here with me. Laura, I prayed, had gotten her revenge when I'd screamed like a madwoman and driven off the cliff. If she had come back with me, I thought I'd simply make myself stop breathing.

People came and went. I had no particular interest in any of them. I suppose they examined me and did things to me, but nothing really mattered at all.

Then suddenly everything changed. My brother Ford walked through the door and I saw him clearly. He was real, he had substance and an expression that was so filled with fear that I would have given quite a lot to be able to reassure him, but of course I couldn't. He was big and good-looking, my little brother, better-looking even than our father, who'd been a lady killer, our mother had always said fondly. Mother and Father were dead, weren't they?

Ford didn't look quite himself. Perhaps not as buff, not as commanding, not as massive. Hadn't he been hurt or something? I didn't know, couldn't grasp much of anything. But Ford was here, I was sure of that. I also knew that I was the only one who called him Ford and not Mac. He'd never been Mac to me.

How was this possible? He was here and I could see him, but I couldn't make out any of the others.

If I could have shouted to him, I would

have. But I couldn't move, couldn't really feel anything at all except this quiet joy that my brother had come when I needed him.

I was shocked again when I heard him say close to my face, "Jilly, my God, Jilly, I can't bear this. What happened?"

I clearly heard his words, understood them. I was even more shocked when I felt — actually felt — his big hands covering one of mine; I'm not sure which one. I felt a shot of warmth from him, and the warmth stayed with me. It was remarkable. I didn't know what to think. How had Ford come so clearly to me when none of the others had? Why Ford and no one else?

"I know you can't answer me, Jilly, but perhaps somewhere deep inside, you can hear me."

Oh, yes, I wanted to tell him, I can hear you, yes I can. I loved his voice: deep, resonant, and mesmerizing. I think I'd told him once how much his voice warmed me to my toes. He'd told me it was his FBI interviewing voice, but that wasn't right. He'd always had that intimate, soothing voice.

He sat down beside me, always talking, deeply and slowly, never letting go of my hand, and the warmth of his hand was dizzying. How I wished that I could at least squeeze his fingers.

"I was with you, Jilly," he said, and I nearly stopped breathing.

What did he mean?

With me where?

"I was with you that night. Scared the shit out of me. I woke up in the hospital sweating my toenails off, so scared I thought I'd die. I went over the cliff with you, Jilly. I believed at first that I died with you, but neither of us died. That highway patrolman saved you. Now I've got to find out how this could have happened. Damnation I wish I knew if you could hear me."

Ford paused, still staring down at me, and I wished with everything in me that I could give him some sort of sign, but I couldn't. I was just a lump lying there in that hospital bed that was probably very uncomfortable, if I could have felt it. I wasn't anything really but my brain and one of my hands that he was holding.

What did he mean that he'd been there with me going over the cliff? That didn't make any sense, not that anything happening right now made any sense.

A white shadowy figure came into my line of vision. Ford patted my hand, pressed it down against the bed. He walked to the figure and said, "Paul, I just arrived. I was talking to Jilly."

Paul. He was here in my room. I couldn't understand what he was saying to Ford, but from Ford's long silence, he must have been saying quite a lot. He and Ford moved away from me and I couldn't even hear Ford speaking anymore. I wanted more than anything for Paul to leave, but he didn't. What was he saying to Ford? I wanted my brother back. He was my only connection to what was real, what was out there beyond myself.

After a while I gave up and went to sleep. Before I slept I prayed that Ford wouldn't leave me here alone, that he would come back to me. I felt great sorrow for my Porsche, lying there at the bottom of the ocean, seafood now.

I pulled the Ford into one of the six empty parking spaces in front of the Buttercup Bed and Breakfast, a whimsical name for the ugly, gothic Victorian house that was hanging nearly off the edge of the cliff. There couldn't have been more than twenty feet between the house and a thick stone wall that you could jump off of directly down to a narrow strip of rocky beach a good forty feet below.

Just as whimsical was the name of the main street in Edgerton — Fifth Avenue. The one time I'd been here before, I'd laughed my head off. Fifth Avenue, with four parallel streets running on either side of it, dead-ending at the cliffs, bisecting streets running north and south a good distance each way.

Nothing much had changed as far as I could see.

There were small cottages dating from the 1920s lined up like pastel boxes along Fifth Avenue. Ranch-style homes from the sixties sprawled, with larger plots of land along the back streets. Wood and glass contemporary homes, the immigrant style from California, perched on higher ground lining the cliffs, while others dotted the shallow valleys that dipped away from the water. There were still a few odd shacks and cottages tucked in among the thick stands of spruce, cedar, and western hemlock.

I went into the Buttercup B&B and was told by a thin woman who sported a line of black hair above her upper lip that they had no vacancies. I thought about all the empty parking spaces out front, saw absolutely no one at all in the house, and said to the woman who was standing behind a stretch of shiny mahogany, looking wary and stubborn, "Busy time of year, hmm?"

"There's a convention in town," she said, turned pink, and studied the wall behind my left shoulder, papered with huge Victorian cabbage roses.

"A convention in Edgerton? Maybe they moved the Rose Bowl up here?"

"Oh, no, these aren't florists, they're, well, most of them are dentists, orthodontists, I believe, from all over the country. Sorry, sir."

I wondered what was considered the low season in Edgerton as I walked back to my car. Why hadn't the woman wanted me to stay there? Had it gotten around already that an FBI guy was in town? Nobody wanted a cop hanging around? It seemed to me that I was the safest customer to have sleeping in your house.

I turned left off Fifth Avenue and drove north up Liverpool Street, a steep winding road that ran parallel to 101 for a good ten miles before swerving eastward to join up once again with the highway. There were new houses along this stretch, spread far apart, most tucked discreetly out of sight from the chance runner or driver. At a particularly lovely spot, I saw a small hill that rose up some fifty yards back from the cliff. The hill was covered with spruce and cedar. At its base there sat a large dark red brick house. Except for a narrow driveway, the house was surrounded by dozens of trees, the outer perimeter trees partially stunted, leaning inward, battered by storms off the sea.

It was 12 Liverpool, Paul and Jilly's house. It couldn't have been built more than three or four years before. If I hadn't been looking for it I wouldn't have seen it.

I was surprised how much it looked like their home back in Philadelphia. It was then I saw a police car parked across the street from the house.

I pulled into the empty driveway, wondering how much longer Paul would be at the hospital. I walked to the cop car, a white four-door Chrysler with green lettering on the side: SHERIFF.

I stuck my head in the open passenger window. "What's up? You here to see Paul?"

She was a woman in her late twenties, wearing a beautifully pressed tan uniform, a wide black leather belt at her waist, a 9mm SIG Sauer Model 220, a sweet automatic pistol I knew very well, holstered to the belt. She said, "Yes. And just who might you be?"

"I'm Ford MacDougal, Jilly's brother, from Washington, D.C. I'm here to see her, and find out what happened to her."

"You're the FBI agent?"

There was deep suspicion in her voice.

"Word gets around fast," I said. I stuck my hand through the open window. "Just call me Mac."

She was wearing black leather driving gloves that felt very cool and soft to the touch when she clasped my hand. "I'm Maggie Sheffield, sheriff here in Edgerton. I want to find out what happened to Jilly as well. Did you just come from the hospital?" At my nod, she said, "No change?"

"No. I left Paul there with her. He's pretty upset."

"No wonder. It's got to be hell for him. It's not every day that a man's wife drives off a cliff, ends up in the hospital rather than the morgue, and leaves her Porsche twenty feet underwater."

She sounded like she wanted to cry. About Jilly or about the Porsche?

"You've driven Jilly's car?"

"Yeah, once. Funny thing is that I never speed unless I have to, which isn't often. But I got behind the wheel, looked out the windshield, and my foot just hit the gas pedal. I was doing eighty before I even realized it. I was grateful there were no cops around." She smiled and looked away from me for a moment. "Jilly was so excited about that car. She'd drive it down Fifth Avenue, hooting and shouting and honking the horn. She'd swerve it from one side of the street to the other. People would come out of the grocery store, their houses, laughing, betting with her that she'd wreck the car with her shenanigans."

"She did."

"Yes, but it wasn't because of her having fun like a crazy teenager. It was something else entirely." Her voice had lightened up just a bit, but now it was low and suspicious again. To my surprise, she suddenly smacked the steering wheel with her gloved fist. "It's just plain nuts. Rob Morrison, the state cop who pulled her out, said she speeded up as she went toward the cliff. It's a pretty sharp incline at that particular spot, so that means she had to push down on the gas, like she wanted to go over. But that doesn't make any sense at all. Jilly wouldn't have tried to kill herself." She paused a moment, frowning over the steering wheel into the forest across the street. "I don't suppose you've got any ideas about this?"

I should have just said no, because I didn't want this sheriff to think I was crazy, but what came out of my mouth was "Yes, I do. It's just that I don't understand my ideas either."

She laughed. It was an honest laugh that

filled the car. "I think you'll need to explain that. Listen, you're a Fed when all's said and done. Sure you're Jilly's brother, but you're a Fed first. What's going on here?"

"All that's true, but I'm on leave from the FBI. I'm here as Jilly's brother, nothing more. I'm not going to throw my weight around, Sheriff." My stomach growled. "Tell you what. Paul's still at the hospital. Actually I'm going to stay here with him since the Buttercup B and B is filled up with the orthodontist convention. It's time for lunch and I'm starving."

"Orthodontist convention, huh? That's how Arlene got rid of you? The woman's got no imagination."

"She tried. I think I frightened her. Is it because I'm an outsider? A Fed?"

"Oh, yes. Arlene Hicks doesn't want you anywhere around her fine establishment. She's weird that way about cops."

"Word got around really fast."

"Yeah. Paul told Benny Pickle down at the gun shop that you were coming. That's all it took. Benny's got the biggest mouth west of the Cascades."

"But what's wrong with being a Fed? I'm clean, I'm polite, I don't spit. I wouldn't run out without paying my bill."

"Arlene doesn't even like me hanging around, and I'm a friendly face. You're not. She probably believes you're as bad as the IRS. You're from Washington, right? Place of sin and corruption."

"You've got a good point there. Maybe Arlene's on to something."

She waved that away. "Okay. You're here, Mac, and you want to find out what happened to Jilly. I want the same thing. It makes sense that we join forces, at least a bit. The thing is, are you willing to play level with me?"

I arched an eyebrow. "I hadn't really thought about playing with anybody. But if I do play, it's usually level. Any reason why it shouldn't be?"

"You're a Fed. You're a big footer. You're used to taking over, used to making local cops your gofers. I'm not a gofer."

"I told you, I'm not here as a Fed. I'm here only as Jilly's brother. Like you, I want to know what happened. Actually I'm pleased that as the local cop you haven't just kissed the whole thing off — attempted suicide — and called in a shrink.

"Sure, I'll play level with you. Do you know anything I should know? Is there any reason to believe Jilly didn't go over that cliff on purpose? You want to start sharing right now?"

She seemed to relax a bit. "When were you hurt and how?"

"How do you know I was hurt? Do I still look like week-old oatmeal?"

She cocked her head to one side, fully facing me, looking me over. I realized that she was probably younger than I'd first thought. It was impossible to be really sure because she was wearing the dark glasses favored by highway patrol officers to intimidate the folk they stopped. I could see my reflection in the lenses. Her hair was thick, dark reddish-brown and curly, plaited into a thick French braid and pulled back up on top of her head, wound around itself and fastened with a clip carved as a totem pole. She was wearing pale coral lipstick, the shade my British girlfriend Caroline had favored. But Caroline, a clothing designer, had never looked as tough or self-reliant as this woman.

Of course she knew I was studying her, and she let me, saying finally, "I've always hated oatmeal. Fortunately, you don't resemble that at all, but you don't move all that easily, you know? You walk like you're twenty years older than you are. There are faint bruises along the left side of your face. You favor your right arm and you're a bit crabbed over, like you're worried you'll hurt your ribs. But not oatmeal. What happened to you?"

"I got in the way of a car bomb."

"I didn't hear about any federal guys being blown up."

"I was over in Tunisia. Bad place. You get hot sand in your mouth when you talk. The people I had to deal with weren't what you'd call very good-natured." I'd just told this woman, a perfect stranger, all sorts of stuff that wasn't any layperson's business, a local cop's least of all. Well, I was playing level, I was *sharing,* as politically correct folk would say. Even thinking that soppy word made me wince. If she knew anything at all, my spurt of openness — something I hoped wouldn't happen again — should help me worm it out of her.

"I'll take you to The Edwardian for lunch. It sounds like an English gentlemen's club, but it isn't. The food isn't great, but there's a lot of it, and you look like you could use the calories. You dropped what, a good fifteen pounds?"

"Yeah, about that," I said. It was only two o'clock in the afternoon and I wanted a soft bed, a dark room, and no interruptions for about three hours.

"Follow me. Fifteen minutes?"

"Thanks," I said.

I watched her turn the key in the ignition and smoothly do a U-turn on Liverpool Street.

Some twenty minutes later, once I'd ordered meat loaf, mashed potatoes, and green beans, and she'd ordered a huge chicken salad from Mr. Pete, a grizzled old varmint who was the only waiter for all ten patrons at The Edwardian at the moment, I leaned back against the hard wooden back of the booth and said, "I visited here about five years ago, as I said. I'd just gotten back from London, and Paul and Jilly invited me out here to meet his parents. I remember this place well. Nothing seems to have changed. How long have you been the sheriff?"

"Going on a year and a half now. The mayor of Edgerton is Miss Geraldine Tucker. Evidently she was going through a feminist phase, said she'd missed it when it first came around, and decided what the town needed was a female sheriff. I was a cop in Eugene at the time and had run into some bad trouble. I wanted out of there. This seemed a perfect opportunity." She shrugged. "I have one deputy and a secretary and about a dozen volunteers whenever I put out the call, which hasn't happened since I've been on the job. There's little crime, as you'd expect, just parking or speeding tickets, kids raising occasional hell, a couple of burglaries a month, probably by transients, normal stuff like that. There has been a rise in domestic cases recently, but nothing like it was in Eugene." She gave me a look that clearly said, *How much more level can you get?*

I smiled at her and said, "What happened in Eugene?"

Her lips were suddenly as thin as the soup an old guy was eating at the next table. "I think I'll keep that to myself, if you don't mind."

"Not at all. Hey, I'm just hoping that the meat loaf will stick to my ribs. They need all the padding they can get right now. What did you want to talk to Paul about?"

Before she could answer, an old man sauntered up, holding an Oakland A's baseball cap between his hands, big hands I saw, gnarly and veined but still strong. He had a full head of white curly hair, tobacco-stained teeth, and he was smiling at me. I put him in his seventies, a man who'd spent many years working hard.

"Charlie," Maggie said, leaning forward to take his hand. "How's tricks? You seen anything interesting I should know about?"

"Yes," he said, his voice all scratchy and thin as old drapes. "But it can wait. Is this the young feller from Washington?"

Maggie introduced us. He was Charlie Duck, a local who'd been here fifteen years. He nodded, never taking my hand, just twirling that Oakland A's baseball cap around and around in his hands. "You're all tied up now, Mac, but later, when you've got some time, I wouldn't mind having a talk with you."

"Sure," I said, and wondered what kind of tall tales I'd be hearing.

He nodded, all solemn, and sauntered back to a booth where he sat down, alone.

"You see, not everybody doesn't like me."

"Charlie's a real neat old guy. You'll enjoy him if you two get together."

I said again, "What did you want to talk to Paul about?"

Maggie picked up her fork and began to weave it through her fingers, just like the old man had done with that baseball cap. She'd pulled off her driving gloves. She had elegant white hands, short nails, calluses on her thumb pads. "Just talk," she said. "I still can't believe how lucky Jilly was. Rob Morrison, the highway patrolman who saved her life, came in third in the Iron Man Triathlon over in Kona last year. That means a two-mile swim, a hundred miles on a bike, then twenty-six point two miles of running. He's in awesome shape. Anyone else, and they'd probably still be trying to get her out of the Porsche. The luck involved, it still boggles the mind."

I felt both grateful and envious. "The Iron Man. I had a friend who tried that. He made it to Kona, but he got cramps in the marathon leg. I want to meet this guy. I wish I had something more to give him than just my heartfelt thanks."

"After lunch." She picked up her glass of iced tea, just delivered by Mr. Pete, now wearing a bright red apron and chewing on a toothpick. He called her Ms. Sheriff. "Rob is working nights right now, sleeping during the day. He should be awake soon. I want to hear him go through what happened again so I'll take you with me. You very slickly asked me why I wanted to talk to Paul." She shrugged a bit. "I want to know who or what sent Jilly over that cliff. If anyone should know, it's Paul."

I couldn't face that, not just yet. "They've only been here about five and a half months. Paul grew up here, you know."

"Yes, but he has no more relatives here. His parents died about three years ago in a private plane crash over the Sierras near Tahoe. They were big-time skiers. Their bodies were never recovered, which is odd since most of the time planes that go down are found after the snow melts.

"Paul's uncle died of cancer about two years ago, and his cousins are all scattered across the country.

"Why'd he come back here? No offense, but it's the middle of nowhere and there isn't, frankly, much of anything here to interest two big-time researchers, which Jilly told me they both were."

My salad was delivered, a huge bowl filled with lettuce, red peppers, boiled potato chunks, and green beans, all topped with a heap of ranch dressing. I thought it looked wonderful. "Go ahead, get started," she said, and I forked down a big bite. "It isn't bad," I said, closed my eyes, and shoveled down six more bites. "Much better. When Jilly called me six months or so ago, she told me that VioTech — the pharmaceutical company where both of them worked — didn't want Paul to continue with the project he was involved in. Jilly said he was pissed and wanted to come back here and continue his work."

"What about Jilly? What were her plans?"

"She said her clock was running out. She wanted to have a kid."

"Jilly said that?" Maggie Sheffield was just swiping butter on a dinner roll. She stopped cold and stared at me, shaking her head even as she said, "Oh, no, that's impossible."

"Why?"

"If she told me once, she told me half a dozen times, that neither she nor Paul had ever wanted rug rats. She said they were too selfish for too long a time now to think about changing to accommodate a child."

Well then, she'd obviously changed her mind since she'd spoken to me about it.

"Meatloaf's all gone," Mr. Pete announced, as if he was pleased as punch about it. "Pierre didn't make enough. It got eaten mostly by the breakfast crowd. How about some nice fish 'n' chips smothered in onion rings?"

All that fat swimming around in my arteries didn't sound like such a bad thing at that moment.

4

Rob Morrison lived in a small wooden clapboard house tucked in among a good dozen spruce trees about two miles south of town. A narrow dirt road, posted as Penzance Street, snaked through the valleys and hills, and his house was at the end of the road. A wide gully lay just beyond. I turned when I got out of the car and stared over the western horizon. I felt a moment of deep envy. When Rob Morrison awoke in the morning, it was to an incredible view of the Pacific Ocean through the skinny spruce trees. It felt like being at the edge of the world.

Maggie knocked on the unpainted oak door. "Rob? Come on, wake up. You'll be on duty again in another four hours. Wake up."

I heard movement from within the

house. Finally, a man's deep voice called out, "Maggie, that you? What are you doing here? What's going on? How's Jilly?"

"Open up, Rob, and I'll tell you everything."

The door opened and a man about my age stood there, wearing only tight jeans with the top button open and a heavy morning beard. The sheriff had been right, this guy was in awesome shape. Thank God he'd been there at exactly the right moment.

"Who are you?"

I stuck out my hand. "Name's Ford MacDougal. I'm Jilly's brother. I want to thank you for saving her life."

"Rob Morrison," the guy said and took my right hand in a very strong grip. "Yeah, hey, I'm sorry it ever happened. How is she?"

"Jilly's still in a coma," Maggie said.

"Can we talk?" I said. Rob stood back and waved us in. "Mr. Thorne was here just two days ago so the place is still as clean as a virgin's memories."

Maggie said to me, "That means there isn't anything of interest anywhere, particularly dirt."

"A blank slate," I said.

"An unsoiled blank slate. Right. I'm

making coffee. Any for either of you?" At my nod, he said, "Black and strong as tar?"

"That's it."

"Maggie, Earl Grey tea for you?"

She nodded. Both of us followed him through the painfully neat living room to the small kitchen just beyond.

"Nice place," I said. "Who's Mr. Thorne?"

Rob turned and smiled. "He's my house-keeper. Comes twice a week, keeps me from living like a pig. A retired salmon fisherman from Alaska. He calls my place his petri dish."

We sat on bar stools at the kitchen counter that separated the kitchen from the small rectangular dining area in front of two wide windows looking toward the ocean.

Soon the smell of coffee filled the air. I breathed in deeply. "The coffee at The Edwardian tasted like cheap watered-down instant."

"It was," Rob said. "Mr. Pete loves instant, makes it with lukewarm water, but only when Pierre Montrose, the owner, isn't there. I wouldn't be surprised if he stirred it with his finger." He poured the coffee and gently shoved a cup over to me.

He poured a cup of hot water over a tea bag. He added a single bag of Equal, stirred it, and gave it to Maggie.

We drank. I sighed deeply. "The best ritual in the world."

"Why don't you go get a shirt on, Rob?" Maggie said. "Mac and I won't move a muscle."

Rob just shrugged his superbly muscled shoulder. "Nah, I've got to take a shower. Let's talk. I can get dressed after you guys leave."

I not only felt like a slab of cold oatmeal, I felt really pathetic. This guy could probably shove me over with one hand and walk away whistling. It was depressing as hell. At least the coffee was waking me up, aches and pains and all. I still wanted that nap, but with Rob Morrison sitting across from me, his legs crossed at the ankles, holding his coffee cup against his bare muscled belly, I wasn't about to slouch or yawn.

At least the guy had to have a house-keeper to keep from living like a slob in a cave.

"Rob," Maggie said, leaning forward, cupping the tea mug between her hands. "Tell us everything you can remember, every detail. I'm going to record it, okay?"

"Yeah, sure, but you already know every-thing."

"Let's do it again. I want it on record this time. Mac needs to hear it too." Maggie made preliminary comments into the recorder. After a couple of false starts, Rob sat forward and said slowly and very clearly, "It was nearly midnight on Tuesday, April twenty-second. I was cruising north along the coast road. I didn't see anybody or anything until I came around a deep curve and saw Jilly's white Porsche in front of me. I saw the car go toward the railing. It didn't slow, just kept going, right on through. Then the Porsche speeded up. I was right on its tail. When it went over the cliff I was there in just a couple of seconds. I saw the headlights through the water and dove in right at that spot. It went down about fifteen, sixteen feet, I'd estimate, before the car hit the sand and settled. The driver's-side window was completely open. I managed to pull Jilly through the window with no loss of time since her seat belt wasn't fastened. I kicked off the bottom and headed straight up. I estimate that she wasn't under water more than two minutes, tops.

"I towed her to shore, made sure she was breathing. I climbed back up the cliff and radioed for an ambulance from my patrol car. They arrived about twelve minutes later and took her to the Tallshon Community Hospital. At least it was close by.

"That's it, Maggie. I can't remember anything else."

"Did you recognize Jilly when you realized it was a white Porsche?"

Rob nodded. "Oh, yeah, I'd know Jilly's Porsche anywhere, just like everyone else in this town would."

"What did you think she was doing?" I asked.

"I didn't have a clue. I yelled and yelled at her but it didn't do any good. It was like she didn't even see me or hear me. Maybe she didn't."

"Did you see anything or anyone else?"

"No, no one."

Maggie said, "In your opinion, was Jilly Bartlett willfully driving the Porsche over the cliff?"

"It looked that way to me," Rob said.

"Is there any doubt in your mind," I said, "that Jilly was attempting to kill herself?"

Rob Morrison raised weary eyes to my face. He rubbed his fist over the thick dark whiskers on his chin. "No," he said finally, "I'm really sorry, but in my opinion, she

65

was trying to kill herself."

"What about a mechanical problem that caused her to lose control?"

"Her car's still twenty feet under water, but I didn't see any signs of mechanical problems. No exploding tires, no smoke coming from the hood, no skid marks, nothing like that. I'm sorry, Mac."

Half an hour later, Maggie and I were sitting in her car outside Paul and Jilly's house.

"You look ready to fold in on yourself," she said. "Why don't you rest for a while before Paul comes home?"

"I don't have a key to the house," I said. "If it weren't for the big tooth convention in town I'd be at the Buttercup B and B. So I didn't think I'd be staying here with Paul."

"So no key?"

"No key. I figured I'd just curl up on one of those chairs on their front porch."

"You're too big to do much curling," she said, and drummed her gloved fingers on her steering wheel. "Actually, since we're sharing information, why don't you just tell me your ideas about Jilly? You know, the ideas you told me you didn't under-stand. Then you can head for that porch chair."

"You've got a good memory."

"Yes. What ideas, Mac?"

"Even if I tell you, you'll think I'm a nut case, or you'll just dismiss it because I was in the hospital when it happened, and you'll think it was a psychotic reaction to a drug."

"Try me."

I looked away from her, then inward, back to that night. "I was in the hospital. I dreamed about Jilly being in trouble that night. Somehow I was with her when she went over the cliff." I wanted to laugh myself at what I'd just said, but I just shook my head. "You think I'm psychotic, right?"

She said slowly, staring at me, "I don't know what to believe. What did you do?"

"The next morning I called Paul right away, found out that my dream had actually happened. I've got no clue as to why I hooked up to Jilly like that, none."

"Jesus," she said.

"I had to get out there."

"You shouldn't have left the hospital."

"There wasn't a choice. As it was, I waited another two days. The longest two days of my life."

She didn't say anything for a very long time. She rubbed her palm on her thigh.

The crease in her tan pants was still sharp. The pants looked as fresh as if she'd just put them on.

"And you and Jilly never had any sort of link before this?"

I shook my head. "There are just us four kids now. Our folks have been dead for some time. Jilly's three years older than me. I'm the youngest. We weren't all that close really, both of us busy over the past several years, but that's normal I guess. Then this damned dream happened. The thing is, I feel like something made Jilly go over that cliff — or someone. She was alone in that car, but she wasn't, not really."

"That doesn't make much sense."

"I know," I said. "I know. At least it doesn't yet. You want the kicker? At the end of the dream I heard a man yelling." I drew a deep breath. "It sounded like Rob Morrison. I recognized his voice just now."

"Jesus."

"There's no way I can just accept this as a suicide attempt, not unless Jilly tells me it was."

I sipped a rich Pinot Noir from the Gray Canyon vineyard in Napa Valley.

"You like the wine?" Paul asked.

"It's darker than the deepest sin," I said, gently swirling the wine in its crystal glass, watching it glide smoothly over the sides. "I met Rob Morrison today, the man who saved Jilly."

"Yes," Paul said. "I met Rob just after Jilly and I moved here. He gave me a speeding ticket. I hear you also spent time with Maggie Sheffield."

"Yeah. I don't know what to think of her just yet, but she seemed okay, once she got over her gut suspicions of me as an FBI agent."

Paul sat forward, his hands clenching. "Watch out for her, Mac."

"What does that mean?"

Paul shrugged his shoulders. "Please don't think that I'm being harsh or a woman hater. I'll just come out with it. She's a bitch, a ball-buster."

"I didn't get that impression at all." I cut another piece of the thick sirloin steak. It was even better than the lettuce and green bean salad at The Edwardian. "She wants to find out why Jilly went over that cliff. I appreciate that. You should too. What'd she do to you? Give you a speeding ticket like Morrison?"

"No, nothing like that. She wants to blame me for Jilly's accident. She's never liked me, believes I'm not good enough for Jilly. I don't appreciate that at all."

It was my turn to shrug. "She didn't say a word about you, Paul. She was waiting here in her car when I drove up. She wanted to talk to you."

"I'd have her fired if I could talk Geraldine into it. The woman's a menace. She doesn't like men in general, always giving them grief. Have you seen that damned gun she wears on her belt? It's ridiculous. Edgerton is a small, peaceful little town. No one — man or woman — should be wearing a damned gun, but she does. Of course, I already spoke to her at the hospital after Jilly was admitted."

"It's not odd at all for a cop — male or female — to want to question someone more than once," I said mildly, surprised that Paul would spew out that sexist crap. I'd gotten no hint at all that she didn't like men. "In the excitement and stress of the moment, people tend to forget things. I'll bet even you will be able to tell her more now than you did then."

"About what, for God's sake? Jilly went over that damned cliff and I don't know why. She was a little depressed, but every-one's down once in a while. That's it, Mac. There's nothing more."

I took the last bite of my steak, sat back in my chair, rubbed my belly, and took another sip of my Pinot Noir. Paul looked pale, his skin drawn tight over his cheekbones. He looked ill, frightened. Or maybe I was just seeing myself in Paul. Lord knew I looked sick enough. "Are you certain there's nothing else, Paul? What was Jilly depressed about? Was she taking any medication for the depression? Was she seeing anyone professionally?"

Paul laughed, a tight, constipated laugh. "Just listen to you. SuperCop with his load of questions. No, she wasn't. I'm exhausted, Mac. I don't want to talk anymore. There's nothing more to say. I'm going to bed." He shoved back his chair and stood up. "Good night. I hope you don't mind the double bed in the guest room. It'll be a bit on the short side for you."

"I'll do just fine, Paul. I slept some this afternoon on that big front porch chair of yours. I think I'll go to the hospital to see Jilly. Good night."

Ford was here again, holding my hand like he had before. The warmth of his hand was indescribable, just like before. Thank God I hadn't just imagined it that first time. I didn't want to lose my brain the way I'd lost my body.

But when was before?

It could have been this morning or last year for all I knew. It was odd, but I had no sense of time at all. I knew what it was, but it had no meaning to me.

There were other shadowy creatures behind Ford, then finally they left, and we were alone.

"Jilly," he said, and I wanted to cry with the sheer relief of hearing his voice, but I didn't know if this body I couldn't feel was even capable of yielding up tears.

I wanted to ask him if they'd gotten my Porsche out of the ocean.

Ford said, "Sweetheart, I don't know if you can hear me or not. I hope somehow that you can. I spoke to Kevin and Gwen and gave them an update. They send their love and their prayers.

"Now, Jilly, tell me about why you were depressed."

Depressed? What was this about being depressed? I've never been depressed in my life. Who said anything about being fucking depressed? I yelled it at Ford, but naturally, he didn't hear me because my words were only bouncing about inside my skull.

"I've got to find out why you drove your Porsche off that cliff, Jilly. I find it hard to believe that you were depressed. I can't remember when you were ever depressed, even when you were a teenager and Lester Harvey dumped you for Susan, that friend of yours who had the big breasts. I remember you just shook your head, said he was a worthless shit, and moved on.

"But things change. We haven't seen all that much of each other in the past five years or so. You've been with Paul. Dammit, Jilly, what happened to you?"

Ford was leaning his forehead on my hand. I could feel the soft whistle of his breath against my skin. I wasn't depressed, I wanted to tell him. He wanted to know what had happened to me so I said, "Listen, Ford, do you like sex? I didn't used to like it all that much, but then something happened. A wonderful something."

I wondered if my mouth was curving at all into a smile. Probably not. I heard Ford's quiet, steady breathing. He was asleep. Why had he fallen asleep? Then I remembered something about him being sick. Had he been injured somehow? I seemed to remember that.

I wish I could have run my fingers through his hair. Ford had lovely hair, all dark and longer than the FBI would like it to be. But it was his eyes I'd always liked best. Dark blue eyes, just like Mom's, at least I think they were

*like Mom's, she'd been dead for so very long.
Yes, his eyes were deep and mellow and too
intense on occasion. I remember hearing he
was dating a woman named Dolores from
Washington, D.C. Every time I thought of her
name I pictured a Spanish flamenco dancer in
my mind. I wonder if she liked sex with Ford.*

*When it comes down to it, who cares? I'm
here, a prisoner, and Paul's alive, free to do
whatever he wants. But it's not Paul I'm
afraid of, goodness, never Paul. It's Laura. She
was dangerous, wasn't she? I knew she'd
betrayed me. She'd gotten into my head and
nearly killed me. Oh, Ford, if she comes back,
I won't be able to bear it. I'll die.*

*I'm lying here, just floating about, and I
think of Laura. Laura, who betrayed me.
Always Laura.*

I woke up with a start some hours later
at the touch of a nurse's hand on my
shoulder. I raised my head, looked at her
face, and said, "Always Laura. Laura
betrayed her."

She arched her right eyebrow, sleek and
black. "Laura? Who's Laura? Are you
okay?"

I looked down at Jilly, silent, pale, her
skin nearly translucent. "I'm fine," I said.
Who was Laura? I looked up again at the

nurse. She was very short, a tiny bird of a woman, and her voice was soft and sweet as a child's. I nodded at her, then looked at Jilly, whose features were barely visible in the dim light from the corridor. Evidently someone had come into the room, seen me asleep on Jilly's hand, and turned off the lights.

"It's time to turn her over," the nurse said quietly, "and to massage her. Bedsores will come eventually if we don't take care now."

"Tell me," I said, watching her untie the back of Jilly's hospital gown, "what you know about coma. The doctors spoke to me at some length, but it was difficult to understand exactly what to expect."

She began to rub thick white cream into Jilly's shoulders and back. "Remember that movie with Steven Seagal a while back where he'd been in a coma for seven years, then awakened?"

I nodded, remembering how much I'd admired Steven Seagal when I was a boy.

The nurse said, "He had a long beard and he was weak, had to practice to get his strength back, and of course he did. He was jumping around, maiming folk after just a week or so. Well, that's Hollywood. Actually, if a person's in a coma for longer than, say, a few days, the risk increases dramatically that something will be seriously wrong when and if the person ever comes out of it. I'm sorry to tell you if you don't know, but all sorts of brain damage is possible — retardation, inability to walk, to talk — any number of dreadful things.

"Most of the time, people come out of a coma very quickly, and they're usually okay. If Mrs. Bartlett comes out of this in, say, the next day or two, her chances are good that there won't be any terrible damage; but it's very possible there will be some. We just don't know. We make assumptions and predictions based on statistics, but in the end, everyone is different. We can hope and pray, and little else.

"In Mrs. Bartlett's case, there was no major damage they could see on any of her test results. Actually, she really shouldn't be in a coma at all. That just goes to show that there's so much we don't know about this sort of thing. I'm sorry, Mr. MacDougal, there's nothing else to say about it."

She'd given me a lot to think about. I didn't leave the hospital until the next morning, and then I drove slowly back to 12 Liverpool Street. When I fell asleep again I dreamed about Maggie Sheffield. She was screaming that Paul was a bastard and she was going to run him out of Edgerton.

5

When I drove back into the driveway at ten o'clock the following morning, I saw Maggie Sheffield's car parked across the street as it had been the day before.

I heard her say as I walked quietly into the living room, "Paul, I called the hospital on my way over here. Mrs. Himmel told me there was no change. She said that Mac was still with Jilly, had been since last night."

I heard Paul grunt.

"Mac spends a lot more time there than you do, Paul. How's that?"

"Go to hell."

Paul didn't sound particularly pissed off at such a question, just incredibly tired. Personally, if she'd said that to me, I would have been tempted to slug her. I walked into the living room, a long narrow great room that ran the entire front of the house, facing the ocean. It was all windows across the front; where there had to be walls to hold up the house, they were stark white. Large square white pavers covered the floor, and all the furniture was black. It was a minimalist designer's wet dream — no compromises with kitsch or newspapers or photos anywhere. Just all these clean stark lines that set my teeth on edge. I couldn't imagine cozying up with a good book in here or setting a nice big TV set in the corner and watching football. Actually, I didn't want to be anywhere near this room when I could help it. It was a testament — not to living, but to someone's idea of perfection. Even the paintings, all of the dozen or so abstracts, were made up of paint slashes, primarily black and white, lined up like perfect little soldiers along a long white wall. I couldn't imagine how anyone could live in this sterile space, particularly Jilly. I remembered Jilly's room growing up — bright teal blues and oranges and greens. Of course she'd also had punk-rocker posters on the walls. People changed, but this much? Was this all Paul's doing?

I said to Maggie, who was seated on a long black leather sofa, a small notebook open on her lap, "Sheriff, I hope you're well." She was wearing her tan uniform, running shoes on her feet. For just an instant, I saw her without the tan uniform, just as she'd been in my dream the night before. Her hair was ruthlessly pulled back, fastened with one of those things that my FBI friend Sherlock called a banana clip. Sherlock had a rainbow of colors in her banana clips.

"Mac," she said, rising. "I'm just fine. How's Jilly?"

"The same. No change."

"I'm sorry. How are you feeling?"

"Fine, no problem."

"You're looking a lot better, not quite so ready for the grave as yesterday. Come sit down, Mac. I just need to go over a few more things with Paul."

Paul hadn't stirred. He was seated forward in a black tufted leather chair, his hands clasped between his knees. He appeared to be studying a white paver at his feet. "There's a small scratch," he said.

"Scratch? What scratch?" Maggie asked.

"There," Paul said. "Right there, in the top right corner. I wonder how that could have happened."

"Tell you what, Paul," I said, not joking

at all, "I'll get a load of newspapers and we can pile them up over the scratch."

"Yeah, Mac, sure. You're a philistine. You've got a messy, unsophisticated soul. Come join the fun. Let's get this over with. I've got to get back to work."

"Jilly told me that was why you left Philadelphia and VioTech — you wanted to continue work on this project and they wanted you to stop."

"That's right."

"What's the project?" I asked, walking over a black-and-white geometrical carpet to stand by one of the large glass windows that looked out at the ocean.

"It's all about the fountain of youth. I'm developing a pill that will reverse the aging process."

"My God, Paul," Maggie said, nearly falling off the sofa, "that's just incredible! Why wouldn't they want you to continue on that? That would be worth not just a fortune, it would be worth the world."

Paul laughed at her. "Everyone bites big time on that one. Everyone wants youth back." He touched his receding hairline. "I'd rather come up with a pill to regrow hair myself."

"If Jean-Luc Picard on *Star Trek* is any indication, we still won't have a pill to grow hair even in the twenty-fourth century. You're out of luck, Paul."

"What are you really working on then, Paul?" I asked.

"Look, it's privileged information and it's really none of your business, either of you. It's got nothing to do with Jilly. Now please get off my back."

Maggie sat back down on the sofa and clicked her ballpoint pen. "I want to know what you and Jilly did last Tuesday night. Think back. It's dinnertime. Did you eat in or go out?"

"For God's sake, Maggie, why do you want to know what we did for dinner?"

"Did you eat in, Paul?" I asked, still standing in front of the window, my arms crossed over my chest.

"Yes, we did. We broiled halibut, squeezed on lemon. Jilly made garlic toast. I tossed a spinach salad. We ate. I had work to do after dinner. Jilly said she was going to drive around, nothing unusual in that. She loved driving the Porsche. She left here about nine o'clock."

"Rob Morrison said she went over the cliff at about midnight. That's three hours, Paul. That's an awfully long time to drive around."

"I went to work. I fell asleep at my desk,

even left my computer on. If Jilly came back and left again, I wouldn't know. If she stayed out the full three hours, I wouldn't know that either. All I know is she left at nine."

"What was her mood at dinner?"

"Maggie, you know Jilly. She's never serious, always joking around. She told me a Viagra joke, I remember that."

"So what is it you're working on, Paul?" Maggie said. "You want to clone little Paul Bartletts?"

"No, Maggie, I wouldn't want to clone myself until I figure out how to regrow hair." He looked over at me. "Now you're a possibility. You've got good genes, Mac. The Germans would have approved of you, or the FBI. You interested?"

"So you put the FBI right in there with the Nazis, do you?" Why was he stonewalling? How could a drug he was developing have anything to do with Jilly driving over a cliff?

Paul just shrugged. "Lots of parallels, as I see it."

I let it go, just shrugged. "Well, maybe I'll consider it three lifetimes from now if I turn real weird, but probably not. So you're saying that during dinner Jilly seemed perfectly normal?"

"Yes. She ate lightly. She wanted to lose five pounds."

Maggie said, "Was she taking any weight-loss pills?"

"Not that I know of. I'll check in the medicine cabinet and see what's there."

"Okay."

"Is it true you made love to Jilly every day, Paul?"

I'd swear that Paul turned red to his receding hairline. "What the hell kind of question is that, Mac? Why is that your business?"

"In February, Jilly told me about her love life. She'd never spoken so frankly about sex with you before that. Thinking back on it, something was off. She spoke about a number of things, going from one subject to the next, without pause, without emphasis on anything."

"What did she say, Mac?"

I looked at Maggie. In that moment, I would have sworn she had more than just a professional interest in what was going on here. Well, why not give her details? I said, "She spoke about her new dress, how Paul made love to her all the time, how she loved her Porsche, and she spoke about a brother and sister, Cal and Cotter Tarcher. Everything she said was in the same tone of voice, almost without emotion. Now, in hindsight, it wasn't quite right."

The doorbell rang.

Paul jumped to his feet. "Oh, God, what if something's happened to Jilly?"

He ran out of the living room. Maggie said to me, "I realize you don't want to hear this, Mac, but there was talk. Just maybe it wasn't Paul she was having all that sex with."

I wanted to punch her. Jilly screwing around? I'd never believe that. Not Jilly. I didn't have time to question Maggie about it before Paul returned to the living room. Standing beside him in the doorway was a small girl — no, a woman — perhaps twenty-five. She had dark brown hair, thick and curly, pulled back with two plastic clips. Her skin was whiter than a pair of my boxer shorts fresh out of the drier. No freckles. She wore glasses with rounded gold frames. She was wearing jeans that were too loose on her and a white shirt, probably a man's, that hung halfway down her legs and was rolled up to her fore-arms.

"Hello, Cal," Maggie said, rising slowly. "What brings you here?"

Good grief. Cal Tarcher, in the flesh. The girl who was going to be jealous of

Jilly's new dress. Sister of Cotter, the vicious bully.

I watched Cal raise her head, look furtively toward Paul, and say, "My father sent me. I'm glad you're here, Maggie. All of you are invited to our house tomorrow night." She looked toward me. "Are you Jilly's brother?"

"Yes. I'm Ford MacDougal."

"I'm Cal Tarcher. Is Jilly all right?"

"She's still the same. In a coma."

"I'm so sorry. I went to see her last night. The nurse told me to talk to Jilly, just talk about anything — the weather, the latest Denzel Washington movie — whatever. Anyway, the party. Will all of you come?"

"Of course we'll come," Paul said, a hint of impatience in his voice. "Your father commands and we struggle to be first in line."

"It's not like that, Paul," Cal said, without looking at any of us.

Cal looked over Paul's right shoulder, toward a painting with two long diagonal slashes of stark black paint slapped on dead-white canvas. "We're all very worried about Jilly, Paul. Dad hopes you'll be able to make time and come to our house for at least a little while tomorrow night. He really wants to meet Jilly's brother. Maggie, do you know if Rob is working tomorrow night?"

"That's a loaded question. What makes you think I know his schedule?"

Cal Tarcher shrugged. "You're both law officers."

"Yeah, right."

Cal Tarcher was very uncomfortable with this, probably embarrassed. What was going on here? I felt as though I'd been dumped in the middle of a play and I didn't have a clue what the plot was. "I'll call him," Cal said in a low voice. Then she raised her head and looked directly at Maggie. "It's just that he's more likely to come if you ask him. He'll do whatever you ask. You know he doesn't like me. He thinks I'm stupid."

"Don't be ridiculous, Cal," Paul said. "Rob doesn't dislike anyone. It would take too much mental energy and he's got to conserve all he's got. I'll call him for you, all right?"

"Thank you, Paul. I'm off to invite Miss Geraldine. She's had a bad cold, but she's better now. I'm taking some homemade coffee cake to her. My father admires her so very much, you know."

"Beats me why," Paul said. He added to

me, "Miss Geraldine Tucker is our mayor and a retired high school math teacher. She also heads up the Edgerton Citizen Coalition, better known as the BITEASS League. Its members range in age from in vitro to ninety-three — that's Mother Marco, who still owns the Union 76 filling station downtown.

"And no, there's no correlation between the letters and the name of the group. Didn't your dad come up with that, Cal?"

"It was my mom, actually."

"Your mother? Elaine?" There was surprise and disbelief in Maggie's voice.

"Why, yes," Cal said. "My mom's got a great sense of humor. She's also very smart. Actually you, Mr. MacDougal, are the only one coming who isn't a member of the League."

I said, "You need to come up with words to fit the letters."

"People have tried," Paul said. "Is that all, Cal? We're really busy here. Maggie is acting like I'm responsible, like I drove Jilly off that cliff. She's asking all sorts of questions."

Maggie waved her ballpoint pen at him. "That's right, Paul. You're a big suspect, particularly since Rob had to pull you out of the Porsche too. Before you go, Cal, did you happen to see Jilly last Tuesday evening?"

"There was lots of fog that night," Cal said, looking, I thought, at her Bally shoes. "I remember Cotter's date canceling because she didn't want to drive in it."

"Jilly went over about midnight," I said. "Was there fog then?"

"No," Maggie said. "It was nearly gone then." She added, "It's very changeable around here — the fog flits through like a bride's veil or it settles thick as a blanket, then all of a sudden it vanishes. It was like that last Tuesday night. Cotter's date was driving to your house?"

Cal nodded. She was, I saw, finally making eye contact with me. "Cotter likes his dates to pick him up," she said, seeing my raised eyebrow. "He says it makes women feel powerful if they're the ones driving. If they get annoyed with him they can just drop him off and leave him on the side of the road, no harm done."

"So did you see Jilly or not?" Maggie asked. She didn't like Cal Tarcher, I thought, looking from one woman to the other. I wondered why. Cal Tarcher seemed perfectly harmless to me, just painfully shy, just the opposite of Maggie, and that was perhaps why she didn't like her.

Cal Tarcher made her impatient.

"Yes, I saw her," Cal said. She took two steps toward the door. It seemed that now she wanted to get out of there. "It was around nine-thirty. She was driving her Porsche down Fifth Avenue, playing her car stereo real loud. I was eating a late dinner at The Edwardian. There were maybe ten, twelve people there. We all got up and went outside to wave to Jilly. She was singing at the top of her lungs."

"What was she singing?" I asked.

"Songs from the musical *Oklahoma*. And laughing. Yes, I remember she was laughing. She shouted at everyone, told them she was going to go serenade all the dead folk in the cemetery. Then she did a U-turn and headed back east on Fifth Avenue."

"That's what everyone else said, more or less." Maggie added, "The cemetery is just south of the main part of town, really close to the ocean, so it's possible that's what she did. But then, much later, she was driving north up the coast road."

I remembered that Rob Morrison lived south of town. No, I thought, Jilly wouldn't break her marriage vows, not Jilly. She wanted to have a kid. She wouldn't screw around with anyone else.

But I knew I wouldn't be able to leave it alone. I'd have to ask Maggie.

"Maybe she went to the cemetery and something happened to her," Cal said.

"Like what?" Maggie said, her words bitten out.

"I don't know," Cal said slowly, ducking eye contact with every one of us. "But sometimes you can see odd shadows there, hear things, soft-sounding things. The trees whisper to each other, I've always thought. The hemlocks always seem to be crowding in toward the graves. You can imagine that their roots are twisted around a lot of the older caskets, maybe cracking them open, maybe releasing —" Cal shrugged. Then she tried to smile. "No, that's silly, isn't it?"

"Yes," Maggie said. "Very silly. Dead people don't hold any interest, and that's all there is at the cemetery. Just moldy old bones. Now, Cal, Mac here doesn't know you're an artist and you have flights of fancy. Stop acting weird. You know you're not, really."

"I still wouldn't want to go there at night," Cal said. "Even if I was drunk. It's a creepy place."

"Are you saying that Jilly seemed drunk when you saw her at nine-thirty?" I asked.

Cal was silent. Maggie said, "Nobody else said anything about her being drunk. Just high spirits, Mr. Pete said, and that was just Jilly. I asked the doctors at the hospital after they'd done tests on Jilly. Her blood alcohol level was consistent with a couple of glasses of wine. And the toxicology screen was negative. So forget the drunk thing. Now, Cal, you didn't see her after that?"

Cal shook her head. She took a step toward the door. I stepped forward. "Maggie, why don't you and Paul continue your chat. I'll walk Miss Tarcher to her car."

I thought she was going to make a mad dash for the front door to escape me. What was wrong with the woman?

"Wait, Cal," I said, and pitched my voice low, filled with cool authority, the perfect FBI voice. She reacted instantly to that voice and came to a dead halt. I cupped her elbow in my right hand and went outside with her.

It was a cool, very clear morning, just a light breeze to ruffle the hair on your head. I breathed in the ocean smell, still new in my lungs.

I didn't say anything until we reached her car, a light blue BMW Roadster, its top down. She was looking at her feet again, walking quickly, eager to get away from me. I lightly touched her shoulder when she opened the car door and said, "Hold on a minute, Miss Tarcher. What's wrong? Who are you so afraid of?"

For the first time, she looked up at me with a straightforward look, no eye-shifting. I saw that her eyes were a pale blue behind the glasses, with shades of gray. Cool eyes, intelligent. And something else I couldn't pinpoint. She straightened, her shoulders going back. She wasn't as short as I'd thought. In fact she suddenly looked tall, standing there with a very conscious arrogance. Her voice was as cool and intelligent as her eyes. "That, Mr. MacDougal, is none of your business. Good day to you. I will see you tomorrow night, unless you decide to leave town before then." She looked back toward the house for a moment, and added, "Who cares?"

"I do," I said.

She gave me an indifferent nod, climbed into her Beemer and was around the curve in Liverpool Street in just under ten seconds. She didn't look back.

Cal Tarcher seemed to be two distinct, two very different people. It drove me nuts not to know anything or anyone, not to be able to root about to put things together.

I stood staring out over the ocean. The water was calm, placid, reaching into an endless horizon. There was one lone fishing boat out some two hundred yards from land. I could make out two people from this distance, sitting motionless in the boat. I sighed and turned slowly to walk back to the house.

Maggie was putting her cell phone back in her jacket pocket as she came running down the stairs. "See you later, Mac," she said. "Doc Lambert just called to tell me someone struck Charlie Duck on the head. Thank God Charlie lives right next door to Doc Lambert. Charlie managed to crawl over just before he fell unconscious. Doc said it didn't look good. I'm heading over there now."

"He's the old guy I met at The Edwardian yesterday at lunch. I remember he wanted to talk to me. Who would hit him? Jesus, Maggie, that doesn't make sense."

"I agree. I'm out of here. See you later."

I hoped the old guy would be all right, but serious head wounds seldom turned out well. I wondered what he'd wanted to talk to me about. I wondered why anyone would hit him on the head.

6

I picked up two sandwiches from Grace's Deli on Fifth Avenue and brought them back to Liverpool Street. I rousted Paul out of his lab and we sat down at the dining room table at twelve-thirty.

Paul set a cold can of Coors in front of each of us. "I accomplished next to nothing," he said as he sat down. "I can't seem to think, to solve the easiest problems." He peeled back the foil on his sandwich. "Ah, rare roast beef, my favorite. How'd you know that, Mac?"

"I remembered Jilly telling me some time ago. She said you would only eat it half-cooked and slathered with mayonnaise. The woman at the deli knew exactly how you liked it."

Paul's face became still. "I can't believe Jilly's not here, telling me I'm a jerk because I forgot to do something she'd asked me to do, telling me to leave her alone because she's working and who says my work's more important than hers? She could be yelling at me one minute, then she'd just start laughing, lean over, and bite my ear. Jesus, Mac, it's hard."

"Paul, who's Laura?"

I thought Paul was going to have a heart attack. His hand jerked and he spilled his beer onto the back of his hand and wrist. He didn't curse, didn't say anything at all, just looked down at the beer dripping off his hand onto the shining mahogany table-top.

I handed Paul his paper napkin. When he'd finished mopping up, I said again, "Paul, tell me about Laura. Who is she?"

Paul took a bite of his sandwich, chewed slowly, not looking at me, just chewed. He swallowed, took a long pull of beer, then said finally, "Laura? There isn't any Laura."

Paul Bartlett was thirty-six, skinny as a post, at home in preppy clothes — this morning a dark green Ralph Lauren T-shirt and khaki slacks, light tan Italian loafers with tassels.

He was a genius, Jilly had always said, simply a genius. Well, that could be, I thought, but he was a lousy liar. I wasn't about to let this slide. "Laura, Paul. Tell me about her. It's important."

"Why would Laura be important to this? How the hell do you even know her name?"

"I heard it from Jilly," I said. I wasn't about to tell him that I'd come suddenly awake at the hospital, my face on Jilly's hand, saying Laura's name aloud. It sounded too off the wall. I leaned back in my chair and added easily, "She mentioned Laura's name. Didn't say anything else about her" — except that Laura had betrayed her — "just said her name."

Did Paul look relieved? I realized I'd blown it. I never should have told him that the woman's name was all I knew. I was an idiot. I was supposed to be trained to lie and bluff well. I was losing it. But why did Paul feel he had to lie? And then of course I realized what Jilly had meant. Laura had betrayed her with her husband, Paul.

Paul took another bite of his sandwich. Some of the mayonnaise oozed out the sides and fell to the napkin. He chewed slowly, buying time, I knew, an old ploy to gain time to think, to make the other person begin to question himself. He said finally, after a long stretch of silence,

"She's not important, just a woman who lives in Salem. I don't even know if that's the Laura Jilly mentioned. As far as I ever knew, Jilly never even met Laura, never even heard of her. I don't understand why she'd say her name." He sipped his beer, his hand steady as a rock now.

"How did you meet her? What's her last name?"

"More questions, Mac, about a person Jilly only mentioned in passing? What's this all about?"

"Jilly said to me, 'Laura betrayed me.' What did she mean, Paul?"

Paul looked like I'd socked him in the jaw. He shook his head as if to clear it and said, "All right, dammit. There was a Laura, but I haven't seen her in several months. I broke it off. I just lost my head for a while there, but then I realized that I loved Jilly, that I didn't want to lose her. I haven't seen Laura since March."

"Laura was your mistress then?"

"You find that hard to believe, Mac? You look at me and you see a nerd who's a decade older than you are, and not a thing like you? No bulging muscles? No big macho cop with broad shoulders and a full head of hair who goes chasing after terrorists, for God's sake? The only thing good you can say about me is that I'm at least an evolved nerd since I attracted your sister."

I forced myself to take another bite of my tuna salad sandwich. So both this Laura and Paul had betrayed Jilly. I wanted to jump over the table and tear Paul Bartlett's head off. I made myself chew slowly, just as Paul had done. It gave me time to cool down. What I needed most of all was control. I said after just a moment, no anger at all in my voice, "Let's get something perfectly straight here, Paul. I find it hard to believe you'd sleep with another woman because you're a married man, supposedly a happily married man. A married man isn't supposed to screw around on his wife."

"Shit, I'm sorry." Paul rubbed his fingers through his light brown hair. "I didn't mean all that, Mac. I'm upset, you can see that."

"What's Laura's last name?"

"Scott. Laura Scott. She's a reference librarian in Salem. I met her there."

"Why were you at the Salem Public Library?"

Paul just shrugged. "They've got great science reference materials. I do some research there once in a while."

"How did Jilly find out about you

sleeping with Laura?"

"I don't know. I didn't tell her. Of course Laura knows Jilly. They're friends."

"So Jilly went to the Salem Public Library too?"

"Yes, she liked to go there. Don't ask me why, but she did. Look, Mac, Laura is shy, withdrawn. She wouldn't have told Jilly. I just can't imagine how she found out. The two of them, they're opposites. Jilly is beautiful, talented, outgoing, like all of you — you, Gwen, and Kevin. She never just plain walks, she struts. She oozes confidence, is immensely sure of herself. She believes she's the best. Laura isn't any of those things. She's so self-effacing she could be a shadow."

"Why did you sleep with her, Paul, if she's so damned self-effacing?"

Paul looked down at the remains of his roast beef sandwich. "What is that old saw about having steak all the time? Maybe I just needed a change from Jilly for a while."

"Is Laura Scott still in Salem?"

"I don't know. She was upset when I told her it was over. I don't know if she stayed or not. Why does it matter? I tell you, Jilly should never have found out about her. Maybe I dreamed about her and happened to say her name, with Jilly overhearing. But it doesn't matter. It's not important, Mac. It wasn't important as of over a month ago."

I didn't let on to Paul that it was more than important to me. Jilly had known that Laura had betrayed her. Laura was so much in Jilly's mind that I'd somehow picked it up from Jilly when I'd been with her in the hospital. Was Laura the reason Jilly had driven her Porsche over the cliff?

An hour later, I was on the highway heading to Salem.

Salem, the capital of Oregon, sits in the heart of the Willamette Valley, on the banks of the Willamette River. It's only forty-three miles southwest of Portland, just a short hop as the natives say. I remembered Jilly telling me once, on her third glass of white wine, that its Indian name, *Chemeketa*, meant "place of rest" and had been translated into the biblical name of Salem, from the Hebrew *shalom*, meaning "peace."

When I reached Salem, I pulled off the road into a small park and dialed 411. There was no Laura Scott listed in the Salem phone directory. There was one unlisted number for an L. P. Scott. I asked for the main number of the Salem Public Library. Ten minutes later I found the big concrete building between Liberty Street and Commercial. It was only a short drive from Willamette University, just south of downtown. On the north side there was a big open courtyard that connected the library to City Hall. Too close to the bureaucrats for my taste. Once inside, you forgot how ugly the outside was. It was airy, lots of lights, the floor covered with a turquoise carpeting. The shelves were orange. Not what I would have picked, but it would keep students awake. I walked to the circulation desk and asked if a Ms. Scott worked there.

"Ms. Scott is our senior reference librarian," a man of Middle Eastern extraction told me in a thick accent, pointing to the right corner of the main floor. I thanked him and headed in the direction of his finger.

I paused a moment beside the Renaissance art section and looked at the woman who was speaking quietly to a high school student with bad skin. He looked ridiculous to a man of my advanced years with his pants pulled down to nearly the bottom of his butt, bagging to his knees and beyond.

The student moved away, ambling toward the magazine section. I got my first good look at Laura Scott. Paul had said she was painfully shy and withdrawn, that she disappeared, like a shadow. My first thought was: *Is the idiot blind?* Truth was, I took one look at her and felt a bolt of lust so strong I had to lean against the nineteenth-century English history section. How could he say that she was nondescript? She was slender, tall, and even though her suit was too long and a dull shade of olive green, it simply didn't matter. She'd look great in a potato sack. Her hair was made up of many shades of brown, from dark brown to a lighter brown to an ash blond. It was all coiled up and smashed close to her head with lots of clips, but I could tell that it was long and thick. Lovely hair. I wanted to throw all those clips in the wastebasket under her desk. I understood how Paul had taken one look at her and lost his head. But why had he said she was plain? Had he said it so she'd hold no interest for me? So I'd dismiss her?

Actually, Laura Scott looked restrained, very professional, particularly with her hair scraped back like that, and she shimmered. I leaned against the English history section again. Shimmered? Jesus, I was losing it. Was her unremarkable presentation to the world calculated? To keep men in line around her? Well, it evidently hadn't worked with Paul.

It wasn't working with me. I said to myself three times: *She and Paul betrayed Jilly.* I said it a fourth time to make sure it got through.

I waited until the high school student in his low-slung jeans disappeared behind an orange shelf, a magazine in his hand.

I approached her slowly and said, "High school students today — sometimes I just want to grab their jeans and give them a good yank. It wouldn't take much. That boy you were speaking to, I think if he coughed his jeans would be around his knees."

Her face was smooth and young and she didn't change expression for about three seconds. She just stared at me blankly, bland as rice pudding, as if she hadn't heard me. Then she looked to where the boy was leaning down to pick another magazine off the shelf, the crotch of his pants literally between his knees. She looked back up at me and after another three seconds, to my surprise, she threw back her head and laughed, a big full laugh. That laugh broke through the silence like a drum roll.

The Middle Eastern guy at the circulation desk looked over, his mouth opening, his surprise evident even from across the room.

What was coming out of her mouth wasn't at all a nondescript laugh. It was full and deep and delightful. I smiled at her and stuck out my hand. "Hello, my name's Ford MacDougal. I'm new in town, just started teaching at Willamette University. Political science, primarily Europe, nineteenth century. I just wanted to see what sorts of public resources the students had off-campus. I like the orange shelves and the turquoise carpeting."

"Hello. Is it Mr. or Dr.?"

"Oh, it's Dr. MacDougal, but I've always thought that sounded phony, at least off campus. To me, a doctor means doing proctology exams. I can't handle that thought. I'd much rather talk about the Latvian drug wars."

Again, she didn't move, didn't change expression for a good three seconds. Then she opened her mouth and a short ribald laugh came out. This time, she clapped her hands over her mouth and just stared up at me. She got herself together. "I'm sorry," she said, nearly gasping with the effort not to laugh. "I'm not like this, normally. I'm really very serious. I never laugh." She cleared her throat, straightened her suit lapels, and said, "Very well, I'll just call you Mr. MacDougal. My name's Laura Scott. I'm the head reference librarian here."

"You've got a great laugh," I said as we shook hands. She was strong, her hands narrow, her fingers long, nails well manicured.

"How long have you worked here?"

"Nearly four months. I'm originally from New York, came out here to go to Willamette. I graduated with a degree in library science. This is my first job here on the West Coast. The only bad thing about working here is the less-than-princely salary they pay me. It barely keeps me in cat food for Grubster — he's my sweetheart alley cat. There's Nolan too. He's got quite an appetite. Oh, he's my bird."

I'd heard every word she'd said. Grubster and Nolan. I liked pets. It was just that I couldn't keep from looking at her mouth. She had a full mouth, a bit of red lipstick left, beautiful. I cleared my throat. I was acting like a teenager. "You're right," I said, "money's always a bitch.

Lucky for me, since I eat a lot, I don't have to share my Cheerios with a Grubster or Nolan. I just have to worry about feeding myself. The university is hard up too. My office has a view since I came in as a full professor, but the heating system is so antiquated you can hear the steam whistle when it comes out of those ancient pipes."

She blinked this time, rapidly, at least half a dozen times. She didn't burst into laughter, but she did giggle. I'd made her laugh. It felt good. Evidently, she found me amusing.

I'd come here ready to play a role, to get the truth out of this woman, to charm her, whatever. Instead, I wanted to scoop her up and take her to Tahiti. I hated this.

"Do you have plans for dinner?" At her pause, I added, "As I said, I'm new here in town and don't know a soul. I realize you could be worried that I'm another Jack the Ripper from London, so maybe we could just stay around here. That way I couldn't kidnap you or mug you or do anything else to you that you might not think appropriate. You know, fun stuff that isn't supposed to happen when you've only known someone an hour. How about the Amadeus Café I saw on the lower level?"

"If I'm forced to eat another salad down

there in the twisted-bowel café, I'll die," she said.

She looked over at the large institutional clock on the wall just above all the medieval reference books. She smiled up at me and nodded. "I know a great place just down the street."

An hour later, after a solitary tour of the Salem Public Library, we walked down Liberty Street to the *Mai Thai*, which turned out to be an excellent restaurant even though it was so dark and dusty I was afraid to order any meat dish off the menu.

She'd taken her hair down before we'd left the library. I wanted my face and my hands in her hair. She was leaning toward me, her long hair falling over her left shoulder. Laura Scott hadn't shown me a single shy, withdrawn bone. She was open, responding to me with laughter and jokes, making me feel like I had to be the most fascinating guy in the known universe. She'd just turned twenty-eight in March, she said. She was single, lived in a condo right on the river, played tennis and racquetball, and loved to horseback ride. Her favorite stable was just five miles out of town.

She was at ease with me. I didn't want that to stop.

For myself, I made up a wonderful academic life, replete with stories that friends and siblings had told me of their college experiences over the years. She was down to the last few bites of her chicken satay when I knew the party was over. I was here for a reason, not to flirt and start a relationship with this fascinating woman. I said easily, watching her as closely as a snake watches a mongoose, "I have relatives down in Edgerton, a little town on the coast of Oregon, just an hour from here."

She kept chewing her chicken, but I saw the change in her, instantly. Shit, I thought. Her eyes, to this point rather vague and soft, were sharp, attentive behind her glasses. But she didn't say anything.

"My cousin — Rob Morrison — is a cop. He says everyone calls the town The Edge. He's got a little house very close to the cliffs. You look out the window and think you're on a boat. If you keep staring at the water, pretty soon it feels like you're really on a boat rocking back and forth. Have you ever heard of the place? Do you know anyone from there?"

Would she lie?

"Yes," she said, "I have, and yes, I do."

I nearly fell out of the booth I was so surprised she'd admit it, to me, a perfect stranger. Well, maybe that was why she'd admitted it — I was a perfect stranger. There was no reason to distrust me.

I said, "Do you know my cousin?"

"Rob Morrison? No, I don't believe I've ever met him."

"You wouldn't forget him if you had — he's a triathlete, a hunk."

She sighed deeply, her hands over her breast, and rolled her eyes. No one in the known universe could ever believe her to be nondescript. She sparkled. "No, sorry. I know the Bartletts — Jilly and Paul Bartlett."

"Small world," I said, wondering if my voice was shaking. "I know them as well." I took a bite of coconut soup and said, "You're a bit younger than Jilly, so you didn't go to school together. How did you two meet?"

"We met about five months ago when she was here in Salem, at the library. We got to talking. She was looking for articles on infertility. I asked her about using the Internet, offered to show her how to go about it in the library, but she said that computers were beyond her. I saw her once or twice a week ever since then, sometimes here and sometimes in Edgerton. I met Paul about three months ago for the first time."

I sat back against the dark red vinyl of the booth. I picked up my fork and fiddled with it. Jilly told Laura that she didn't know anything about computers? Why had she told Laura that lie? Jilly was a whiz at computers, always had been. And what was this about infertility? Finally, I said, "So Jilly was your friend."

"Yes."

"You weren't Paul Bartlett's mistress?"

She cocked her head to one side, sending her beautiful hair spilling over her left shoulder nearly to her plate. "What is this, Mr. MacDougal? Did Jilly send you here? What's going on?"

"Ms. Scott, I lied to you. I'm not a professor at Willamette University. I don't know a thing about Latvian drug wars. I came into the library specifically to meet you. My name is Ford MacDougal; I didn't lie about that. I'm Jilly's brother. She's in the Tallshon Community Hospital, in a coma."

She dropped her thick-bowled white spoon into her soup. She turned perfectly white. I thought she was going to pass out. I was halfway out of the booth when I

111

managed to stop myself. She was fine. I was the one who was the mess.

"I'm sorry I lied to you but I'd do it again no matter what I felt about you." If my boss heard me say that, he'd have laughed his head off.

She got hold of herself. "My God, Jilly's in a coma? That's crazy. No, it's impossible."

"Why?"

"I just saw her Tuesday night over in Edgerton."

7

I hadn't felt so stupid since my high school English class when Mrs. Zigler told me *Wuthering Heights* wasn't a fancy district of London.

I stared blankly at Laura Scott, and eventually my mouth moved. "You were with Jilly and Paul on Tuesday night?"

"Yes, it was a party of sorts, at least that's how they billed it. I had to leave so I don't know what happened after I was out of there."

"Who all was at this party?"

"Well, it was just Paul, Jilly, and I. I understand that other people were supposed to be coming by. When I left it wasn't very late. You see, Grubster — my cat — is on medication and I had to get home to give him a pill. It's not important. Tell me about Jilly. What happened to her?

Is she going to be all right?"

"She's in a coma. No one knows much of anything about her chances for recovery."

"But what happened?"

"She drove her Porsche off a cliff, landed in twenty feet of water, and a cop managed to pull her out. She told me a short time ago that you'd betrayed her. What did she mean by that?"

She shook her head, sending her hair perilously close again to her chicken satay. "What a strange thing for her to say. That's why you came to meet me? To see if I'd somehow betrayed your sister? I don't know what you're talking about. I just don't know." She was suddenly very still, staring down at her dinner plate. "It just doesn't make sense. She was an excellent driver. I can't believe it. She was laughing the last time I saw her. Did someone force her off that cliff? Was it an accident? Was she hit by someone?"

Even I, the cop, hadn't first thought that someone forced her off the cliff. Why had Laura? "No, she went flying off a cliff some ten miles north of Edgerton just before the junction east back to 101. It would appear that she was trying to kill herself."

"How could she possibly have survived that?"

"As I said, a cop saw her go over and managed to pull her out before she drowned. No one disagrees that it was a miracle."

Laura Scott slowly rose and stared down at the platters still piled high with Thai food. She shook her head and stuck her hand in her purse. She pulled a fifty-dollar bill out of a very fat wallet and dropped it beside her soup bowl. She said, not looking at me, "She was always driving that car too fast, hooting and hollering, yelling at the top of her lungs. She liked danger, she told me. She said driving the Porsche at a hundred miles an hour was like flying, only without having to wear a parachute. Jilly wouldn't try to kill herself. She lost control of that damned Porsche. I want to see her. You said she was in Tallshon?"

"Yes, that's where she is." I rose to stand beside her. I lightly touched my fingers to her forearm, holding her still for a moment. "Before we go anywhere, tell me the truth, Laura. Are you or were you sleeping with Paul?"

She looked up at me like I'd lost my mind. "No," she said, "of course I wouldn't sleep with Paul. That's ridiculous."

I realized I was still touching my fingers to her forearm. I didn't stop. I didn't want to lose the connection to her. "Paul says you were his mistress up until last month. Then he said he broke it off. And Jilly told me you had betrayed her."

She shook off my hand. I thought for a moment that she was going to smack me, but at the last moment she held herself back. "No, I didn't sleep with Paul. He lied. Why? I don't know. As for Jilly claiming I betrayed her, I don't know what she meant."

"Why would Paul lie?"

"Ask him, damn you. I'm going to see Jilly."

"I'll drive you."

"No," she said. "You've done quite enough."

I couldn't believe it. Laura was here, standing beside Ford. I saw her as clearly as I saw Ford. I couldn't believe it was that betraying bitch, Laura. But it was. She was here and I saw her. She was saying something to Ford. What was she telling him?

I felt my flesh crawling, felt bile rise in my throat, felt the fear begin to wash through me, and yet I felt nothing at all. I was apart from her now and she couldn't hurt me. She was coming closer, and she was saying my name over and over. Why did I still feel the fear so strongly?

I wanted to scream that I would kill her, but I couldn't. Why in God's name was she here with me? How could she still have the power to terrify me? It shouldn't be happening. She should have been long gone by now, nothing more than a stupid memory. She was reaching out her hand to touch me as she spoke to Ford. I couldn't stand it.

"Her eyes are open. Look at that. Her eyes are open!"

"They usually are," Ford said. "It doesn't mean anything."

I felt her fingers touch my shoulder. Her fingers were cold as death.

I screamed.

I whirled around so fast I nearly landed on my butt. My heart was pounding out of my chest. I was at Jilly's side in an instant, shouting over my shoulder, "Laura, get the nurses, quick. And the doctors, too. My God, hurry! Move it!"

I gathered Jilly up in my arms and pressed her tightly to me, trying to hold her steady. She was heaving against me, flailing her head from side to side, and she was screaming — screams that came out like low harsh bleating sounds. It sounded like someone was torturing her. She ran out of strength fast and slumped against me. I was relieved because I was afraid she would hurt herself. Very gently, I laid her back against the pillow. "Jilly," I said as I leaned down and kissed the tip of her nose. "No, don't close your eyes. Keep looking at me. Stay awake. Don't fall back asleep. You might not wake up again. Jilly, you've got to stay awake. Do you understand?"

"Yes, I can hear you, Ford," she said to me. Her voice was wispy, thin as a piece of paper, almost too faint for me to hear.

I patted her cheek, stroking my fingers through her hair. She felt alive, solid, back with me. I felt ready to burst with relief. "Good." I leaned closer. "Listen to me, Jilly. You were in a coma for four days. You've come out of it. You'll be just fine now. Jilly, keep your eyes open. Blink at me. Yes, that's good. Can you see me clearly?"

"Yes, Ford. I'm so glad you're here."

Her brain was all right, I was sure of it. Jilly was back with me, all of her. There was awareness in her eyes and she was staring hard at me, willing herself to be here, and she was. "You're the only one who still calls me Ford," I said, and kissed her cheek.

"You've never been Mac to me. I'm so thirsty." I quickly poured water from the carafe into the small glass on the table beside her bed and held her up while she sipped. I wiped the water off her chin when she finished drinking. She cleared her throat, swallowed a couple of times, and said, "When you first walked through that door I couldn't believe it. You were real, unlike all the others. To have you here was wonderful. I felt so alone."

I wasn't really surprised that she'd seen me, that she'd heard every word I'd said, seen the expressions on my face. Actually she could have told me what I'd eaten for breakfast, that she'd tasted it right along with me, and I wouldn't have doubted her for a moment. I said only, "I was real? Unlike the others? What do you mean exactly?"

"Oh, yes," she said, and managed a small smile. "You were very real. The others weren't. Everyone else who came in here was a white shadowy thing, but not you, Ford, not you. You were all here. You touched my hand and I felt warmth. Thank you."

I wasn't surprised, but I did wonder if I hadn't gone off the deep end after the car bomb in Tunisia. Psychic communication with my sister? I wondered what the FBI profilers would say about that.

I heard shouting and running feet. Two nurses and a doctor all tried to squeeze through the doorway and into the room at the same time. I nearly laughed, remembering the Three Stooges.

Things quickly degenerated from there.

Dr. Sam Coates had a 1930s black pencil-thin mustache and a bald head. He said, "We'll be running lots more tests, but given how she appears now, I'm just about ready to say she's pulled through this with no physical or mental deficit." He sounded all cool and professional, but I could tell he was pleased beyond anything, the nurses too. They were hopping about beside him, nodding, smiling, looking ready to burst into song, probably the "Hallelujah" chorus. Dr. Coates continued, gesticulating with his hands, unable, I guess, to keep himself quiet, just like the nurses. "It really is a miracle, you know, Mr. MacDougal. No other way to say it. A miracle and we were all here to witness it. I've seen this complete recovery before with a drug overdose, but not after a head trauma. I'd begun to believe she wouldn't wake up."

He stuck out his hand and I obligingly shook it. I was grateful to all of them. Jilly's room was filled with people. Maggie and Paul had arrived not fifteen minutes before. I watched Dr. Coates shake Paul's hand. He nodded to Laura Scott and said to Maggie, "Sheriff. Now, I suggest all of you go home. Mrs. Bartlett will sleep soundly until morning. Go home."

"But what if she doesn't wake up again?" I asked, terrified when I'd seen Jilly close her eyes, her head falling to the side.

"Not to worry," Dr. Coates said. "Trust me on this. A coma's like a nightmare. Once you wake up, it's over. Memories of the nightmare or the coma might remain but it rarely comes back. Really."

Maggie said, "You're wrong about that, Doctor. Nightmares do come back."

Dr. Coates just shrugged. "Sorry, I'll have to dig up another analogy."

"It's still great news," Maggie said, and shook his hand again. She said to Laura, "Why don't you come home with me? It's pretty late."

"No, thank you, Sheriff," Laura said. "My cat needs his medication. Also I have to work tomorrow." She walked to Paul, and I wondered if she was going to hit him. But she didn't. She just frowned at him for a moment, then stepped back. I watched her walk out of the room. I was right behind her. I said over my shoulder to the doctor, "I'll be back in a moment."

I waited until Paul and Maggie were out of hearing distance, then I gave Laura's hand a tug and stopped her. I pulled her over to a window. "You said you weren't sleeping with Paul. Either you are a remarkable actress and liar, or you're really not sleeping with him."

"I'm a decent actress and liar when I have to be. One more time, Mac. I didn't sleep with Paul. I can't imagine sleeping with Paul."

I believed her and that raised more questions.

"Ask Paul."

"Yes, I will." I forced myself to walk away from her. I stopped to look out the window at the cloud-strewn dead sky. A stand of spruce stood beside the parking lot, thick leaves rustling. The wind was rising. It was pitch-black out there.

I heard her walking toward me. I could feel her. She vibrated with life. I wondered what she'd feel like if I touched her, really touched her.

"Good night, Mac. I'm glad Jilly woke up." She lightly patted my cheek, turned, and walked away. I watched her push open the exit door and ease through a small crowd of off-duty hospital personnel and a couple of late visitors. I couldn't stop myself. I came up behind her, my hand out to stop her when she suddenly turned back to me and said, "I understand from the sheriff that you're FBI. You're a big federal cop. She said you were here to help find out what happened to Jilly that night. Ask her. Find out what happened. Then tell me, please. You might consider believing me about Paul. Actually, truth be told, the only man I've met in the past year or so that I'd even consider going to bed with is you. Good night. Grubster is waiting for his pill. Nolan has probably torn the bars off his cage."

"He's sure been on those pills a long time," I called after her.

"Now you're a veterinarian? Give it up, Mac. I'll be back tomorrow to see Jilly."

"Why didn't Paul call you to tell you what had happened to Jilly?"

"I don't know," she shouted back, not turning. She kept walking. "Ask him. He's your damned brother-in-law. Don't you know him?"

I let her go. What else could I do? I watched her walk to her car without another word, without a backward glance at me. She was looking down as she walked, her shoulders slumped. I stood in the middle of the parking lot, staring after her until her Toyota turned out of the gated opening and disappeared into the night.

I found Paul in Jilly's room, sitting beside her bed, holding her hand. "I wish they'd kept her awake," he said. "It's like she's back in a coma. It's like she's gone again. I don't care what Dr. Coates said. I don't think any of them know much of anything. Why didn't you stop them, Mac?"

"She had a killer headache, Paul. They hadn't expected her to fall asleep so quickly, but Dr. Coates said it wasn't anything to worry about. Knowing the hospital routine, they'll be here to give her a shot in the butt at about three A.M."

"Yeah," Paul said, looking up at me. "You'd know, wouldn't you? How long were you in the naval hospital in Bethesda? Two, three weeks?"

"Too long, however long it was," I said, knowing that it was exactly eighteen days and eight hours. "I don't like to think about it. Jilly's awake now, Paul. Everything will be all right." He looked so painfully hopeful that I dropped my hand to his shoulder and squeezed. "Jilly's back with us. She'll tell us exactly what happened. It's over now, Paul." He looked like he was going to cry. For the life of me, I couldn't bring myself to demand that he explain Laura.

"Well, you look tired yourself, Mac. It's been a long day. You've been pushing yourself too hard. Why don't you have the doctors here check you out?"

I declined and sent Paul home. He looked ready to pitch forward onto his face. I'd nail him about Laura tomorrow. I wanted to know about the damned party on Tuesday night, the same night Jilly drove her Porsche off the cliff.

I realized that I didn't have to know any more about anything right now. Who cared what Paul had told me, what Laura had told me? It didn't matter. Jilly would live. She was the only reason I was here.

I was so tired my eyes hurt but I was too restless to sleep. I ended up wandering the hospital corridors, looking into every room that had windows, except for the morgue in the basement. I had a tough time dealing with the morgue anytime, but now, not a chance.

I went back to Jilly's room a little after

one A.M., still wide awake, still restless. I sat down at the small table in front of the window, pulled out my notebook, and began to write. I wrote down what people had told me. I wrote down some of the questions I still had.

I laid down my pen. I shook my head. My written questions sounded like a soap opera. *Was Jilly sleeping with some other guy? Who is Laura Scott, really?*

I wrote one final question: *Jilly's awake. What the hell am I still doing here?*

When Jilly awoke at two A.M. I was in a semi-stupor, feeling a strong pull from my cracked ribs because I was stretched out in a long deep chair pulled from the doctors' lounge, alongside her bed. I was holding her hand.

"Ford?"

It was her voice and it sounded to me like old knotted threads, ready to unravel at the first pull. She spoke again, and I knew she'd heard the weakness in her own voice and was concentrating on sounding stronger. "Ford?"

I gave her a big smile, which I didn't know if she could even see because the room was shadowy, with only a lamp in the far corner of the room lowered to dim. But my eyes were used to it. I could see her clearly. "Jilly, hi." I squeezed her hand, leaned up and kissed her forehead.

"You stayed with me?"

"Yeah. Paul looked ready to drop so I sent him on home. You want me to call the nurse?"

"Oh, no, I just want to lie here and be alive and start to believe it. The headache's gone. I just feel sort of weak, nothing more."

I gave her more water and rubbed my knuckles over her smooth cheek. "I was with you, Jilly. I was with you when you went over the cliff, when you hit the water. I felt that huge impact."

She said nothing, just looked up at me, waiting.

"I was in the hospital myself, remember?"

She nodded. "The car bomb explosion, in Tunisia."

"Yes. That dream or vision — whatever — was more than real. I came awake and I couldn't breathe. It scared me shitless, Jilly. What I can't figure out is why you hooked up with me. How you were able to connect to my mind. Were you thinking about me at all at the time?"

She shook her head. "You told me about this already, Ford. I heard you clearly, that first time you came to see me. Do you believe me?"

"Of course I believe you. I'd be pretty stupid if I didn't, since I was with you in the Porsche, going over that bloody cliff."

"It's all very confusing, Ford."

"Jilly, the truth now. Were you thinking about Laura?"

I thought she'd pass out. She turned utterly white, her breath wheezed out, and she was shaking her head back and forth on the pillow. "You brought her here. She was with you. I saw her as clearly as I always saw you. No one else, Ford, just you. And then Laura was with you, and I saw her clearly too. And I started screaming —"

"And you came out of the coma screaming," I said slowly, my eyes never leaving her face. "You saw Laura and you couldn't bear to have her here, and then you woke up. Was she the one who brought you out of it?"

I didn't think she was going to answer me, then she whispered, "I had to get away from her, that's all I know. I just couldn't believe she was still here. What were you doing with her?"

Only the truth, I thought, but what was the truth? There were so many lies swirling about that I couldn't be certain exactly where the truth lay, but I could at least tell her what I thought of things. "When I was here yesterday, I fell asleep holding your hand."

"I know. I saw you."

"We'll talk more about that later. I awoke suddenly and heard you saying that Laura had betrayed you. At dinner last night I asked Paul about Laura, said that you'd told me about her. It took a while, but he finally admitted that he'd had an affair with her, once he admitted that she actually existed. Then he said he'd broken it off. He told me she wasn't important. He didn't believe that you knew about it. But you see, I knew that you had at least heard her name. I wanted to see her, so I went to the public library in Salem."

Suddenly, Jilly was nearly gasping for breath. She was wheezing. "Ford, you've got to believe me. Stay away from her. She's very dangerous."

And I was thinking: *I've never met anyone less dangerous in my life.* What was going on here?

"Did she sleep with Paul?"

Jilly shook her head, her skin so pale I thought she would faint. Then she nodded. Was it a yes or a no or just more confusion? In any case, she was tired, upset, and I backed off. I patted her hand and covered her with a light blanket. I stood and felt my body creak. "You're exhausted. It's very late. I'll let you rest awhile. Let me get the nurse."

I watched her for a moment, seeing the waves of fatigue wash over her, dragging her under into oblivion. The nurse could wait. All my questions could wait. She needed sleep. I turned to see Nurse Himmel standing in the open doorway.

"Don't worry. I won't wake her up again. That's what you were coming to tell me, wasn't it?"

I nodded and stepped back so she could come into the room. I liked Nurse Himmel. She was short, built solid as a Humvee, and she'd always been kind to me, and to Jilly. Like Midge, Mrs. Himmel would have brought me a beer.

"She's sleeping, Mr. MacDougal," Mrs. Himmel said quietly as she gently pulled the blanket up to Jilly's neck. "She's just fine. Her pulse and oxygen level are normal. Goodness, it's wonderful to see a recovery like this. She'll be up and walking around soon. Now you should go home and sleep in your bed. You're looking just a bit slack in the jaw."

"You're right, my jaw could use a rest."

She just smiled at me.

Whatever. I knew she was right. It was just that there was so much Jilly had to tell me. It could wait. It would be stupid if I got myself laid flat again. The people I called friends would never let me live it down. I could hear Quinlan, another FBI agent, calling me a wimp in that easy dark voice of his. I drove into Paul and Jilly's driveway twenty minutes later. I shucked off my clothes, down to my boxer shorts, and was in bed only five minutes after that.

I dreamed I was a waiter in a nightclub, with a white towel over my arm, carrying a tray of drinks, but I couldn't remember who had ordered them. I just kept walking around this huge room, looking and looking, not knowing, and I was getting frantic. There were dozens of customer drink-tables, all of them circular, people crowded around them. There was Jilly, tap-dancing from one table to the next. She was dancing like a pro. People were whistling and clapping. She was also stark naked except for her black tap shoes. A man whose face I couldn't see clearly was running after her, holding a long cloak toward her, waving it at her actually.

When I woke up it was nearly nine

o'clock the next morning. I hadn't slept so soundly since before I'd been blasted in Tunisia. For the first time I felt nearly back to normal. I stretched, flexed my muscles, even smiled at myself while I shaved. I didn't look like oatmeal anymore, thank God.

Paul wasn't home. I imagined he'd gone to the hospital to be with Jilly. I could speak to him there.

I was at the hospital a half hour later.

8

As I was turning the corner to the third-floor waiting room, I heard Maggie Sheffield's voice. "I can only tell you, Cotter, that someone hit Charlie Duck over the head and he died shortly after he managed to crawl over to Doc Lambert's house."

"You've got no clues? Nothing?"

"I'll just tell you that it's the damnedest thing, this murder of a harmless old man. It's not like this is Salem or Portland, for God's sake. This is Edgerton, small-town USA. I don't know if a murder has ever happened here before, but someone killed Charlie Duck and then ransacked his house."

I came into the waiting room to see the sheriff speaking to a young man I'd never seen before. He was about my age, on the short side, built like a bull — obviously a weightlifter — with a manner and look that were dangerous. Strange that a guy would think that, but it was true. I disliked him on sight.

"Cotter Tarcher," the man said and nodded to me. "You're Jilly's brother?"

"That's right. Ford MacDougal. And you're Cal's brother?"

"Yes. I forgot you met Cal. She went over to Paul's house and caught all of you there. You're coming to the party tonight? It's Miss Geraldine's birthday and we always celebrate every year. My folks decided that we'd go ahead, despite Charlie Duck's death."

"It was murder, Cotter," Maggie said.

"To be honest, I forgot all about it," I said. "Jilly's awake. I've been thinking about her." Cotter Tarcher looked dark from his dirt black hair to the heavy growth of beard on his cheeks. I bet that women sensed danger in him and were drawn to it. At the same time they'd be wary, if they had half a brain. Cal had said that he let the women he dated do the driving, to make them feel like they had the power. It was a smart move on his part, the prick. He would need to mellow them out. I remembered that Jilly didn't like him either.

"Of course," Cotter said easily. "I saw Jilly just a little while ago. She's looking really good. She got one of the nurse's aides to wash her hair. She looks normal. It's amazing."

I said to Maggie, "I heard you talking about Charlie Duck. It really is a shock for a little town like Edgerton. Did you bring in the crime-lab people from Portland? They're top-notch. The medical examiner — Ted Leppra — is one of the best M.E.s on the West Coast."

She shook her head. "I know how he died. He got bashed on the head, his brain filled up with blood and smashed bone, and that was the end of him. I don't see any need for an M.E. to translate that for me in medicalese — it's a waste of time.

"Poor old Charlie. He's been here for at least fifteen years. The funeral's on Tuesday. Everyone will be there at the League's Christian church."

"The League?" I asked.

"The BITEASS League, remember? Since everyone in town is a member, the League keeps up one central place of worship. Different religions can have the building at different times. In the case of funerals, it's an interdenominational service. Representatives from all the religious groups will take a few moments to speak. Since old Charlie was an agnostic, everyone will get equal time. If he'd been a Baptist, say, they'd get the lion's share of the time. Come if you can, Mac. You can meet the rest of the folk in town.

"Or are you heading back to Washington? Since Jilly's awake again, there's no reason for you to stay, is there? Has she told you about what happened Tuesday night? Does it match your dream?"

"I'm going to speak to her about it right now," I said, wishing Maggie hadn't said anything about it in front of Cotter Tarcher. But in the long run I couldn't see that it would make any difference. Who cared if anybody thought I was nuts? As for Tarcher, he hadn't acted like an ass, at least not yet.

"I hope she'll talk to you," Maggie said to me. "When I was in there this morning, she claimed she didn't remember a thing. She acted shocked when I told her we were worried because it looked to Rob like she'd driven over the cliff on purpose. She didn't say another word. If there's something more, maybe she'll tell you, Mac."

I said, "Maybe nothing's going on, Maggie."

"I hope you're right. I'm just worried she

might try to hurt herself again."

Cotter looked back and forth at each of us. "Try to drop by tonight, Mac. My parents would like to meet you." He shook my hand, harder than necessary, nodded to Maggie, gave me a look that said he could whip my ass anytime, and left. He was easy to dislike, on spec.

"Maggie," I said. "Were you invited over to Paul and Jilly's house on Tuesday night?"

"No. Why?"

"Laura Scott told me Paul and Jilly were expecting other people. She had to leave early, so she didn't know how many people or who they were."

Why did I have to know? It didn't matter. What mattered was speaking to Jilly, making sure that she was okay now, that she wasn't depressed or bent on trying to kill herself again.

I thought about Laura, about how I'd never before met a woman who drew me instantly as she had. No, I wasn't going back to Washington just yet. There was the Tarcher party tonight. It should prove interesting.

"Mac, before you go see Jilly, there's something else about Charlie Duck's murder, something that's really weird. I didn't want to say anything about it in front of Cotter, but hey, you're a cop too."

"You know something?"

"Yeah, but I don't know if it means anything. Someone killed Charlie, then ransacked his house. I've had my guy dust for fingerprints. I've made a search myself. I didn't find anything, nothing that might have been of interest to anyone. Whatever the murderer was looking for, he probably found it. He took the murder weapon with him."

She drew a deep breath. "Maybe you can help me figure this out. After Doc Lambert called me, he said that Charlie regained consciousness just a moment before he died."

My heart speeded up, I don't know why. I waited.

"Doc Lambert said Charlie was real frantic, mumbled a whole lot of stuff, but the only thing he could really make out was 'a big wallop, too much, then they got me.' Doc Lambert said he died then. Does that make any sense to you?"

"Have the M.E. in Portland do an autopsy," I said. "Do it right now."

"Why?"

"Because I've got this feeling, a real burning in my gut, that this wasn't a random killing and burglary. Charlie Duck wanted to speak to you. He wanted to speak to me. I wish he'd done it yesterday, but he didn't, obviously because he didn't think he was in any danger. But he was. Someone walloped him, it was too much, then they killed him."

"Mac, you make it sound like some sort of B movie. You know, the murdered guy trying to tell someone who it was who killed him? It doesn't happen like that in real life."

"Who was Charlie Duck?"

"He was a retired cop from Chicago. More than fifteen years ago."

My heart speeded up again. "Look, Maggie, Jilly goes over a cliff. Someone murders a retired cop. Maybe the two don't have anything to do with each other, but I'd rather know for sure than guess about it."

"Surely his death can't have anything to do with Jilly driving off that cliff. It doesn't make any sense."

"Have the M.E. do an autopsy. His name's Ted Leppra. Call him now, Maggie. Get it done."

A big wallop, too much, then they got me.

What was going on here?

Jilly was alone. She was reading a news-

139

paper. When she saw me, she grew very still. I was at her side in two big steps. "What's wrong?"

She smiled up at me and laid the newspaper aside. "Nothing at all, Ford. I'm looking human again, don't you think? Did you come to tell me good-bye?"

"No, I came to talk to you."

Again she grew still, as if she didn't want to see me, didn't want to talk to me. Why?

"Jilly, you're my sister. I've known you all my life. I love you. If you tried to commit suicide, just tell me why. I'll do what I can to help. I want to help. Please talk to me."

I knew her well enough to see the lie in her eyes and quickly added, "No, don't tell me you can't remember, like you told Maggie. Tell me the truth. Did you try to kill yourself, Jilly?"

"No, Ford, I'd never try to do such a ridiculous thing. Truth of it was that I lost control of my Porsche. I was singing as loud as I could, driving much too fast, and I lost control coming around a corner. That's it, Ford, I swear."

"Rob Morrison said you speeded up when you drove toward that cliff."

"He's wrong," Jilly said. "Absolutely wrong. I lost control. Maybe I hit the gas when I went through the railing, I don't remember. I suppose it's possible.

"Ford, I'm all right, truly. Go home now. You're still not back to one hundred percent. Better yet, take another week off and go down to Lake Tahoe and get some fishing in. You know you'd really like that."

"I'll think about it."

"Well, if I don't see you again, take care of yourself. You, Kevin, Gwen, and I — we'll get together at Gwen's in Florida at Christmas."

It was a tradition, one we'd missed this past year and thus the get-together in February. I leaned down and hugged her hard against me. "I love you, Jilly," I said.

"I love you too, Ford. Don't worry about me anymore. Be sure to call Kevin and Gwen, tell them everything is all right."

The Tarcher house sat on a cul-de-sac at the end of Brooklyn Heights Avenue. It clearly dominated the other three or four pretenders set far apart from one another, separated by spruce and hemlock. The mansion was a good three times larger than Paul and Jilly's place, and looked like an honest-to-God Victorian transplant straight from San Francisco. Its basic color was cream, but there were another four or five accent colors used on the various window frames and sills, door frames, balcony railings, arches, cornices, and various other whimsical things whose names I didn't know. It looked like a huge, fascinating, over-the-edge birthday cake. It had been designed by people with lots of money and an equal amount of imagination.

Four young guys dressed in red shirts and black pants were valeting all the guests' cars. By the time Paul and I pulled up in his Ford Explorer, there must have been thirty cars parked all along both sides of the winding avenue. It looked like the whole town had turned out for the event.

Jilly had wanted to come. She wanted everyone to see she was back in action again, even though her Porsche wasn't. She told me she'd already gotten a towing service to figure out if they could get her Porsche out of the ocean. I'd said fine, you can come if you can walk without assistance from here to the end of the hall. She made eight steps and drooped. But she was fine, according to all the tests Dr. Coates had done on her since early that morning. I'd asked him if he was coming to the Tarchers' party and he'd said he wouldn't miss it unless a set of triplets was ready to slip out. My sister Gwen, who'd had three kids, none of whom, I was sure, had just slipped out, would have slugged him.

I turned to Paul as we stepped out of the Explorer in front of the Tarcher house. "Tell me about Tarcher, Paul."

"His full name's Alyssum Tarcher, and don't ask me where he got the weird name. He's been here some thirty years and he's filthy rich. I wouldn't be surprised if he owns half the state. Everybody here owes him, probably without exception. Nothing happens in this town that isn't run by him first. The mayor, Miss Geraldine, is at his beck and call. She'll do anything he wants. Actually, most of us will."

"Did you have to ask his permission to move back out here from Pennsylvania?"

"As a matter of fact, he helped me come back," Paul said, all cool and formal. "No secret there. He's invested in my current project. He sold Jilly and me our house."

"Ah," I said. So that's how he and Jilly were surviving. But that beautiful house and Jilly's Porsche were far above the survival line. "This is the fountain of youth formula?"

"Good try," Paul said, slamming his door. "Jesus, Mac, I'm so relieved that Jilly lost control of the Porsche. If she'd tried to kill herself, I don't know what I would have done."

"Me either."

One of the young valets dashed up, out of breath, gave Paul a big purple ticket, and drove the Explorer away. "Some house, huh?"

"Incredible," I said, climbing up the deep half-dozen front steps. Lights and mellow chamber music poured out of the house. When we walked into the huge vestibule, I paused a moment, just breathing in the incredible smell of the house. It smelled like standing in the middle of a deep forest with a sliver of sunlight on your face — a hint of flowers, of water-drenched moss, of trees and light, pure air. I inhaled deeply as I turned to see a tall, hawk-nosed man walk toward us. It was, I had no doubt, Alyssum Tarcher, the patriarch of Edgerton, Oregon.

I am six feet, two inches tall, one hundred eighty-five pounds before the car bombing. He was at least two inches taller than me but not any heavier. He was probably around sixty years old, his hair thick, mixed black and white. He was a strong, vigorous man, no paunch, no softness on him. He looked potent. His son, Cotter, was standing behind him — thick-necked and dark, he looked like a thug. It was quite a contrast. He'd probably just shaved, but there was a hint of dark growth on his cheeks. He cracked his knuckles, his eyes studying my face.

"Ford MacDougal?"

Alyssum Tarcher's voice was as deep and rich as the smoothest Kentucky bourbon.

"Yes, sir," I said. He stuck out his hand and I shook it. An artist's hands, I thought, slender, narrow, long-fingered. Too smooth.

"You and Jilly don't look a thing like each other," Alyssum Tarcher said, looking through to my molecules, I thought. This was a dangerous man. Far more dangerous than his bully of a son.

"No," I said. "We don't."

"Of course you're both fine-looking young people and your general coloring's the same. You've met my son, Cotter?"

I shook Cotter's hand and smiled down at him, content to wait to let him begin the pissing contest, which he did, quickly. I managed to twist my hand slightly so that I had better leverage than him. I looked him straight in the eye and proceeded to crush his fingers. I let his hand go when I saw the strain around his mouth. I think Paul was the only one who noticed the locker-room behavior. As for Cotter, oddly enough, he looked both homicidally furious and curiously absorbed. He slowly rubbed his hand, staring at me. It was as if he was trying to get inside my head, trying to see how he could best go about smashing me. I knew I'd made an enemy, didn't really care, but I did wonder what he was thinking now. I hadn't met up with a verifiable sociopath in at least six months.

Cotter never looked away from me. I turned when I heard Alyssum Tarcher say, "Well, Paul, now that Jilly's back with us, you can get to work again. I understand all this has been hard on you, but now, finally, everything will be all right."

"Yes," Paul said. "Jilly wanted to come tonight, but she couldn't walk more than a few steps. Mac and I left her nearly asleep and disappointed. She wants me to assure everyone that she didn't go over that cliff on purpose. She lost control of the Porsche. She also swears that she won't go a hundred miles an hour around any more curves as long as she lives. She sends her love."

"That's a relief," Alyssum Tarcher said. He picked up two flutes of champagne from a waiter's tray and handed one to me and one to Paul. Then he picked up one for himself, raised it, and said, "To the future. May our project succeed beyond our wildest imaginings."

"I'll drink to that," Paul said.

Neither Cotter nor I said anything, merely sipped the champagne, nasty stuff, I'd always thought, remembering fondly the Bud Light Midge had brought me in the middle of the night. Her husband, Doug, was a lucky man. I placed the flute back on the waiter's tray. Alyssum had a dark brow raised, but I didn't give a shit.

Paul said, "It's a real tragedy about Charlie Duck getting killed. Not something you'd expect to have happen in a great town like Edgerton."

"Bad, bad thing," Alyssum Tarcher said, nodding that leonine head of his. "Everyone's been talking about it, trying to figure out who could have done such a thing, and why."

"He was a nosy old man," Cotter said. "He was always pissing people off when he pried into their business."

"A stranger went to his house and killed him, a random thing," said Tarcher. "It must have been. No one in Edgerton would have hurt a hair on his head."

"He didn't have much hair left," Paul said.

He received a strained smile from Tarcher.

I turned to see Rob Morrison, looking like a hunk from Southern California in a black T-shirt, black slacks, and a black sports jacket, speaking to Maggie Sheffield. It was the first time I'd seen her out of uniform. She was a knockout. A red dress on a woman, especially one without much front or back, has an amazing effect. Her hair was piled up on top of her head and she was wearing three-inch heels. I had an urge to walk up to her, bite her earlobe, and go from there. Then I saw Rob Morrison's hand on her back, very low on her bare back. Very proprietary.

"Hello, Mac. You look very nice in that dark suit."

I turned to see Cal Tarcher, dressed like a frump in a long skirt with a black, high-neck, long-sleeved silk blouse and ballet flats. At least the skirt and blouse fit her, more or less. Her red hair was flat against her head, pulled back and tied with a black ribbon at the base of her neck. Her glasses had black frames. Well, at least she was color coordinated. "Hi yourself," I said. I wondered what had happened to that young woman I'd seen briefly outside Paul and Jilly's house, the one who'd suddenly looked taller and arrogant and cold as ice.

We were back to little miss prim and dowdy.

"I saw you staring at Maggie. She looks beautiful, doesn't she?"

"Oh, yes. I like a woman out of uniform. Maybe soon you can get out of your uniform. Maybe you could try a red dress like that."

The cold, arrogant young woman flashed across her face, then smoothed away. "Have you met my mother, Elaine?"

"No, not yet. The originator of BITEASS?"

"Yes," she said, and seemed delighted that I remembered. "I hear that Jilly is just fine now. I tried to get to the hospital today but what with the party, I didn't have time. Mother had me running around all day long. You wouldn't believe how much food is going to be consumed tonight. Can you believe someone killed poor old Charlie Duck?"

"No, I can't."

"You hungry?"

"I can't wait to attack the food. Oh yeah, do you know if Paul slept around on Jilly?" I watched her eyes widen behind her glasses. Just shock at what I'd said? It wasn't exactly acceptable party talk. Or was it surprise that I knew that? I realized then that I just had to let it go. Jilly was fine. There was no damned crime here, except for the random murder of Charlie Duck.

"Paul loves Jilly," Cal said after a moment. "He wouldn't ever sleep with another woman. Besides, Paul's too skinny. He does enjoy sex, that's what Jilly told me. She said he was really good."

"Were you jealous of Jilly, Cal?"

9

She didn't skip a beat, just said in a very nice, indifferent voice, "Not at all. I liked Jilly. She was always so gay, always singing. Would you like a beer?"

I stared down at her a moment, waiting her out, but she beat me in that staring contest. Finally, I nodded.

"Let's go to the kitchen. Cotter and I keep our stash hidden behind Father's mango supply. My mother hates mangoes so we have to hide the beer where she won't see it. She disapproves of beer, you know. It's low-class."

I followed her through the crowd of at least fifty people, all different ages, dressed to the hilt, all of them seeming to be enjoying themselves, digging into an incredible array of food — from oysters Rockefeller to trays of chilled fish smothered in limes to heaping platters of pesto pasta dotted with sun-dried tomatoes — set out on a wide table at least twenty feet long.

The kitchen was the command center. Cal didn't slow, just wove her way through the caterers to a huge refrigerator, opened it, and leaned inside. She was in there awhile, scrounging around. She came out holding two Coors. "Cotter's already been here. This is the end. We've got another six-pack out in the garage if we really get thirsty."

"This is great," I said, popped the lid, toasted her without saying anything, and drank. I loved beer.

"How old is Cotter?"

"He's twenty-eight, two years older than me. I know, I only look like I'm eighteen, but I'm not. You're also wondering what we're both doing still living at home at our age."

"I did wonder. But I'm not rude enough to ask."

"You were rude enough to ask me if I was jealous of Jilly. Why'd you even think of such a thing?"

"I heard something, I guess. Why are you and Cotter still living at home?"

She laughed, drank more of her beer,

and led the way from the noisy, chaotic kitchen to a small back room, a library from the look of it. It was empty, dark. Cal shut the door and turned on a small Tiffany desk light.

She set the beer down on a desktop, then turned to face me. "Well, Jilly was wrong. I'm not jealous of her. Actually, I want to paint her. She just keeps putting me off."

"Paul and Maggie said you were an artist. What do you paint?"

"I usually do landscapes, but people's faces fascinate me. Jilly has incredible bones. I want to paint them, and her eyes. Her eyes are the key to her. It's the same with you, Mac. You have beautiful eyes. Dark, stormy blue, romantic eyes."

"Don't make my beer go down the wrong way."

She stopped then, shook herself, and gave me a bright smile, a really fake smile. "How are you feeling? You're looking stronger and more fit than you did yesterday."

"I feel fine."

"Cotter lives at home because Father wants him to. He wants Cotter to learn all about his business holdings. He did allow Cotter to leave the state to go to UCLA, even pushed him. Cotter got his undergraduate degree in business and then an MBA, all in four years. The thing is, though, I don't believe Father will ever think Cotter competent enough to take over. He'll just have to die before Cotter can get anywhere. Then, of course, it would be moot. But Cotter thinks our father will live forever."

"So Cotter wants out?"

"No, Cotter wants to run everything. I've told him he's too short. It would help if he'd wear elevator shoes. Tall men, like our father, like you, get all the respect. Cotter's too dark as well. He looks like a gangster."

"What did Cotter say to that?" I asked, fascinated.

"I believe he ordered some elevator shoes from a catalogue. He might wear them now for all I know. He still looks like a thug though. No way he can ever change that."

"You're very informative all of a sudden, Miss Tarcher. What's Cal stand for?"

"You don't want to know, trust me." She took two steps toward me and very slowly laid her open palms on my chest. "It stands for Calista. I like you, Mac."

I closed my hands over hers and lightly tugged them away. "Thank you. Actually,

Calista isn't bad, but I like Cal better. It sounds more natural. I don't know what to think of you, Cal. I think that the picture you present to the world and how the world responds to that picture must amuse you tremendously."

She drew her hands free of mine and backed up until she was leaning against the desk.

"Don't bother to deny it. I saw the real you yesterday. You forgot to hide yourself for a moment there when I walked you to your car. I saw arrogance in you, certainty. I have this feeling that you're laughing at the whole town, that you think they're all fools. Maybe you are jealous of Jilly. Or maybe she's seen the real you and she's jealous of you. What do you think?"

"Is this the FBI speaking?" There was amusement in her voice and a smile on her mouth.

"Nope."

"You a profiler?"

"I'm in Counter-Terrorism. Jilly is very beautiful. Why would she be jealous of you?"

Cal just shook her head, the abrupt movement clearly telling me that she was tired of this game. Standing there in the shadows cast by the Tiffany lamp, she said

155

suddenly, "Please don't move. I just want to sketch you. Is that okay?"

I was too startled to say anything. She dashed out of the room, leaving me there alone with two nearly empty Coors cans.

She came back into the room a couple of minutes later, holding a large sketch pad and a thick charcoal pencil in her hand. "Don't move, please," she said, walking quickly toward the desk.

I nodded. I looked at her as she flipped open the sketch pad, flipped through several pages, and propped the pad up on her thighs. Her face changed completely. There wasn't a hint of frump. I saw an intense woman who bristled with focus. This was a strong woman. I started to raise my hand, but she said, "No, Mac, don't move, please."

"I've never had anyone sketch me before. Can I at least talk?"

"Yes," she said, not really paying any attention to me, just drawing on the paper.

"Why do you dress like this?"

"Shut up."

"You said I could talk. The jeans you wore yesterday, they were huge, baggy. You were wearing a man's shirt. Why, Cal? Why were you hiding yourself?"

"I want men to desire me for my brain."

I laughed, I couldn't help myself. I tried to think of a less controversial question and said, "Do you think Maggie is sleeping with Rob Morrison?"

Her charcoal stopped cold in mid-stroke. She stared at me, her lips pursed. "He's so beautiful he could sleep with any woman he wanted. Why not Maggie?" She began sketching again, more quickly now, her strokes deep and fast, rather like really good sex, I thought.

She stopped suddenly, the charcoal pencil poised over the paper, and she stared at me. She was breathing hard. Her hands were shaking, her lips slightly parted.

"Done?" I asked, looking at her hands.

She didn't say anything, just set down the charcoal and the pad and flipped off the lamp.

"Mac," she said, in a voice low and harsh, and she jumped me.

I tried for about three and a half seconds to pull her off me, then a good wallop of lust changed my mind and I gave it up. She kissed me all over my face, ran her hands over my chest, then down, unzipping my slacks, and then her hands were inside my boxer shorts. I nearly lost it when her fingers went around me. I felt a wildness in

157

her, a frenzy, and in her fingers. Dear God, it had been too long and I was a mess. I pulled on her clothes, ripping her blouse, but she didn't seem to care. She pushed me down onto the carpet, climbed on top of me, and straightened over me. I could see her outline, her head thrown back, her throat white and smooth. I could hear her breathing — like someone running a race — hard and deep, jerking with effort.

"Cal," I said, trying to hold her still for just a moment. "Cal, listen to me. I don't have any condoms."

"Don't worry about it. I'm on the pill."

In the next instant, she'd pulled down her panties, kicked off her ballet slippers, and spread her legs. She straddled me, and brought me up and into her. I went in high and deep and I could feel her, every slick bit of her, and I groaned with the effort of not coming right then. "No," I said, "no." I lifted her off me, nearly throwing her onto her back. I watched her raise her hand, jerk off her glasses, and toss them across the room. She stopped cold then, just staring up at me. "I don't understand," she said.

"You don't have to," I said, and brought her up to my mouth. I wondered a few seconds later why the entire household didn't come rushing into the room, she screamed so loudly. I managed to fit my hand over her mouth, felt her hot breath lacing through my fingers, felt her cries nearly liquid against my skin. When she collapsed, all boneless, I came into her, wild and hard. I didn't stay long, I couldn't.

It always takes me a while to get my brain back together. I didn't really want to this time; I didn't want to think about any consequences. I just wanted to keep floating free, not thinking, just mellowing, drifting away. Eventually she moved and then I did. She was wide awake, looking up at me in the shadowy light. "You came down on me," she said, unexpectedly.

I still tasted her, a lingering scent of dark promises and bone-deep lust. It was amazing, that taste of hers, and it made me hard again. "Yes," I said, and managed to slide off to her side. I leaned down on my elbow, and kissed her mouth. I kissed her several times, lazy kisses, and I said against her lips, "You draw a picture and it makes you horny?"

"Not usually," she said, kissing me back, all the while stroking her fingers over my jaw and back into my hair. It was like she was drawing me all over again. "But you, Mac, you were different. I sketched your mouth, then your jaw, and it was all over for me." She sighed and curled onto her side facing me. "That was very nice, Mac. Come into me again."

"All right," I said. This time didn't last much longer than the first time, and I was ready this time to muffle her cries when she climaxed. I knew her scent, the taste of her, would stay with me for a very long time. I'd learned two very important things about Cal Tarcher: She really liked making love, and she had long thin legs that fit nicely around my neck.

I found out she wasn't much for conversation either, which I appreciated since I didn't have a thing to say. She kissed me once more, patted my cheek, and rose. I watched her blot herself with kleenex, watched her dress and slide her glasses up her nose. She left the small room first to go upstairs and straighten herself up, she told me. I moved more slowly. I finished my beer, now warm, and tossed it in the wastebasket beside the desk. I zipped up my pants, found a bathroom just down the hall, and tried to wipe the just-fucked look off my face. It was difficult because it had felt so good, still felt good. So good if she'd been there I would have asked for more.

When I went back into the huge great

room, confident that I looked normal again, except for the lingering glazed stupor in my eyes, the first person I saw was Maggie Sheffield, standing right in front of me. She frowned a moment, then looked me up and down. Then she smiled. "Well, Mac, who just put you out of your misery?"

It was impossible. There was no way she could tell what I'd been doing. No way.

"You want to dance, Maggie?"

"I wonder," she said, tapping her fingertips on her cheek, her head cocked to one side.

"All right. No dance. I'd like to meet Elaine Tarcher," I said. "Could you introduce me?"

"Why not? Come along, Mac, that's Elaine over there, in the midst of that group of men. She's a middle-aged femme fatale. I think she's ridiculous with all her little coyness, a little pathetic actually. She's old enough to be my mother."

The first thought in my brain when I saw Elaine Tarcher up close was that if she wanted to jump me, I wouldn't have hesitated any longer than I'd hesitated with her daughter. The woman wasn't anywhere near her husband's age. I knew she had to be at least in her late forties, given Cotter's age, but still, she just didn't look it. There wasn't anything pathetic about her. I had nothing against cosmetic surgery, if that's what she used to stop the march of gravity. If so, Elaine Tarcher had an excellent cosmetic surgeon. She looked to be in her thirties, no older. She was wearing a black cocktail dress, sheer black panty hose, and black high heels. She had Cal's rich brown hair, short and styled in a mussed-up fashion that made her look very natural and, at the same time, eminently sophisticated. At least half a dozen men were standing around her in a circle, and she let them admire her. I heard her laugh, a charming sound, full and deep and very personal. I didn't agree at all with Maggie that any of her moves were ridiculous.

I heard Alyssum Tarcher call out Maggie's name. She shrugged, pressed my hand, and left me. I stood there observing Elaine Tarcher's magic.

"Everyone thinks my mother is just a silly, useless ornament, but it's not true."

I smiled down at Cal Tarcher, who'd come up behind me. I couldn't see any just-had-sex signs on her face. She was back in her frump mode, neat as could be, her glasses firmly in place. She had changed her blouse since I'd ripped hers.

This one was just as bland.

"Introduce me, Cal."

She looked up at me, silent for a moment, and said, "I wish you weren't staying with Paul."

I felt her lurching upward, bringing me deeper inside her body, and swallowed hard. "I agree, but there's nothing to be done for it."

"Old Charlie Duck adored my mother. She'll be one of the main speakers at his funeral tomorrow. I hope you'll be there? That's all she's talking about tonight, his murder. She's really mad about it."

"Oh, yes, I won't miss it. Perhaps Jilly can come as well."

"When are you going to leave? To go back to Washington."

"I don't know," I said. "Maybe I'll stay on a couple more days. I thought of Laura and felt a hard dash of guilt for having sex with Cal. I shouldn't, I knew that, but it was still there.

I met Elaine Tarcher, all of her gathered admirers, and Miss Geraldine, the leader of the town League and the mayor of Edgerton. She was a well-dressed old bat with a sharp tongue and faded blue eyes that I bet never missed a thing. She said, "Well, boy, I understand you came to see

163

what happened to your sister. Well, I'll tell you what happened. She was going around a corner in that Porsche of hers and lost control. I've told Jilly a dozen times to be careful, but she just sings and dances away. She's fine now, I hear. That's good."

"That's exactly what Jilly said happened," I said.

"How long are you staying in Edgerton?"

"You'll make Mr. MacDougal feel unwelcome, Geraldine, and he's not," Elaine Tarcher said. She'd not said anything up to now. She'd been studying me, assessing me, calmly. There was nothing at all flirtatious in her manner. I wondered if she was seeing me as a possible mate for her daughter. I saw her group of friends fade back when her husband came over.

Alyssum nodded to his wife, then kissed Miss Geraldine's parchment cheek. "You've met our guest here, Geraldine?"

"He appears to be a good boy. Or maybe he's just tall and good-looking and nothing else interesting. I've heard he wants to solve the puzzle of our key letters."

"I've been working on it," I said.

"So did Charlie Duck," Elaine Tarcher said. "He told me just a couple of days ago that he was getting real close. I know I never should have thought it up since I didn't have anything to go with it, and I've thought and thought, but without reportable results."

"BITEASS — not easy," Alyssum said. He was impatient with this nonsense, I could see. Where was that prick, Cotter?

"Edgerton Town League," said Elaine. "That would have been better. Simpler. Short and to the point."

"Not as clever," said Miss Geraldine. "I've always admired clever. Don't worry, Elaine. I'm counting on our nice-looking fellow here. So you're with the FBI. Is that right?"

"Yes, ma'am."

"I also heard you were in the hospital until just before you came here."

"Yes, ma'am. I'm just fine now."

"Are you some sort of hero?"

"No way, ma'am, just in the wrong spot at the wrong time. How about Better Information Through Elucidation And Sober Selection?"

"That's not bad," Elaine said, nodding. God, she'd taken me seriously. No, I saw a flicker of amusement in her eyes.

"It doesn't mean anything," Alyssum said. "It's just nonsense."

Elaine Tarcher gave me a sweet smile. "Keep working on it, Mac. Do you mind if I call you Mac? Good. It's a nice solid name. Poor Cal, now she's got a burden to bear —"

"Please, Mother, don't."

"All right, dear. I forgot."

"Maybe," I said, "if you could tell me the purpose of the BITEASS League, I could come up with something better."

I know I didn't imagine it. Elaine Tarcher shot a look toward Miss Geraldine, who just smiled and said, "We do a bit of everything, Mac. I originally organized the League to force a local chemical plant to clean up its waste. With Alyssum's help, we got them to do it. We discovered we had clout. With an entire town focusing on one specific problem, we could accomplish quite a lot. Now we use it whenever anyone in town needs help or there's another problem common to all of us. Nothing more than that. It's worked very well."

"Usually we're just a big social club," Elaine said. "Tomorrow we'll hold a wake for poor Charlie. The funeral will be the next day. We want to give him a good send-off."

"Poor old man," Cal said.

"It's time for Geraldine to cut her birthday cake," Alyssum Tarcher said.

I walked with them to the long table where a large three-tiered cake sat, weighted down by more candles than I could count.

"Don't think we're insulting her," Cal said. "Geraldine always insists that the number of candles equal the number of years."

I saw Paul out of the corner of my eye, cutting through the crowds of people to get to me.

"What's the matter, Paul?"

"Mac, I just got a call from the hospital. Jilly's gone. They don't know where she is. Do you know anything? Did she tell you where she was going?"

10

It was after midnight when we'd all come back to Jilly's room. I stared down at her bed. It looked like Jilly had simply stood up, lightly smoothed her hand over the covers, and left the hospital room.

"She had no clothes," I said as I touched my hand to her pillowcase. "She couldn't have just walked out of here in her hospital nightgown."

Paul said, "She asked me to bring her clothes this afternoon. I did. I didn't want to make her feel like she was some sort of prisoner. Believe me, she never said she was planning on walking out of here."

"This is weird," Rob Morrison said, walking into the hospital room. "Was she even strong enough to walk out of here?"

"Yes," Maggie said. "She was getting stronger by the minute. Her muscles hadn't given out on her. She was only here for four days, Rob. Does anyone here know anything?"

"Nobody saw a thing," Rob said, rubbing his hand across the back of his neck. His neck cracked. "Man, this doesn't make any sense. Why would she leave? Why didn't she say anything to the nurses? She's got to be here somewhere. I've rounded up everyone I could find to search the hospital, top to bottom. Two of the security guys have established grids in the parking lot and the grounds and are walking them off. They won't miss her even if she's hiding under a car."

"I'm talking to everyone," Maggie said. "Someone must have seen her leave. She's not a ghost."

Paul said suddenly, "Maybe somebody took her." It was the first time he'd said anything like that since we'd all run out of the Tarcher party more than three hours before.

I turned slowly to face Paul. "Why would anyone take Jilly?"

"I don't know," Paul said. "But somebody may have been afraid she'd remember everything that happened Tuesday night. She was gone for three hours, dammit. Where did she go? What did she do?" He added on a whisper, "Maybe it was Laura. I don't understand what was going on between Jilly and Laura anymore. Who else would have done it?"

I pictured Laura in my mind and I couldn't begin to believe she could have done anything like that. But Jilly had said that Laura had betrayed her, that Laura was dangerous.

"Fine," I said. I took Paul's arm and pulled him out of Jilly's room as I said, "Excuse us, Maggie, Rob, but I've got to clear something up with Paul, and it just can't wait."

"Maybe Laura took her," Paul said again once we were in the empty hospital corridor.

"Let's say that Laura did take her. Did she have a gun to her head? Maybe Laura was carrying her over her shoulder? That means that someone must have seen Laura with her. It's ridiculous, Paul, just plain ridiculous. Now, I dragged you out here because I want the truth out of you and I want it now. Did you sleep with Laura?"

"All right, so I didn't sleep with her," he said, and my nerd brother-in-law actually flushed up to his eyebrows.

"Why would you tell a lie like that about an innocent woman?"

"I wanted to sleep with her, but she turned me down. I wanted to get even."

"That doesn't make sense, Paul. You never knew I'd even meet Laura Scott. How would that be getting even?"

"It wouldn't. Look, Mac, I wanted to sleep with her. It was a fantasy, nothing more really, just lay off. It's not something I'm proud of doing, but I did it. Now I'm undoing it."

I said slowly, "Jilly told me that Laura had betrayed her. If you didn't sleep with Laura, if you made it all up, then what did Jilly mean?"

Paul shrugged. "I guess Jilly must have believed that Laura was my mistress."

"I suppose you made some comments that Jilly might have misinterpreted?" I wanted to slug him. It was hard not to.

"Look, Mac, Jilly and I were married for eight years. You can't be married that long and not have some problems. We had our share."

"According to Jilly in February when I saw her, you and she were in the sack all the time, having a fine time."

"Yeah, well, sex isn't everything."

"Paul, was Laura at your house last Tuesday night?"

"Of course she wasn't there. Why would

she be? I already told you, Mac, it was just Jilly and me and the halibut we broiled. What the hell does that matter anyway? I'm going back to Jilly's room."

I watched him until he disappeared around the corner at the end of the hall. I heard Maggie speaking to Rob as they walked out of Jilly's room, over the security guards' voices, all of them talking over one another, making no sense really.

Mrs. Himmel caught sight of me and waved me down. I saw at least half a dozen hospital personnel milling about behind her. She was wringing her hands. I'd never seen Mrs. Himmel flustered before. She looked like she was going to burst into tears. Her pallor worried me. "Mrs. Himmel," I said, gently touching her shoulder.

"Oh, Mr. MacDougal, it's all my fault. Oh, God, Mrs. Bartlett is gone and it's my fault."

I pulled out my firm, very matter-of-fact voice that sometimes worked to calm things down. "Let's go someplace quiet, Mrs. Himmel. I need your help." I followed her to the nurses' lounge. There were two nurses inside, drinking coffee. I heard one of them say, "People said that she'd tried to kill herself. Well, now she just left to do it right this time."

The other nurse jumped to her feet when she saw me. "Oh, Mr. MacDougal."

"Excuse us, please. Mrs. Himmel and I need to be alone for a moment."

The nurses were out of there in under two seconds. I led Mrs. Himmel to an old brown vinyl sofa that had seen better days maybe three decades ago. "Tell me what happened," I said, sitting down beside her.

She drew a deep breath, her fingers curling into a fist. I saw that she was a strong woman. Her biceps rippled as she clenched and unclenched her hands. She was regaining some healthy color, thank God. "Mrs. Bartlett was very quiet," she said finally. "I just thought she had a lot on her mind, and no wonder. I've heard a lot of the stuff that's been going on, so many questions, so much that people wanted her to tell them. I heard her say today that everything from that night was blurry. Well, I suppose that's possible, but I really don't think so.

"Oh damn, let me just get it off my chest. It is all my fault. If I hadn't eaten shrimp for dinner, I would have been at my station just down from Mrs. Bartlett's room or actually with her in her room, tending her, and nothing would have happened!"

173

"Shrimp?" I must have blinked because she leaned over and patted my hand. She was in control again. "How could you possibly know? I've had a bad reaction to shrimp in the past, but it looked so good that I wanted to eat just a little bit. Well, I did and it hit me really hard. I was in the bathroom most of the time, sicker than Mr. Peete down the hall who just had a chemo session. Because I wasn't at my post, Mrs. Bartlett could have just walked out with no one stopping her or asking her questions, probably with no one even noticing her. And of course she had her own clothes. Dr. Bartlett brought her a suitcase this afternoon. She'd been fretting about it, you know, so he gave in and brought her the clothes she wanted."

Paul could describe what Jilly was wearing.

"When we walked in here just a few minutes ago, I heard Brenda Flack, one of the ICU nurses, talking about Mrs. Bartlett leaving to kill herself. I hate to say this, Mr. MacDougal, but it's possible."

"No," I said. "Jilly told me very clearly that she lost control of her car. She didn't try to kill herself. I believe her. Why did she walk out of here without telling anyone? I don't know. But count on it, I'm going to find out everything. Can you think of anything that happened today or this evening that wasn't quite right?"

"Well, there was a phone call from that young lady who was here yesterday."

"Laura Scott?"

"Yes, that's her. She asked to speak to Mrs. Bartlett, but there was a foul-up and she never got through to her. But why would that be important? They were friends, weren't they?"

At three in the morning we still had exactly zilch. No one had seen Jilly. No one had seen anyone carrying her out of the hospital or carrying much of anything, for that matter. Maggie Sheffield had an APB out on her. Since we had no clue about a car, there wasn't much to say other than to give a description of Jilly, and from Paul, a description of the clothes she was wearing, a gray running outfit with black trim and black-and-white running shoes.

I put pressure on the phone company and found out that there'd been a phone call to Jilly's room from the single pay phone on Fifth Avenue, downtown Edgerton, at 8:48 P.M. Laura's call had come in about eight, but she hadn't spoken to Jilly.

I found Paul sitting in the chair in Jilly's

room, his head in his hands.

I said, "Someone called Jilly from a pay phone in Edgerton earlier this evening."

"There's only one public phone," Paul said. "It's on Fifth Avenue, right in front of Grace's Deli."

I said, "Anyone could have ducked out of the party to go make the call. You included, Paul."

"Yes," he said, not looking at me. "Cotter disagrees with me. He thinks Jilly was pissed off that everyone had assumed she was trying to kill herself. She wanted to make all of us worry that she just might try it again. She wants to make us suffer. She'll show up soon, laughing at us. Oh, yeah, Cotter was here earlier, helping look for her."

I said, "Let's get some sleep. It's late. My brain's scrambled. There's nothing more we can do until morning. Come on, Paul, let's go home."

I wanted at least three hours' sleep before I went to Salem to see Laura.

11

It was just after seven the next morning when I pulled my car into a guest parking spot in front of a parkside condo complex. I got out and looked around. The complex didn't look more than three or four years old, designed in a country French style, three condos to each building, all of them garnished with pale gray wooden siding. The park was quite pretty, all pine and spruce trees, and playgrounds for kids, and even a pond for ducks and lily pads. As I walked into the complex, I saw a swimming pool off to the left, a clubhouse, and a small golf course. I remembered Laura saying that the library didn't pay much. That was interesting. This place wasn't cheap.

Laura Scott opened the door and blinked at me as I said, "Nice digs."

"Mac, what are you doing here?"

"Why didn't you go to see Jilly yesterday? You told me you were going to visit her."

She just shook her head at me. It made her long hair swing and lift. She was wearing nice-fitting jeans and a loose T-shirt, and running shoes on her feet. I thought she looked elegant and sexy.

"Come in, Mac. Would you like a cup of coffee? It'll take me just a few minutes to brew."

"Yeah," I said and, having no choice, followed her into one of the most beautiful homes I'd ever been in. The foyer was small, tiled with country peach-shaded pavers and whimsical accent tiles of French country scenes. Off to the left was a beautiful oak staircase leading upstairs. I followed her through an archway into a living room that was octagonal-shaped, giving it complexity with lots of nooks and crannies. There were bright colors everywhere, window seats, small flashes of scarlet pillows, and richly colored South Seas–patterned material on a sectional sofa. There were lamps and chairs and small groupings and nearly every inch of the room was filled with something extravagant, brightly colored, and utterly useless. It coaxed you right in.

There were plants and flowers every-where. A mynah bird stood on the back of a chair watching me. He squawked, then began poking under his wing feathers.

"That's Nolan," Laura said. "He doesn't talk — which is probably a good thing — just squawks occasionally."

"Squawk."

"That's his greeting."

"Hi, Nolan." I followed her through the dining room into a small kitchen that looked right out of *Bon Appétit* magazine. All in all, the condo was a good-sized place, not as big as my own house, but not bad.

"How many bedrooms?"

"Three upstairs and a study downstairs."

I accepted a cup of coffee, shook my head at the offer of milk or sugar. "You've got a really nice place here, Laura."

"Thank you."

"Did I see a two-car garage for each condo?"

"Yes. Before you raise that sarcastic eyebrow of yours even higher, let me tell you that my uncle George left me this condo in his will. About eighteen months ago, just in case you wondered."

As, of course, I had. It was at least something solid and real that I could check out.

179

"So Uncle George lived here?"

She nodded and sipped her coffee. Her head was cocked to the side, sending her loose hair hanging like a shining curtain beside her face. I wanted to roll around in that hair of hers, smooth it over my hands, let it tumble over my face. I'd noticed immediately that she wasn't wearing a bra. I noticed again, and swallowed.

I forced my libido back into its case and got back to what I'd come for. "I was thinking that the complex doesn't look more than three years old."

"That's about right. My uncle George bought it when they'd just begun building. He died a year and a half ago. I'll never forget the first time I walked in here. The place was painted dark colors and filled with heavy, old pieces. I just shoveled everything out and had the greatest time making it mine." She motioned toward the living room, and I followed her back out.

"Squawk."

"Nolan likes coffee but I only give him a tiny taste just before bedtime."

I elected not to sit in the chair that was Nolan's current hangout. I sat opposite Laura on a pale yellow silk-covered chair. There was a hand-painted wooden magazine holder beside the chair. I saw two suspense novels, a world atlas, and three travel books. No magazines or newspapers to be seen.

"I didn't go see Jilly yesterday because I had to work. There was a meeting with the Board of Trustees in the afternoon and I had to make a presentation. I didn't go last night because, frankly, I didn't feel well. I'm going to see her this afternoon."

Ill? Had she eaten some of Mrs. Himmel's shrimp and spent the night in the bathroom?

"You look just fine now, Laura. The flu bug gone? Or was it food poisoning?"

"No, it was a bad headache. Not quite a migraine, but still unpleasant. Maybe it came from all the stress. I came home about four in the afternoon and slept on and off until this morning. I called the hospital just an hour ago to see how Jilly was doing, to see when I should come, but no one would tell me anything. Of course, it was only six o'clock. The most anyone would say was that Mrs. Bartlett was unavailable. Why are you here, Mac? Tell me what's going on."

"What was your presentation to the Board of Trustees about?"

Her mouth curved into a grin. "It was titled 'Into the Next Century' — on library economics in the next decade and what the library should do in order to survive."

"I'm here because Jilly's gone."

She jumped to her feet, took two steps toward me, leaned down, and yelled in my face, "No! That's impossible, she couldn't have died. She just woke up. She was bloody fine, the doctor said so. I called her last night. The nurse I spoke to said she was doing very well."

"You never actually spoke to Jilly last night?"

"No, there was some sort of screwup. One nurse answered the phone, then another picked it up instead of Jilly. What happened, Mac?"

"She's not dead. She's gone, just disappeared out of the hospital."

She lurched back, knocking her coffee cup off the table. The cup shattered on the oak floor, the coffee snaking toward a small silk Persian rug. She made a small sound of distress in the back of her throat and stepped back, staring down at the coffee. I got up and moved the rug out of the way. Then I just couldn't help myself. I took her left wrist and slowly pulled her against me. She resisted, then finally she came to me, wrapping her arms around my back. I said against her hair, "She's not dead, Laura, but she is gone. I came because I wanted to know if you knew why she left the hospital."

Laura was tall. She fit against me very nicely. I held her away from me. I had to or I'd never even be able to keep a modicum of objectivity.

"When?"

"About ten o'clock last night," I said, taking a step back from her. "We don't know where she is. I'd hoped you'd know."

She hadn't moved. She just stood there where I'd put her. "Why should I know? Naturally I don't have any idea where she is. How could I possibly know? She's really missing? Just a second, Mac. I'd better clean that up."

I waited until she returned to the living room with a paper towel. She went down on her knees and wiped the floor clean. I said, "No one has a clue where she is. No one saw her leave, by herself or with anyone else."

She was cleaning up the shards of the cup, wiping more spilled coffee off the oak floor. She sat back on her heels and looked up at me. "And you think I'm involved," she said at last.

"I came here because I hoped you'd know. You called her last night." I raised my hand to cut her off. "Yes, I know, you never really spoke to her. But hear this, Laura. Jilly didn't like you. She might have been afraid of you. I know she believed you betrayed her somehow. I know she didn't want to be anywhere near you. Surely you realize it was you being there that helped bring her out of the coma. She wanted to get away from you.

"Your story to me about meeting Jilly at your library — she was looking up articles on infertility of all things, you told me. I don't buy that, Laura. To the best of my knowledge Jilly only realized she wanted to get pregnant about six months ago, at the outside. She wouldn't even have started to worry there was a problem yet, would she?"

She rose slowly to her feet. She took a hard breath, her face set. "I'm not lying to you. That's exactly how I met Jilly. I don't personally know much of anything about infertility. How long does it take for someone to become concerned about not conceiving? I haven't a clue. Maybe she's been trying for quite a while and just didn't tell you. That's certainly possible, isn't it? Jilly might not have been very well educated, but she wasn't stupid."

"You really believe Jilly was uneducated?"

"That's what she told me. She said she barely scraped through high school, said that one of her teachers wanted to get in her pants and so he passed her, helped her graduate. She was always talking about how brilliant Paul was, what a genius he was, and how she was content to just be in the background and take care of him. I thought that was ridiculous, but it was what Jilly really believed, evidently what she really wanted. She said she wanted his child. She asked if I could begin to imagine how bright his child would be? Then she'd shudder and say that if the kid had her brains and her no-talent they'd all be in big trouble. I didn't tell her that I think Paul is too skinny, doesn't take proper care of himself, that he's losing his hair, and that I hope he doesn't pass that along to a kid."

If she was lying, I'd never in my life heard anyone better. I said, "This is all pretty strange, Laura. I guess then Jilly never told you that she's a scientist, a researcher with a master's degree in pharmacology? That she'd completed all her course work for her Ph.D. but put it on hold because she was more interested in the projects she was doing than writing a silly thesis, her words?

"Why would she lie to you? Why would

Paul back up her lie when you were with the both of them? Come on, Laura, if someone saw you last night, you'd better dredge him or her up because, frankly, I don't believe you. There's no proof of any crime yet, no proof that someone took Jilly from the hospital against her will, but as far as I'm concerned, I'd say you need an alibi."

"Wh-what?"

I thought Laura was going to pass out. She turned utterly white and leaned at the last minute against a white wall, barely missing a mirror with a brightly colored frame. She was shaking her head slowly, back and forth. The thing was, I wanted to comfort her, to hold her and pat her back. I wanted to bury my face in that long straight hair of hers.

"Squawk."

She looked wildly over at Nolan and spread her hands in front of her. "No, you're making that up, Mac. Jilly told me she was a housewife, that she didn't have a single skill. I always just laughed at her when she went off on those self-bashing kicks of hers. She was so very beautiful, you see, and she had this natural confidence that made everyone respond so eagerly and positively to her. She was bright, well spoken. I can't believe it. A scientist? A master's degree?" She looked suddenly as if she was going to cry. She was still shaking her head, her hair swinging. She looked shaken and confused. It couldn't be an act, I told myself. No one was this good.

"I was sleeping all evening, all night. I was alone. Why did Jilly lie to me?"

I said, "Paul told me there was no party at all last Tuesday night, the night of Jilly's supposed accident. He said that they ate dinner alone. He said that Jilly left at nine o'clock to drive around in her Porsche and he was in his laboratory, working.

"He also admitted, finally, that he hadn't slept with you, that he'd wanted to but you weren't interested."

She looked like a blind person, feeling her way along the back of two chairs until she finally collapsed onto a section of the sofa. She lowered her head to her hands, her hair falling forward. "This is crazy," she whispered through her hands. "I don't understand any of it."

"That makes two of us. But the fact remains that Jilly is gone. Vanished." I had to attack straight on, I thought, whether I liked it or not. "I want to know where she is, Laura. I want to know how you convinced her to leave with you. I want to know how you managed to get out of the hospital without anyone spotting you."

She looked up at me, eyes focused and hard. Her voice was fierce. No more shock or palpitations out of her. "Listen up, Mac. I didn't lie to you, about any of it, the party included. I told you I had to leave early to give Grubster a pill. If there turned out not to be a party, that has nothing to do with me or with what Paul and Jilly told me."

"Where is Grubster?" I asked, looking around. Who would have a cat around when Nolan was sitting quite at his ease on the back of a chair, looking at my coffee cup?

She shook her head as she rose from the sofa. "Now you don't even believe I have a cat." She left the living room. I heard her light steps up the stairs. When she returned a couple of minutes later she was carrying a huge calico cat. "This is Grubster. As you can see, he likes his food. He weighs eighteen pounds. He doesn't move very quickly anymore. He's nearly eleven years old. He just looks at Nolan and yawns. Sometimes they just have staring contests. Sometimes Nolan even deigns to sit on his back and dig around behind his ears with his beak."

"Squawk."

Laura looked over at the bird. "Come here, Nolan, and say hello to Grubster."

The cat yawned and curled up next to Laura on the sofa. The mynah bird hopped from chair back to sofa section until he was finally looking down at the cat. Grubster cocked an eye open and regarded the bird with complete indifference.

"Would you like some more coffee, Mac?"

I just nodded, staring from Grubster to Nolan. Someone was hanging me out to dry. Someone was playing a very big game with me and I didn't have a notion yet about the rules. I didn't know where the game left off and reality kicked back in. I also had no clue where Jilly had gone. Laura's claim that she'd had a bad headache and slept throughout the night was a good one, one I couldn't check out.

Laura handed me a new cup of coffee. Steam was snaking off the top of it. I took a sip. It was delicious. Maybe she'd tossed in a dash of Amaretto. I drank some more, trying to get my brain back on track. She handed me a chocolate chip cookie. She couldn't have known they were my favorite. I ate two, to help soak up the dash of alcohol in the coffee, then said, as I watched her drink her own coffee, "When you were at Jilly and Paul's last Tuesday night, what did you do after dinner?"

She took another drink of her coffee. "Very well. There were just the three of us. I got there about six-thirty. Jilly wanted fish. Paul made a salad, spinach, I think. I sliced and garlicked some bread. We ate, then listened to some music. Jilly and I even danced a couple of numbers. Paul drank a good bit. Jilly knew I couldn't stay late because I had to work at the library the next morning and because Grubster needed meds. She told me that some other people were coming, but later, so I'd have to meet them another time. We'd have another party in Edgerton real soon, she said."

I leaned forward in my chair. "Is this the truth, Laura?" She remained silent for a long time. I sipped more of my coffee, watching her.

"There's more, isn't there?"

She looked down at Grubster and began to scratch behind his ears. I could hear the cat purring from where I sat.

Finally she nodded. "Yes, there is more. I really don't want to talk about it, but Jilly's gone, and I know you won't be happy until you know everything, even if it doesn't have anything to do with what happened to Jilly." She sucked in a hard breath. "When Jilly went to the kitchen, Paul grabbed my breasts and pushed me down on the sofa. He started kissing me, tried to shove his knee between my legs. Then he heard Jilly call out something from the kitchen, and he jumped back away from me. He was breathing real hard. I looked at him and told him he was a creep.

"When Jilly came back to the living room, I made up the story about Grubster needing medication earlier than he really did. I just wanted to get out of there. I didn't want Jilly to realize what her precious husband had done, the jerk. She adored him. She worshiped him. She wanted to have a kid with him. God, it was awful."

"And you never got the impression that Jilly was more than an infertile house-wife?"

She shook her head, mute. "No. Neither of them ever said anything to make me believe what Jilly had told me wasn't the truth."

"Them's all the facts?"

"Yes, them's all the facts, the whole truth. I swear it."

"All right. Tell me, Laura, what kind of fish did you have for dinner?"

"Fish?" Her face was blank. "I don't particularly go for fish, so I really didn't pay any attention. Maybe it was bass, or halibut."

She'd gotten the fish right on the second guess. At least the rest of the meal was as Paul had described it to me, whatever good that did.

I felt suddenly so tired that I couldn't seem to think two words ahead. It crashed over me, dragging me under. I stood up quickly and began pacing. It didn't help. I felt like I was slogging through mud.

"Mac, what's wrong?"

I just kept walking around her living room. "I've got to go," I said. I needed to get out of there, breathe in some fresh air. What the hell was wrong with me? That was stupid, I knew exactly what was wrong. I'd been pushing my body too hard and now it was getting back at me. I hadn't felt this dragging sort of fatigue for more than a week, until now. I knew that I should keep questioning her, but for the life of me I couldn't think of anything else to ask.

"I'll see you later, Laura," I said and left. I heard her call my name, but I didn't stop or look around. I heard Nolan give a final squawk toward my back.

I rolled all the windows down in the Taurus, turned the radio onto a rock 'n' roll station, and cranked the volume up as high as it would go. I even stopped at a McDonald's and got more hot coffee.

I sang "King of the Road," and when I forgot the words, I hummed as loudly as I could. I couldn't keep my eyes open. I kept banging my forehead against the steering wheel. Three or four times I went off the road and scared the shit out of myself before I managed to twist the car back. I nearly hit a truck, which would have smashed me six feet under. The sound of his horn zinged through my head. Fear cleared out my mind for a few minutes. Then it was back, this overpowering, brain-numbing fatigue.

I knew that I wasn't going to make it back to Paul's house. I was sweating, remembering how close I'd come to biting the big one with that truck. The hospital, I thought. Yes, I could make it to the hospital. It wasn't more than six minutes away, maybe seven minutes. I managed to keep the car reasonably in my own lane. Only about half a dozen oncoming drivers honked at me. Finally, disbelieving that I'd really made it, I pulled into the Emergency Room parking area, clipping a bush on the way in. I watched my fingers try to turn the key off and fail. I felt like I was folding in on myself, that whatever strength I'd had until this minute was gone. I just let go because I didn't really have any other choice.

Odd, but I heard a horn blasting in my eardrums. It was the last thing I remembered.

12

"Mac. It's time for you to wake up. Come on now, you can do it."

I didn't want to move. I didn't want to open my eyes. The voice came again, low and insistent. I recognized that twangy voice vaguely, and I hated it. It made my head ache. Finally, I managed to get words out of my mouth. I said, "Go away."

Twangy Voice said, "No can do, Mac. Open your eyes. Let me see that you're alive."

"Of course I'm alive," I said, pissed now, wishing I could lift my arm and punch the voice out. "Just leave me the hell alone."

I heard the man speaking to someone else. "Slap his cheeks," a woman said. It was Mrs. Himmel.

Smack the man — that was a woman for you. "No," I said. "Don't hit me."

"He's coming around," Twangy Voice said, and I swear I could feel his breath on my skin. Skin? What did that mean? I felt something cold touch my bare chest. I didn't have my shirt on. How did that happen?

"Vitals are stable," another man said. I didn't recognize his voice at all. "Yeah, he's coming back now."

It pissed me off even more that this damned stranger would stick his oar in.

"Mind your own business," I said. "Nobody asked you."

Twangy Voice chuckled. "It will take him awhile to get back to normal. Just give him a few more minutes. He's coming out of it just fine."

"Yes," I said. "Go away." Then I opened my eyes and stared up at Dr. Sam Coates, Jilly's doctor, Mr. Twangy Voice.

"Ah," he said, smiling down at me. "You're back. Can you understand me, Mac?"

"Yes, I can understand you. What's going on? What are you doing here? Where's my shirt?"

"It seems you managed to drive nearly into the Emergency Room itself before you collapsed. You smashed down the horn with your forehead. There were a dozen nurses, orderlies, security, patients, and doctors with you within two seconds."

I remembered the loud noise. The horn blasting in my ear. "I've been pushing too hard, haven't I? My body's angry at me and finally just shut down?"

"Paul told us you'd been in a terrorist attack out of the country, and in the hospital until very recently. But no, this had nothing to do with any relapse. Actually, you had a high level of phenobarbital in your system. You've been out of it for about three hours now. Once we guessed the problem, we began treating you, but this kind of thing takes time. You're going to feel groggy for a while."

I thought about the likely treatment and nearly turned green. "Tell me you didn't pump my stomach. I saw that done once and nearly puked."

"Sorry, Mac, we had to. We didn't have a choice. But hey, you were unconscious. We also put some activated charcoal in your stomach. There's still some flecks of black above your mouth and a bit dried on your chest. Pretty gross, but it soaks up all the poison. Don't worry about the IV and the oxygen. That's just in case something goes wrong. We'll keep them in for a while longer. Does your throat hurt?"

It did hurt. I nodded. My brain was finally kicking in again. "I was drugged, you said? With phenobarbital?"

"Yes. No one's suggested yet that you were trying to kill yourself. Who gave you the drug, Mac?"

I looked up at Dr. Coates, then over at Mrs. Himmel, whose face was shocked and still, and at a man I didn't know. "Well, damn," I said.

A few seconds later, Dr. Coates knew I was very much awake because I had his wrist in a vise as I said, "This is important. The cops need to get to Laura Scott's house in Salem. That's where I was this morning. She may have tried to kill me."

Dr. Coates wasn't a young man, but he could move fast. He was out of the room in a flash. Mrs. Himmel patted my hand. "You'll be all right now, Mac. Oh, this is Dr. Greenfield, he's the one you told not to butt in."

I looked at a skinny older guy who wore a thick black beard and sported a green and white dotted bow tie. "I'm alive," I said. "Thanks."

He said, "Your body's still not fully recovered. That must have been some terrorist, er, incident."

"Yeah, an incident."

"You're young and strong, Mr. MacDougal. You'll pull through this just fine. I'll leave you in good hands." He turned on his heel, gave Mrs. Himmel a little salute, and left.

"He's our resident guru," Mrs. Himmel said. "Now you just rest, Mr. MacDougal. Why would this woman try to kill you?"

"I don't know. I drove to Salem early this morning to speak to her. I'd like to think she had something to do with Jilly's leaving the hospital last night, but I didn't find out anything. I drank her coffee, then got really tired. I left." I wanted to cry or howl, I didn't know which. How could I have been so wrong about her?

"You almost didn't make it back, Mac," Dr. Coates said, coming back into the hospital room. "Why didn't you just pull over and go to sleep?"

"I didn't think of doing that, for some reason. I just thought about getting back. I guess I was blurry because stopping wasn't an option in my mind."

"Well, you made it back. Some of that road you were driving is tricky enough when you're not drugged to the gills."

"A truck nearly got me and the adrenaline surge bolstered me up for a few minutes. I was singing, shouting, anything to

199

keep myself awake. I just couldn't go over a cliff in the car, like Jilly. I had to make it back." I drew a deep breath. "All right, what about Laura Scott?"

"Detective Minton Castanga will get back to us as soon as they get to her house and find out what's going on. I got him when I mentioned the words *attempted murder and FBI agent all in the same breath.*"

"She could be long gone. If she wanted to kill me I don't think she'd hang around." Then I thought that if Laura had done it, she'd go to prison. I wondered: *In prison for what? What has she done? It had to be something bad enough to make her believe she had to kill me.*

Dr. Coates said, "As to that, there's no way to know if her intent was to kill you, unless she's caught and admits to it. You had a butt-load of the drug on board, but you probably would have survived the dose even without us. Your blood level was never that high, and you were never really unstable. They'll have to find her and see what she says."

I shook my head as I said, "I just don't think they're going to find her. She's a very smart lady. She won't be there and they're not going to catch her."

Dr. Coates listened to my chest again

and Mrs. Himmel took my blood pressure. Then he said, "Oh, I nearly forgot. Dr. Paul Bartlett was here, pacing and upset, until finally we got him to go home. I'll call him and he can bring back the sheriff and some of your other friends who were trying to pile into your room. Maggie did tell me she was going to call the FBI and tell them what happened."

"Oh, no," I said. "I don't suppose you tried to talk her out of that?"

If Maggie did call the FBI, she would have gotten my supervisor, Big Carl Bardolino. I looked at the phone beside my bed. I didn't see much choice now. I made the damned phone call and got put on hold by his secretary. Big Carl was a man I respected, a twenty-five-year veteran, a canny team player but not a yes-man, and I really didn't want to talk to him about this.

"Yeah? Is this you, Mac? What the hell's going on? I get this call from a sheriff out there in the boondocks telling me about your getting yourself poisoned."

"Yes, sir, that's why I'm calling. I wanted to let you know that I'm fine. The local cops are on it. No need to worry."

"Damnation, you got yourself involved with a woman, didn't you? How many times have I told you young people that

201

you've got to be careful about letting your hormones go on a rampage and getting you compromised. Or should I say poisoned?"

"Yes, sir, you've told all of us that at least half a dozen times. That isn't exactly what happened."

"Yeah, right. I can hear the truthfulness in your voice. You're a lousy liar, Mac. How many times have I told all of you that only vigilance conquers lust?"

"At least half a dozen times."

"Right. And none of you ever listens. I'm fifty-three years old, thankfully beyond all that sort of thing, but you're not. You're supposed to be on leave. You're supposed to be taking care of yourself, not getting poisoned. How are you feeling? How's your sister?"

"Well, she was in an accident and she's okay, but she's out of the hospital right now, and I'm not sure just where she is. I'm sorry the sheriff called you. I really don't think the drug I took was meant for me. There really wasn't any need to call you."

"Mac, I'm going to ream you if you get yourself hurt, you understand me? The FBI is a team, not a bunch of hotdoggers doing their own thing."

"I understand, sir. I'm not hotdogging. This is all about my sister, and where she's gone. It's not an official investigation. I'd appreciate it if you'd let me deal with it for now. I don't see any need to call in the cavalry."

He grunted. Finally, after I knew he'd chewed his unlit cigar nearly through, he said, "You will keep in touch with me, you understand?"

"Yes, sir. I understand."

I was so thankful I fell asleep, the oxygen still up my nose and the IV still dripping into my arm.

I woke up to see another man I didn't know staring down at me. His expression was thoughtful, and his long fingers stroked over his clean-shaven jaw. He had light hair, a narrow nose, and an obstinate look. He was dapper, no other way to say it, from his French-cuffed white shirt to his highly polished Italian loafers. I put him at about forty, on the lean side, probably a runner, with smart, dark eyes that had seen more than their share of the world. He didn't look at all like a doctor.

When he saw that I was back among the living, he said quietly, in a lazy drawl that shrieked Alabama, "I'm Detective Minton

Castanga from the Salem Police Department. I understand that your name is Ford MacDougal and you're an FBI agent here to find your now-missing sister."

"That's it exactly."

"Well, not all of it. You're flat on your back because someone laced your coffee with phenobarbital."

"Laura Scott," I said. "Did you find her?"

"Oh, yes, I was at her condo within ten minutes of Dr. Coates's phone call. However, she didn't tell us a thing."

"She's very smart. I doubted you would find her."

"You don't understand, Agent Mac-Dougal. Laura Scott was lying unconscious on the floor of her living room, a huge calico cat curled up on her back and a mynah bird squawking on the seat of a chair just a foot from her head.

I couldn't take it in. "No," I said, struggling up to my elbows. "She's not dead. She isn't dead, is she?"

He cocked his head to the side, and I could nearly see his mental wheels turning. "No, no, she's not dead. She's at Salem General Community Hospital. They're still working on her, lavaging her stomach, the whole bit you went through with the nasogastric tube, the oxygen up the nose, and the rest. They said she's going to make it.

"So, Agent MacDougal, she gave you coffee, you drank it, and she drank it as well, in front of you?"

"Yes." I thought back. "She had only about a half a cup, at least while I was there. I got more of the phenobarbital than she did. I drank two cups."

"Was anyone else there in the condo? Or was it just the two of you?"

"No, no one else that I saw. Just me, the bird, the cat, and Laura."

"One of two possibilities, then," he said, smiling down at me. It was a smile filled with irony and a good deal of understanding. "Someone wanted both of you dead, which doesn't ring true unless that person knew you were going to visit her."

"I didn't tell anyone I was going to visit her."

"All right then. It appears that you were an accident and it was Ms. Scott they were after."

"But who would want to kill Laura?" Saying the words made me crazy with worry, and guilt. Because I'd blamed her.

"Not a clue yet. We have to wait to talk to her. You don't think she did try to kill you and then gave herself just a bit of the drug to fool us?"

"No," I said. "Absolutely not. Now that I've got my brain back in gear, I realize there was no reason for her to try to kill me. As far as I know she isn't guilty of a thing. Don't get me wrong, Detective, there's lots of stuff going on here, stuff I haven't figured out yet. My sister, primarily. Why she went off a cliff and now has vanished. I know she believed that Laura betrayed her. She didn't want to see her. Perhaps she was even afraid of Laura. Or was that a lie? No matter how I slice it though, there's no reason why Laura would try to kill me."

"Maybe you were getting too close — to something, Agent MacDougal." I heard the tinny ring of a cell phone. He excused himself and walked over to the windows. He pulled a small cell phone out of his jacket pocket and spoke quietly.

I couldn't just lie there like a piece of meat, just like I had back in Bethesda for more than two weeks. Slowly, I slid my legs over the side of the bed. They'd left me stark naked. I looked around for anything to put around me.

Detective Castanga said from behind me, "Ms. Scott is waking up. Oh, yes, I had my forensics folk check over her condo. They found a bottle of phenobarbital in the medicine cabinet of the second bathroom. It didn't have many pills left in it. It was prescribed to a George Grafton, and expired at least a year ago."

George Grafton had been her uncle George who'd left her the condo in his will. But how did it get in the coffee?

I said it aloud. "Laura isn't stupid. The more I think about it, the more certain I am that someone else did it. And whoever did it meant for Laura to die, just like you said."

I stood slowly as I spoke, bringing the sheet and thin hospital blanket with me and wrapping them around my waist.

"Was Ms. Scott expecting anyone else to come see her?"

"Not that I know of."

"I'm going to speak to Laura Scott, Agent MacDougal, but first I want you to fill me in on everything so I don't have to start all over."

I told him everything I'd heard, everything I'd verified and realized that there was precious little. For an attempted murder investigation, the tangible, solid facts in my pocket were pitifully few. "Bottom line, the first crime I can point to for certain is what just happened."

Detective Castanga jotted some notes and asked a few questions, but mainly he just listened to me. I could feel the weight of his attention. He was good. He was just putting his notebook into his pocket when I heard a sharp indrawn breath from the doorway.

I looked up to see Maggie Sheffield in her sheriff's uniform. She wasn't looking at me. She was staring at Detective Minton Castanga.

"Hello, Margaret," Detective Castanga said, taking a step toward her. He stopped cold at the look of mean dislike on her face, obvious even to me. "I wondered if I'd see you here."

"Of course I'm here," Maggie said. "I'm the damned sheriff. Where else would I be? The question is, what are you doing here?"

"We found Laura Scott on the floor of her living room, doped with phenobarbital, just like Agent MacDougal here. You're looking well, Margaret."

"Yes. So are you, Mint."

Mint? Margaret? What was this all about? "You two know each other?"

Maggie Sheffield turned to face me as I stood beside my bed, a sheet and a single blanket knotted around my waist. "Hi,

Mac. You've still got some impressive battle scars. You steady on your feet now?"

"I don't know about how steady my feet are, but at least they're holding me up."

Detective Minton Castanga finally answered my question, as he gave Maggie a long, cool look. "Margaret was my wife at one time, Agent MacDougal."

13

Laura was in room 511 at Salem General Hospital. I stood quietly by her bed looking down at her. She was breathing smoothly and slowly. They still had the oxygen tubes in her nose and the saline IV in her arm. She was alive and would recover, just as I had. I was surprised that I'd never felt so thankful in my life as I was at that moment, except when Jilly woke up. Someone had smoothed down her hair and pushed it back from her face. All that beautiful hair was strewn over the hard hospital pillow. Unlike me, they'd put her in a hospital gown and pulled the light covers up to her shoulders.

I leaned down, lightly touched my palm to her cheek, and said, "Laura, I'll tell you what they said over and over to me when I was lying helpless flat on my back. It's time for you to wake up now. You've been sleeping long enough. Come on, come back to me."

Her lips moved slightly, forming my name.

I leaned closer, without conscious plan, and lightly kissed her pale mouth. "That's it. Yes, it's Mac. I like the way you say my name. Say it again. Come on, Laura. Come back to me."

"We were just coming in to wake her up again, but it sounds like you're doing a fine job." I turned to see a tall woman in a white coat. She smiled. "Just keep encouraging her to open her eyes. Are you her husband?"

"No," I said, for the first time in my life thinking maybe that didn't sound so bad. I'd known Laura two days. Funny how that didn't seem to matter. "She's a friend," I said, smiling now. "I'm a friend."

"I'm her doctor, Elsa Kiren. Do you want me or one of the nurses to spell you?"

I shook my head. "No, I'll stay. I came out from under the same drug just a while ago. I know what's going on in her head."

"If you need any help, just call out," Dr. Kiren said. "I'll be close by."

I turned back to Laura. I wondered if I'd been as pale as she was now before I'd come out of it. "Laura, listen to me now.

I've been thinking about things and here's the bottom line. Somebody drugged you. I was an innocent bystander. Now it's time to wake up so we can figure this mess out. Come on." I lightly slapped her cheek. "Someone tried to kill you, Laura, wake up."

"Stop hitting me, you jerk."

I grinned from ear to ear. "That's right, it's me, the jerk." I slapped her lightly on her other cheek.

She growled deep in her throat, probably just like her cat. "After I leave you, I'll go back to your condo and take care of Nolan and Grubster. You've got to tell me what to do for them. Wake up, Laura, think of your bird and your cat."

Her eyes slowly opened. She looked at me without recognition, then I saw the light slowly rekindle in her eyes, saw memory return. I would swear that I could feel the exact moment that vivid intelligence of hers was under full sail again.

"Hi," I said. "Keep dialing your mind back in, that's it. It just takes a bit of time, but you'll get there."

"I don't believe that you would drug me, Mac, but if you did, why?"

"Keep not believing it because I didn't. Until a couple of hours ago, I was lying on my back, just like you are. Someone got both of us."

That opened her eyes really wide. Any vagueness was now long gone. "My head hurts."

"Yeah, I know. It lessens. Don't worry about it, my headache's nearly gone now. Who got us, Laura?"

"I don't know. It had to be in the coffee. Both of us drank it, you more than me, if I remember correctly."

I saw a shadowy movement off to my right and jerked around to see Detective Minton Castanga standing just inside the hospital room doorway.

I felt Laura tense, readying for battle, beneath my hand.

"He was here before but I was out of it. I don't like him. Send him away, Mac."

"I can't. But don't worry, Laura. This guy isn't bad. He's a cop, Detective Castanga, from the Salem PD. He's here to find out who dropped us both in our tracks. Detective, this is Laura Scott."

I straightened and turned to face him. "She just woke up again," I said. "Come on over and she can talk to both of us at once."

Detective Castanga stood on the other side of Laura's bed. He studied her silently for a moment, then said in that soft, end-less drawl, "It's true I was here earlier. I stood right where I'm standing now, looking at you. I tried to imagine what you'd look like awake. I was off on all counts." He smiled then. "I'm glad you made it, Ms. Scott. You really do need to talk to me this time."

There was no expression whatsoever now on Laura's face. She was still pale, but her eyes were bright, focused. I couldn't begin to tell what she was thinking. She merely nodded her head very slightly and said finally, "All right, Detective."

"Agent MacDougal told me he believed that both of you were alone at your condo, except for the bird and the cat. Is this correct?"

"That's right. As far as I know, no one was lurking in a closet. If they were, they were certainly very quiet."

"You're right about the phenobarbital being in the coffee. It very probably came from an old prescription bottle in your medicine cabinet."

"No, I don't keep stuff like that. Oh, that's right, you're thinking about my uncle George."

"That's right. Why did you still have the pills?"

She shrugged. The covers slipped down just a bit. Without thinking, I pulled them back up and patted her cheek. She leaned her cheek against my hand.

"I don't know," she said. "They were just there. I've heard that phenobarbital is good if you really have a hard time going to sleep. I suppose I kept them just in case of insomnia. Not very bright of me, I suppose."

Suddenly, in the blink of an eye, Detective Castanga's Mr. Cool and Nice Guy was gone, and in his place was a hard-nosed son of a bitch whose voice and very stance were cold and sarcastic. "So, Ms. Scott, let me see if I get this right. Someone came into your house, rifled through your medicine cabinet, came up with the phenobarbital, stirred the stuff into your coffee, all without you ever seeing him or her?"

"I guess there's no other conclusion, Detective."

"Oh, yes there is. Seems just as likely to me that you're the one doing the drugging and that you tried to cover yourself by drinking a bit yourself."

I gave him a sharp look, but he was focused on Laura.

"From your tone I take it you want me

to confess to feeding Mac the drug, then drugging myself. Or maybe you want us both to tell you it was a suicide pact between two lovers? Tell me, Detective, why would I want to kill Mac?"

"Because he knew something about you and he was going to take you down." His voice was like nails now. He leaned down, right in her face. I would give him three more seconds of this bullshit.

"Sorry, Detective. I just don't have any fatal secrets like that," Laura said, and I could tell she was getting pissed. The three seconds were up. I was on the verge of interrupting this interrogation when she added in a voice as cold and sneering as Detective Castanga's, "Get out of my face, Detective. My head hurts. I'm cold and I still feel groggy. My stomach feels like it's caved in on itself, and you're treating me like I'm a failed murderer who ended up really fouling things up. Go away. I have nothing more to say to you. Go do your job and stop squandering precious time."

Detective Castanga slowly straightened. He was surprised, I could see it in the sudden twitch in his cheek, the slight hitch in his breathing.

"I think you tried to kill Mac, Ms. Scott. I'm going to prove it."

"Yeah, right. Run along, Detective, and search out every dead end you can find. Waste the taxpayers' money. You look like the type who would get off on that. That makes a lot more sense than finding out who drugged Mac and me. Cops like you make me want to spit."

Detective Castanga, very suddenly, with no warning at all, turned from a bad-ass to a man trying not to laugh, and failing at it. He did laugh. He rubbed his hands together. "You're very good, Ms. Scott. You're a reference librarian? At the public library? Hard to believe. You just took me apart very cleanly and smoothly." He was right. She'd sounded more hard-ass than he had.

Then Detective Castanga's laughter dried up. "Okay, so you were the target, Ms. Scott. I'll buy that now. Let's get down to business. Mac, pull up a chair, you're still looking pretty shaky. Hey, you were ready to belt me. Come on, she didn't need you to ride in and save her from the nasty cop. Now, Ms. Scott, do you want a couple of aspirin?"

Laura got her aspirin, Dr. Kiren finished checking her again quickly, nodded, and left us. Detective Castanga sat down with an open notebook on his leg. As for myself,

I was just trying to sit straight in the chair. "Talk," he said to both of us. "You two seem joined at the hip. Tell me why someone wants Ms. Scott dead."

Laura and I both remained silent as a tomb. Finally, I shrugged. "I already told you why I came here to Edgerton in the first place, Detective. It was all about my sister, Jilly. I just met Ms. Scott a couple of days ago."

Detective Castanga didn't believe me. He turned to Laura, a dark eyebrow cocked up a good inch.

"No, there's no reason I can think of. I'm a reference librarian, for heaven's sake."

In that instant, I knew she was lying. It was clean and fast, but it was a lie.

As for Detective Castanga, I don't know what he thought. He looked at her thoughtfully for a long time.

"It seems to me the shit hit the fan with your arrival, Mac. Give me names of people you've met in Edgerton."

Laura was relieved at that, I could tell. I hauled out the names of everyone I'd met in Edgerton. After I finished, he looked up and said, "All right, you've given me about twelve names. I'm going to read this list out loud. Add or subtract anyone you want to. Let's start with your heavyweight,

Alyssum Tarcher. This guy is big bucks. His financial assets are far-reaching. He's got lots of power with a lot of folk here in our state government, and even in Washington, I'm told. You've got him on the list along with all his family members."

"Well, there's no way around it," I said. "Wait, obviously something else has happened since I came to Edgerton. There was Charlie Duck's murder just a couple of days ago. Maggie can't find a reason either for the attack, or for why his house was ransacked." I shrugged, and because I was good, I looked him straight in the eye as I added, "She thinks it was just a random killing, and she may be right, but who knows?"

Detective Castanga said, sitting back in his seat, "Yeah, it was a real shame. He had quite a reputation back in the bad old days. The old guy was a retired cop."

"Yeah, Maggie told me."

"He left the Chicago PD a long time ago. I'll speak to Maggie about what she's found out about it. She told me she'd sent the body to Portland to the medical examiner even though it was obvious old Charlie had been struck on the head. She was right. You never know what will turn up. She told me she was pushing to have his body back by Tuesday. That was the day his funeral had been set."

He turned his attention back to Laura. "Now, Ms. Scott, you claim you have no enemies. Still, I'll need a list of the people you know in Salem, and I'll need to go over that list with you."

Laura nodded, then closed her eyes. She looked pale and exhausted. I bet I looked about the same.

I wondered if I should tell Castanga all the rest of it, including Charlie's dying words. No, I'd leave that decision to Maggie.

I thought of Jilly and Paul. Could either of them hate Laura so much they'd want to murder her? Had Jilly left the hospital on her own, driven up to Salem, managed to get into Laura's apartment, and poured phenobarbital into the coffee can?

"Did Jilly have a key to your condo, Laura?" I asked finally, hating the words as they left my mouth.

"No," she said. "I don't think so. She visited me there, of course, from time to time. I need a better painkiller. My head is killing me."

Detective Castanga stood and slowly slipped his notebook back into the inside pocket of his coat. "We have time for this later, Ms. Scott, when you feel better. In the meantime, I'll post an officer by your door."

"Thank you, Detective," she said and closed her eyes again, turning her head away from him on the stingy hospital pillow.

"Mac, are you coming?"

I said, "I don't want to leave her here alone. Someone tried to kill her. It'll take a while for you to get someone over here."

"Not long," Detective Castanga said. "I got a guy who's a little burned out right now, but he'll guard her well." He said to Laura, "His name is Harold Hobbes, a nice guy, tough as nails, and he won't let his own mother into your room."

"Thank you, Detective," she said.

I went with Detective Castanga to the door and partway down the hospital corridor. Our footsteps sounded on a background of muted groans, one loud shout, the low hum of music, beeping machines, and an occasional curse. When I returned to Laura's room, I saw a tall woman bending over Laura.

"Hey," I said and ran forward.

The woman straightened and cocked her head at me in question. It was Dr. Kiren. "She's tired but wanted to ask me a question. I had to lean over to hear her."

"Sorry," I said.

Dr. Kiren smiled. "She'll be just fine by this evening, maybe even ready to go home."

Home, I thought. No, that wouldn't work. I had to think about this.

Dr. Kiren's pager went off. On her way out, she told Laura to rest.

I thought about Charlie Duck's funeral. Hopefully Charlie would arrive back in time for his scheduled send-off.

I leaned over Laura and stroked my thumb over her eyebrows. I said very quietly, "I'll see you later this afternoon. Then we'll talk. Just rest. Harold Hobbes will be outside your room. If anyone comes near you, it means they've gotten past Harold, so scream your head off."

"All right," she said, not opening her eyes. I'd nearly made it to the door when she called out, "Thanks, Mac."

"Sure," I said.

"I'm sorry I nearly got you killed."

"Yeah, I know."

I stopped at Laura's condo. Castanga's people had finished with it, but I still had to show my FBI badge so the manager would unlock her door. Grubster was standing directly in front of the door, waiting for Laura. He saw me, meowed once, then turned around and walked away, his tail high in the air. "I'm here to feed you," I called after him.

To my surprise, Grubster stopped, raised his left paw, licked it, and took two steps back toward me. Then he just sat there. "Okay," I said. "Let's find your cat food."

I watched Grubster chow down an entire can of salmon and rice and a big handful of dried stuff that looked so bad I poured some non-fat milk over it. Grubster purred the whole time he ate. I gave him a ton of fresh water and eyed his cat box, which needed changing. Grubster watched my technique. He must have approved because on his way out of the kitchen he stopped a moment and swiped his whiskers against my leg.

"Now for you, Nolan." When I said his name, Nolan filled the air with loud, sharp squawks, probably a bird's equivalent to orders. I changed his water, crumpled up a thick slice of bread into small pieces, and sprinkled sunflower seeds on the floor of his cage. Nolan obligingly hopped in to dine.

I stopped at the front door, looked from Grubster to Nolan, sighed, and went back to scratch and pet Grubster while Nolan serenaded me with squawks between bread bites.

I'd always had dogs growing up. During the past four or five years, though, I hadn't had a pet of any kind around. As I left, it didn't seem strange to call back to the two of them, "I'll be back to get you guys later."

"Squawk."

Nothing from Grubster. He was asleep.

I got back to Edgerton in the early afternoon. I stopped at Grace's Deli and ordered up a tuna salad sandwich on rye bread, with lots of tomatoes and dill pickles. While I ate, I asked Grace how to go about renting a home or an apartment here in town or just out of town, maybe near where Rob Morrison's small clapboard cottage was.

Grace was strong-willed as a mule, tall and very thin, with a head of salt-and-pepper hair. She smiled at me and said, "Well, I reckon you could go over to the Buttercup Bed and Breakfast, but Arlene Hicks isn't really high on you being here. Never got it through her head that money is money. She already told you she was all filled up, didn't she?"

I nodded. "I should have told her that if

she wasn't running drugs, she has nothing to fear."

"Well, she just might be, you never know. Arlene's full of deep shoals, lots of secrets. I've got it, Mr. MacDougal. Mr. Tarcher owns a little house like Rob Morrison's. It's called Seagull Cottage, to the south of town, nearly right on the cliff. It's empty right now. The last tenants left about a month ago."

"Excellent." I finished off my sandwich and rose. "Are you coming to Charlie Duck's funeral?"

"Wouldn't miss it," Grace said. "I have a three-minute eulogy to give." She smiled, seeing my confusion. "I'm the town Buddhist."

"You're a Buddhist?"

"I haven't made up my mind, but I'm close enough. The thing is, though, that the Buddhists make it very simple for you to reach your heavenly reward. To reach Nirvana, all you have to do is live right, think right, and deny yourself just about everything. That's something, isn't it?"

"Where does the line begin?" I asked, looking around.

Grace just cocked her head at me, and I smiled and left. I called the Tarcher house and was surprised when Alyssum himself answered the phone. I told him I wanted to rent Seagull Cottage and I told him why. If he was the one behind having Laura drugged, well, it hardly mattered. He'd find out soon enough anyway where she was. Besides I wanted everyone to know that Laura and I were together and planned to camp right in their own backyard.

"So that's why I can't allow Ms. Scott to return to her place. It was Grace who kindly told me about the house you're renting down on the cliffs."

Alyssum Tarcher said, "Well, Agent MacDougal, this is a surprise. So you'll be guarding Ms. Scott then?"

I told him there'd be a lot of people near her, that Maggie was setting up a schedule, but I was going to be the main one baby-sitting.

"I'll tell you what, Agent MacDougal," Tarcher said, pausing for a deep, stentorian breath, "to do my good citizen's part, I'll grant you a month's free rent on the house." I didn't have a problem with that at all. I thanked him and made a date to pick up the house key. The only problem I foresaw was getting Laura away from her condo in Salem and down to Edgerton with me. And maybe getting the truth out of her.

I returned to Salem General Hospital, Nolan and Grubster on the backseat of the Taurus, the trunk loaded down with three suitcases holding just about everything I could imagine she'd want and need.

I decided on my way up in the elevator how to get Laura to Edgerton.

14

Laura was sitting on the edge of the bed, her feet dangling, the green hospital night-gown falling off her left shoulder. When she saw me in the doorway, her face lit up.

"Mac! I was just going to get myself together. Would you mind taking me home?"

I told her I wouldn't mind at all. The clothes she'd worn when they'd brought her in were hanging in the closet. I spoke outside with Harold Hobbes while she changed.

"Hell of a thing," Harold said, as he nodded toward the door. "Some jerk trying to ice a pretty lady like that." I agreed that it was.

"No one even came by to sniff."

I knocked, heard Laura tell me to come in, and went in to fetch my new roommate.

Laura was still a bit on the shaky side, but she looked much better. They made her ride down in a wheelchair, which she didn't like at all. I put her in the passenger side of the Taurus and quickly shut the door.

"What is this, Mac?" — her first words to me when I slid in behind the steering wheel. I turned to the backseat and said, "Hi, guys. Everything okay?"

"Squawk."

"Grubster, you got any news from the front?"

Nothing from Grubster.

"What's going on here, Mac?"

I drove out of the parking lot. "You're on vacation as of right now, Ms. Scott. I've rented us a small house just south of Edgerton, on the cliffs. It's called Seagull Cottage, and Mr. Alyssum Tarcher has given it to us rent-free for a month. I'm going to be your roommate."

She chewed this over for about twenty-two seconds. "No way. I live in Salem. I'll lose my job."

"No. I got you a two-week vacation, without pay. I told them I was your brother and you'd come down with Lyme disease. They were suitably impressed. It was a Mr. Dirkson who cleared you. All right?"

"My condo."

"I told the manager you were going out of town. He's going to keep an eye on everything."

"I don't have any clothes."

"All in the trunk."

She was done, for the moment. We were out of Salem now, heading toward 101.

"It's okay, Laura," I said, giving her a quick smile. "Really, it's better this way. Except it's interesting about Alyssum Tarcher being our landlord. Hey, if he had anything to do with this, he would have found out that you'd flown the coop. Now everyone knows you're not alone, that you've got protection, namely yours truly."

"You don't know anything, Mac."

"I will, soon enough. I don't want you thinking that you're walking right into the bear cave, what with us going to Edgerton. I'll be in that cave with you and I'm mean. Besides, I've got a big spear. Running away is not the way to find out what's going on in Edgerton, or to find my sister." I waited, but she didn't say anything, just nodded after a bit.

It had started raining, just a drizzle at first, but now it was really coming down. "I didn't bring you a raincoat, sorry."

She didn't say a word for at least seven

miles. Finally, I said, "Laura? Is this okay with you?"

"Are you really going to let people know — the whole town — that someone tried to kill me? Or are you going to leave it as both of us?"

"I already told Alyssum Tarcher that it was just you. When we get to Edgerton, I need to stop off at Paul's house to pick up my clothes. Then I need to see Maggie, find out if she's heard anything about Jilly. Also, Charlie Duck's autopsy report should be coming in soon."

"You think the old man's death is somehow connected, don't you?"

"My boss, Big Carl Bardolino, at the FBI, likes to say there's no such thing as coincidence, at least in our line of work."

"Squawk."

"Nolan's got some more sunflower seeds in that lunch bag on the backseat if you think he's still hungry."

A car came around to pass us, not too wise since we were on a curve. I slowed down just a bit and gave it plenty of room to go around.

Laura started to say something as she turned around to reach for the bag of sunflower seeds. In the next instant, there was a popping sound, then another. I jerked back. I realized that a bullet had gone through her passenger-side window. It had crashed through my window and missed my neck by a couple of inches, leaving a spiderweb of cracked glass in its wake.

I pulled the steering wheel hard right, then corrected to the left, just missing an oncoming car. I saw a man in my mind's eye, on the passenger side, raising what had to have been a gun. I saw the car just ahead of us, a dark red Honda. I gunned the Taurus and winced. In this rain, if I wasn't careful, we'd go skidding right off the road. The Honda roared ahead, cutting hard and fast around a sharp turn. I knew the Taurus wouldn't make it. I had to slow a bit. When I got around the curve, the Honda had widened the distance.

"My God, Mac, are you all right?"

"Yep. You?"

"I think so. If I hadn't turned in just that moment to get Nolan some sunflower seeds —"

"I know. Laura, sit back down and fasten your seat belt."

"Squawk."

"It's all right, Nolan. Think of this as an adventure."

Laura was strapped in and I passed two cars, nearly skimming off the paint on the second one. Horns blared loudly in our ears.

We were getting closer. "Laura, I don't think we can catch them, but we can get the license plate."

"I can try," she said, and buzzed down what was left of her electric window to lean out. Rain flew in the open window, hard and heavy.

I tried to keep my hands loose and relaxed on the steering wheel even though my heart pounded faster in anger each time I saw that webbed bullet hole out of the corner of my eye. I passed another car, a Land Rover. The driver gave me the finger and shouted a curse. I didn't blame him.

There were just about forty yards of highway between us and the Honda. I saw a man leaning out the passenger window, looking back. He had a gun. "Laura, down!"

She jerked back in and flattened herself against the seat as the man fired five or six rounds.

"Mac," she said, "you've got a gun, don't you?"

"Yes, but I've got to concentrate."

"Give it to me. I know how to shoot."

I didn't want to. It was the last thing I

wanted to do, actually. I felt her hand pulling it out of my shoulder holster.

"Laura," I said, "I'd rather you didn't. Please, be careful."

"Just get us closer to that damned Honda."

We closed to within fifteen yards of the Honda. This stretch of 101 was all curves and inclines and twisting hills. The rain had lightened up a bit, thank God. I'd be just on the verge of seeing the license plate when the Honda would disappear again around another curve.

Laura hugged the passenger door, waiting. She seemed very calm, perhaps too calm. Something was strange here. "Laura, are you all right?"

"I'm fine, Mac. Just keep up with them. Yeah, just a little bit closer." Suddenly, she reared up and halfway out the open window, rain curtaining her face. She shot off half the clip, fast.

The Honda's back window exploded. A man came out of the passenger-side window, a gun trained on us. Before he could fire, Laura shot off another three rounds. I saw his gun fly out of his hand and skitter across the highway. She'd got him. Then the Honda disappeared around another turn.

I gunned the Taurus. We came around the bend and skidded out to see the Honda disappear on the short straight stretch in front of us.

"Damn, I wanted to get a back tire."

When we last saw the Honda, it was weaving back and forth, the driver sawing the steering wheel to get it out of a skid. He straightened over a crest and the car shot forward. I gunned the Taurus. Just one more try. But the rain did us in. We hit a slick patch. The car spun in a full three-sixty. We ended up on the side of the road, about six feet from a ditch, facing back toward Salem.

"We didn't get the license plate," Laura said. "Well, damn."

"After this I'm going to rent a Porsche. Bastards got away."

And Laura laughed.

We were still pumped with adrenaline. I started laughing too. It felt good. We were alive.

It took petting Grubster and calming Nolan to get ourselves back down.

"You okay?"

She nodded as she continued scratching behind Grubster's ears. "That was a close one, Mac. My heart's pounding louder than a runaway train. My adrenaline level

235

was so high there for a while, I bet I could have flown right out of this busted window. Oh, Jesus, Mac."

She leaned over to me to put her arms around my back, her elbow hitting the steering wheel. Grubster was between us, purring loudly. I held her tightly, feeling her heartbeat against my chest, her warm breath against my neck, grateful that we'd survived this. It had been close. I took a quick survey of the Taurus. One busted window and a driver's-side window that was spider-webbed, with one small hole right in the middle. Too bad it hadn't stopped the bullet. Some sort of tangible evidence would have been nice.

"What are we going to do?" She didn't move while she spoke, and I liked that.

"I guess if I had my cell phone with me, I'd call Castanga, the President, and the Joint Chiefs of Staff."

"I don't have mine either," she said against my neck. "It's on the dining room table at my condo."

"Squawk!"

"Oh dear, I forgot about Nolan and Grubster."

She lifted Grubster off her lap and hefted him onto the backseat. She gave Nolan more sunflower seeds. I turned to see Grubster stretch his front legs against the front seat. I'd swear that cat was as tall as I was. Then he lightly jumped up front again and curled in Laura's lap.

I raised my hand and picked up a strand of hair that had come free of the clip at the back of her neck. I rubbed the hair between my fingers.

She grew very still.

"I'm glad we're both still alive."

"I wonder if you could be more pleased than Grubster here." The damned cat was purring so loudly she'd had to raise her voice. I sat back, tapped my fingertips against the steering wheel for a moment, and said, "That was excellent shooting."

"Thank you."

I smiled at her and wondered just how much of a smile it had turned out to be. "At least now I know what you lied about. You're a cop, Laura. Since you were a reference librarian at the Salem Public Library, it means you were undercover. Isn't that right?"

A myriad of expressions crossed her face, from doubt, to dread, to guilt. I guess she finally realized it was just too late to go in any direction but toward the truth.

"Laura? You really can trust me. I have no intention of hurting you, or compromising your case, or blowing your cover, or getting you into trouble with your superiors. You've just got to deal me in. We've been through too much together for you to leave me blowing in the breeze any longer. I don't want to be helpless, and that's what I am if you keep me in the dark. Come, it's time."

I took her hand as I watched her take a very deep breath. I watched her come to her decision. I swear her eyes turned two shades lighter because she knew the incessant lying was over. "Yes," she said. "Yes, I'm a cop."

I just nodded for her to continue. Grubster continued purring at high volume, his tail thumping up and down.

"They wanted to kill me," Laura said, her fingers tightening in Grubster's fur. "If I hadn't turned to get some more sunflower seeds for Nolan —"

I quickly took my gun from between us on the seat and eased it back into my shoulder holster. "Meet me halfway," I said as I smoothed down my jacket, and she did. I pulled her against me, Grubster between us again, and lightly pressed her head against my shoulder. I pulled back, touched my forehead to hers, and cupped her head with my hands. "You've been alone in this for too long. You've got me in it now. Can you imagine what you and I can accomplish together?"

"There's really nothing more to accomplish. My cover's blown now. That's another reason for me to tell you the truth. My orders don't make sense anymore."

"Tell me then. All of it."

"I'm DEA, Mac. Even when I called my boss from the hospital and told him I'd been poisoned, that obviously my cover was blown to hell, he told me to lie low for a couple of days, that he'd try to find out what they know and how they'd found out. Of course I told him about you. That made him even more adamant. He said we'd worked too hard to have this case blown by the FBI. I'm sorry I had to lie to you, Mac."

"This guy sounds like a real winner. For God's sake, they tried to poison you."

"I was getting to be a pretty good reference librarian. I read just about all the assigned texts for a degree."

"What's your real name?"

"I'm really Laura. They just changed my last name. My real last name is Bellamy. I've been undercover for nearly four months now. It involves drugs, of course."

"And it has to do with Paul and Jilly," I

said slowly, looking closely at her. She paled and hesitated because what she was about to say was going to bring me pain.

"Just spit it out."

Grubster meowed loudly. "It's all right, Grubster. Take a nap. You've been through a lot." She closed her eyes a moment and ran her fingers through his fur. His loud purring soon filled the car again.

"About five months ago an electronic surveillance unit picked up a rumor that a new drug was being developed, one that is highly addictive and cheap to produce."

"A drug dealer's wet dream."

"Yes. A man called John Molinas was said to be bragging about it. We think Molinas is a major drug distributor, but we don't have anything solid on him. He's been in business in the past with a cartel headed by Del Cabrizo."

"I've heard of him."

"Del Cabrizo occasionally comes to the United States just to shove a finger in our face. And now the reason I'm here. The word was that there was a wealthy local man involved. It's none other than Alyssum Tarcher."

I must admit I was staring at her now. "Tarcher involved with Del Cabrizo?"

"There's more. John Molinas is Alyssum

Tarcher's brother-in-law. That's probably why Tarcher's involved in this thing."

"A real kicker," I said. "I knew Tarcher was powerful, but this? He's a damned crook too?"

"Evidently so. All of this came as a bit of a surprise to us too. You see, John Molinas hasn't been active for a few years as far as we could tell. Maybe he got religion, maybe he got cancer, we just didn't know. But when we threw Alyssum Tarcher into the mix, it didn't take us long to find out that Dr. Bartlett and his wife, pharmaceutical researchers, had just moved to Edgerton from Philadelphia into a house that Tarcher sold them for a nominal price. We put two and two together and put pressure on their employer in Philadelphia, VioTech, to tell us what they had been working on. Paul and Jilly had been working on some sort of memory drug. It sounded nuts, but still, our people went over all the research Paul and Jilly had submitted. It was obvious why VioTech had pulled the plug. Whatever else the drug did, it was toxic as hell, turned some lab animals completely nuts. They'd sunk millions of dollars into a drug that was going nowhere.

"Still, why had the Bartletts suddenly

moved to Edgerton? We found out that Paul had grown up there, but there wasn't anything to draw them back."

"Alyssum Tarcher was behind it," I said.

"Right. I set up in Salem posing as a reference librarian because there was no better way I could get closer to Edgerton, to the major players there. I did go to Grace's Deli to see if she needed help, but she didn't. I couldn't just move to Edgerton. Everyone would have known I was up to no good. It's too small and tight a community."

"Why the library?"

"God, I'm so sorry, Mac. The reason I became a reference librarian was that we found out that Jilly Bartlett was coming to the library in Salem. At least three days a week, like clockwork. Our surveillance showed — oh God, Mac, I'm so sorry about this — she was meeting a lover there, always in the reference section. If I became the reference librarian, I'd have a good chance to meet her, to make friends with her, and I did. The regular reference librarian got a very nice open-ended holiday, with pay."

I had only heard one thing. "A lover? Jilly met a man in the library three days a week?"

"Yes. He's a local thoracic surgeon. No one could find out how they'd met, but as yet we have no reason to think he's involved in anything going on down in Edgerton."

I looked up to see a police car cruising slowly by, his eyes on us. I waved and turned the ignition key. "Let's go to that McDonald's we passed. I need some breathing space and then a cup of coffee."

The McDonald's was about six miles down the highway off Exit 133. It was tucked between a Denny's and a Wendy's, with three gas stations completing the grouping.

Grubster slept through being put back into his carrying case. Nolan didn't even squawk once when Laura slipped his cover over the cage.

Over Big Macs and coffee, I said, "You've been undercover for four months. What have you come up with?"

"You mean against Jilly and Paul?"

"Believe me, I don't give a damn about Molinas or Tarcher or this Del Cabrizo character."

"Again, Mac, I'm sorry, but the truth is that Jilly lied to me from the beginning, told me she was here because she wanted to get pregnant. She told me she was the uneducated one in the family. I don't know if she did this to protect herself or me.

"I like Jilly. When you told me she was in a coma, it really hit me hard because I do like her so much. She's funny, lights up a room when she swings in, her skirts swishing, her hair bouncing. We did get close, but not close enough that she ever really let me in."

"Bottom line, Laura, you didn't have squat on either Jilly or Paul, and that's because there isn't anything to get. I don't believe my sister would be involved with drug dealers, for God's sake. Both she and Paul are scientists, not criminals. They're moral people, not people who'd develop a drug to feed to kids. You're wrong about them, Laura. At least you're dead wrong about Jilly."

She knew I was being a brother, defensive and angry, but I didn't care. I didn't want to accept it, couldn't accept it. I looked at Laura, felt mean as a snake, and said, "Did you sleep with Paul? As a sort of quid pro quo?"

"No," she said matter-of-factly, but I felt her surprise and hurt at my question. She dropped the french fry she was holding back onto her plate. "Jilly never mentioned anything like that to me. Actually, she's very fond of Paul."

I said slowly, "Jilly said you'd betrayed her. I assumed it meant you'd slept with Paul, but that isn't it at all. She found out you're a DEA agent, didn't she?"

"She must have but I don't know how. Maybe I gave myself away somehow, I don't know. But she must have found out that very night. Both she and Paul must have known since then. One of them may have made a phone call to Molinas. He's perfectly capable of everything that's happened since."

"So now you're saying that my sister conspired to commit murder. I'll never believe that. Probably Molinas found out about you. Jilly wouldn't blow the whistle on you."

She took my hand and held it between hers. "She came out of the coma, Mac, and disappeared just as soon as she was able. She knew we were getting close. She went into hiding."

"Then why didn't Paul leave with her?"

"I don't know. There's still no direct evidence against either of them. I thought about that, a lot. Something else I wanted to tell you. Over the past couple of months, Jilly didn't seem quite right. She talked about sex a lot, how much more she liked it than before. Not just one conversation, she went on and on about it. And she seemed somehow off, the way she spoke of other things, mixing in non sequiturs, like she wasn't really with me."

"You think she was experimenting with her own drug?"

"I don't know what I'm saying, but she was different, Mac."

I let it go. It was just too close to my own memories of Jilly's visit the previous February. "Where is Molinas? Has he met with Jilly and Paul? Has he showed up at their house or at the Tarcher house?"

"No. But there's just no getting around the fact that it was Alyssum Tarcher who got Paul and Jilly back to Edgerton. He bought Jilly the Porsche, gave Paul and Jilly the house. I'm sorry, Mac, but you just don't do that for no reason.

"Our assumption is that Paul and Jilly are working on this drug, that they're trying to make it less toxic or more addictive, and then it'll be mass-produced and sold on the street."

"For argument's sake, let's say you're right about all of it. To get people hooked, a drug has to produce a high that will knock the user's socks off. Does this drug do that?"

"We don't know, but we think it has to do with sex."

No, I thought. Jilly and all her talk about sex to both Laura and me. No.

"You mean the user shoots up and just lies there in a semi-stupor having orgasms?"

"Maybe. We don't know. Some of the VioTech data showed some very significant changes in lab animals' sexual drive. It went off the charts and frequently showed itself by intense sexual aggression. There's got to be more to it than that, of course. Jilly and Paul probably took some of their records with them.

"My boss told me to lie low, but I just can't do that. I don't know how close they are to perfecting the drug. If I can help it, that drug isn't going to make it to the streets. I just don't know how to go about that anymore."

"I'm not going to stop looking for my sister, Laura. I guess I don't see any other choice but to join forces with you."

"You could get in big trouble with your people too, Mac. But more than that, I don't want you in any more danger. You've been an innocent bystander in all of this and it nearly got you killed. I couldn't bear that."

I gave her a crooked grin. "We've known each other for two days."

"That's strange, isn't it?"

"Look, Laura, you know as well as I do that if you don't get on a phone and tell your boss you've been fired at in a car on a public highway, you can forget about your long-term career in the DEA. You're the one in jeopardy. You've got to think about covering your butt, driving to a motel on Bainbridge Island or somewhere and hiding until it's all over. That's what's safest."

"I don't want to call in the cavalry," she said. "I want to find Jilly. I can't just head off to parts unknown and forget about this. If I call my boss, I'll be out of here for sure and the DEA will be all over town. These people are too smart. The DEA won't find a thing that way."

"And Jilly and Paul might get railroaded. I want to find out whether Jilly and Paul are up to their necks in this, or if they're just innocent bystanders, like I was two days ago."

Laura's eyes sheened, and her hands curled into fists.

"Laura —"

"No, this has to be my decision, Mac. I can't turn my back on Jilly. Or on you. I'm in this with you, for the long haul."

I smiled over at her. "All right. We're both professionals. We both know the risks we're taking." I took her hand, slowly smoothing away the fist. "You want to come to Edgerton with me?"

"Yes. I don't see anything else to do."

I took the last drink of my coffee. It was cold. I gave her a sideways look. "Did Paul really put the moves on you last Tuesday night?"

"Yes he did."

I sighed. "I thought so. Paul's not as good a liar as you are."

"That's because he's a scientist and not a federal agent. It's in our genes. I've had to weave so many lies in with the truth on this case that it's sometimes confused me. Mac, if we go to Edgerton, we're thumbing our nose at them."

"I honestly don't think they'll try anything in Edgerton, not when Alyssum Tarcher is our landlord and everybody knows we're there and I'm protecting you. It's our best cover."

"They could shoot us down on Fifth Avenue. That's not much more gall than trying to kill us on 101. This isn't your assignment, Mac."

"No, you're right. It's more than an

assignment. This is about my sister. Give it up, Laura. Consider, you need me. Remember, I'm FBI. Now, I've got the beginnings of a plan. I'm calling two friends of mine in Washington, D.C., Savich and Sherlock, FBI agents."

I had to call collect since I didn't have enough coins for the pay phone. Thank God they were home. It took me fifteen minutes to cover all the ground.

When I returned to our table, I smiled down at Laura. "Our numbers are soon doubling. Sherlock and Savich will be here soon."

When we reached the outskirts of Edgerton, I said, "We'll need to stop by Tarcher's house to get the key to Seagull Cottage. I won't bait him, at least not yet. But he'll know, Laura, he has to. I can't imagine that Molinas has kept him out of the loop."

It had started to drizzle again. Laura was beginning to shiver. I turned up the heater. "It'll be better in a few minutes, I hope."

"I'm fine." She leaned back and petted Grubster's head. She hadn't put him back in his carrier. He was sprawling his full length along the backseat, his nose pressed against Nolan's cage.

Even the magnificent Tarcher mansion looked desolate in the thick dark rain. No hope for it, I thought, and sprinted from the car to the porch. I turned and waved to Laura to stay put, which she did.

Then I realized she was alone, vulnerable to attack. I dashed back through the rain to the Taurus, opened the door, drew my SIG Sauer, and handed it to her. "Keep it close," I said, and closed the car door again.

A maid, who was dressed in jeans and a sweater, let me into the large foyer and asked me to wait. It was better that I drip on the marble than on the highly polished oak floors in the living room just beyond.

Cotter Tarcher was whistling as he came from the kitchen at the back of the house. He stopped dead in his tracks when he saw me.

"What's going on? Have you found Jilly?"

"No. I'm here to get the Seagull Cottage key from your father. Laura Scott and I will be staying there for a while."

"Why?" he asked, watching me drip on the floor. He was wearing sweats and running shoes. He was perfectly dry. I didn't answer him. "Do both you and your father work here at home?"

"For the most part. I usually knock off about five o'clock to either go to the gym or out running. Why are you and Laura Scott staying at our cottage?"

"Because someone tried to kill her and it seems safer if she's here, with me, than in Salem by herself. It's a bit on the wet side to go running, isn't it?"

"Yes. I'm working out downstairs in the gym. Where's Laura Scott?"

"In the car."

"Does she know Jilly?"

"Oh yes, she knows Jilly very well."

Alyssum Tarcher came striding down the stairs off to my right. He looked arrogant and intelligent, his eyes at that moment maybe even harder than his son's. He seemed somehow taller to me than he had just the night before.

"Agent MacDougal," he said, and shook my hand. "Here's the key to Seagull Cottage. I made sure the place was cleaned up and the phone works. Given this weather, I checked to make sure there's heat as well. This Laura Scott, she's with you?"

"Yes, waiting for me in the car. Since someone tried to kill her, she's keeping my gun on her at all times." I suppose I should have mentioned Grubster and Nolan, but you never knew about a landlord, and I didn't want the pets to give him an excuse for us not to use his property. I thanked him and turned to leave.

"Agent MacDougal, call me if there's a problem — of any kind at all."

"Yeah," Cotter said. "My father chews on problems and spits out solutions."

Alyssum Tarcher laughed and buffeted his son's shoulder with a light shove.

"Who is it, Aly?"

Elaine Tarcher didn't wait for an answer, just came running lightly down the stairs. Like her son, she was wearing sweats and running shoes, and she didn't look much older than Cal. I realized I hadn't thought about Cal since, well, for a good while. "Mrs. Tarcher," I said, nodding. "Don't come any closer, I'm wet."

"I see that you are. We heard about your problem with that drug. Are you all right?"

"Yes, I'm just fine. Did Mr. Tarcher tell you that Laura Scott and I will be staying for a while at Seagull Cottage?"

"Yes, he did tell me. He also told me that someone is trying to kill Ms. Scott. This isn't what we're used to, Agent Mac-Dougal. You seem to have brought a good deal of trouble with you. We've never liked violence, only rarely seen it here in Edgerton. Until poor Charlie Duck. Have you heard anything about Jilly?"

I said no and left three minutes later, sprinting back to the car under thick, cold rain that was coming down harder than ever and had me shivering even after five minutes with the car heater turned on high. Laura had put one of her jackets up against the shattered window. It kept the rain out but the heat from the car seeped out quickly.

I stopped off at Paul's house. I was relieved when he wasn't at home. Truth be told, I wasn't ready to confront him. The last thing I wanted to happen was to scare him into running, maybe even disappearing like Jilly.

I packed up my clothes, left him a note telling him where I was, and didn't give him any explanation at all.

We drove to a small grocery store called The Cove to stock up. Laura remained in the car both times, my SIG Sauer on her lap.

It was dark when we arrived at Seagull Cottage, not more than fifty feet from the cliffs with, I imagined, a sweeping view up and down the Oregon coast. But not tonight. Only heavy, cold rain tonight that covered everything, leaving the ocean black and flat. There wasn't any wind at all and surely that was odd. The rain just came straight down, striking the ground hard as a slap. There were only about half a dozen spruce trees to soften the barren landscape.

I unlocked the door, checked out the inside, and waved Laura in.

15

At seven that evening we ate our dinner in front of the fireplace, chicken noodle soup and English muffins with butter dripping over the sides. Grubster lay sleeping at Laura's feet, sated from two cans of cat food, with just an occasional twitch. Nolan was under wraps for the night. "That was delicious," Laura said as she sat back on her hands and yawned.

"Yes, it was," I said, barely managing to stifle my own yawn. "It's been a long day."

She cocked an eye open. "You're being the master of understatement here?"

For the life of me I was too tired to think of something clever to say to that wonderful straight line. I said, "You ready to hang it up?"

Laura looked toward the cottage door. I could see the tension in her. "No," she said. "They wouldn't dare try anything here, in Edgerton."

"I don't think so either. Tomorrow is Charlie Duck's funeral. I want to introduce you to everyone and start getting in Tarcher's face. As for Paul, I want to handle him very carefully. I don't want him running."

"He'll never admit to anything, I'd swear to it. He'll protect Jilly."

She was probably right. I was imagining what it would be like to put my hands around his neck, lift him off the floor, and shake him.

"When Savich and Sherlock get here, we'll all discuss what's the best approach. They know we've got to act quickly."

"Your friends sure have a lot of flexibility."

"Yeah. They're both in the same unit and he's in charge. Savich's boss, Jimmy Maitland, usually gives him as much leeway as he wants. Besides, they're coming as my friends, not an official assignment.

"Sherlock and Savich are first-class agents and very good friends. It's possible that they'll see things as outsiders that you and I have missed. They'll have some great ideas, you can count on that."

"I don't know anyone like that in the DEA." She put her fingers on my lips. "No, don't you dare start up again on my agency."

"I wouldn't dream of it, Laura. Now, I'll hook a chair under the doorknob and I'll put my SIG right beside the bed. We've got the curtains pulled over the windows and everything's locked up tight. It'll be okay."

"I guess there's nothing more that we can do. Goodness, it's only eight-thirty. It feels like it should be at least midnight, I'm so tired."

"Why don't you take the bathroom first? I want to check around outside."

"Be careful, Mac." She lightly touched her fingers to my face. "I mean it, be very careful. You've gotten kind of important to me, real fast."

I wanted to kiss her and not stop, so I got out of there fast. The rain had stopped for the moment. Low-lying black clouds were shifting in thick, grotesque shapes across a huge fat full moon.

It looked like a werewolf kind of night.

In that instant I heard something, something not far away, just off to my left, away from the cliffs, something rustling, then moving, perhaps a heavy foot thudding on the ground, then silence, then more rustling.

I waited, so still I could hear my own breath. Nothing more, as if whatever it was that was coming toward me had stopped. I waited longer, then longer still. Still nothing. I wondered if my brain had obligingly conjured up the bogeyman.

I remembered Cal saying that she never wanted to go anywhere near the cemetery, that the trees were growing inward, pushing so close that the roots probably had split through the coffins. I'd thought she was nuts then. Now I was hearing things, and terrifying myself. Jesus, I was losing it.

I walked to the cliff and stood looking out over the flat, black water. It went forever, well beyond those distant low dark clouds that tricked the eye, making it appear that the water simply disappeared into them. Looking north and south, I could make out the coastline — primeval mists, driftwood strewn over and sprawled out in piles on the beach. Black rocks rose out of the water like misshapen sentinels, groups of them hovering, just below me, the water scaling them, then crashing back, gushing white foam. Again and again, never stopping, never changing. I thought about what it would be like to be here every day of my life and wondered if my soul would be calmed, or if I'd go mad.

I turned to go back, pausing a moment to get my bearings. Seagull Cottage sat at the very end of a narrow, rutted dirt road, winding south and west toward the cliff, just to this small cottage. I couldn't see the half-mile back to the road this one split off from. There were no car headlights that I could see even in the distance. I walked to the back of the cottage, checked the windows, and looked south to the wild barren hills that rose and fell as far as I could see. Anyone could hike to the cottage over those soulless hills. I didn't like it. I wondered if we weren't the biggest fools in Oregon, staying here right in Tarcher's face. I was putting my life on the line, but more important, putting Laura in danger as well. I shook my head. I wasn't going to back down and I couldn't imagine Laura backing away now either.

I looked at the cottage. All the windows were secure, covered with patterned cotton curtains, faded from many years in the sun. There was nothing else I could do.

My head had started aching again. No wonder. My body felt like it had been hit by a wrecking ball. I was so tired I could barely stand. But I also felt jumpy.

When I walked into the small bedroom, Laura was standing in a long nightgown by the side of the bed, looking at me.

"Hi," she said, her voice deep and rich, making that small word sound sexy as hell. I was at her side in just under four steps. She moved against me, raised her face, and kissed my mouth.

In an instant my fatigue was gone. I'd known this woman for a matter of days and I wanted her more than any woman I'd ever met in my life. There were no more lies between us, I thought, not a single one.

My hands were all over her, in her hair, stroking and rubbing that thick smooth hair on my face even as I kissed her, and down her back, cupping her tightly against me.

"This is crazy right now," I said, and smiled at her beautiful face, now flushed with color. She was breathing fast, as excited as I was.

"Crazy is as crazy does," she said, bit my ear, hooked her leg behind mine, and knocked me onto my back on the bed. She fell on top of me, kissing me, yanking on my hair to get more of me. I was kissing her and laughing at the same time. I was roaring with power.

I had my clothes off in just under a minute and her nightgown over her head and tossed to the far corner of the small bedroom in another ten seconds flat. "I don't believe this," I said, looking at her, wanting all of her at once, not knowing where to start. She laughed as she kissed me and then her hands were all over me.

We were laughing and moaning together when I came into her and she arched up sharply, biting and licking my neck, nipping me with little kisses. I forced myself to stop. "I've got to get a grip here," I said, "I just want to feel you around me. God, Laura, I've wanted to make love with you from the moment I saw you talking to that teenage boy in the library."

"I wanted you over the chicken satay," she said and tightened her arms around my back. "Yes, hold still, Mac, and let me feel you. I hadn't imagined this tonight, I really hadn't, I —"

She climaxed. I watched the pleasure take her, felt her tightening around me and knew I couldn't hold on much longer. Wonderful thing was, it didn't matter. In a frenzy, I joined her.

"It's the two of us now, Laura."

"That's more than fine by me," she said. "I'm really glad you came to the library, even if you don't know a thing about Latvian drug wars."

At ten minutes after one o'clock in the morning, we were both awake again, still not going slow and easy but frenetic and urgent. There wasn't any laughter this time, just the darkness surrounding us, Laura's lovely flesh, and the lovely groans coming from her mouth. Afterward I came up on my elbows and touched my forehead to hers. "It's all over for me, Laura."

"Yes, I can feel that it is."

The damned woman had the gall to laugh.

"That isn't what I meant."

"I know." She kissed my chin, bit my earlobe, and polished it by chopping my elbows so that I fell on top of her again. She wrapped her arms tightly around my back and held me close. "It was over for me, Mac, when you walked into the reference section and made me laugh with the first thing out of your mouth. The truth is, for me, this is a rather incredible thing."

"Yes, for me as well. I just wish we could have met in a more normal way. Getting poisoned and shot at during the courting period tends to make a guy look over his shoulder a whole lot, and it wasn't even your dad."

"I forced it on you. Every time I think of all the lies I told you — had to tell you — it makes me furious and sad. Promise me that you've forgiven me."

"Since I'm lying naked on top of you and you've kissed me just about everywhere, I guess I'll have to. But no more lies or evasions, Laura, ever. Okay?"

"I promise. Now you make me a promise, Mac. Promise me that everything's going to turn out okay."

"I can promise you that we're going to survive this, Laura. But how can it ultimately end well if Jilly's involved?"

She kissed me again in answer, and we fell asleep, her warm breath against my neck.

I had incredible dreams.

There weren't any more werewolves prowling around outside the cottage, trying to peer in.

I came awake suddenly to the sound of loud banging on wood, and a voice calling out.

My brain woke up in high gear. I pulled on old cotton sweats, grabbed my SIG off the nightstand, and eased out of bed. Laura was still asleep, sprawled on her back. She was naked and my hands were on her before I could stop myself. I covered her quickly.

Daylight hadn't made it through the curtained windows. It was dull gray and cold in the small living room, the fire in the grate long cold. Where was Grubster?

Someone banged on the door again. "Open up. Come on, Mac, open the bloody door."

I recognized that irritated, sweet voice. I jerked the chair away from under the doorknob, turned the lock, and pulled open the door. Standing on the small porch was Special Agent Lacy Savich, known as Sherlock by everyone except her parents. Early-morning sunlight backlighted her. With all that red hair, she looked like a Titian painting come to life.

She was on me in an instant, hugging me tight. "Hi, Mac," she said, drawing back, giving me a big smile.

"My angel," I said, grabbing her up in my arms, and swinging her around. "I hadn't expected you this soon. What did you do, immediately hop a plane?"

She kissed my ear. "Yes, we took the redeye." Then she said over my shoulder, "Hello, who are you?"

I let Sherlock slowly back down on her feet. We turned together to see Laura, in her sweats, her hair tangled around her flushed face, Grubster curling around her bare feet.

"So soon, Mac?"

"This is Sherlock, Laura. I got her through her final physical exam at the Academy. She would have failed miserably if I hadn't been there."

"Ha. He was noted for his magnificent brawn, but I had the brain power." Sherlock and Laura shook hands, Sherlock eyeing Laura like you'd expect a mother to do.

"Where's Savich?" I asked, giving Sherlock a final hug. "You did let him come with you, didn't you, Sherlock? I mean rather than leaving him home to take care of Sean? He's come in handy before, hasn't he?"

She laughed and poked me. "That man is a dream and don't you ever doubt it. We took Sean over to his grandparents, Savich's folks, who couldn't wait for us to leave so they could spoil him rotten.

"Hey, it's after eight o'clock in the morning, Mac. Dillon is walking the cliffs, checking for any recent signs of people close to the cottage. He wanted me to wait, to give you more sleeping time, but hey, I couldn't. I was worried about you. You're okay, Mac, really? And you too, Laura?"

I was wondering if Savich knew werewolf tracks when he saw them. "No one came back last night. Maybe the bears are hibernating."

"Both Dillon and I are good at finding bears. We're all together now, Mac, not just you two alone anymore." Sherlock began to examine me, not saying another word, just lightly touching my arms, my face. She pulled up my sweatshirt and began looking me over. "Your ribs okay now?" I felt her fingertips lightly brushing over my still-bruised middle.

"Yeah, I still get tired quicker than I used to, but it's better every day. Hey, Sherlock, don't pull down my pants."

"Oh, all right." She straightened again, then gave me several long looks. "How do you guys feel now after all that phenobarbital?"

Laura said, "I'm still just a bit on the groggy side, but it's nearly gone."

"Since I'm a manly man, I had almost no aftereffects."

I got a punch in the arm.

"I'm off to make some coffee," Laura said. "Everyone want some?"

I heard her moving around in the small kitchen that was separated from the living/

dining room by a bar with three stools bellied up to it.

"Squawk."

"That's Nolan, and his first word of the new day." Laura had pulled off his cage cover.

Laura called out, "You can open his cage if you want to. All the windows are closed, he'll be just fine. Also, if you could sprinkle some sunflower seeds for him. I'm making him some toast right now. Yes, Grubster, I hear you, the world hears you. I'm going to open some cat food for you. Don't fret."

I watched Sherlock open Nolan's door, saw him stare at her a moment, then, a step at a time, venture outside his cage. He cocked his head at Sherlock. "Squawk."

He jumped to the back of one of the love seats. He took a sunflower seed from Sherlock's outstretched fingers, carefully dropped it on the sofa back, then hopped up on Sherlock's shoulder and began chewing on her hair. Sherlock began to laugh.

"Squawk."

"Eat your breakfast, Nolan," Sherlock said, and set him on the sofa back.

Grubster was meowing his head off. Then, suddenly, there was silence from him. He'd doubtless buried his face in a bowl of cat food.

"Come sit down, Sherlock," I said. "I don't remember how you like your coffee."

"Just a bit of fake sugar and a dollop of milk," Sherlock said to Laura. "Oh, if you don't have any of that stuff, black is just fine."

"No, we're in luck," Laura said. "That's the way I drink my coffee too. Mac?"

"Don't pour me any yet, Laura," I called from the cottage door. "I want to see what Savich is up to."

"Put on some shoes before you head out," Sherlock said, absorbed with putting another sunflower seed in Nolan's mouth.

When I walked outside, I was surprised to see a beautiful clear morning, the sky as blue as Jilly's eyes, with just a light breeze. I turned south to see Savich striding toward me. He saw me and waved.

Like his wife, when he reached me he studied me closely. "You okay?" Thank God he didn't feel it necessary to feel me up.

"Yeah, nothing to worry about. Did you see anything? Sherlock's already inside drinking coffee. Come on in. I'm surely pleased to see both of you."

"I didn't see any signs of anyone out

here. The ground's still soft from all the rain. There would have been footprints if anyone had come close. But you've already checked out here, haven't you?"

"Not this morning."

"Now you don't have to. Sounds like you guys are in deep shit. I'm glad you called us. But it's going to be sticky, Mac. We're both really sorry about Jilly and any involvement she may have in all this. I want you to know, too, that we talked it over on the way here, and for Jilly's sake, we're with you for a day or two. I agree with you we should be safe enough for that long. Someone would have to be crazy to come after four federal agents when everyone knows why we're here.

"I said as little as possible to Jimmy Maitland. For the moment, at least, since you're on leave and have already talked to your boss, Carl Bardolino, he's going to let us go with this. As I said, Sherlock and I discussed this situation thoroughly on the flight to Portland. We've got more questions. Then we can discuss strategy." He paused a moment and gripped my shoulder. "I'm very sorry about Jilly, Mac. No word about where she is?"

"No. I'm sorry about your having to leave Sean."

"He'll do just fine. Sherlock says he's too young to be ruined just yet, so it doesn't matter how often they tickle his stomach and tell him he's the prince of the world. I sure hope she's right."

It sounded so normal, so very unlike the past four days of my life. I sighed. "Come meet Laura Scott?"

16

After we'd each drunk a cup of coffee strong enough to cut through sludge, I said, "There's a whole lot we need to do today. Since we don't know how long we can count on staying here, we've got to make good use of every minute."

I looked over at Savich, who was staring into his nearly empty coffee cup. He looked every inch a mean son of a bitch, big and lean, wearing jeans and a dark blue turtleneck sweater, short boots. You could count on him to cover your back. "It's fifteen minutes after eight o'clock in the morning, Mac. I ain't going nowhere until I get food in this empty belly."

Sherlock said, "Before we do anything, you guys need to go shower. A shave for you, Mac. Your hair's standing on end. Actually, both of you could use some more sleep. But it's odd. You both look real relaxed." She raised her eyebrow, blinked twice, and walked quickly into the kitchen.

"She knows," Laura said to me.

"I hope she approves of you."

Laura and I didn't share the shower, but it was a temptation. We brushed our teeth together. When we returned, I inhaled the smell of bacon and eggs and nearly cried. I saw that Nolan was riding around on Savich's shoulder. Grubster was sitting on Sherlock's lap.

"Quite a menagerie you've got," Savich said, and lightly stroked his fingertip down Nolan's breast.

"Squawk."

The table was set. We all sat down like grown-ups. Savich brought out the plates of food he'd kept warm in the oven. "Eat up." Savich ate for five minutes, then said, "Mac, you mentioned this old fellow, Charlie Duck, who was murdered. What about him? How does he fit into all of this?"

"All we have is his dying words to Doc Lambert: 'a big wallop, too much, then they got me.' He knew something about Laura's drug case, no question at all in my mind about that. But what?"

Laura said, "There hasn't been a whole

lot of time to think since I met Mac, but I agree with him. Charlie found out something he shouldn't have and that's why they killed him."

I said, "After breakfast I want to call the M.E. in Portland and see what he has to say. I want to speak to Maggie Sheffield, the sheriff, and see if she's learned anything. I'd assume that she would have called here if she'd gotten any leads on Jilly."

"Charlie Duck's funeral is this afternoon," Laura said as she fed a sunflower seed to Nolan, who was seated on a chair arm. "We can go see what's in the pot and maybe stir it up."

"We're going to start stirring the pot much sooner than that," I said. "Paul's first on the list."

Savich reached down and fed a bit of bacon to Grubster. He said to Sherlock, "Do you think they'll keep us as interested as Sean does?"

"He's already a hell-raiser," Sherlock said. "Savich is trying to find some weights light enough for him so he can begin his training." She looked at Grubster, who was now washing himself on one of the love seats. "That's some cat," she said. "Big varmint but a sweetie."

"I found him when I was a sophomore in college. He was so tiny and skinny then, not larger than one of his legs is now. The vet thinks he's about ten or eleven years old now. Once Grubster trained me with a can opener, he never stopped eating."

Sherlock made more coffee. I lit the logs in the fireplace. The room was soon warm and cozy. Sherlock said unexpectedly, "It was probably a good thing you saw Laura use a gun. She was forced to tell you everything. I hate to go into situations blind."

"My wife," Savich said, patting her thigh, "can find a silver lining in a ditch. But you know, it's probably better that the shooters got away. If you'd taken them in, the shit would have hit the fan and you'd be sitting here watching yourself on national news. The agency directors would be arguing about who should be in charge, and the criminals would probably disappear while all the bureaucratic chaos was going on. You and Laura would be separated and sent to different sides of the country for endless debriefings that would ultimately lead nowhere. So Sherlock's right, as usual."

He stood up and picked cat hairs off his jeans. "I do have an announcement to make. Laura is nuts about you, Mac, so there's one good thing in all this mess. Now, let's get this show on the road."

I heard a car coming down the dirt road. I reached automatically to my belt. "Where did you park your car, Savich?"

"Behind the cottage."

"Good," I said. "Everyone stay put." I pulled out my SIG, eased open the front door, and stepped outside, pulling the door closed behind me.

17

Cal's light blue BMW Roadster convertible roared toward me. The earth was still damp from the rain, so the car didn't kick up any dust though she'd jammed on the brakes to do just that. I remembered our own party at her parents' house and winced.

I quickly tucked my SIG into the back of my pants, called out, and waved to her. Cal got out of the little car and looked at me, but didn't wave or say anything, just waited for me to come to her. She was wearing baggy jeans and a huge sweater that came nearly to her knees. Her glasses were firmly on her nose. Her hair was scraped back in a ponytail.

When I was nearly to the car, she jumped me, just as she had the night of the party. Her legs went around my waist, her arms around my neck. She started kissing me enthusiastically all over my face.

I gave her a hug and peeled her off me. "Hi, Cal, what's cooking?"

"What's wrong, Mac? Don't you want to make love? How about over on the edge of the cliff. It's warm enough, or I'll get you warm soon enough. How about it?"

"I've got company, Cal."

"Oh yes, Mom told me you were here at Seagull Cottage with Laura Scott, that you were playing FBI agent and protecting her. That right?"

"Yeah, that's right. It's early, Cal. What can I do for you?"

"I just came around to see if there was anything I could do to help. Where's this Laura Scott you're protecting?"

"I'm right here."

Sure enough, Laura was standing on the single step that led to the front door. "Hi," she said. "I'm Laura Scott."

"I'm Cal Tarcher. No one can figure out why anybody wants to kill you."

"Easy enough," Laura said. "I'm a DEA agent. I was undercover until just last week, when my cover broke down. See, I was getting too close to something. Would you like to come inside? I think there's some breakfast left. You and Mac seem to be great friends."

"You're a DEA agent? Does that mean you're a drug cop?"

"That's exactly what I am."

"What are you doing here, with Mac?"

"That's a very long story. Would you like to go on in?"

I said in Laura's ear after Cal passed us both and went inside the cottage, "You didn't have to invite her in, dammit."

"Why not? You two sure do seem on very good terms. I'd be almost tempted to say intimate terms. Sherlock and Savich are holed up in the bedroom. Can we expect any more of your conquests to show up, Mac?"

"Cut it out, Laura. It's not what you think. Besides, I'd barely met you when Cal nailed me."

"She nailed you? Usually it's said the other way around. Poor Mac, all these women after your body."

"You're the last so you'd better not put too many holes in me."

She lightly patted my cheek and followed Cal into the cottage.

Laura had removed all signs of Sherlock and Savich. I wondered why they hadn't wanted to stay out here. "How about some bacon and toast, Cal?"

"Thanks, Mac. Hey, who's this?"

"That's my cat, Grubster."

Cal immediately broke a piece of bacon in half and fed it to Grubster. "He's a pig." Having said that, Cal took a big bite of toast. She leaned down and gave Grubster the other half of the bacon.

"He'll kill for you now."

"He's beautiful. Who's that?"

"Squawk."

"That's my mynah bird, Nolan. Would you like some coffee, Cal?"

She nodded and Laura soon returned with the coffeepot and poured, then went back into the kitchen.

Cal took a drink, then sat forward on her chair and whispered in a very loud stage voice, "I know you have to protect her, Mac, but just maybe we can get rid of her for a while? She seems nice, she'll probably want to take a walk on the cliffs. She won't have to stay out long. I figure I can have you out of those pants in under three seconds."

Stones were piled on top of my tongue.

"It might be nice to have a bed this time instead of the floor. What do you think?"

"Cal," I said, "this isn't the time, really. Laura can't be alone. This isn't a game — someone's trying to kill her."

"Oh, I don't know, Mac," Laura said, grinning, not six feet away. "I think I'd like a walk on the cliffs. You two can just go tangle up the sheets. Would you like me to make the bed before I leave?"

I knew it. I just knew it. There was no justice, no fairness in the world. What there was, was Laura standing two feet away from Cal, no expression at all on her face, and I knew that was a bad sign.

"You see, Mac?" Cal said. "Laura doesn't mind. You'd really make up the bed for us?"

"It's not all that messed up," said the woman I'd made love to the previous night, the woman who Savich said was nuts about me. "We both slept like logs, little movement. Hey, I could just spread the covers and you two could tussle on top. How about that?"

Cal was suddenly very quiet. "You two slept together last night?"

"Yes," I said, standing. "We did. Now, Cal, we've got lots of stuff to do. Was there anything specific you wanted?"

"No, just you, Mac." Cal slid off the bar stool. She took the last bite of her toast. She wiped her hands on her jeans' leg. "I thought this was just a cop assignment for you, Mac," she said slowly.

281

"It's a lot of things, Cal. Is there any word on Jilly?"

Cal shook her head. "Surely Maggie would call you first if she found out anything." She looked over at Laura, for a very long time. "Do you know what, Laura?"

"No, what?"

"I sure would like to paint you. Your face isn't all that interesting, but your clothes are so tight I can tell you've got a great body. How about it?" I pictured Cal jumping Laura after she'd sketched her body.

Laura was staring at Cal like she was two boards shy of a floor. Then, slowly, she turned to me. "What do you think, Mac?"

"Cal's a good artist," I said.

"No, do you think I've got a great body?"

"Yes, and Cal's still a good artist."

"Okay," Cal said, rubbing her hands together. "We can set up a time for next week. About us, Mac, we can talk about it another time, since you say you're so busy. Oh yeah, I got some of those French condoms, you know, the ones that are real slippery and ribbed?"

I thought I'd be smart and not say a single word to that. I don't think I even breathed for at least ten seconds. I watched

Cal leave the cottage, heard the soft roar of the BMW's engine.

"Well," Laura said, eyeing me, then the toast crumbs all around Cal's plate. "I guess that took care of my idea of actually questioning her."

I grinned at her, grabbed her, and jerked her into my arms. I was kissing her when Savich and Sherlock walked back into the room.

Sherlock said, "How long did you say you'd been here, Mac?"

I kept kissing Laura until I saw that she was laughing. "Good," I said, and rubbed my hands down her arms. "I barely knew you, Laura. It just happened. Okay?"

"No, it's not at all okay, but I won't break you into parts about it just now."

"What sort of punishment do you have in mind?"

She laughed again and poked me in the belly.

I said to Savich, "Why didn't you guys stay out here to meet Cal?"

"You had a great dynamic going there, Mac. If we'd come out, everything would have changed."

"Thanks for the entertainment," Sherlock said.

"You guys just keep enjoying your own

283

jokes," I said as I dialed Ted Leppra, the M.E. up in Portland.

A minute later, Ted Leppra, boy wonder, told me it was indeed a blow to the head that had killed Charlie Duck. "He survived maybe ten to twenty minutes after someone hit him," Ted said in his smoker's hacking voice, "and bought it, I was told, on the floor of the local doctor's house. It was a pretty fast bleed into and around his brain. His brain was crushed by blood, if you prefer a more colorful description."

"You're sure?"

"Oh, yes. Funny thing though, Mac. As you probably know, the old guy was a former cop from Chicago. One of the detectives was cruising through here during an autopsy and we got to talking about him. Do you think there's a tie-in? Someone out for revenge after he got out of the can?"

"Could be," I said, all neutral. "The local sheriff is looking into all of that, naturally."

"Hey, you don't sound happy, Mac."

"No, I'm not. I was hoping there was something else involved here."

Ted coughed, holding the phone away while he hacked. "Sorry," he said. "I know, I've got to stop smoking."

"You of all people have seen enough smokers' lungs," I said mildly.

"Yeah, yeah. Listen, maybe there was something else."

Hot damn, I thought. "Hang on a minute, Ted. I'm going to put you on speaker. There are some other folk here who need to hear what you've got to say."

"Okay. Mac, you were right about that. We found some sort of drug in his system. It appears to be an opiate or related to an opiate. At least it tested positive on the opiate screen. I haven't been able to identify it yet. It's maybe some sort of drug we've never seen before. Weird, huh?"

"Not really," I said. "It's very possible it's a brand-new drug that isn't on the market yet. When will you be able to give me more information, Ted?"

"Give me a couple more days. Call me on Friday. If I find out anything sooner I'll let you know."

"Stop smoking, you moron."

"What did you say? I can't hear you, Mac."

I hung up the phone, turned, and looked at everybody. "Charlie was on to them. He had some sort of drug in his system."

"He either found out about it and wanted to see what it was, or someone forced it down him," Laura said. "Remember what he said when he was dying — 'a big wallop, too much, then they got me.' "

Savich was scratching Grubster's ears. "Or maybe lots of people around here want to try it and damn the side effects."

"More likely he discovered something and that's why he wanted to talk to me. But he didn't think it was all that urgent."

"He was wrong," Laura said.

"Yes, the poor old man," I said. "Now we know that they killed Charlie Duck. The drug in his system pretty well proves that. Damn, I wish I'd collared him that first day, but you know, I just thought he had some fishing stories to tell me. I was an idiot."

"He did try to tell the doctor what had happened," Laura said. "It's too bad he couldn't say more before he died."

I picked up the phone again. "Just maybe he's got some friends he still talks to in the Chicago Police Department."

I identified myself to three indifferent people at the Chicago Police Department, in three different departments, including Internal Affairs, and finally ended up in Personnel, where I identified myself to yet another indifferent person. Finally, I got hold of Liz Taylor. She was a real charmer, no sarcasm, she really was.

"Nope," she said cheerfully, first thing off the bat, "I'm no relation at all, so you don't have to wonder. Now, you say you want to know about Charlie Duck?"

"Yes, please. I understand he was a detective with the CPD until about fifteen years ago?"

"Yeah, I remember Charlie well. He was a homicide detective, sharp as a tack. It's funny, you know? Usually, the bosses want the old guys to retire just as soon as they can plunk a gold watch on their wrist and push them out the door. But not Charlie. Everybody wanted him to stay. I bet he could have continued here until he croaked, but he wanted to leave. I'll never forget on his sixtieth birthday, he gave me a big kiss and said he was out of here, no more dealing with scum bags, no more weeping over plea bargains that let criminals back out on the streets faster than it took the cops to catch them. He didn't want any more winters in Chicago, either. They aged his skin, he said. He was gone by the following week. Hey, who are you anyway? I know you're FBI, but why do you want to know about Charlie?"

"Charlie's dead," I said. "He was murdered. I'm trying to find out who killed him and why."

"Oh no," Liz Taylor said. "Oh no. I got a Christmas card from him just this last December. Sweet, sweet old Charlie." I heard her sniff.

"Tell me about him," I said. "I heard he wasn't exactly the trusting type."

"That was Charlie," Liz said, sniffing some more. "Some people didn't like him, called him a snoop and a son of a bitch, and I guess he was. But he'd never hurt you if you hadn't done anything wrong. He had the highest homicide clearance rate of any detective in the department. In fact, he still holds the record. Poor Charlie. I'll tell you, nothing could stop him if he smelled something rotten."

Not only had he been a detective, he'd been in homicide. He was smart and relentless. It had been a deadly mix for the old man.

"I need the names of friends he's still close to in Chicago. Some other cops. Can you give me some names?"

"Wait. Is that what happened? He smelled something rotten? And that's why someone killed him?"

"Probably," I said. "Do you know of any family or friends he still kept up with?

Maybe confided in?"

"No family left," she said. "His wife died before he left the force. Breast cancer, poor woman. He went out west somewhere when he retired, to live with his parents, somewhere on the West Coast. In Oregon, right?"

"That's right," I said, my jaw nearly locked with impatience. "Liz, any friends?"

"Just a couple of older guys still on the force. But I don't think they've spoken to him in years. I can ask around, see if any of the old guys have spoken to him recently."

"Yeah," I said, "I'd really appreciate that." I thanked her profusely, gave her my phone number at the cottage, and hung up.

"Interesting," Laura said. "Too bad she couldn't give you anything."

"She's got to come up with something pretty quick," Savich said, "or it'll be too late."

"Amen to that," Sherlock said, turning to Savich.

I walked to Laura, lightly lifted her chin in my palm, and said, "Forget Cal Tarcher. Forget all those hundreds of other women."

She laughed so hard I had to squeeze it out of her. She still thought I was funny.

At two o'clock, Laura and I were seated next to Savich and Sherlock in the League's Christian Church on Greenwich Street, just off Fifth Avenue. There was a small park opposite the white brick church, and lots of parking space. The building itself looked strangely unchurchlike, I supposed because it was used by so many different religions.

I'd introduced Laura to everyone as a DEA agent I was currently working with, Savich and Sherlock as FBI agents who were here to help us look into things. What things? Who had tried to kill Laura? I'd been as vague as possible as I'd smiled into Alyssum Tarcher's face with that news. It was an I'll-get-you-later smile and I'd swear he knew exactly what I was thinking.

Charlie Duck held the place of honor in the nave of the church, his beautifully carved silver urn set in the center of a circular piece of glass balanced on top of a hand-carved rosewood pyramid at least five feet tall. I couldn't tell how that round piece of smoky glass balanced on that pyramid point.

While we sat waiting for the service to begin, I gave them all a running commentary on the people I'd met.

Paul came in, but he didn't sit down beside me. In fact, he didn't even acknowledge me or Laura. He looked tired, his face gray, harsh shadows scored deeply beneath his eyes. More than that, he looked scared.

I looked around to see that every pew was filled. There were at least a hundred folk, a good two dozen more lining the back of the church. Everyone had left work and come here. All of a sudden conversation stopped.

Alyssum Tarcher, dressed in a black suit that quietly announced English bespoke, strode to the pulpit, which really wasn't a pulpit, but rather a long, thick mahogany board set atop marble pillars. The interior of the church was all like that — a mixture of styles and materials, announcing all sorts of possibilities but nothing specific, like an onion dome or a menorah.

Alyssum Tarcher cleared his throat and raised his head. Sunlight poured through the high windows and flooded over him. The air was perfectly still. There wasn't a sound.

He gave an almost imperceptible nod. Bagpipes sounded, low and raw and savagely beautiful. No one seemed surprised, evidently used to this. The pipes played a wrenchingly sad set of chords, then grew more distant, softer, leaving only echoes.

"Charles Edward Duck," Alyssum Tarcher said in a rolling, powerful voice, "was a man who lived a full and rich life."

I tuned him out, studying Paul's face in profile. What was going on?

"He was a police detective in Chicago until he retired to Edgerton to live with his aging parents, now deceased, some sixteen years ago. We will miss him. He was one of us."

I heard the scrape of bagpipes again, minor chords sliding into one another, then nothing. Alyssum Tarcher, the patriarch, returned to sit in the first row.

Elaine Tarcher rose next. She looked slim and well groomed and rich. Her dark suit was elegant, somber. She wore pearls. When she spoke, her voice was full and deep with emotion. "I first met Charlie Duck at our annual New Year's Eve party back in the mid-eighties. We were having the party that year at The Edwardian. Charlie played his guitar for all of us. Good-bye, Charlie."

A dozen townsfolk followed, the first representing the Anglican Church. It was Rob Morrison. He spoke briefly of Charlie's good nature, his acceptance of others, his tolerance.

Miss Geraldine, the leader of the town League, mayor of Edgerton, represented the Jewish religion. She spoke of Charlie's lack of anger toward anyone, his gentleness.

It appeared that everyone had seen Charlie Duck differently.

The final speaker was Mother Marco, ninety-three, who owned the Union 76 station. She was small and frail, and her pink scalp showed through soft, sparse white hair. "I don't represent any religion," she said in a surprisingly strong voice. "Well, maybe you could say I represent old age and the brink of death. I feel older than the rocks on the shore below Edgerton." The old lady grinned out at us all, showing big, very white false teeth. "And I'm proud of it. I knew Charlie Duck better than any of you. He was smart, was Charlie. He knew a bit about everything. He liked finding things out. If he didn't understand something, he dug and dug until he found his answers. Because he was a police detective in Chicago, he didn't have a high opinion of anybody. He wasn't blind about people."

Of all the speakers, I thought that old

Mother Marco had hit Charlie right on.

Alyssum Tarcher walked to the wooden pyramid and picked up Charlie's silver urn and held it over his head. "To Charlie," he shouted. Everyone cheered, filed in behind Alyssum Tarcher, and marched out of the church.

"My, oh my," Sherlock said.

"Some show," Savich said.

I felt Laura's fingers close around my hand. "I don't want to go there," she said. "To the cemetery. I don't want to go."

"No, we don't have to. No one will expect us. After all, we are outsiders." I saw Rob Morrison beside Maggie Sheffield, and I thought of Detective Castanga. *Margaret was my wife at one time.*

"Who the hell are you?"

"This is Cotter Tarcher, guys. He's Alyssum's only son."

Cotter dismissed the two women and eyed Savich, his eyes dark and hot. Savich arched a dark eyebrow.

"Here we have the weakest link," I whispered to Laura.

"I asked you a question, buddy. What are you doing here? You don't belong here. Nobody invited you."

"Actually, I did," I said. I nodded toward both Sherlock and Savich, and showed

Cotter that I was holding Laura's hand. "They're friends of mine."

Cotter said, "None of you should be here."

Savich smiled, a kick-ass smile that should have alerted Cotter but didn't. Savich knew exactly what he was doing. He'd taken Cotter's measure very quickly. "I enjoyed the performances, sport. Everyone who spoke was very talented. Why didn't you speak? No religion? No talent?"

Cotter's eyes flamed. He was quickly going beyond anger, to nearly out of control. What had happened to him? Cotter had a hair trigger and Savich had baited him well, but no one was more surprised than I was when Cotter took a swing at Savich. I didn't move; I even felt a bit sorry for Cotter. As for Sherlock, she said, "Oh, no. You idiot," but not in time.

Savich smoothly caught Cotter's wrist and squeezed it back down to his side. Cotter tried a kick but didn't make it. Savich grabbed Cotter's leg just behind his knee and flipped him into the air. He released Cotter's wrist only at the last minute before he landed on his back in a marigold bed, the move smoother than a twelve-year-old scotch.

Sherlock looked down at Cotter, her hands on her hips. "Why are you acting like an adolescent?"

"Get a grip on yourself," Savich said. "Consider growing up."

"None of you is worth a piece of shit. Big federal agents, that's a laugh. You'll never find out anything." Cotter dragged himself out of the flower bed and stomped away.

"That man has real problems," Laura said.

"He's the local sociopath," I said. "So he doesn't think we're going to find out anything, does he?" I watched him speak to Alyssum Tarcher, and the older man shook his head. "When I first met him I thought he was just an immature hothead. But after seeing him perform today, I wonder if he's involved in all of this, his daddy's right hand?"

"His father looks like an aristocrat, a sleek greyhound among a pack of mutts," Sherlock said. "As for Cotter, he looks like a little bulldog."

"I think Cal and Cotter are different," Laura said. "Cal acts weird too, but Mac's never called her a sociopath."

"Hey," I said. "I only calls 'em like I sees 'em. At the very least we know that Cal's got great taste in men."

I saw Alyssum Tarcher look back at me. His face was cold but his eyes were suddenly as hot as his son's.

18

It was just after five-thirty in the afternoon when Savich and I pulled into the driveway of 12 Liverpool Street. Paul was indeed at home. Actually, both his car and Maggie Sheffield's sheriff's car were side by side in the driveway. We heard them yelling at each other from the front porch and stopped a moment beside a hanging plant that looked a lot happier than I did. We stood quietly outside the front door, listening.

"You damned little worm," we heard Maggie scream at the top of her lungs. "Don't say or do anything like that again, Paul, or I'll take your head off. Are you nuts? How long has Jilly been gone?"

"What do you know? You don't know anything. You like to play at doing a man's job, but you don't do it well. But as a woman, Maggie, you really suck. Maybe this is the ideal job for you. What are you, a dyke?"

We heard a crash. I sighed, opened the door, walked into the small foyer, and looked to the right, into the living room. There I saw Maggie straddling Paul, who was lying flat on his back in his black-and-white living room. She had him by the neck, his head pressed against the floor.

Savich calmly walked over to her, grabbed her under her arms, and pulled her straight up. She turned on him, fists raised. He held her up by her armpits and said in that deep, smooth voice of his, "Not smart. Don't do it."

"Enough, both of you," I said, and gave Paul a hand up. "Now, what's this all about? We could hear you screaming at each other from the front porch."

"He's a stupid prick," Maggie said. "Let me down, you jock. I'm the sheriff. I'll arrest you."

"I'm not a jock, ma'am. I'm a Special Agent, Dillon Savich, FBI."

"Oh," she said, and immediately went still. "I'm sorry. You're here for Mac, aren't you? I saw you at Charlie Duck's funeral but I was late and didn't have a chance to meet you."

"That's right. Can I put you down now?"

"Please do. I won't hurt that little wimp." She looked over at Paul like she wanted to spit on him.

"Paul," I said, "go sit down. We need to talk. Maggie, you sit over in that chair. Either of you makes a move toward the other and Savich or I will flatten you. Well, Savich will for sure. My ribs are a bit on the sore side. Got it?"

"I'm the sheriff," Maggie said, tucking her blouse back in. "I'll do whatever the hell I want to."

"Fine," Savich said. "That's the spirit. What we'd really like is for you to sit down and tell us if you've heard anything about Mac's sister."

"Not a blessed thing," Maggie said, looking over at Paul. "I even spoke to Minton this morning, not something I was crazy about doing, but he didn't have anything new, just sputtered and whined about not knowing what you and Ms. Scott are up to. I told him that if it had been any of his business, you would have told him." She smiled. "He called me a bitch. Made my day. I'm leaving now. If I stay in the room any longer with this jackass, I'll lose it. Call me if you find out anything, Mac."

She nodded. "Agent Savich, thank you for your generous help. I'm sure you'll let me know if you need anything."

"Wait a minute, Maggie, I'll walk you out," I said.

"He's a pathetic jerk," Maggie said in my direction as we walked out of the house.

"What did he say this time to make you blow up?"

"You won't believe it, Mac. He tried to get in my pants. Well, to get under my uniform so he could find my pants. The little jerk. It took me a while to get him off me, so I could beat the crap out of him."

"Why would he do that?"

"God knows. I've always thought he was weird."

"Okay, Maggie. We'll keep in touch."

I waited until she drove off, waving at me. When I came back into the living room, Savich was waiting. "All right, Paul," he said as I came in, "tell us about the drug you've developed."

"Yes. We're real interested in that, Paul."

Paul just sat there, staring down at his hands that were clasped between his legs. "I don't have a damned thing to tell either of you. Go away."

"No, we're not going anywhere until you tell us about it."

Paul looked as if he wanted to fold in on himself. Again, I thought he looked scared. "Talk," I said.

He walked around the room a couple of times, pausing in front of one of the stark modern paintings. We waited until finally he turned back to us and said, "It's all experimental, Mac. It's doubtful anything will come of it, truth be told. You know the odds against developing successful drugs these days. The business of pharmaceutical research is astronomically expensive, demands incredible numbers of man-hours and highly specialized computer programs. And then there's the FDA to contend with."

He paused a moment and pulled at a loose thread on his tweed jacket. "I wanted to continue along a certain line of research. The people at VioTech deemed it too expensive to continue the research, not enough projected payback even if the drug could be perfected, and so they canceled it. They wanted Jilly and me to go into AIDS research. Our interests just don't lie there. When Alyssum Tarcher offered to finance us, we took him up on it."

"What exactly is the drug, Paul?" I asked.

"It's a memory drug, nothing more than that."

"I don't know what you mean by a memory drug," Savich said. "We know so little about the mind, about how memory even works. What does it do to the memory?"

"It's meant to take away the physical responses to bad memories when they surface. You see, the drug seems to be activated when there are sudden physical manifestations of distress — heightened adrenaline levels, rapid heartbeat, dilated pupils — things like that. Its purpose is to shut down the power of the memory by reducing the physical distress and substituting a sense of well-being.

"The benefits might be enormous in treating someone who has lived through something terrible, for example, soldiers surviving battles, or physical or sexual abuse as a child. Once the emotional baggage of the memory is dissipated, so is its physiological power."

I sat forward on the sofa, my hands clasped between my knees. Finally he was talking. I had to keep him going. "The physical reactions you're describing, Paul, aren't just prompted by a bad memory. They can happen with a whole lot of things, like fear, excitement, tension."

"True enough, but you see, the drug is

meant to be given in a controlled setting in which the memory is repeatedly triggered. So the drug is focused."

"It sounds incredible," Savich said slowly. "But how can you continue research by yourself, in a home laboratory?"

"I was very close to success when I left VioTech, although none of the decision makers at VioTech agreed. It's just a matter of fine-tuning some of the drug's side chains."

"Would the drug be addictive?" I asked.

"Oh no," Paul said, shaking his head. "Oh no."

"What about military uses?" Savich asked. "After all, if you can lessen all the physical manifestations of distress, why, then you could give your soldiers a shot and produce a battalion of heroes."

"No, I won't ever have anything to do with the military."

Paul looked incredibly tired, his voice flat, as if he simply didn't care about anything anymore.

"When I asked you about this before," I said, "you just laughed it off as a fountain of youth drug. This is something else entirely."

"It doesn't matter. None of this has anything to do with Jilly's disappearance. It doesn't have anything to do with anything at all. Go away, Mac. I don't want to talk to either of you anymore. Please leave now."

"Oh?" I asked, an eyebrow up. "You just want to attack women who happen to wander into your house?"

"Maggie told you about it all wrong. She was coming on to me and when I decided to do something about it, she turned on me. A man gets horny, you know that. Maggie's nothing but a tease, Mac."

"Tell me where Jilly is, Paul."

"I don't know. If I did, I'd be with her."

"Look, Paul," I continued after a moment, "it's time to drop the pretense. Laura told me she's DEA, that she was undercover. They know about this drug. They know about Molinas. There were then two attempts on Laura's life after Jilly disappeared. Who ordered them, Paul? You? Tarcher? This arch criminal, Del Cabrizo? Tell us how Tarcher's involved. Tell us about John Molinas."

"I don't have to talk to you, and I want you to go away, both of you." With those words, Paul got up and walked out of the living room.

I went after him. When he heard me

305

coming, he broke into a run, took the stairs three at a time. By the time I caught up to him, he was locked in his laboratory. Jesus, I thought, this was nuts. It was a steel-reinforced door. I didn't have a prayer of breaking it open. I told him to let me in, pleaded with him to tell me what was going on before they came in with a search warrant, but he remained completely silent.

After ten minutes, I felt Savich touch my arm. "Let's go," he said. "We need to regroup. Maybe it's time for Laura to call her boss at the DEA and let them take over. A search warrant doesn't sound like such a bad idea. They can haul both him and Tarcher in and interrogate them big time. Jesus, I'm tired. That late flight is catching up with me."

"Maybe you and Sherlock can rest a little when we get back to the cottage."

19

Laura and I held hands while we watched the sun sink into the ocean. The evening was mild with only a light breeze coming off the ocean. We walked along the cliffs, stopping every couple of steps to talk or kiss.

"You're right," she said, her arms clasped tightly around my back.

"About what this time?" I kissed her silly before she managed to pull back. "We've talked to almost everyone today. You baited Tarcher. You went after Paul and he's locked himself up. It's hard to know how to make any more progress. Unless you've got a better idea, maybe it's time to call my boss and let the DEA come on out and kick butt."

Savich agreed with her. I agreed with her. But what hit me full in the gut in that moment was that I had met Laura less than a week before. Yet I knew she was honorable and, I'd wager, as loyal as a tick. After less than a week, I knew I didn't want to let her get away from me.

I couldn't stop looking at her. She was wearing Nike running shoes, tight jeans, and a long, loose white shirt. She'd pulled up her long hair and fastened it with a banana clip. She wore a bit of coral lipstick and no other makeup. I'd nearly kissed all of it off. I looked at her mouth and decided it was my duty to get the rest of it. I closed my hand over her forearm and pulled her to a stop. We looked out over the ocean, following the flight of several seagulls that were cruising for dinner in the water below. It was quiet and peaceful, tastes of salt blowing in the wind.

"Let's sit down," I said. We found a trio of rocks leaning into one another, back about fifteen feet from the cliffs.

"Talk to me," I said.

"You want me to tell you how sexy you look?"

"Yeah, but it can wait a minute. Tell me about yourself, Laura."

"Nothing wild in my youth, Mac. Actually, I had a pretty normal life growing up in Tacoma, Washington. My mom and dad were close to me and my older brother.

"I played the clarinet growing up. I had great technique but my tone wasn't very good. I could never be first chair because of that."

"You couldn't play those sweet solos, huh?"

"Only once in junior high. I was a pretty sight, my mom said, but my clarinet wasn't a pretty sound. I went to Boston College, dropped the clarinet — no loss to the music world — and got a degree in psychology. I always knew I wanted to be a cop. I love my job, Mac. My older brother, Alan, is a homicide detective in Seattle. My dad was a cop. He's dead now. My mom lives near my brother and his family in Seattle."

I noticed how the wind, stiffer now than just five minutes before, lifted some stray hair and blew it across her face. I watched the fading daylight shadow-play across her face.

In that instant, a bullet struck the rock not an inch from her hand, spewing out sharp shards. She looked at me blankly as I grabbed her and hurled her to the ground, rolling back behind those rocks. Not much cover, but it was all we had.

Two more shots rang out, one striking the rocky ground and flinging out clumps of dirt and shards of stone, and the other probably high and wide. I grabbed Laura's head and flattened her face against the ground. I had all of her covered with my body, I hoped.

I leaned close to her ear. "Damn, we're about twenty feet from the cottage and there's not even a stump for cover."

There was another shot, this one thudding solidly into the ground beside us. I pulled her back farther under me.

I looked back at the cottage, beyond that huge expanse of naked ground, and saw the front door slowly open. "Sherlock, Savich," I shouted. "Keep inside. Call the cops."

I saw a good half-dozen bullets slam into the cottage. Those shots came from my right, near the cliff. I squirmed around, pulled my SIG Sauer, rose up on my elbow, and fired off six rounds in that direction. I heard a yell.

I smiled. "Maybe I got one of the bastards. Now they know we're armed, they won't take the chance of rushing us. They might have heard me yell for Sherlock and Savich to call for the backup. Just hold tight, Laura. Think of me as your Kevlar vest."

Her face was covered with dirt. She spit some out. "Damn, that was close. This is incredible, Mac. Who are these people coming after federal agents? What good does this do them?"

I was lying only half on top of her now. Three more shots sounded, these toward the cottage. I wasn't surprised to hear return fire from the cottage, fast, an entire clip in a matter of seconds. I knew I wasn't mistaken — there was a shout of pain. Sherlock or Savich had hit one of them. How many were there?

There was silence now. Even the seagulls were quiet. Laura began to squirm away. "No," I said, grabbing her shoulder. "Don't move, not yet. Wait a few more minutes."

I yelled, "Savich, did you get through?"

He yelled back, "The cops should be here in three minutes, no more." But there was something about his voice I didn't like, something that didn't sound right.

"Those guys must have thought they'd died and gone to heaven when you and I came trooping out here."

I looked up at the sky. We had another fifteen minutes of daylight. Laura and I had three rocks for cover. A piece of cake.

She twisted about to get more comfortable, lying fully beneath me now, and said, "How many are there?"

"I don't know. At least three. Two of them may be hit. Now we wait for Sherlock and Savich. It shouldn't be long."

We waited stiff and silent for two more minutes. Laura spit out some more dirt.

The door to the cottage opened. I heard Savich yell, "Come on in, Mac. Run!"

We ran hunkered over, zigzagging over the ground as we'd been trained to do, Sherlock and Savich covering us. They fired off another clip each, fanning the area behind us. There were three or four stray shots that didn't come near us, several more that struck the cottage, then silence again.

I literally threw Laura through the door, turned and fired as Sherlock and Savich eased back into the cottage. I slammed the door, crouched to the floor, and turned to see both women laughing.

"Well done, you two," Laura said, her arms around Sherlock. "You really saved our hides."

Well, I thought, staring at the women, everyone reacts differently to being shot at. I checked out the other narrow window that looked toward the cliffs. Nothing. I pulled the curtain tightly over the window. Savich nodded. "All clear from here." He was staring from his wife to Laura. Laura's face was dirty, her hair hanging in tangles. Sherlock was grinning at her like a loon.

"You've got a clot of dirt in your ear," Sherlock said and picked it out.

"So who did you call, Savich?" I said.

He pulled the curtain back into place. "They cut the phone lines, Mac. It's just us in this little box of Cracker Jacks."

"Damn," I said. "These guys are good." I got to my feet and went into the kitchen to check the back of the house. I brought the two beers left in the refrigerator back into the living room. I looked from Laura to Sherlock, knew there was no hope for it, and pulled a quarter out of my pocket. "Call it in the air, Sherlock," I said.

So much for fairness. They started on the beers without the slightest guilt.

"They've got balls," Savich said, looking up from cleaning his gun by the window. "They can't shoot worth a shit, but they're serious about this."

"Please tell me your rental car has a cell phone, Dillon," Sherlock said.

"I'd tell you so if it were true," Savich said.

"This is very depressing," Sherlock said.

"I wish I hadn't finished my beer off so fast."

I checked the dead bolt again and shifted the chair more firmly beneath the knob. "When it's dark we've got to try to get out of here."

"It's dark enough," Laura said. "We'll all go right now. Let's try to make it to your car, Mac. We can get the hell out of Dodge." I saw she was chewing on her bottom lip, looking toward Savich, who'd been silent. He said finally, "I agree. It's been nearly a half hour that we haven't heard a thing. If they wanted to kill us, they'd still be shooting. Yeah, why not try to get out of here?"

I opened the front door very quietly. I waited, then eased outside, looking toward the cliffs, sweeping my SIG Sauer slowly around in a wide arc. There was a big moon floating over the water, but roiling dark tattered clouds kept sliding in front of it. The night was blessedly dark. I waited until the moon was covered, then ran low to the Taurus, Savich, Sherlock, and Laura on my heels.

Both women were in, down on the floor of the backseat, Savich in the passenger seat as I turned the key in the ignition. Nothing. I tried again, then stopped.

"Somebody disabled the car," I said.

"They must have been very quiet about it," Savich said. "Let's get back inside. I'll cover you."

No one tried to shoot us on our mad run back.

Once the four of us were back inside the cottage, the front door closed and locked, Savich said, "This is interesting. We're in America and we're as effectively cut off from help as you were, Mac, in North Africa." I remembered that day when I thought my ticket was punched. There'd been help there though.

Laura shook her head, her face drawn. "This should have been just me. It doesn't matter that you're cops too, this wasn't your assignment. You're innocent bystanders. I'm sorry you got tossed into the middle."

"I made the decision with you," I said. "It's Sherlock and Savich who are the innocent bystanders."

"Shove it, Mac," Savich said.

"Coffee," Sherlock said. "We might as well start making some. We're just going to have to wait for the sheriff. You do think she's coming to check on us, don't you?"

"I don't think they're going to let us just sit here and snooze all night, Sherlock,"

Savich said. "They're going to come for us."

"Interesting how they got off at least a dozen shots at us, Laura, and missed. Don't you think that's strange?"

"They don't want us dead for some reason?" Savich said, a dark eyebrow hoisted up an inch.

"Maybe not," I said.

In the next instant, all three windows across the front of the cottage imploded, spewing in shattered glass, tattered bits of curtains, and heavy metal canisters that struck the floor and rolled. They made loud popping noises and gushed out smoke. The smoke was something caustic, bitter, something that burned the very air, something that burned the breath in your mouth.

There was no time. I looked at Laura, who was staring down at one of those small egg-shaped gray cylinders that was releasing a steady stream of the pale blue smoke not six feet away from her.

"It's ice acid," she said. "I'm sorry, guys. I'm very, very sorry."

I wanted to tell her it wasn't her fault. I opened my mouth, inhaled some of the ice acid, and thought my tongue would burn off. I wanted to yell with the pain, but my throat was burned closed. I was shutting down and it was the strangest feeling. I was beginning to feel cold, my mouth was numb, my teeth chattering. That's why they called it ice acid. It did that to you before it laid you flat.

Before I closed my eyes, I saw Savich holding Sherlock tightly against him, his head against the top of hers. Laura was on her side on the floor, her legs drawn up. She wasn't moving. I tried to get to her. Then I couldn't see her. My eyes were freezing shut, tears seeping out, ice cold on my cheeks. I wanted to tell Savich that we had to get out of here.

Then I didn't feel a thing.

20

I knew I was awake because I heard myself moaning. But there wasn't any pain. Laura was calling my name, over and over. "Mac, don't do this. Please, please, Mac, stop. Wake up!"

I opened my eyes and stared down into Laura's face. "Oh God, you're awake. Mac, you've got to stop."

For a moment I didn't know what she was talking about. Stop what? "Mac, please, get away. Stop it, Mac."

No, I wasn't feeling any pain, but what I was feeling was harsh and real. It was shattering me. I didn't understand it.

"Mac, wake up!"

I was on top of her. She was naked and I was naked as well and between her legs. I was poised to come into her. I felt such overwhelming lust, I didn't think I could stop.

"Laura, my God, Laura."

"Mac, stop!"

"Oh, God, I don't think I can." I was panting, trying to slow the movement of my body. The urge to come into her was killing me. I locked my muscles and yelled. I wasn't going to rape her. I wasn't. The need to do just that was beyond what I could understand. It was pushing me, driving me, and I yelled again, trying to get hold, to get my mind, my will, back. I could feel her flesh against me and I didn't think I could hold back.

I looked down at her, saw she was crying, tears rolling down her cheeks.

"NO!" I yelled, my head thrown back.

I jerked myself off her, falling beside her on the wooden floor. I lay there panting, cursing, feeling the urge to come inside her pounding through my body.

"Mac."

Her voice seemed a long way away, but I knew she was lying beside me.

"Are you all right?"

There wasn't any more fear in her voice, just relief. I turned onto my side to face her. She was looking at me, and she was smiling. It was then I saw that her hands were tied over her head, her legs open and tied at the ankles. She was helpless. I wasn't. I wasn't quite naked. I still had on my running shoes and shirt.

I took deep breaths, over and over, just kept sucking in air and blowing out, trying desperately to clear my mind.

I reached out my hand to touch her, then pulled it back. I wasn't strong enough yet.

Tears were still on her cheeks. I couldn't bear it. I touched her then, wiping the tears away with my fingers. "I'm so sorry, Laura. What happened?"

"They drugged us."

I made the mistake of looking down her body. I gritted my teeth and rolled away. I was still hard. I jumped to my feet, grabbed my clothes off the floor, and quickly pulled my shorts and pants on.

I felt more normal now that I was dressed. Fight it, I said to myself over and over. Just fight it.

I came down on my knees beside her. Her legs were wide apart, her ankles tied to small rings fastened in the floor.

"I'm sorry," I said. "God, I'm sorry. I didn't realize, didn't know —"

"You weren't the one who tied me down, Mac. I'm all right. You managed to stop."

My hands were shaking. It took awhile for me to untie the knots around her wrists and ankles. Slowly, she pulled her legs together and sat up. She was rubbing her wrists. "Thank you, Mac."

"Where are your clothes?"

"I don't know."

I stripped off my shirt and handed it to her. As I watched her pull it on and fasten the buttons, my mind started to feel heavy and dull. The urge to have her was receding now. I could control it.

She rose and walked to the narrow bed in the corner of the small room we were in. My shirt came down to her thighs. She sat on the side of the bed, rubbing her wrists.

I sat beside her. I wasn't about to touch her. I was afraid that if I did, I'd lose it again. "Tell me what happened. Where are we?"

"I don't speak Spanish so I don't know what they were saying.

"You were awake but still very groggy. I watched them inject you." She shuddered.

I pulled her against me, holding her tightly. "We beat them," I said as I rubbed her back, "we're both all right."

She said against my shoulder, "I think it was all a game to them. They wanted to have some fun. They took my clothes and tied me down. Then they set you on me like a stallion over a mare. They put your face between my legs. When they pulled you back, they were laughing. Then one of the men, probably the leader, said something and they left us alone." She was silent again. I kissed her hair, kept rubbing her back. "It's all right," I said.

"Only because you came out of it enough to see what you were doing. I didn't think you'd be able to stop, Mac. Oh God, it was awful."

She'd been tied down, naked, helpless. I closed my eyes a moment against the enormity of it. If I hadn't been able to stop myself, then — "They wanted me to rape you?"

"Apparently. Funny thing, knowing it was you but that you weren't really there made it worse. You weren't my Mac. You were a stranger who didn't care who I was. You had my scent, knew I was female, and that was enough. That drug was in control."

"The drug," I said slowly. "Remember you told me the drug had some effect on sex?"

"Yes. This had to be it, what we've been looking for. They used it on you to see what it would do to you."

I wanted to kill them. They'd treated us like animals. We'd been used for sport to see what the damned drug would do.

"They probably gave you a lot more than one would inject for a sex high."

"That figures. I didn't really feel like I was having the time of my life."

I felt her smile against my shoulder. I squeezed her. "Did they hurt you?"

"Not that I can tell. I don't know how long we've been out. But they brought me out of it with smelling salts. They wanted me fully awake when they set you on me. God, Mac, it was awful. I couldn't do anything and you were gone. Then I saw you come back, just a bit, and that's when I talked to you until finally you got control back."

"Do you know where we are?"

"No. I've just been clearheaded for about an hour. It's night, I do know that much. My watch says it's just a bit after ten."

There were no windows in the small room. It was nearly square, not more than twelve by twelve. There was just the one single bed, an ancient rag rug beside it, and a toilet and sink in the far corner.

"It was about eight at night when they threw the ice acid into the cottage," I said.

"So how much time has passed? Hours? A day? I don't know, Mac. But I'll tell you one thing. Right now if I had my gun, I swear I'd blow off the head of the first man who came through the door. I just can't believe what they did. And they laughed about it."

"How many?"

"There were three men, then the man I think was their leader came in and made them leave." She paused a moment, then added, "They were all speaking Spanish. I doubt we're still in Oregon."

"Mexico, maybe," I said.

"Could be," she agreed. "Or Colombia. Remember the DEA agent who was tortured and murdered in Mexico some years ago? And nothing at all happened?"

I held her away from me. "Listen up, Laura. Don't think like that. It does no good. You haven't seen Sherlock or Savich?"

She shook her head. "When I woke up, I was alone. When they brought me here to this room, it was empty. I don't know where they were keeping you, but two of the men half-dragged you in here. It was like you were in a stupor. They tossed you on that bed and injected you. Five minutes later they put you on me. They're animals."

"I wonder what would have happened if

I hadn't gotten control? The way I felt, I would have kept at it until I was dead or the drug finally wore off. Maybe that's what they wanted to see. I wonder if they were laying bets."

She pulled back. "But you stopped yourself, Mac."

I kissed her mouth. I smoothed back her hair, lightly ran my thumb over her eyebrows. "I finally realized it was you. I love you, Laura. I couldn't have hurt you."

"Well then, let's take care of this mess and then get married. Can we do that, Mac?"

I couldn't believe it had taken me until I was twenty-nine years old to find this woman. I kissed the tip of her nose. "In exactly that order."

I looked over to the small rings screwed into the wooden floor. Had they done this before? Brought in some women and taken turns, enjoying the hell out of it? The drug was something. I was still hard.

I looked at Laura again. Her hair was curtaining her face, hanging long and loose, real shiny. I couldn't believe it. "They combed your hair?"

"Yes," she said, not looking at me. "More than that even. They bathed me, washed my hair, and sprayed some perfume on me. They let two women do this while they watched. Neither of the women spoke any English. Then they brought me to this room. I got the feeling that they've done this before with other women."

I pulled her close again, and this time I really smelled the musk on her. I felt a wave of lust. It wasn't overpowering, but I didn't want to test myself. "I'm thirsty," I said. Just having a bit of distance between us made it easier. I walked to the sink. It was as ancient as the rug by the bed, cracked and rusted. But the water was cool enough and clear. I washed my face. Laura's scent was gone. The heavy feeling in my brain was easing. I could think more than one thought at a time now, glean more than one impression. But my only thought was that I wanted to kill them. I couldn't seem to get beyond that and I knew I had to. We had to get out of here.

Laura stood up. "Did you walk away because the drug hit you again?"

"Yeah, but it's better now. Don't worry about me." Then I shook my head and said, "No, forget that. If I start looking at you funny, or talking funny, anything that isn't right, you get away from me, fast. If you can't, knock me silly. Protect yourself. All right?"

She studied my face for a long time, then nodded. When she walked toward me, I took an outside route back to the bed. I said while she was cupping water in her hands, "We've got to figure out how to get out of this bloody room."

We both looked at the one door, no windows.

"Do you think they'll feed us?" I was starving, my stomach nearly beyond the growling stage, but that wasn't the point. "If they bring us food, we'll have a chance to get out of here."

They fed us, not ten minutes later. The door simply unlocked, very quickly, and a young boy carrying two big plates in his skinny arms walked in. Behind him stood another man holding an AK-47 at the ready. He didn't come into the room, just stood there in the doorway, aiming his weapon at my belly, watchful and ready.

I don't even think I heard them close and lock the door. My eyes were on the food. There were stacks of soft tortillas and beans, strips of beef, and thick pepper-and-onion-filled potatoes. I was so hungry it tasted as good as anything I'd ever eaten.

They left a large pitcher of cold water. We drank the whole thing since the peppers were hotter than pitch. There wasn't a bit of food left. Laura looked down at the empty plates and said, "I hope we don't get sick from stuffing ourselves."

"Not a pretty thought," I said, remembering the Montezuma's revenge that had me dehydrated and ten pounds lighter a couple of years before when I'd been fishing off Cozumel. "One guy with an AK-47. I think we should move over by the door so that if he comes alone again, we'll have a chance at the guy with the gun."

Laura nodded. "There's only this one skinny pillow and the blanket. I'll mold them under the sheet. Maybe for an instant they'll think we're on the bed, asleep."

We did that and stood back to look at our handiwork. "Not very good," I said, "but hopefully it'll work. Which side of the door would you like?"

I ended up on the side of the lock, Laura behind the door. She'd taken off the heavy porcelain toilet lid and held it against her chest.

"They must know that we won't be sitting here idle," she said. "They'll expect us to try something. It's even possible that they're watching us even now."

I'd thought the same thing. I got up and went over that small room, inch by inch. I didn't see anything that remotely resembled a camera lens or a peephole. I sat back down. "I sure to God hope that Sherlock and Savich are all right."

"Maybe Sherlock's sitting by the door as we speak, a toilet lid hugged to her chest."

We waited. For a very long time. We slept. We awoke early the next morning. My watch read about 6:30 A.M.

We took turns using the toilet and washing up. At exactly seven o'clock, we heard them coming.

21

A key turned in the lock. The door slowly opened. But no one said a word, no one moved in. A canister of gas rolled through the doorway. I jumped to my feet, grabbed the thing up, and threw it in the toilet. I flushed it. Smoke gushed out of the bowl. I slammed down the toilet seat. Thankfully it contained most of the smoke. I'd inhaled only a bit. I didn't feel a thing.

I heard a man laugh. I turned to look at the two men who stood watching me from the doorway.

"*¡Así se hace!*" one of them said. He had a deep bass voice. He was a short, wiry, dark man, dressed in army fatigues, like his partner. He said in strongly accented English this time, "*Sí,* that was well done. We knew you would be waiting for us. And now you have finished. Move." He waved the AK-47 toward me. "The woman is still sleeping? You wore her out, eh?"

I took a step, watching the men. The man with the bass voice raised his weapon, but he didn't say anything more because Laura rose up, whipped around the side of the door, and smashed him in the face with the porcelain toilet lid.

The other man leaped through the doorway, his eyes on Laura, his AK-47 up, ready to fire.

I yelled and ran straight at him. He whipped the gun around, only to moan and fall hard to the floor when Laura hit him hard on his temple with the porcelain toilet lid.

The first man tried to struggle up. Laura calmly leaned over and smashed him hard again with the toilet lid. Then she kicked both of them hard in the ribs.

"Close the door quick," I said. I grabbed the larger man under his arms and began dragging him inside the room. Laura grabbed the other guy.

I picked up one of the AK-47s and looked out the door. There was a long narrow corridor on either side of the room. No one else was in sight.

"We need their clothes," I said.

Five minutes later, we were buttoning

our camouflage pants and lacing up our combat boots. Laura had ripped the sleeves off my white shirt to stuff in the toes of her boots. She stamped her feet a couple of times and smiled at me. "Good fit now. I'm glad one of the men was bigger. The fatigues nearly fit you."

It took us longer to tie up the men. Laura stripped them both to their skin and tied one of each of their legs to the rings in the floor where she'd been shackled. She rose and dusted her hands and looked at me.

"Okay, let's get out of here. Savich and Sherlock have got to be somewhere close by."

We locked the door and turned to the left, for no other reason than I am left-handed and that was the way I'd turned first. We each had a full magazine in the AK-47s and another magazine from each man's belt.

I was armed and dangerous, feeling more pissed than prudent. Laura had tucked her hair up beneath the army camouflage cap. From a distance of ten feet, I guess she could pass for a man for at least a few seconds.

"The stupid goons," she whispered, "dressed up like army militia."

"Don't complain. It might help us if we get out of here." My boots were hurting my feet already. I was going to get blisters.

We heard booted feet tramping toward us. There was a door on our right, the third one along this side of the corridor. I opened it as quietly as I could and we slipped inside. We listened. Then we heard a noise, just the clearing of a throat.

Both of us whipped around to see an old man sitting at a small table in the corner, tucked away in shadows, just beneath a narrow, high window, eating a bowl of soup. He was bald and his face was scored with lines, the color of brown leather. He had a long dirty-gray beard. He was wearing an old dark brown wool robe, a rope tied around his waist.

He was staring at us, a tortilla halfway to his mouth. I whispered in Spanish for him not to move, "*Quédate,* Father. Don't even twitch your beard."

I looked up at Laura. She was standing pressed to the door, still listening, her fingers pressed against her lips for quiet. The boots marched by. No one stopped. The priest didn't move.

"Who are you?" he asked me in Spanish in a deep and ancient voice.

"We're American federal agents. They

drugged us and brought us here as prisoners. They're going to kill us if they get ahold of us again. We're trying to get away. Are you a prisoner too, Father?"

He shook his head. "No, I come to the compound once a week to minister to all the people. When I arrive, one of the women gives me breakfast." His words rolled into one another, nearly slurring. It was hard for me to understand him. But I understood enough.

"What day is it?"

He had to repeat it twice before I understood. Thursday. We'd lost a day.

"Where are we, Father?"

He looked at me like I'd lost my mind. "You're just outside of Dos Brazos."

More boots were marching this way. They were slowing. We were trapped. The one narrow window wouldn't let a skinny kid through it. The old man looked at us, then said slowly, "There's no more time. Both of you, get under the bed, quickly. I will deal with the men."

If he betrayed us, we had less of a chance pinned under the narrow sagging bed in the far corner. We had no choice. Laura and I scooted under it. At least the stringy blanket fell over the bed nearly to the floor. We fit, barely. I was nearly lying on the

AK-47, Laura pressed against my back, her weapon pressed against my spine.

The door opened, no knock. I saw at least three pairs of boots. I heard a man with a shrill voice say in Spanish, "Father, have you been here long?"

"*Sí.* I am still eating my breakfast."

"You haven't heard anything, no people, no running?"

"Just you, *señor*, and your men. *¿Qué haces?* What is the matter? Is there a fire?"

"Oh no, nothing like that. Some people — a man and a woman — we were holding them for the *policía.* They've gotten away. Don't worry, Father. We'll find them."

The priest didn't say anything. Was he giving them a sign? No. The men turned and marched back out the door. Then, suddenly, one of them said, "Father Orlando, the woman Hestia told me that her son is in great pain. She wants you to see him now. Can you come? My men will escort you to keep you safe from the foreign man and woman."

"I will come," said the priest. He was wearing old Birkenstock sandals, no socks. His feet were as worn and scarred as a tree trunk.

The door finally closed. We slowly moved out from under the bed.

"That was close," Laura said, wiping herself down. I stared toward the small table. There were three soft tortillas just lying there. I was still hungry. I grabbed them up, rolled them, gave Laura a big bite, and stuffed the rest in my mouth.

"I'm starting to feel human again."

22

We were in some sort of old wooden barracks that turned and twisted about like a rabbit warren. The first two rooms we looked into were empty, but in the third one there was a man sleeping in a lower bunk, his back to us. He didn't stir. We quietly closed the door and kept looking. Savich and Sherlock had to be in one of these rooms.

We eased out into the corridor again. We came to a corner, and I motioned Laura to stay back while I went down on my haunches and took a quick look. I nearly lost my tortillas I was so startled. Not fifteen feet from me were at least ten men of all ages, dressed in fatigues and combat boots, all at stiff attention, their weapons held against their shoulders, their backs to me. They were silent, not a single twitch. I couldn't even hear them breathe.

An older man, in his early fifties, stood in front of them. He wore civilian clothes, a white linen shirt open at the neck, tan slacks, and Italian loafers. He was perfectly bald. It looked like he shaved his head for effect. He was a large man, nearly as tall as me, and solid with muscle. He was carrying a white lab coat over his arm. He was speaking quickly in Spanish. I understood most of it. I slowly eased back as he said, ". . . we must find the man and the woman. They are dangerous American agents here to destroy us. If you see them, you must not kill them. That is forbidden."

I whispered to Laura, "A dozen soldiers ahead. The man who called the others off us, was he really big, muscular, and bald?"

"No, it was another man."

"This one seems to be the boss. He's giving them orders about us. He doesn't want us killed. I suppose that's good news. Oh yeah, he's a sharp dresser."

"Let's get out of here." We came quickly to the other end of the long corridor, to a big double door. I tried the shiny brass doorknob.

It turned easily and silently. I went in low and swung around, fanning the room with my weapon. It was a very fancy office at first sight, with lots of gold-trimmed antique furnishings and several incredible Persian carpets. It wasn't much of an office. There wasn't a telephone or a fax or a computer, nothing to use to get help.

We eased inside and closed the door. I turned the lock. "*El jefe's* office," I said. "The boss of this place. Probably it's the bald guy out there with the soldiers. I wonder who the hell he is. Damn, I don't even see a phone. They must communicate by radio."

Laura was already behind the huge Louis XIV desk, going through the papers. Behind her was a large glass window looking out over a small walled-in, English-type garden filled with tropical flowers and plants. "Damn, it's all in Spanish and I can't read it," she said. "Quick, come here, Mac."

Someone tried to turn the handle on the door.

I heard shouts. More pounding. A gun butt smashed against one of the doors, then another. The expensive wood splintered.

No time. I prayed and grabbed Laura's left hand. We took a running start, crossed our arms in front of our faces, and crashed through the huge glass window behind the Louis XIV desk.

We thankfully landed on grass, rolled, and came up instantly into a run. We were in a private flower garden, perfectly manicured and maintained, and I, who loved flowers, didn't give a shit.

Ain't nothing easy, I thought, as I smashed the butt of my weapon against a small gate in the far corner of the garden. The aging wood splintered and fell outward. We were out of the compound, only to stop cold. There was absolutely nothing in front of us except jungle and a three- or four-foot-wide moat of sorts, probably to keep the jungle from encroaching into the compound every few days. It was filled with brackish water that looked like it could kill anything that even got close to it.

I took her hand again, and we jumped the moat. We heard shouting behind us. Guns were fired over our heads. Good, they hadn't forgotten *el jefe* had told them to keep us alive.

We ran into a dense green wall of vegetation that blocked out the sun within a couple of minutes. It was going to be a race, us against a dozen men native to this place.

I'd never been in a jungle before. The floor wasn't a thicket of plants and trees and bushes as I'd expected. We didn't need a machete like the movies I'd seen had portrayed. It was nearly bare, only a single layer of leaves covering the ground. But even that single layer was rotten. Everything around us was alive and green or rotting.

It got darker as we ran, the green over our heads forming an opaque canopy. Only the thinnest slivers of sunlight managed to get through. No wonder everything rotted so quickly — there was no sunlight to dry anything out. People would rot too, I thought, and there were a lot of creatures to help them. This was not a good place to be.

We ran another twenty feet into the jungle and came to a dead stop. We couldn't go farther without a machete after all. It was impossible to pull away the branches and vines that were in front of us, an impenetrable wall of green. I'd never imagined anything like this. We stopped and listened. For a few moments, we didn't hear anything, then I heard a man shout. It was in very fast Spanish and I couldn't make it out. I heard men crashing through the dense foliage, not paying any attention to where they stepped, just coming toward us.

"It's time to try to hide," I said. We went

exactly ten big steps to the right, careful not to leave any signs of our tracks to this spot, and hunkered down behind a tree. I looked up and saw a frog staring me right in the eye. At least this little guy wouldn't try to eat us. He looked like he belonged on that old Bud commercial.

We were ill equipped, just our clothes and guns. There was no way we could survive for any time at all in this alien place. I didn't want to think about it. I had no intention of staying here any longer than necessary.

The men were close now, not more than twenty feet away from us. Two of them were arguing about which direction to take. Ants were crawling over my feet. Laura swatted the back of her hand. A coral snake, its beautiful bright bands announcing that it could kill you fast, slithered by not six feet from Laura's foot. I wrapped my arm around her shoulders.

I realized I was so hot my blood seemed to swell in my veins. Sweat pooled under my arms and at the small of my back. I hated the heat. Why couldn't drug runners deal out of Canada? A lovely little insect the size of a fifty-cent piece dropped from a branch above my head onto my forearm. It took a good-sized bite out of me, then lightly dropped to the ground where it scurried off to hide beneath a leaf.

Finally, the men fanned out, several coming our way. It made sense. I would have done the same thing. I listened carefully to every boot crunch.

Only two men were coming our way. I raised two fingers to Laura and she nodded, readying herself.

I pointed to the guns and shook my head. She nodded again. A minute later they were not a foot from us, sweeping their guns around, swearing at all the bugs, all the dripping leaves overhead, all in Spanish. If they found us, I knew we had to be fast and quiet as the dead. One of the men yelped. Maybe the insect that had just bitten off half my forearm had gotten him.

Then one of the men looked down and we stared at each other. Without a sound, I reared up and smashed the butt of the AK-47 under his jaw. It cracked real loud, but he only let out a whiff of a yell before he fell.

Laura moved fast. She butted the other man in his gut, then raised her weapon and slammed it down against his temple.

We stood over the two men, trying to control our breathing.

We heard men calling to one another.

They apparently hadn't heard these two go down, thank God. Of course they'd be missed soon enough. We quickly stripped the man Laura hit, because he was very small. Laura pulled on his pants and his boots and threw the pants and boots she'd been wearing into a bush that, I swear, quivered when the boots struck it. We relieved both of them of their weapons.

It took three minutes, no longer. We began to make our way due west, going by small glimpses of sun. Every dozen or so steps, we wiped away the marks of our passage. Our progress was slow. Both of us were dripping wet, so thirsty our tongues felt swollen. We heard the chattering of monkeys high above our heads in the interlocking tree branches, and the constant calls and shrieks of animals we'd never heard in our lives. We heard a low, warning growl. A puma, Laura whispered. They knew we were there and were announcing it loudly to their cousins.

Birds checked in — squawking louder and more ferociously than Nolan ever had even at his crankiest.

"Just listen to them," Laura said. "They're all around us and loud as can be. Oh, Mac — what do you think the ice acid does to animals? Like Grubster and Nolan?"

I stopped cold and stared at her. "I hadn't thought about them. Doesn't it make sense that they'd sleep just like we did? That they'd wake up, just like we did? That they'd be all right?"

I thought she was going to burst into tears.

"That was a stupid question," I said without hesitation. "I'll wager my AK-47 that they're just fine." The panic calmed in her eyes. "Maggie's probably feeding them. Don't worry, Laura."

We kept walking, looking carefully down and around before we took each step. To walk a mile would take three hours, I figured, cursing at the boots rubbing my heels.

Then, suddenly, with no warning, it started to rain. We just looked at each other, tilted our heads back, and opened our mouths. The water tasted wonderful. Suddenly, something with a dozen skittering legs landed on my cheek. I shook it off, cupped my hands together, and drank.

The rain was so heavy, even coming through the dense canopy of green overhead, that in just a minute or two we weren't thirsty anymore. We were also sodden and nearly steaming, it was so hot. It felt miserable. God, I couldn't wait to be on a ski slope, puffs of cold air streaming out of my mouth.

I raised my hand and rubbed my fingers over a dirty smudge on Laura's cheek. "You know, Laura, when I flew from Washington just a week ago, I never imagined ending up in a rain forest with the woman I love, someone I had to come three thousand miles to meet."

"This isn't anything I'd anticipated either," she said, and kissed my fingers. "We'd better get to work on finding Savich and Sherlock."

I laid my weapons on the ground and buttoned her shirt up to her neck, then raised the collar. It touched her chin. "Let's keep as much covered as we can," I added, and buttoned my own shirt up to my chin. Our sleeves were fastened at our wrists. At least our fatigues were tucked inside our boots and the boots were sturdy. It was good protection from all the creatures that slithered close to us.

We started walking northeast, roughly parallel to what looked like clear-cut land just outside the rain forest, not more than a hundred yards distant. We wanted to stay hidden until we were well beyond the compound. After another hour, we turned south again. It didn't take more than twenty minutes to reach the edge of the rain forest. The thick foliage suddenly thinned. The sun was bright overhead, the air immediately drier. The difference in the landscape couldn't have been more dramatic. The lush, dense forest simply gave way to an indistinct barren patch.

I figured we were at least a hundred yards northeast of the compound.

23

There were mountains in the distance, their tops shrouded with clouds.

There was no sign of people, of any habitation at all. We'd stepped out of a green world filled with more creatures than anywhere else on the planet into desert terrain. The sun dried our clothes in less than fifteen minutes. It also made us thirstier than hell.

"We need water," Laura said. "Then some shelter." She pointed toward a copse of trees not too far away. The copse was on a small hill. From there we might see some sign of life, perhaps even the compound.

"Listen," Laura said. She pointed up. Above, a small plane was coming closer.

It was then I saw the empty airstrip a few hundred yards from where we stood. A four-seat Cessna was coming in.

We ran back into the rain forest until we heard the plane land, then slowly eased out on our bellies. We could barely make out three people getting off the plane, walking to a jeep, and getting in. Men or women, we couldn't be sure. The jeep drove off, due east from the airstrip.

To my disappointment, the Cessna was in the air and gone beyond the mountains in a matter of minutes.

"I wish," Laura said, "that the plane had hung around. We could have persuaded the pilot to get us out of here."

"All we need is Savich," I said. "He's got a license. He can fly anything."

Laura and I walked slowly out of the rain forest again. The dry air felt wonderful on my face. I saw Laura raise her face to the baking sun high overhead.

"It's around midafternoon," I said. "At least four and a half hours until it gets dark."

"We can scout around, try to see the best way to get back into the compound."

"I'm hungry," I said, and rubbed my fist against my belly. My hand stopped. I saw her eyes follow my hand, then widen with alarm. Coming from nowhere, just suddenly upon me, I felt a bolt of incredible lust. I was almost instantly as hard as the rocks I was standing on. Jesus, I was losing it. Laura was staring at me.

"Mac, what's wrong?"

I grabbed her, flattened my hand over her mouth, and said in a raw voice, "Laura, there's time for us to make love. Let's do it right here, right now. I've got to —"

"Mac, stop it!"

I heard her voice, but what she said made no difference. There was only one thing I wanted, only one thing I was going to do. I was trying to pull her shirt off and unzip my pants at the same time. I didn't even think about touching her, no, I just had to get inside her, right that instant. She twisted away from me.

I grabbed a moment of reason and choked out, "It's hit me again, Laura. I don't know if I can control it. I'll hurt you. Get the hell out of here, now. Run!"

"Mac, you can control it, you did it before!"

"Please, Laura." I was on her again, knocking her backward. She hit a tree but didn't fall. Instead of running, she stepped forward and kicked me in the balls. My breath whooshed out. The pain blanked anything in my brain. And I stood there, bent over like an old man, knowing the pain was going to get worse, much worse. And it did. I moaned, clutched myself, and folded over. I waited for the god-awful agony to lessen. I simply tried to breathe and not fall on the ground and weep like a baby. Laura was standing not three feet in front of me, not saying a word.

"Good shot," I said when I could get the words out.

Neither of us moved. I just stood there, still hunkered over, trying to get hold of myself.

"It's not so bad now, thank God," I said, slowly straightening. "Jesus, I can't believe a drug can do that to me. You feel like an animal in pain, and just have to get out of it. You might have had to kill me to stop me if you weren't so smart. You knocked every thought, every urge, out of my brain."

"I didn't know what else to do. You sure you're all right, Mac?"

"You don't have to kick me again, at least for the moment. I'm back together again. It was just there for a moment that I wanted sex more than I wanted life. Hell, I thought having sex at that very moment *was* life. How can there be people who would pay for this drug?"

She lightly touched her fingertips to my

mouth. "Just let me know if I have to kick you again."

"I don't think so," I said slowly. We sat down and leaned against a scrubby tree I couldn't identify. It gave about as much shade as a single leaf on one of the trees I couldn't identify in the rain forest.

"They didn't kill us, Mac. They brought us down here and they haven't done anything but play with us, ugly games, but no torture. Drug dealers don't do that. Drug dealers eliminate anyone they perceive as a threat to their operation. When they fired on us at Seagull Cottage, they weren't trying to kill us. They just wanted us under wraps, inside the cottage, so they could use the ice acid and bring us to wherever we are."

"Maybe they took us because they wanted guinea pigs for the drug."

"They can pull people off the street to experiment on. They wouldn't take four federal agents to do that." She took my hand. "I know this is tough, Mac. But someone gave them orders not to kill us. The only person I can think of who cares whether or not you live or die is Jilly. If you weren't involved, I think we'd be dead."

"No," I said. "It had to be Paul. He gave the order because he knew how much Jilly would be hurt if I was killed."

She swatted an insect off her knee. "I'm sorry, Mac. But you've got to think objectively about this. Four federal agents are in Edgerton, Oregon. Things are getting too hot. It's Jilly, Paul, Molinas, and Tarcher whose butts are on the line. They've got to buy some time so they can shut things down and clear out before the cops come to get them. There's another guy I told you a little about: Del Cabrizo, the head of the Maille cartel. We believe he's the kingpin behind the development of this drug. John Molinas is just one of his flunkies. He probably used Molinas just to get to Tarcher and to Jilly and Paul. As to Alyssum Tarcher's exact role, I'd say he cut himself in by getting Paul and Jilly out to Edgerton.

"But I do know that Jilly is the only one who has the power to keep us alive. She's the only one with the leverage. We're kept alive or the problems getting the drug ready for the streets won't get solved.

"She left the hospital to get away from you, Mac. She knew you wouldn't stop pushing. She had no choice but to leave and hide out, and hope you just went home."

"My sister, no matter whatever else she

possibly could have done, wouldn't drug me and set me over you like a dog in heat. She hates you because you betrayed her, not me."

"Jilly doesn't have a clue what they'd do to us. She's in Oregon, not here. But I'll tell you, Mac, she knows what kind of people they are. She had to have guessed they wouldn't treat us as valued guests."

She knew I didn't want to hear this. Bless her, she didn't say anything more about Jilly's role in all this mess. She knew I'd think about it.

"Who is that bald man in the compound?" I asked.

"I've been thinking about that. From your description, I'd say it has to be John Molinas. In the photo I saw of him he had a lot of thick black hair."

"I guess he thinks the shaved head is more intimidating."

Laura said, "If it is Molinas, I think he's here to make sure no one kills us. Maybe Jilly demanded insurance, insisted he be here to run the show. She wanted to make sure that Del Cabrizo wouldn't just have our throats cut. Maybe it was her way to protect you."

I rested my head on my crossed arms. I felt a huge wave of fatigue wash over me.

No sex in this, no prodding lust, just sudden, utter exhaustion. "Laura," I said, trying to raise my head. "Laura, what the hell am I feeling now?"

I heard her voice, thin, far away, calling my name. I tried to look up but I didn't have the strength to lift my head. I clearly saw the terrorists in Tunisia, heard their voices, wondered if I would ever escape this mess alive, then there was the car, driving toward us, only there was no driver, and then it was a ball of flame and I was gone. Unholy fear ate into me. It seemed stronger, more corrosive now than when it had actually happened.

It was the effect of the damned drug again, I thought, but it didn't make any difference. The sun grew hotter, the air even drier. The heat was inside me, filling me. There was desolation everywhere and I was part of it. I had flown to the sun and fallen in.

"Mac!"

Laura's voice was high, terrified.

I tried to look at her, but her face blurred, then faded into a strange sort of gray whiteness that seemed endless and cold, but it wasn't any of those things, and on some level I knew it. I just didn't know what it was, and I didn't care.

I was floating now, and it was very strange to be staring down at a large man, and I knew the man was me, only he was just lying there, his eyes closed, his chest heaving with the effort to breathe. Then I knew he was me because suddenly I couldn't breathe. I was dying.

Then there wasn't any more pain, just a gray-white void that didn't go anywhere. I was cold. That made sense, I was naked. I wanted covers but couldn't seem to move my arms.

I felt fingers on my forearm, soft fingers, loving fingers, fingers so gentle I wanted to see who they belonged to. It became more than that. I had to know who was touching me like that. I forced my eyes open, forced myself to look through the gray-white, to find the person whose fingers were so gentle, so tender.

I saw Jilly standing over me, looking both frightened and angry. Why would she be frightened? Or angry? It made no sense at all. I had to know. I concentrated with everything in me and whispered, "Jilly? You're all right. Thank God. I've been so worried about you. Why are we here, Jilly? Where are we?"

She just smiled down at me and lightly touched her fingertips to my cheek. "It'll be all right, Ford. Listen to me now. You're coming out of it, very soon now. No, keep your eyes open, Ford, listen to me. You mustn't drink or eat anything. Do you understand me? *Don't even drink out of the tap. Nothing.*"

"Laura, Jilly? Where is she?"

"It will be all right, Ford. Laura's here. Get strong, Ford. Just lie still and get strong."

And then her fingers left my arm. When I looked up, she was gone. The gray-white void thickened around me until I disappeared into it, just eased into it and let it swallow me. I wondered why I wasn't cold any longer.

I opened my eyes and realized that no one was standing over me. I felt clear-headed, but so hungry I could have eaten just about anything. I shook my head. What had happened? "Laura?"

I saw her lying on her side on a folded blanket on the floor beside the bed I was lying on. She was naked, just like I was. I was down on the floor next to her in an instant, panicked. "Laura?" I lightly pressed my fingers against the pulse in her throat. It was strong and steady.

I knelt over her, wondering what the hell to do, then wondering where we were.

357

Something was very wrong here but I just didn't get it yet. I lightly stroked my hand over her shoulder and turned her onto her back.

"Laura," I said again, and leaned down to kiss her mouth. Her lips were dry. She was so pale. "Laura," I said, and watched her eyes slowly open.

I saw the scream in her eyes and quickly pressed my palm against her mouth. "No, be quiet. I don't know what's going on here yet. Are you all right?"

She looked confused, her brows drawn together. Her long hair was in tangles around her head. "Mac," she said at last, and her voice sounded beautiful to me.

"It's all right, sweetheart. We're both alive. I just don't know where or why. Somebody stripped both of us naked."

She didn't move, didn't try to cover herself. I saw her draw in a deep breath and knew she was searching for control, for something to latch onto, something that made sense.

"I saw a man, standing behind you. He was just there, suddenly. I never heard him coming. And he sprayed something at me. Before I went out, I saw him strike you on the back of your head. I don't remember anything else. I want to get up now, Mac."

I gave her my hand. She was looking at me and I realized that I was hard again. I was embarrassed and frightened as hell. Pain was one thing, but not knowing what was real and what wasn't, that was beyond anything I'd ever experienced in my life. God, I hated it.

I turned away from her, grabbed a blanket off the bed, and wrapped it around my waist. There was only a dingy sheet for Laura. I pulled it off the small bed and handed it to her. She wrapped it around herself, tucking in the ends over her breasts.

She sat beside me on the bed. "I'm dying of thirst," she said, not looking at me but down at her bare feet.

I said without thinking, "We're not going to drink anything at all. Not even tap water."

"Why?"

I turned to face her. I lifted her hand and held it between mine. She leaned forward until her cheek was touching my shoulder.

"Listen, Laura. Jilly came to see me. She's here. She seemed upset. She told me not to eat or drink anything."

"Jilly, here? But when could you have seen her, Mac?"

"I don't know but it makes as much sense as you and me being here, wherever here is."

"It means she is involved," Laura said finally. "You see that now, don't you, Mac? If she was really here, with you, then she's in on all of this, somehow."

"Yes, I know," I said.

"They've got us again, haven't they? What are we going to do?"

But how did they have us again? They just walked up to us and turned off the lights? What was going on here? Was it all somehow planned with a drug whose effects diminished, then came roaring back?

I stood and began pacing the twelve-by-twelve room. "We've got to find Sherlock and Savich," I said over my shoulder. "We know they're real."

It was odd but even though I was walking around and speaking to Laura, I knew that somewhere inside my brain something still wasn't right. I remembered reliving that horrible few moments in Tunisia, how it had somehow been magnified.

I looked over at the tap in the small sink.

Neither of us was going to touch another drop of water, at least not in this place.

24

What about the food? Jilly hadn't said anything about food, had she? Yes, she had, I remembered. I looked down at the plate of steaming rice, tortillas with small pools of melted butter, and the small bowl of beef in some sort of red sauce. I held out my hand and stopped Laura from using her fork.

"We just can't take the chance. They could put drugs in the food as easily as in the water." I smelled those tortillas and wanted to curse, which I did under my breath.

Two men had stood in the doorway, their weapons pointed right at us, as a young girl, not more than twelve years old, looking so scared I thought she was going to pass out, brought us the meal.

"There's something else," I said, and got to my feet. I gently put the two trays of food on the floor. "Let's look around again for cameras or listening devices. There weren't any last time, but who knows?"

We didn't find anything. Even so, I kept my voice down. "We need to get ready for any opportunity, just like the first time."

"Can we be so lucky again? There were two guys this time with AK-47s." She looked over at the toilet. "The porcelain lid is gone."

"I never said they were stupid. We'll have to find something else. We do have an advantage here."

"I'd bet the farm that they put drugs in the food and water. Someone will come sooner or later to see how we're reacting. It won't occur to them that we wouldn't eat or drink anything. They'll be expecting us to be out cold or having sex on the floor or whatever the hell else this drug does to you."

Her shoulders were slumped. I'd never seen her look so defeated. "Laura, listen to me. Our brains will straighten up again. No more drugs. We're pros. If anyone can get out of this place, we can. Now, come here and hold me. I'm feeling a bit off balance right now. I need you."

She came to me, clutching the sheet over her breasts. She didn't say anything, just held me against her. I felt her kiss my bare shoulder.

Suddenly I was so pissed I could have easily killed the first person through that door. I kissed Laura and set her away from me. I got up and tore off a leg of the bed. My blanket fell off but I didn't pay any attention. I hefted that leg. It made a solid club. I handed it to Laura. "Hit me if I try to take you down again. Please, I'd much prefer that to being kicked."

She took the club and hefted it. Then she smiled at me. "Give me a bad guy instead."

It was such an excellent weapon that I took off another leg for myself and swung it around a bit, liking the solid weight of it in my hand. I smiled at Laura, standing not six feet away. She still had that old threadbare sheet wrapped around her, her hair was in tangles, and she looked ready for anything. The woman was tough. I realized then that she wasn't looking at my face. I picked up my blanket and wrapped it around me again.

"You're the best, Laura," I said. "I can't imagine having a better partner. Now we wait again."

We waited.

We dozed. Since there were no windows,

we had no clue if it was night or day. There was a lamp in the room and it gave off a sluggish sixty-watt light.

The sound of at least three pairs of boots thudding on the wooden floor snapped me alert. I couldn't wait to get a shot at the bastards.

I raised a finger to Laura. She nodded. I could see she was ready. I wondered if she was as angry as I was, and imagined that she was.

The door handle turned. There wasn't a sound. Both Laura and I were staring at that turning knob.

A woman wearing a white lab coat stepped in. She had a small silver tray in her right hand. I moaned loudly and clutched my throat.

She came down to her knees beside me, and I moaned again. But I was looking behind her at the same two men who'd accompanied the breakfast or lunch or whatever meal it had been. When the first man came through the door, his gun was down because he was staring down at me and the woman. I grabbed her under the arms and threw her at him. She yelled as she hit him squarely in his AK-47.

He screamed out the other man's name: "Carlos!"

Carlos was through the door in an instant, the weapon raised to mow me down. Laura rose up behind him, and the club came down in a hard, graceful arc against the side of his head. His eyes bulged. Blood poured out of his mouth, then he fell against the door. The other man had gotten his AK-47 free of the woman and was swinging it up. I wasn't in a good position. I managed to roll to my left side and kick up as I moved. My foot struck the weapon but didn't knock it from his hands. He fired two rounds, a loud, obscene sound. One bullet smashed into the floor beside my head, spewing splinters of wood into my arm and chest. The other bullet struck the woman. I heard her cry out as I gained the leverage I needed. I kicked him solidly beneath his chin at the same time Laura clubbed him in his kidneys.

His eyes rolled back in his head and he went down like a stone. I slowly rose. "These guys were serious." I knelt beside the woman. The bullet had struck her forearm. She'd be all right. I told her in Spanish to be still. As for the two men, all I wanted from them were their clothes.

Laura went right to the smaller man and stripped him. We both tucked the legs of our fatigues into the boots at about the same time. I saw Laura lean down next to the woman. "What is it?"

"Look," she said, raising a pistol, a Bren Ten, a 10mm automatic that held eleven rounds.

"The woman had it on her tray along with some needles and bottles. I haven't seen one of these guys for a long time. It's a good combat weapon."

I grabbed the two small vials on the tray.

"Good idea," she said, smiling at me. "You ready?"

I turned left and stopped cold.

"What's wrong, Mac?"

"Just an attack of déjà vu," I said, and slithered out the door. We left the men completely naked and tied up as best we could with strips of the bed sheet Laura had been wearing. Laura had tied the woman up with her underwear.

"Let's go to Molinas's office," I said. "If there's someone there, we can force them to take us to Sherlock and Savich."

We passed a window. It was dark outside, and that was good. How much time had passed?

The office was empty. They'd boarded up the glass windows behind the desk. "Maybe they've hidden a phone," I said, and began opening drawers.

Suddenly I felt dizzy and unfocused. I just stood there, waiting to see what would happen. Was this death coming? A numbing cold overwhelmed me. I felt it chewing at the edges of my brain. My heart pounded. Laura was staring at me, her hand out. I knew she was talking but I couldn't make out her words. To die like this, I thought, as I went to my knees.

I wasn't dying. It was the drug again. I fell back against the wall. I saw Laura over me even as I sat there, my head to one side.

She was shaking me as hard as she could. "Mac, listen to me. I know you can hear me, you're looking at me. Blink at me. Yes, that's right. Whatever's going on in your head, you've got to control it. We've got to get out of here."

I looked over at the glass windows. They weren't boarded up. The glass was solid, whole. And I wondered: Did we really crash through it the first time?

"Mac, blink at me again."

I evidently did because she started speaking again. Her voice was low. She was close to me. I could feel her breath on my face.

"I want you to raise your hand now, Mac."

I looked down at my hand lying limp on the floor. I looked and looked at it and then I thought, Just raise your damned hand. My hand came right up. I cupped Laura's face with it. "Whatever it is, it's going away. It's a weird feeling. Laura, we didn't use anything when we made love at Seagull Cottage. If I made you pregnant, I don't want you to worry about it, okay? We're going to get married. It'll all be okay."

She grinned at me, leaned down, and kissed my mouth. It was a sweet kiss and I felt it throughout my body, and the feeling was healthy and real. "I'm better," I said.

"Good. I want you to stand up now, Mac. Do you think you can do it?"

I felt the journey of coming back into myself, of retaking control. I doubted in that moment if I would ever again even willingly take an aspirin. There is nothing more terrifying than losing control of your mind.

I got up. I stood staring at the boarded-up windows. "My memory went haywire. I felt numb and everything was different. This damned drug is a killer."

"Let's find Molinas, Mac."

I picked up my AK-47. I felt strong again. In control. But for how long this time?

25

I was frankly surprised when we went through a corridor on the far side of the office and found ourselves in an antique-filled bedroom. The man we believed to be Molinas was sitting on the side of a bed, leaning over a woman. Not a woman, she was young, perhaps eighteen. She had a white sheet pulled to her chin. Thick, shiny dark hair fanned around her face on a white pillow.

Molinas hadn't heard us. All his attention was focused on the girl. He was wearing black pants, a loose white shirt, and his bald head gleamed beneath the mellow bulb just above the bed.

He was speaking quietly, but I couldn't make out his words. I watched him stroke her hair, lean down to kiss her. He continued speaking in a low, warm voice even as he straightened again. I couldn't tell if he was speaking Spanish or English. I saw the girl's hand come up and lightly touch his shoulder.

I nodded to Laura and pointed to the Bren Ten she held lightly in her right hand. She frowned a moment, then reluctantly handed it to me. How could she know what I intended?

"Take the girl, Laura," I whispered.

She nodded again. I left my AK-47 on the floor just outside the door. We went as silently as we could into the still air of the room. It smelled sweet in the bedroom, a vague rose smell. I didn't like it. It was cloying.

He was completely focused on the girl, leaning over her, speaking. My boots creaked. I froze, but he didn't move. What were they talking about?

I gently pressed the Bren Ten against his left ear. "Hello," I said. *"¿Cómo le va?"*

The girl was sitting up now, pressed against the bed's headboard, her eyes wide, silent as death. She was terrified.

I felt him coil then relax again. He said, "If you kill me you'll never get out of here alive."

"It won't matter to you, Molinas," Laura said very calmly.

"How do you know who I am?"

"Who else would they send down here?" Laura asked. "You were assigned to keep us. As for all the fun you had with us, that was your own idea, wasn't it?"

"Some of the men are animals. I protected you."

I looked over at the girl, who still clutched the sheet to her throat, her narrow hands clenched. I said in Spanish, "Don't be afraid. We're not going to hurt you."

Slowly she nodded and said in perfect English, "Who are you?"

"My name's Mac. What's yours?"

"Marran."

Molinas moved and I gave him all my attention. "Keep an eye on her, Laura."

I came down beside him and raised the pistol. "You're going to take us to where you're holding the other two agents."

"They're dead," he said.

"Then so are you." I pressed the pistol against the side of his mouth and cocked it.

"No, don't," he choked out. "They're not dead, I swear it. I'll take you to them."

"Did you drug them like you did me?"

"Yes, but not in the same way. They're all right."

"You'd better hope that we agree. Now, I want you to get up real slow."

"We should probably bring the girl along," Laura said.

Molinas lunged for me as he rose, but I brought the pistol down on the side of his head. The girl groaned. Laura clapped her hand over the girl's mouth, pressing her head back against her pillow.

Molinas went down but not out. He landed on his knees, moaning, holding his head. I knew the pain must be bad, the bastard.

"If you try that again, I'll kill you." I said it in a near whisper. I didn't want the girl to make any more noise. I thought about hauling her with us and decided it wouldn't improve our odds. We'd leave her here. I opened my mouth to tell Laura when I saw that she'd already begun ripping up the sheet. I waited for her, keeping the tip of the Bren Ten against the back of Molinas's head. The girl was silent now. I saw tears running down her cheeks.

"Who is she?" I asked Molinas, who was still holding his head in his hands.

He tightened like a spigot in January. "Touch her, you bastard, and I'll rip your head off your shoulders." I believed him.

It took Laura a few minutes to tie the

girl firmly. I noticed she had skinny arms. They were pale with sharp blue veins running beneath her flesh. Her beautiful shiny hair streamed across her face. Laura smoothed it back after she'd fastened the gag in her mouth.

I hoped Molinas could walk. I started to help him to his feet. He snarled at me and made it himself. A proud man, I thought. I looked back at the girl, who was staring at him, her eyes large and frightened.

"Turn out the light, Laura."

The room went dark.

We heard a whimper from the bed.

I could feel him resist when he heard the girl's distress. "We didn't do anything to her," I said. "She'll be all right, if you don't do anything stupid. Now walk."

The moment we had him back in his office, Laura motioned for me to stop. I kept three feet between me and Molinas. She walked to the door, opened it quietly, and leaned out. She turned back to me and nodded.

"Now," I said quietly, "you're going to take us to the other agents."

He said nothing, merely walked from the office and turned left down the corridor. "You're dead if one of your soldiers tries to take us out."

He stiffened but didn't say a thing.

"If you're dead, what will happen to the girl? She's already tied down. A regular offering, I'd say."

He nodded, and I heard him curse, low and fluently. Even with a Spanish last name, those curses were pure American.

"Who is that girl?"

He just kept walking.

"You might as well tell me."

Finally, not turning to face me, he answered, "She is my daughter."

26

"Where are your men, Molinas?" I said near his left ear. "Some operation you run here. Hard to believe you haven't been run out of town."

"The men are not professionals," Molinas said, and I could tell that disgusted him. "They have courage but no discipline."

"I buy that," I said. "Now, tell us where we are."

"No, you can't kill me. If you do, you won't ever get your friends out of here. I can't tell you anything. If I did, I would be dead and so would my daughter. Very few people know about this place. If you find out on your own, I cannot be blamed. Your friends are just around that corner. There are three guards around the door."

Suddenly, Laura put her finger against

her lips. We heard a man talking in a low voice. She walked quietly to the corner and looked around it. She came back. "There are three guards up ahead, just like he said. They're sitting on the floor outside a door. Their heads are down, but I'm not certain they're asleep."

"The other agents are behind that door?" I asked.

"I wasn't lying."

He was pale now, but he didn't say anything more.

"Del Cabrizo's behind the whole operation, isn't he?" Laura asked Molinas.

"I can't tell you anything. You can kill me if you must but I know that you won't harm my daughter."

"We'll do whatever we need to," I said. "I want you to walk ahead to the men and tell them that you intend to speak to the prisoners. You will tell them to go outside until you come to tell them to return. If you screw this up, Molinas, I will personally shoot you. I won't harm your daughter, but I will shoot you. Trust me on this."

He looked me straight in the face. He had dark blue eyes, and there was something familiar about them. The shape, perhaps, slightly tilted at the corners. They were his sister's eyes, Elaine Tarcher's. He said in a low voice, "My daughter is innocent. She has suffered enough. If I release your friends, will you leave here?"

"You can hardly expect things to go on as they have."

"No, once you escape, my job here is over. Then I will deal with what will happen."

I shrugged. "Your daughter, who is so precious to you — why is she here with you? Have you let her watch you pump drugs into people?"

"No. We have only been here for a short time. We arrived just before you did. I couldn't leave Marran back home. She needs me. You cannot take me with you as a hostage. You cannot leave her here alone. She would be savaged by these men. She would kill herself. She's tried before. I will do as you ask, Mr. MacDougal."

He was pleading with me, his expression as raw as his voice. His daughter was more important to him than his pride, certainly more important to him than his own life. "Let me see what kind of shape my friends are in. Then I'll decide what to do with you. You try to screw me, Molinas, and you're dead. Just think of your daughter before you decide to betray me. By the way, I speak Spanish."

Molinas nodded and straightened. As he walked forward, he looked like a man used to command, a man in charge. Laura and I watched him kick one man in the knee. The man cried out. The other two awoke. The man Molinas had kicked scrambled to his feet, excuses tumbling out of his mouth. I understood only that they were excuses. Molinas raised his foot and kicked another man in the ribs. The third managed to jump away.

He used his hands while he spoke to the men, and his voice was low and angry. If he'd had my gun I wouldn't have been surprised if he'd shot all three of them. He motioned for them to pick up their weapons. He stood there watching them scurry away. He had told them to go outside and stay there. Then, after just a slight pause, he turned and walked back to Laura and me. He held up a key ring, pulled out a long brass key and handed it to me.

"This is the one."

I gave the key to Laura. "Be careful. There might be a man inside."

She nodded. I remained behind with Molinas, the Bren Ten pressed against his neck. "Nice clothes," I said close to his ear while we waited. "I guess dealing drugs to kids lets you hobnob with a lot of Italian designers."

"I haven't been involved in drugs for five years," he said. "I am doing this for other reasons."

"Yeah, right. And you keep American federal agents just for the fun of it." I focused on the slowly opening door. Laura eased inside, crouched low. I saw a light come on, then nothing. "Let's go. One try at me and I'll pull the trigger."

Savich was half-crouched, ready to attack. He looked pale and drawn, his clothes torn and dirty, and there was such rage in his eyes that suddenly I didn't want to know what had been done to him. "I was hoping you'd come," he said, as he slowly straightened.

I came into the small room, pushing Molinas in front of me. Savich's hands closed around his throat and he shook him like he was a rag. Molinas did nothing to defend himself.

"Savich, stop it." I tried to jerk Molinas away from him, but Savich was out of control.

Laura cried out, "Sherlock. Oh, God!"

Sherlock was the only thing that could have distracted him and Laura knew it. Savich dropped his hands and whirled about, dropping to his knees beside Sherlock. She was unconscious, huddled on her side.

He gathered her against him and rocked her back and forth, back and forth, kissing her dirty hair. Savich looked up. His face was battered. He'd been beaten. I nearly pulled the trigger. "By God, what have you done to him? You damned bastard. I should have let him strangle you."

"He is all right," Molinas said, and I knew his throat hurt. Savich was strong, very strong, no matter what they'd done to him.

I shoved Molinas to the floor and closed the door, then walked to where Savich sat, still rocking Sherlock on his legs.

"Thanks for coming, guys. I'm glad to see you, to say the least. I did try, but I couldn't get us out of here. I failed. I took out a couple of them but then four others came in and I got the crap kicked out of me for my efforts."

He was coherent. He was himself.

"They didn't drug you?" I asked.

"Not after I woke up when we first got here, wherever here is. They took Sherlock. I guess they wanted me to be clearheaded enough to see what the drug did to her."

"What happened to her?"

"When she's awake, she just keeps reliving that awful time in the past when she was hunting down that serial killer, Marlin Jones." I was nodding. I knew all about Marlin Jones. Savich explained for Laura. "She was his prisoner. It was terrifying for her. She had nightmares about it for months. With the drug, it's come back, only worse. Jesus, you can feel her terror, her confusion." He looked over at Molinas. "I'm going to kill that sadistic bastard."

But he didn't move, just kept rocking Sherlock.

He said even as he rubbed his cheek against Sherlock's hair, "After they beat me, they left me alone. They never did shoot any drugs into me."

I looked down at Sherlock, and then I struck Molinas, I just couldn't stop myself. I must have gotten him just right because his head fell back against the wall. I drew a deep breath. "I'm sorry, guys. He'll be back with us in a minute. He's going to get us out of here. There's an airstrip out there."

"Thank God," Savich said. He was still clutching Sherlock tightly against his chest. "They drugged you again, Mac?"

I said, as I watched Molinas open his eyes, "I'll tell you about it later." I hunkered down into Molinas's face. "You're going to get on your radio. You're going to get a plane in here. Now."

Savich said, "I want to take him back with us. I want to strap him down and give him the lethal injection myself."

Molinas smiled. "Sorry, Agent Savich. That won't be possible. The plane carries only four passengers. I gather one of you is a pilot?"

"No problem," Savich said. He rose, Sherlock in his arms. "I can kill you myself if I can't take you back. I don't want to think how much dirty money you've got for lawyers. Yes, this is better. I don't want to let the law dick around with you."

"Your wife will be all right," Molinas said. "It will be a bit longer before she comes around, but she will be all right. There are two separate drugs that can be mixed together in varying amounts. We were having trouble with the balance and the dose. Everyone reacts differently. Some people are particularly sensitive. Your wife is one of them."

Very slowly, Savich turned and laid Sherlock on the tattered black blanket spread on the wooden floor. He rose, then faced Molinas and smiled. It was a terrifying smile.

I didn't move. This was up to Savich. I looked over at Sherlock. Laura was kneeling beside her now, stroking one of her hands.

"Get up," Savich said.

Molinas slowly rose.

There was no graceful display of martial arts, just the raw power of Savich's fist into Molinas's belly, then his knee into his groin. Molinas went down like a stone.

"Good," Laura said. "He deserved it, but now we've got to get him into good enough shape to get to a radio and order up a plane."

"I want Jilly," I said.

Savich stared at me. "What did you say, Mac? Jilly? She's here?"

"She came to me when I was just coming out of a session with their drugs. She warned me not to eat or drink anything. Whatever she's doing here, Savich, she kept Laura and me away from another round of drugs."

Laura didn't argue with me, just said, "If she's here then we'll need a bigger plane."

"Jilly's small and so is Sherlock," I said. "We can fit the five of us in a Cessna."

"Mac," Savich said, lightly touching his bruised fingers to my forearm. "Is your brother-in-law, Paul, here too?"

"I don't know," I said. "If he's here I say leave the bastard. He's the one who developed the drug with all its charms. I just want Jilly." I looked over at Laura. She was staring at the floor, and I saw her eyes narrow in fury.

I followed her line of vision. Savich was shackled to a ring in the floor. It was Molinas's bad luck that I'd pushed him far enough into the room for Savich to reach him.

No wonder Savich hadn't escaped. As simple as that.

"Savich, I don't believe this."

"They enjoyed the fact that I could strain and curse, but not reach them. They laughed about it. They knew exactly how far the chain would let me reach. Thanks for bringing that big bastard close enough so I could get him."

"Savich," Laura said quietly, as I tried all the keys on the ring Molinas had given me. "He's Alyssum Tarcher's brother-in-law, John Molinas."

"I remember."

Finally, Laura found the key that fit the shackle on Savich's right ankle. When it fell open, he knelt down and rubbed his ankle. He pulled down his sock. There was dark bruising but no broken skin. "I have

Sherlock to thank for these thick wool socks. It's good to get that thing off me." He sounded like himself, which was a big relief.

We had no choice but to wait for Molinas to come to his senses. There was a bucket of water on a rickety table in the corner. Laura threw it on him.

Savich pulled Sherlock up against him. "Sherlock. Come on, love, wake up. You can do it. Wake up." I watched Savich lightly slap her cheeks. "Come on, sweetheart, open your eyes. Hey, I'll let you throw me the next time we're in the gym, but you've got to wake up for me now."

Finally, she did open her eyes and look up at him. She looked drugged, strung out, and when she whispered, "Dillon?" her voice was slurred.

"She recognizes you," Laura said. "That's a good start."

"It's me, Sherlock. It's all right now. Mac and Laura are here. We're leaving."

"He's here, Dillon," she whispered, rubbing her fingers against her temple. "He's tucked right behind my left ear. He's laughing. He won't leave me alone, and he's still laughing. He won't stop. Please, Dillon, please make him stop." She closed her eyes again and slumped back against Savich's arm.

"Is she talking about Marlin Jones?" I asked, kicking Molinas lightly in the ribs. He was still trying to catch a breath.

"Yes," Savich said, never looking away from Sherlock's chalky face. "The drug they've been giving her brought him back, planted him in her mind and magnified him, made him into even more of a monster than he really was, and that's saying something. He's there in her head, as real as you are."

"It did the same thing to me," I said slowly, "but it just happened once. I relived the car bomb in Tunisia. You're right. It was worse remembering it than when it actually happened. Paul said the drug was supposed to lessen the power of a bad memory."

Molinas struggled to sit up. "Yes, the drug is supposed to relieve the physical symptoms. They promised me it would. But there's something wrong. The drug shouldn't bring the memory to the forefront.

"It's like you said, the drug is supposed to dissipate the physical symptoms, and with repeated doses finally remove the horror of the memory. But it doesn't work.

I tried different doses and even different additives to see if I couldn't fix the drug. But it doesn't work."

I went down on my haunches in front of Molinas. "What happened to your daughter?"

"She was raped three years ago right on campus at her private school. She was only fifteen years old. Four older boys raped her. It destroyed her. They promised me the drug would help her, that's the only reason I got involved with Alyssum and Del Cabrizo in the first place, to help my daughter.

"That's why I gave her the drug. I injected her myself. But it hasn't worked. Her memories of that night have grown worse, not better. The drug is killing her!"

"So you gave Sherlock an even larger dose and mixed in other drugs?" I asked.

Molinas stared into Savich's eyes and saw his own death there. He quickly leaned over and vomited on the wooden floor.

Savich carried Sherlock in his arms. She was conscious now, but her eyes were heavy and vague. He'd wrapped her in all the blankets that were in that cell. She was disturbingly silent, quiescent. That really worried me. My mouthy Sherlock, who usually ordered everyone around, including her husband, was lying like a ghost, not really there. Laura walked behind them, carrying two AK-47s. I marched Molinas in front of me, the Bren Ten pressed against the small of his back, another AK-47 slung over my left shoulder.

"Take me to Jilly," I said to Molinas. "Now. I want to see my sister. She's coming out with us."

"Your sister isn't here," Molinas said. I could tell it hurt him to speak.

I smiled at him. "I don't believe you. She came to me. She spoke to me, she warned me."

He said slowly, "It must have been the drug. Your sister was never here. Never. I have no reason to lie to you about that. It was the drug. It's unpredictable. But I have never heard of it doing that before."

Was that possible? Jilly had been standing over me, clear as day. She'd been with me, speaking to me, dammit.

"She's never been here," Molinas repeated.

"But you know her?" Laura said.

"I know who she is," Molinas said carefully. We stopped and kept silent. There were men speaking not fifteen feet away. About three minutes later their boot steps faded down the long wooden corridor.

We went back to his big opulent office and the huge adjoining bedchamber only to find it empty. His daughter, Marran, must have gotten herself untied because she'd locked herself in the bathroom. Molinas told her to stay there until he came back. We heard her crying.

"Look what I found."

We turned to see that Laura had opened a closet door that I hadn't seen before. "Guns, clothes, and look at this — two more AK-47s."

She turned around, grinning really big. She was holding up a machete. "You never know if we might need it. They all carry knives. Just maybe we should have one too." She looked over at Savich. "You guys need to get out of those clothes. I'll help change Sherlock."

She clipped the machete to her own belt. "There," she said, patting it. "I guess I'm ready now for just about anything."

"I know you've got to have a radio somewhere. Get it." Molinas opened the third drawer of the huge desk and pulled out a small black radio.

"Get the plane here, now."

We all watched him set a frequency and listened to his rapid Spanish, some of which I couldn't make out. He looked up when he finished. "I didn't betray you," he said.

Savich walked to where Sherlock was sitting on the floor, Laura holding her hand. He bent down and picked her up. "Let's get out of here."

"You'd better pray that the Cessna comes," I said against Molina's ear.

"It will come," he said. I saw him glance back at the radio.

He didn't look happy.

27

We reached the airstrip at about five-thirty in the morning, according to the watch I'd taken from Molinas. The half-moon was fading quickly, but still hanging on, and behind it a few scattered stars dotted the gray sky. The mountains in the distance looked like ghosts, stretched up into broad sword shapes, others hunched over, all of them unearthly in the vague dawn light. There would soon be enough light to use the airstrip. Three days ago, I thought, we were in Edgerton, Oregon, buying sandwiches from Grace's Deli.

The silence was profound, just the crunch of our boots on the rocky ground. The rain forest began not a hundred yards to our left, stretching up the flank of the distant eastern mountains. The compound was directly behind us. If anyone was following us, they were staying out of sight. I thought of snipers and moved closer to Molinas. I hoped we covered the others' backs well enough so if there were snipers, they'd be afraid to shoot for fear of hitting Molinas.

When we reached the edge of the airstrip, the sky was a soft gray, with strips of pink streaking to the east. There was no cover. We crouched down against the stark landscape, still too well silhouetted for anyone with a gun.

Savich turned, a black eyebrow raised. "The rain forest begins right over there? Yet it's hot and barren here. How can that be?"

"It's called deforestation," Molinas said. "The people are very poor."

"Mac and I were already in there," Laura said. "It's incredibly beautiful but the humidity strangles you, and there are so many creatures you can hear but can't see, it's also terrifying. I'm grateful we don't have to go back in."

Sherlock laughed, shaky, but it was a real laugh. "I think I just need to kill Marlin again. I can hear his laughter, his shouting. I'm just going to kill him. I'll see if he can come back from the dead a second time."

"Yes, kill him," Savich said, looking

directly into her eyes. "Kill him again, Sherlock. You're the only one who can do it. You did it before, you can do it again. Kill him and kick him a couple of times, then come back to me and stay. I need you here."

"I need you too, Dillon," she said and closed her eyes. The look on Savich's face was terrifying. I gripped his shoulder.

It was in that moment that I knew Jilly had been taking the drug when she went over the cliff. I'd been there with her and the drug had driven her mad, just like Sherlock. When she'd discovered Laura was a DEA agent, that she'd been betrayed, she'd been haunted by Laura in her mind. She hadn't been able to bear it. And that's why she'd driven her Porsche off the cliff.

I looked over at Laura. She was still staring toward the eastern mountains, not moving, just staring. I wanted to tell her that everything would be all right, but there was something about the way she was focused on those mountains, her silence, that kept me quiet. Laura had it together. She was fine. I smiled at her, knowing in my gut that this woman I'd known for less than a week would decide that living with me was better than living without me.

We tried to limit our risks. We sat closely pressed together, Molinas facing back toward the compound. I didn't think any of his men could have gotten beyond us, but I couldn't be sure.

A small plane was coming in, the buzz of its engine sounding rough. I saw Savich frowning at that sound, looking toward the mountains. In a couple of minutes, a sleek little Cessna 310 appeared over the top of the closest peak, banked sharply, and started in to land, the sunrise a halo around it.

I didn't like the sound it was making — the engines sputtering, missing, as if barely hanging on.

Had Molinas screwed us?

I was turning to him when suddenly two helicopters burst over the mountains.

"My God," Savich said, shading his eyes, "they're McDonnell Douglas — Apaches, AH-64 Apaches. They're ours. They've got an M230 Chain Gun, Hellfire missiles, and a stinger. Down! Everybody, DOWN!"

We all hit the ground. In a blink one of the Apaches fired on the Cessna. The small plane sputtered above the ground. I saw two men inside, one of them screaming. I watched the plane explode, showering debris into the dawn sky.

Twisting shards of metal, parts of the engine, the seats, one of them holding what had been a man still strapped in, scattered over the airstrip and the land around it. A part of a wing crashed into the ground not twenty feet from us.

"Jesus," Savich said. "Good old USA Apaches. What the hell are they doing here?"

"Somehow they must have found out where we were." Laura was yelling at the Apaches, waving her arms. I held Molinas close.

I looked up at the helicopters. They came closer and hovered, making no move to land.

Oh, God. "Laura," I shouted, "get away from there! Run!"

Without warning, they fired on us.

"The rain forest!" I grabbed Molinas and shoved him ahead of me. They came around again, firing, the hail of bullets kicking up dirt all around us. We made the rain forest, barely. Then I realized the last thing we needed was Molinas holding us back. He'd betrayed us.

I jerked him around and yelled in his face, "You damned bastard!"

"I didn't betray you." He was panting now. "You saw them. They shot down the

Cessna. One of my men must have radioed Del Cabrizo and told him you were escaping. The cartel ordered it. I didn't."

"That makes me feel a whole lot better," I said. "Well, you can stay and talk to him about it." I shoved him down behind a tree, took off his belt, and tied his hands behind him to the skinny tree. I ripped off his very nice Italian silk shirt and stuffed it into his mouth, tying the rest behind his head.

"You'd better pray they don't think you're disposable. That's about the only thing that would save both of you."

I turned away from him and shouted, "Savich, we're heading north. Keep going, but veer to your left, to the west." Thank God it was light enough now to see where we were going. Northwest, we had to go northwest. Molina's soldiers would be searching for him and then come after us.

Savich nodded, holding Sherlock close. I looked at Laura, wondering why she hadn't come to help me. She was standing about ten feet from me, not moving. I watched her weave where she stood, then drop one of the AK-47s.

"Laura?"

I heard the Apaches overhead, incredibly loud, heard their automatic weapons firing into the forest. Chances were that only an incredibly lucky shot would find us through that thick, nearly impenetrable canopy overhead. But given how our luck had gone so far, I didn't want to take any chances.

"Laura?" I yelled again. "Come on! We've got to hurry. I'll take the other weapon. What the hell's wrong?" She didn't answer. I saw her lean back against a tree, gripping her shoulder.

"Laura?"

"Just a minute, Mac." Her eyes were closed, her teeth gritted.

Oh, God, she'd been hit. The guns kept sounding overhead, the bullets smashing down through the foliage. We were too close to the edge of the rain forest. We had to go deeper. Without a word, I pulled her hand away from her shoulder. "It went through," she said, and I saw she was right after I'd opened her shirt. "Hold still."

I unbuttoned my fatigue shirt and jerked it off. At least it wasn't as sweaty as my undershirt. I wrapped it as best I could over the wound, tying it under her breasts. It was still bleeding. She was trembling. Her blood streaked over my hands. "Can you hang on for a while?"

She gave me a smile that made me want

to cry and said, "I'm DEA. Of course I can hang on."

I smiled at her as I rebuttoned her shirt, picked up both AK-47s, and hoisted her over my shoulder.

"Mac, no, I can walk."

"It's time for the DEA agent to keep her mouth shut," I said, and to Savich, who'd turned back, "Laura's been shot. It's clean, through the upper shoulder. But we've got to take care of it, we've —"

An Apache was coming in fast and hovered right over us. It sounded muffled through all the greenery overhead, but it was close, too close. If it fired downward, it could hit us.

I laid Laura on the floor of the forest, cupped her cheek with my palm, and said, "Don't move, I'll be right back. I'm going to get you a first-aid kit and then I'm going to play doctor."

She looked at me like the drug had captured my brain again. I just smiled at her, grabbed one of the AK-47s, and ran for a small, light-filled clearing just inside the forest belt. I looked up. An Apache was hovering not twenty yards overhead, its rotor blades fanning the thick upper canopy of the rain forest. I heard birds screeching, heard their wings flapping madly to escape. It was just that the growth was so thick off to my left that I couldn't see them. I could make out a man staring downward with binoculars.

"Hey, you bastards!" I fired upward. When I cleared the magazine, I pulled it out and shoved another in, and waited. I needed them closer, and lower. The Apache weaved, plunging side to side. Yes, I thought, you've seen me. Now, come and get me. I could hear a man yelling. They were right over me now. I fired off another twelve rounds, directly into the gut of the helicopter.

I could see the pilot fighting the controls, trying to regain control. I heard the other man yell. Then, like it was released from a slingshot, the Apache rose straight up and then dipped sharply to the left. I fired another half-dozen rounds. It trembled, the rotor grinding, those amazing General Electric turboshafts sputtering, dying now from all the damage my bullets had caused. The Apache lurched and went straight up again, its nose aimed at the sky. It stopped, trembled some more, turned nose toward the ground, and came down fast. I heard the two men screaming.

The helicopter plunged into the rain forest, slashing through leaves and trees. I heard a loud ripping sound — its rotor being torn off. Then silence. I heard the other helicopter, but it wasn't close. Wouldn't it come over us like this one had? Because they saw it go down?

I waited a moment, then ran as fast as I could to where the helicopter lay, nose buried some two feet into the ground, its rotor broken off halfway down, gleaming sharp blade edges embedded in the foliage. Monkeys shrieked overhead. I saw several of them leaping from tree to tree some six feet above my head. I knew the helicopter could explode, but I had to get my hands on a first-aid kit. I couldn't face the thought of Laura wounded in this living hellhole without any medical supplies.

The gunner and the pilot were both dead. They were wearing fatigues, like the rest of Molinas's men. They were in an American helicopter but they surely weren't Americans. They were probably Del Cabrizo's men, sent to take us out, just as Molinas had said.

To my relief, I found the first-aid kit shoved beneath the pilot's seat. On the back of the pilot's chair, to my amazement, were half a dozen containers of bottled water in a net fastened to a strap. There were several blankets strewn over the backseat. I grabbed them up, smelling the fresh, thick scent of sex. Now I knew what these guys had been doing before they'd taken off.

I unfastened the net that held the water from the strap, threw the blankets over my shoulder, and shouting like a madman, I ran back.

We were still too close to the edge of the rain forest. I didn't hear anyone coming, didn't hear the other Apache. But it was stupid to take any chances.

"My God," Savich said. "You've got your first-aid kit, and water. I'm going to make sure you get a promotion and a raise, Mac."

"Can you hold out a bit longer?" I said, coming down to my knees beside Laura.

"Yes, but then I want to relax by the pool with a good book."

"You got it. Let's see what we've got in here. There should be some pain pills to help take the edge off." I found them and gave her three, and all the water she wanted from one of the bottles. Savich had gotten the bleeding stopped, thank God. It was as good as we could do for the moment. I rose quickly. "Let's go north-west about fifty more yards, then I'll back-track and erase our tracks. The good

Lord is looking out for us, guys. Just look at all this bottled water. And it isn't even drugged."

Another fifteen feet ahead and we couldn't get through the twisted and intertwined vines and trees. It was a wall of green. The first time we'd been helpless, but this time we had the machete Laura had taken.

I unfastened it from her belt, kissed her cheek. "You're brilliant," I said. "I can't promise anything, but it seems to me that just maybe you've got the makings of an FBI agent."

"You really think so?" She managed a smile. Laura had to walk since I was carrying the water and the first-aid kit and one AK-47 and hacking our way through the dense green foliage. So much of it. I held her up, my arm around her waist. "You're doing great, kiddo. Just hang in there. Another fifteen steps and we'll rest. That's good Laura, just ten more steps." I took another whack at the twisted vines in front of us. "The sucker's nice and sharp, thank God."

"I'd rather have a margarita, Mac."

"Me too, but I'd rather know for sure where we are. I should have wrung that out of Molinas."

"He got us out of there. We're in Colombia, Mac. We have to be."

I heard Sherlock moan, heard Savich's low voice, but I couldn't make out his words.

He hefted Sherlock over his shoulder and took the machete from me. I was grateful. We kept going, at least another fifty steps. It was Savich who pulled up. He was panting hard. He gently eased Sherlock to the ground and balanced the big machete and an AK-47 against a tree trunk beside her.

"Mac, enough. I'm beat for the moment. Spread out those blankets and let's lay our patients on them. Shush, Sherlock, it's okay."

Sherlock opened her eyes and looked over at me, at the AK-47s I was laying next to Savich's. The only thing was, Sherlock wasn't behind those eyes. I looked away, I just couldn't stand it. I wished I'd killed Molinas.

I leaned Laura against a tree, unwrapped the blankets from around her, and spread them out. I eased her down onto her back. Her eyes were nearly black with pain.

I leaned down and kissed her dry mouth. "Now, you just lie here, make Savich give you some water." I unfolded the other two blankets that I'd been carrying over my shoulder and spread them out over her. I said to Savich, "We've been using the machete, but maybe there's something I can do to lessen their chances of tracking us." Before I left I gave Laura another pain pill.

When I returned some five minutes later, I heard Laura whisper, "I'm sorry, really sorry. I should have dodged better. Maybe I'll be demoted to the FBI."

"You'd have to do something a lot worse than dodge the wrong way to be consigned with the likes of us," Savich said. "Rest now, Laura."

"And hold still," I said. I flipped up the metal clip on the first-aid kit. "I'm going to play doctor now." I looked through the medical supplies. Alcohol, an oral antibiotic, aspirin, gauze, bandages, tape, needles, matches, thread, the pain pills — thank God the helicopter hadn't exploded. I had a feeling this was the luckiest find I'd ever make in my life. After Laura.

Laura focused her eyes on my face. "We could be in Thailand right now. Any place there's a jungle."

"Not with a town called Dos Brazos," I said. "Hold still and swallow these pills.

It's an antibiotic and just one more pain pill." I waited a couple of minutes for the meds to start taking hold, then stripped her shoulder down and examined the wound. It was just a small hole in the front, sluggishly oozing blood. "Hold still," I said again. I wet one of the bandages with alcohol and pressed it against the wound.

Laura didn't make a sound. Her eyes were tightly closed. She was biting her lower lip. "It's all right. I'm not in shock, at least not now. You don't have to look at me like that. I was shot two years ago. I know what shock feels like. Really, it isn't bad this time."

"Where were you shot?" I asked her.

"In my right thigh."

I could only shake my head. "You're doing really good. Don't move." I lifted her up and looked at the exit wound. It was raw and big and covered with shredded, bloody flesh and material from her fatigue shirt.

I said, "I can't put stitches in to close the wound, Laura. There's just no way to get the wound sterile. The chances are the wound would get infected and that would be worse. So I'll just clean it and lay a bandage over it. We'll change the bandage every day. Okay?"

"Yes. I hate needles."

I laid a cloth soaked with alcohol over the wound in her back and gently cleaned the area as best I could. There was an antibiotic ointment, and I smoothed it on. Savich unwrapped a sterilized square of gauze and handed it to me. I gently removed the alcohol pad and pressed the gauze over the wound and pressed strips of adhesive bandage over it.

I repeated the procedure on the small entry wound. I washed the blood off her breast. The dried blood was dark red, nearly black now against her white flesh. I hated it.

I wrapped her shoulder, tying the thick bandage beneath her breasts. I'd done all I could think of. I'd done the best I could.

"Hey, Sherlock, you still there, sweetheart?"

"I'm here, Dillon."

"Do you think we're doing things okay here? Concentrate, Sherlock. Talk to me."

"I'm here," she said in a thin, nearly transparent voice. "I'm concentrating really hard."

After a few minutes, I asked Laura if it still hurt.

"Just a bit," she said, and I believed her. She sounded vague and pleasantly surprised. "Isn't it wonderful how that stuff works? No, it isn't too bad."

28

I had to keep her warm. I got her back into her shirt and covered her with blankets. "You just hunker down and take it easy now." Since she'd taken a bullet in the leg, she knew what that sort of pain felt like. I had no doubt she could deal with it. The thing was to keep her alive in this damned rain forest with more possible ways to die than the LA freeways.

Savich had turned back to his wife. "What do you say, Sherlock? Were we efficient enough for you?"

"I don't know, Dillon. I'm sorry, but I can't seem to concentrate, I —" She was gone from us.

"She'll dream of that lunatic now," Savich said. "Jesus, Mac, it isn't fair."

"She was with us longer this time," I said.

Laura said, "Maybe this time she'll kill Marlin Jones. That would be best for her."

"I hadn't really believed that such a thing was possible, but maybe, just maybe," Savich said thoughtfully. He leaned close to his wife's face. "Did you hear that, Sherlock? Kill the bastard if he dares to come again. Just shoot him right between the eyes. Try really hard to do that, okay?"

He stopped talking and looked up. We listened to the distant sound of an Apache. Not hovering or firing down, just cruising, it seemed to me. Since there was no way they could ever see us through the thick canopy of green, there was no reason to fire.

I told them what I thought had happened to make Jilly drive off that cliff. "There's no doubt in my mind that Jilly was on that drug. I think the night she went over the cliff she was trying to get away from Laura. Laura was in her head, just like Marlin Jones is in Sherlock's head, just like when I relived being in Tunisia. But there's a big difference here. Sherlock will come out of this, like I did. Maybe Jilly took too much of the drug, maybe she was really hooked, because she was still obsessed with Laura when she woke up in the hospital.

"Did she run out of the hospital herself because she didn't want to see me again? I don't know. Maybe. When we find her, we'll get the answer."

"The truth is," Savich said, "we don't have a clue about what the long-term effects of the drug are."

"I'm afraid that even Paul doesn't know that," I said. I saw a beetle, black and orange and green, pause a moment, wiggle its antennae at me, then hurry behind some small orange leaves. I saw several other leaves move. Critters everywhere, I thought, all of them hungry. Everything was alive in this place, everything was hungry, everything was hunted by something else, that or dead and instantly rotting or eaten.

I turned to Laura and lightly stroked my fingers over her mouth. "Since you've been cooperative, I'll give you some more water."

She drank down a good bit. I looked at the half-dozen bottles. Should we conserve? I wondered how long we'd have to survive in this place. Laura was shivering. I started to take off my shirt, but she stopped me. "Not here, Mac. You've got to keep as much of you covered as possible.

There are lots of nasty things around here to bite you. And there are leeches too."

Leeches. Good lord. She was right. I doubled one sex-scented blanket and tucked it around her chest and neck.

"We've got to be very careful," she said. She paused, then frowned. I knew she was trying to get her thoughts together.

"It's okay, Laura. Take your time. We're not going anywhere."

"I was just thinking about my boss, Richard Atherton, wondering if the DEA is all over Edgerton." She stopped then. I knew she was in pain. I couldn't stand it. I gave her another pain pill.

After a few minutes, she opened her eyes, smiled at me, but her face was flushed. From fever or the heat or the tremendous weight of the humidity, I didn't know. "Breathe deeply, Laura," I said. "Think about that margarita I'm going to make for you. Think of me rubbing oil on your back, massaging your shoulders until all the knots are out. Now won't that feel good?" I lightly stroked my fingers over her cheek.

I smoothed the hair back from her face. After a few minutes she looked woozy. I didn't want to kill her with too many pain pills. I looked down at my watch. Nearly eight o'clock in the morning. No more pills until noon. I said, "Just be quiet for a while, Laura. You can tell us all this stuff later, after you feel better. Are you warm enough?"

She thought about it but didn't say anything.

Sherlock was far off in a stupor, no doubt troubled by visions of Marlin Jones.

"How long has it been since they drugged her the last time, Savich?"

He thought a moment. "Actually, she was back with me only about thirty minutes before you and Laura arrived with Molinas."

"So it's only been about six hours."

Savich was staring up into the canopy of trees over our heads. I heard monkeys shrieking, a bird's wings flapping wildly, and other sounds I'd never heard before.

"What is it?" I asked him.

"I hear something," Savich mouthed to me. "Someone's coming this way. We knew they'd come after us. I wonder if they found Molinas."

I squeezed Laura's hand to keep her quiet and listened. Yes, someone was coming, several someones. They were searching blind, not too far away now. Savich had lifted one of the AK-47s. I eased the Bren Ten out of my waistband. "Don't move," I whispered against Laura's ear. She looked at once alarmed, then almost instantly quite calm again. "I might be down, Mac, but I'm not out. Give me a gun."

"Not on your life. You're a patient. You're not to move. Just think about that shoulder opening. It wouldn't be good, Laura. We've got to survive. Now, just lie still and —"

"I don't want Sherlock or me to die because I'm helpless, Mac. Sherlock's out of it. I'm all she's got. Give me the Bren Ten."

I gave it to her without another word.

"They're close, Mac," said Savich. "Let's go."

I slung the other AK-47 over my shoulder, slid the machete through my belt, checked the other magazine in my waistband, and fell in behind Savich. If something happened to us, Laura had the Bren Ten. No, I wouldn't think about that, but I still took one backward look. Laura's fingers were curled around the pistol. I gave her a thumbs-up.

We were nearly on their heels fifty steps later. They weren't trying to be quiet. They were speaking loudly in Spanish, cursing, from what I could make out.

We waited, crouched down beneath some broad green leaves larger than my chest. The heat was rising. The air was becoming so heavy, so filled with water that moving through it was like carrying weights. It was tough to breathe. Thank God for that water I'd found in the Apache. The men kept complaining, coming within a dozen feet of where we were crouched on the floor of the forest.

"Let's get behind them," Savich said.

They were walking single file only about eight yards ahead of us. Their heavy steps covered any noise we might have made. I saw Savich's profile. He looked carved out of stone. Mean, dangerous stone. There was death in his eyes, and utter concentration.

He took the last man down so quickly I heard only a hoarse gurgle. The men ahead didn't hear a thing. Savich sliced his throat with a small scalpel he'd taken from the first-aid kit. Savich quickly dragged him out of sight. There were two others, who could turn around any minute. We didn't want to be standing there just staring at them. He looked up as he laid the guy on his back.

"Let's get the other two."

We heard the two men talking just ahead of us in rapid Spanish. I paused a moment, listening carefully. I said behind my hand to Savich, "They think Leon stopped to piss."

"We'll take them both together," Savich said.

It happened fast.

Savich took one of them cleanly with the scalpel, just like the first man. I quickly sidestepped them when the other one turned, alarm firing his face. He yelled and lunged at me, bringing up his AK-47. I brought up my hand and smashed it into his throat. His head snapped back. He dropped to his knees, gagging and choking. I finished it with a blow with my rifle butt.

I raised my head to see a big cat staring at me calmly. He was stretched out along a low-lying branch, watching the two of us, unmoved. He looked down at us with, at best, mild interest. Was he waiting to eat the guys who lost?

Savich said, "It's just a jaguar, Mac. He won't risk tangling with you. But he might take your prey. Hey, you okay?"

"Yeah," I said.

"Don't worry about him. Now, let's see what we can salvage here."

"Look," I said. "There's a couple of

Baby Ruth candy bars here. Hot damn, we need those. We should check the other guy too. You know, Savich, these wrappers aren't written in Spanish. Neither is anything in the first-aid kit I got out of the helicopter, which was also American. Everything's American except for Molinas's men. Who the hell are these guys? What do they do around here?"

Savich answered me with a shrug. He was right. At the moment, who these goons were wasn't important.

I felt strangely detached from the three dead men, poor bastards. "We got it done. Let's get back to Laura and Sherlock."

When we came through the trees to Sherlock and Laura, I nearly lost it. A man was standing over the women, his AK-47 pointed down at Laura's chest. Laura's eyes were closed. I didn't see the Bren Ten.

He didn't seem to know what to do. He saw us and said, "You will not move, *señor,* or I will shoot the women. That's right, lay down the weapons and step away."

They were the last words he ever said.

Laura pulled up the Bren Ten in a single motion and shot him through the forehead.

29

"That was well done, Laura," I said.

She laid the Bren Ten back against her stomach. "One minute we were alone, the next, he just appeared. You rattled him. It gave me the chance I needed."

We took his weapon and three candy bars from his pants pocket. Soon Savich was stamping his feet into new boots. "They fit perfectly," he said. "And he has water too."

I said, "That shot could attract anyone else out there. Savich and I should look around. We shouldn't be much longer than ten minutes."

Laura said, "Go. We'll be all right."

Savich and I went together, back toward where they'd come from. We saw a green boa wrapped at least three times around a tree we had just passed. I felt a chill slide over my flesh. "There are too many things alive in this place. Every step you take you've got to look everywhere, up and down and sideways, all the time. I just touched a tree that was covered with spikes. It's all so bloody wild and we're not in control here."

"If Laura hadn't taken that machete," Savich said, "we wouldn't be here at all."

I traced the flight of a scarlet macaw, its brilliant red feathers blending down its back into yellow, then blue. He landed, hovering on the very end of a branch not three feet from us that pumped up and down with the bird's weight. I wondered what Nolan would think of this other-worldly bird.

"A trail or two might be nice," Savich said. "There's no sign of anyone else. Let's get back."

It was so hot now it was hard to breathe. The humidity was crushing. Our shirts were soaked with sweat. The sweat was so deep on my forearm I could see insects drowning before they could bite me.

"It's still morning," Savich said. "I can't wait to see how much hotter it gets by this afternoon. Look at this damned soil — it's clay. I don't want it to rain. Maybe it's not the rainy season, you think?" He laughed, shaking his head at himself.

I said to Savich, "It's not even ten o'clock yet, but we shouldn't stay here. What do you think? Carrying Sherlock and Laura and all the supplies, can we make maybe half a mile before collapsing under a tree?"

"At most," Savich said. "If we have to use the machete to get through, we might not make more than a couple of miles all day."

"Better the women are down than us. I can just see Laura trying to tote my carcass over her shoulder."

Savich laughed, then sobered. "If Laura's wound gets infected, she's in major trouble."

"We've got some more shirts. We'll cover every naked bit of her. The shirts might not smell real sweet, but they're blessed protection against the filth and the bugs."

I looked up at the dense canopy overhead, saw a big reddish monkey staring down at us. "There are so many colors," I said, "everywhere. Look, Savich, mangoes. They're even ripe. We can eat our Baby Ruths, then have mangoes for dessert." I picked about half a dozen of the best. I was surprised that some of the critters hadn't already nabbed them.

★ ★ ★

At one o'clock in the afternoon, we broke into a small clearing, maybe two square meters, that wasn't overflowing with growing green things. The canopy wasn't as thick here and more light came through. That light brought us some breathing space, literally. I stood a moment, Laura in my arms, under a thick shaft of hot, clear sunlight. I laid her on a blanket right beneath that blessed shaft of light. "Soak it up," I told her. "Let it dry you to your toes."

I dragged the thick net that held the water bottles over the last thirty or so yards. Two snakes flashed across the ground so fast I couldn't imagine any predator catching them. I had no idea if they'd kill you with a bite or not.

I spread out the blankets, then scraped away more foliage to create a small perimeter. Laura had been largely silent for the past two hours. I think she'd slept part of the time, so drugged that she couldn't stay awake. I laid my palm across her forehead. She was hot as hell, but maybe that was normal in this hellhole. It had to be near one hundred percent humidity on the floor of the rain forest. At least her skin didn't feel clammy.

Sherlock was finally awake. She was sitting cross-legged in the middle of a blanket, staring over at Laura. "Don't let her die," she said to me, and began shredding the ragged edge of one of the shirts she was wearing. She'd torn off a strip of shirt and tied her thick red hair back from her face. Still, strands were curling haphazardly around her ears. "I couldn't have imagined a place like this. I just saw a frog that flew from one tree to another tree. They were at least ten feet apart. It was long and skinny and just about the ugliest thing I've ever seen. I think it was red, maybe orange, I can't be sure, it flew so fast. This place isn't meant for people, you know?"

"I know," Savich said. "Maybe we should think of our little sojourn here as a bizarre sort of vacation. Maybe Club Med would be interested. Mac and I saw a jaguar. You rarely see them, even here. Drink this, sweetheart. No, don't just give me ladylike sips. Gulp it down. That's right."

When she'd drunk her fill, Savich wiped her mouth. She raised her hand and touched his fingers as they lay against her cheek. "Dillon, my brain feels like it's coming back to me. Is that a lemon I see?"

"Good," he said. "That's good. Yep, Mac and I found some lemon and lime trees. We picked both. If we run out of water or need to wash up, we can use them."

"We can use the lime in Laura's margaritas. I can see you now, Dillon, see exactly who you are. I didn't like being away from you like that."

"I didn't like it either," Savich said.

"You don't have to carry me anymore now."

He leaned over and kissed her hard and quick. "Good. That means you can help carry the water bottles."

She laughed, a real Sherlock laugh, and again, it made me wish I'd killed Molinas for what he'd done to her. And what he'd done to me.

Laura's eyes were closed. I knew she was in pain, but I needed to ration the pain pills. I gave her water, antibiotics, and two aspirin.

"It's time for lunch," I said. "It's all sugar and fat. My two most favorite things in the world. We'll be on such highs, we'll be jumping around up there in the trees with the monkeys."

Savich said, "I saw half a dozen red howler monkeys about seventy-five paces behind us. They were swinging around, high above us, interested but not going crazy at the sight of us. It was like we were neighbors they just didn't like. It made me think they've seen a number of people here in their territory. Maybe we aren't deep in a rain forest in the bowels of Colombia, a hundred miles from civilization. Maybe we're close to a village or a town. Though I don't know who would live in a place where taking a breath feels like sucking on a blast furnace."

I frowned over at him, nodding. "You're right. That jaguar we saw just seemed bored, like we were no big deal. Like he'd keep an eye on us because it was part of his job but he wasn't at all worried."

"That's probably how they look just before they spring," Savich said, laughing at my expression. "Nah, I wouldn't worry about the cats. Who knows? Hey, are you guys ready for some lunch?"

"I want my margarita," Laura said, her voice slurred. "I know you picked some limes. I heard Sherlock talk about it." I opened her two shirts and looked at the bandage. No blood, thank God. What should I do for it now? I'd been through some basic survival training, but that was it. I saw a small pool of dried blood on her right breast that I'd missed when I'd cleaned her with the alcohol. I didn't think, just lightly scratched up the dried blood. Her eyes opened.

"Blood," I said. "I couldn't bear to see it on you, Laura."

"How do I look?"

I wanted to tell her that despite everything I was still a guy, with guy thoughts, and I wanted to look at her breasts and smooth my fingers over them while my eyes were closed, and tell her she was beautiful. I felt an insect bite the base of my index finger. "No new bleeding. The bandage is nice and clean. You're sweating and that's good. A nice dry, hot sweat from the sun. I think the best thing is just to leave everything alone. Tomorrow morning I'll change the bandage and see how the wound looks. Now, since you're such a good patient, you get a reward." I peeled a Baby Ruth candy bar and broke off a small chunk. I waved it under Laura's nose. She didn't say a word, just opened her mouth. She smiled while she chewed. I fed her the entire bar. "You're going to want to start dancing from this sugar high," I said.

"She can dance with Sherlock," Savich said. He was sitting on Sherlock's blanket, licking chocolate from his fingers.

"Sherlock, you okay now?"

"I'm a lot better than you are, Laura. Is the pain bad?"

"I can control it. I'm forced to lie here and watch Mac eat one of my candy bars. It's tough. My mouth is watering. If I had the strength, I'd rip it out of his mouth."

I broke off a little piece and put it in her mouth. She closed her eyes in bliss and chewed.

I counted. We had five more candy bars. We needed to find some fruit besides the mangoes. I thought bananas should be all over the place, but I hadn't seen any. I'd seen a small anteater scraping along on the floor, and I tried to imagine baking him over a fire. I said, "Everyone, keep your eyes open for some edible stuff, probably fruit, that we can pull off a tree, peel, and eat, okay?"

"We might as well start on the mangoes," Savich said, as he began peeling mangoes and handing them out. "Nice and ripe. Eat up."

"I've got matches," Sherlock said, mango juice dripping off her chin. "When we stop this afternoon, we'll build a fire. It'll keep the creepy things away."

"I know all about how to do that," Laura said. "I spent lots of my childhood at campgrounds being ordered around by

425

Dad and older brother. I've seen some hickory and beech trees. Even some oak. That's hard wood, good for burning in a fire."

Sherlock crawled over to Laura. "I've got another strip of shirt. Let me braid your hair, it's kind of all over the place."

I watched Sherlock try to make a French braid of Laura's long, very matted hair. She smoothed out most of the tangles and picked away half a dozen insects. The best I could say about the result was that her hair was away from her face.

"How is it?" Laura asked.

"You're gorgeous. Sherlock's got a real talent with hair, particularly really long hair like yours." I dabbed a piece of wet shirt over Laura's mouth to get rid of the sticky mango juice. I could just imagine how all the flying critters would love that stuff.

She smiled and closed her eyes.

I got to my feet and stretched. I packed everything up, then lifted Laura into my arms. I was used to her weight now. It felt good. I looked all around me, carefully. Nothing lethal in sight, man or beast.

Sherlock, thank God, was walking on her own. She kept up with Savich, right on his heels, carrying the first-aid kit and an

AK-47. "Sleep, Laura," I said. "I won't tell any bad jokes to keep you up."

"That's good, Mac," she said against my shoulder. Her voice was weaker.

We kept moving. Laura seemed lighter than she had just an hour before. It was as if she were fading away, slowly, and there didn't seem to be anything I could do to stop it. Except find help.

Savich kept up a steady stride, chopping away the undergrowth ahead of us. We saw very little but we heard scurrying sounds all around us.

Suddenly we heard screaming and barking sounds, high above us. A family of spider monkeys, about ten of them, were jumping up and down, rattling branches. Savich got hit in the middle of his back with a shriveled piece of brown fruit we couldn't identify. They hurled other vegetation and small branches down at us, but nothing that hurt us. I hurried and got a thick, sharp-edged leaf in my face for my trouble. They weren't afraid of us, just pissed that we were in their territory. Once we had moved sufficiently on, they ignored us.

When the rain came in the middle of the afternoon, hot, thick sheets of rain, I would have given two of my candy bars for a big umbrella. Then we discovered that parts of the canopy overhead were so thick, we were able to stay relatively dry if we stayed in the right spots. I covered Laura as best I could. Steam rose off the ground when the deluge finally stopped. The humidity didn't lessen, it just wasn't liquid anymore. Steam rose from our clothes again.

We all smelled very ripe.

I eased Laura onto her feet, holding her upright against me.

"Can you imagine what a cold shower would feel like, Mac?" she asked.

"Right now," I said, and closed my eyes briefly, "it would be on my top-ten list. Maybe top three. I want you in that cold shower with me, Laura, laughing and fit again."

She didn't say anything and that scared me. We kept going.

Now, to add to the impenetrable undergrowth in front of us, the ground was mud. The nicely packed clay was slippery and wet through to a depth of a good six inches. Mud covered us to our knees. It made walking as hard as sucking one of our limes through a straw. I nearly fell once. It was Sherlock who steadied me.

Sweat poured off us. Savich was grunting with each swing of the machete.

Monkeys and birds shrieked and howled above us. We couldn't see even one of them. The racket was nearly deafening at times.

Just when I wanted to stop, go down on my knees, and never move again, I saw butterflies sporting the most amazing colors — reds, yellows, greens. I just pointed at them. One followed us a good distance, gliding beside my face, wide-winged, the brightest blue imaginable, its wings rimmed with solid black. When the butterflies disappeared, taking their beauty with them, I realized we'd moved at least another twenty feet west. The rain forest was deadly, horrific, and those butterflies were the most beautiful things I'd ever seen.

Sherlock spotted two coral snakes. She came to a stop and just stared two feet to her left into some undergrowth. There was no way a coral snake could go unnoticed. The vivid orange-and-white stripes slithered away from us and into deeper cover.

I checked to see that everyone's boots were tightly laced up, the ends of their pants firmly tucked inside the boots. It was hard to tell with all the mud covering everything. At least we didn't have any mud on our skin. Talk about itching. But no insects could get inside, and no snakes. I noticed bites on the backs of my hands. No hope for it.

Survival, I thought. We just had to survive. We didn't hear any helicopters for the rest of the afternoon, or the noise of any other humans. It was just the four of us, alone in this living oven.

"Hot damn," Savich shouted. "Look what I found. Ripe bananas, to go with our mangoes. Now the Baby Ruths can be our dessert."

We also found some *pipas,* a green coconut you can crack open and drink out of. Since Sherlock had taken one of those huge leaves and fashioned it into a funnel to catch rainwater during the downpour, both the empty water bottles were full again. We picked half a dozen *pipas* just in case.

I was doing the hacking now, Savich carrying Laura. I said over my shoulder, after I'd had to whack a welter of green intertwined leaves three times to get them apart, "I wonder if they found Molinas, the bastard. Maybe they didn't. Maybe a coral snake got him. Or maybe he's still lying there with insects crawling all over him."

"Or maybe," Savich said, "this Del Cabrizo character was so pissed that we escaped, he killed him."

I didn't want to think about what could happen to Molinas's daughter.

We stopped to make camp when we came to another small clearing. When we stepped into the sunlight, we saw a flock of wild turkeys running through the deep grass to the other side. They disappeared into the forest. It was late in the afternoon, time to stop anyway.

Laura was getting weaker. It required too much energy for her to talk. I gave her more antibiotics, more aspirin, and two more pain pills. There were only four left. She didn't have a fever, and the bandages looked clean, but she was getting weaker.

Sherlock swept our small campsite clean with the thick net. The ground here was nearly dry because of the direct, hot sunlight. She managed to get it completely bare. "It's important that we leave room so lots of oxygen can circulate. Once we build a fire, it will stay brighter and hotter." I collected tinder: low, dead hanging branches, rotted pieces of tree that were dry. We managed to find some birch that Laura said was good for fires. Sherlock began digging a moat around our campsite. She said it would keep the critters out.

Savich used the scissors from the first-aid kit to make several fire sticks. He shaved the sticks with shallow cuts to "feather" them. "My granddaddy taught me how to do this," he said. "It'll make the wood catch fire more quickly."

We found birch bark and dried grass. I stood back and watched Sherlock build a teepee of kindling over a pile of tinder. I handed Savich the matches from the first-aid kit and watched him light one of his fire sticks, let it burn brightly, and touch it to the tinder. I couldn't believe it actually worked. It bloomed up bright and hot. It must have been ninety degrees, and there we were, sucking up to it.

"A hot dog might be nice," Sherlock said. "Potato chips, some dill pickles."

"Tortilla chips and hot salsa," Savich said, rubbing his hands together, and grinned. Behind him, a branch shimmied. A brown-spotted gecko poked its head around a tree, looked at us, then pressed itself flat against the bark. I swear it disappeared.

"Maybe some pickle relish on the hot dog," Sherlock said. "Forget the dills." As she spoke, she was looking over at Laura, who lay quietly.

We were trapped in a Hieronymus Bosch painting and we'd managed, for a moment, to superimpose normalcy. As evening settled in, the beetles began to move around. You could hear them scuttling to and fro. So many of them, all hungry. I smiled over at Laura. "We're geniuses. Just look at that fire."

But Laura wasn't looking at either me or the fire. She was staring to her right, just beyond the perimeter of the campsite, just beyond Sherlock's moat. Her face was whiter than boiled rice. I heard her say my name, her voice just above a croak.

I pulled the Bren Ten out of my waistband and slowly turned.

30

There, reared up on its hind feet, its claws extended, claws so ragged and huge that one swipe could have taken off my face, was a golden brown armadillo. Not one of those small guys you see as road kill on the west Texas highways, but a giant armadillo. I'd never even seen one in a zoo. I'd only seen pictures of them. It had a long snout and small eyes that never left us. The hoary flesh seemed to retract farther, showing more of its claws.

"It doesn't eat people," Laura whispered. "It eats worms."

"That's a happy thought," I said as I lowered the Bren Ten. Who knew if men were out there to hear the noise? Savich tossed me a rock. I threw it, kicking up leaves and dirt not six inches from where the armadillo stood. It made a strange hissing noise and disappeared back into the undergrowth.

I heard a collective sigh of relief.

It was time to eat. Savich peeled mangoes with the first-aid scissors. A great find, those scissors. Savich assigned me the task of peeling bananas.

I eyed my slice for just an instant before eating it. I didn't think we could get food poisoning or diarrhea from something we had just peeled. We each ate only two mangoes, followed by one banana, and polished it off with one of the precious Baby Ruths.

"It's only eight o'clock," Sherlock said. "Does anyone know what day it is?"

"If it's Friday," Savich said, "you and I would be putting Sean to bed and curling up downstairs with some of my French roast coffee."

Sherlock grinned at the thought, then she scooted over to Laura. She lightly laid her palm on Laura's cheek, then her forehead. "Mac, when did you give her aspirin?"

"Two hours ago."

"She's getting a fever. We've got to dump water down her throat and keep at it. That's what the doctor told me to do with Sean when he had a high fever."

I believed I'd endured long nights before, but this was the longest. At least three dozen different beetles kept up an endless dissonant concert throughout the night. We heard things slithering all around us. I'd swear I heard at least a dozen winged things fluttering over my head. But the noise of those beetles, there was nothing like it.

Savich kept the fire burning bright. No more giant armadillos came to visit. No snakes slithered in to get warm. Just the four of us and the fever that was burning Laura up inside.

I was sleeping lightly when I felt her trembling beside me. The shakes, I thought, from a breaking fever. I got all the water I could down her throat, then eased her tight against me, and perhaps it worked because she stopped moaning and eased into fitful sleep for several hours.

We had to find civilization.

With our luck, we'd probably go loping into another drug dealer's compound.

The next morning, we drank a bottle of our precious water, ate two more mangoes, three more bananas, and savored the last of our Baby Ruths.

When we were ready to head out, Savich

looked at me and held out his arms. I shook my head and pulled Laura closer to my chest.

"Give her to me. You're driving yourself into the ground, Mac. It hasn't been that long since Tunisia. You do the chopping for a while. I'll carry her until noon, then you can take over again."

It was clear ahead, no need for the machete. It was an unlooked-for blessing.

Laura's fever had fallen close to morning and hadn't come back, as far as any of us could tell. But she was weak. The wound was red and swollen, but there wasn't any pus. I rubbed in the last of the antibiotic cream. Her flesh felt hot beneath my fingers. I didn't know how serious it was, but I knew we had to get out of this damned hellhole. I had very little of anything left. I prayed that a real live doctor would suddenly appear in the path just ahead of us, waving a black bag and speaking English.

When Savich was holding her, I took the edge of one of the shirts she was wearing and wet it. I dabbed it all over her face. Her mouth automatically opened. I gave her as much water as she wanted.

"I figure we pulled a little south before we stopped yesterday," I said, once I'd gotten my bearings. "Let's go due west and hold to it."

"Look, we've got to be somewhere," Sherlock said, swiping an insect off her knee. "It's a small planet, right?"

"You're right," Savich said. "Sherlock, lead the way. Mac, you take the rear. Everyone, eyes sharp. I've got a hankering for a banana, so keep a lookout for some ripe ones."

When it rained late that morning, Sherlock managed to capture a good half bottle of fresh rainwater, again using one of those big leaves as a funnel. She stood holding that half-filled water bottle, hair streaming down her face, covered with bite marks, puffed up proud as a peacock, grinning like a fool.

We were wet, but there was nothing we could do about it. Savich managed to keep Laura's wound dry.

The ground turned to mud again and the undergrowth suddenly thickened. I pulled out the machete and began hacking. My arms felt like they were burning in their sockets. When we found a small area that enjoyed, for some reason unknown to me, a patch of clear sunlight, Savich laid Laura on her back on a blanket and wrapped another blanket around a water bottle to put under her head.

We got a small fire going within ten minutes this time. With that sun overhead, we found dry tinder quickly. With the fire burning brightly, the insects backed off.

Savich began peeling mangoes with the first-aid scissors. "I always liked these things," he said. He gave a slice to Sherlock.

He cut off another thick slice and handed it to me. I waved it over Laura's mouth. She opened up. She was still eating. The food seemed to rouse her. She sat up and said suddenly, "Sherlock, have you felt any sort of withdrawal signs? Like you wanted more of that drug?"

"God, no." She shuddered. "Why do you ask? Oh, I see. If a drug's not addictive, it wouldn't be worth the drug dealer's time to sell it. No repeat customers."

"Right. Mac, how about you?"

"I haven't felt anything either."

"Maybe you guys haven't had enough of it," Laura said. "Maybe it takes more than three doses to get hooked."

"Do you think Jilly was hooked, Mac?"

I hated to say it, but I did. "Yes."

"I wonder who else in Edgerton has tried the stuff and what they're doing now," Sherlock said.

"I'll bet you Charlie Duck tried it. The coroner told me there was something odd in Charlie's blood. He was going to run more tests. Maybe he even tried it on purpose to find out what was going on. He was a retired cop, remember."

"Maybe that's why someone killed him," Laura said.

"That works," Savich said, nodding as he ate a bite of banana.

"Mac," Sherlock said suddenly, "you had that hookup with Jilly when she went off the cliff and you were actually in bed in Bethesda. You just didn't understand it. Well, maybe it happened again. Maybe Jilly was just in your mind, warning you."

"There's really no other explanation," Savich said, folding up the banana peel. "Unless you just dreamed it up because you were drugged out of your mind."

"I was drugged for sure. Whatever it means, I hope it also means that Jilly is alive. Jesus, Laura, this is tough to take," I said, leaning over to feel her forehead. "How do you feel?"

"There's something crawling up my leg — on the outside, at least."

I swiped off the salamander, who flicked its skinny tail, then flitted off into the undergrowth.

Savich was carving another feather stick with the scissors. The damned thing looked like a piece of art.

Laura moaned. She was lying on her back, her eyes closed. Her face was paper white, her lips were nearly blue. I shoveled more aspirin down her throat.

There wasn't much of anything left in the first-aid kit. My eyes met Savich's across her body. He was frowning. He was also holding Sherlock's hand, tight.

We slogged through the mud at least another couple of miles before we stopped for the night.

Laura was about the same the following morning, weak, shaky, and feverish. The wound was redder, more swollen. There was no kidding anybody now. It was bad. We had to get her to a hospital. We were up and walking, Savich carrying Laura, by sunrise.

"Due west," I said again, and began hacking.

We found a stalk of ripe bananas at nine o'clock. Savich tore them off the stalk to the accompaniment of screaming monkeys, whose breakfast we were stealing. I was relieved they didn't dive-bomb us.

It was nearly noon when I smelled something. I stopped dead in my tracks, lifted my head, and smelled. It was salt, so strong I could taste it.

I started to let out a yell when I heard men's voices, loud, not twenty feet away from us.

"Oh, no," Sherlock said, and backed up, dropping everything except her AK-47. "How could they have found us? Dammit, it's not fair."

Savich held Laura, who was either asleep or unconscious. He didn't put her down, just drew back so I could come up alongside Sherlock.

"They don't care that we can hear them," I whispered. "Are there that many of them? Have they fanned out?"

"I can smell the salt now, Mac. We've got to be near the ocean."

The voice moved away. Then, to my shock, I heard women's voices. Then laughter. Lots of laughter, yelling, more laughter. I heard screaming, but not in terror, screaming and shouting in fun, and all of it was in English.

Something was very strange here.

The thick foliage melted away, everything suddenly thinning out. I took the lead, my Bren Ten in my hand, Sherlock in the rear, Savich carrying Laura between us. We moved as quietly as we could. I saw a troop of green parrots flying from one banana tree to the next, a phalanx of green with flashes of red and yellow. The salt smell grew stronger, and the sun slashed down through the trees above us as the thick canopy above disappeared.

I felt a breeze on my face. I broke through a final curtain of green leaves and stepped onto white sand. Savich inched out behind me. I heard Sherlock suck in her breath. We just stood there, staring.

We were standing at the edge of the rain forest, a good fifty feet of pristine white sand stretching between us and the ocean. It was the most beautiful sight I'd ever seen.

Some twenty yards up the beach were at least twenty men and women in swimsuits, playing volleyball.

There were beach towels strewn over the sand, a couple of sand castles, half a dozen umbrellas and beach chairs. To top it off, there was a guy on a seat set up some twenty feet above the ground, an umbrella covering him. He was a lifeguard.

Laura made a soft noise in her throat. She opened her eyes and looked at me. "What's happening?"

"I'd say we lucked out, sweetheart. Just hold on. You and I are going to be in that cold shower before you know it."

The laughter slowly died away. The men and women were looking down the beach at us. Two of the men waved the others back and came walking toward us. I dropped the Bren Ten to my side. Sherlock eased down on the AK-47, trying to look a little less terrifying.

I yelled, "We need some help. We've got a wounded person here."

The women came trotting up behind the men. One of the guys sprinted toward us. Short and fiercely sunburned, he was wearing glasses and a slouchy green hat. "I'm a doctor," he said, panting when he stopped in front of us. "My God, what happened to you guys? Who's hurt?"

"Over here," Savich said. He carefully laid Laura down on a blanket Sherlock quickly spread beneath a palm tree.

She was barely responding. I unbuttoned the two shirts and bared the bandages. As he knelt down beside her, I said, "It's a gunshot wound through the shoulder, happened two days ago. I had a first-aid kit, thank God. I didn't set any stitches for fear of infection. I changed the bandages every day and kept the wound as clean as possible. But it looks like it got infected anyway."

In the next minute, at least a dozen men and women circled around us. Savich rose and smiled at them, looking ferocious, I realized, seeing how dirty he was, with mud dried to his thighs and his growth of beard. He looked like a wild man, filthy and dangerous.

Then Sherlock laughed. She tossed the water bottles in their net to the ground and let out a big whoop. "We've been in the rain forest for over two days. Is this Club Med?"

The men and women just looked at one another. A man in a loose red-and-white-striped bathing suit said, "No, we're on a day trip here from up the coast," he said, eyeing us closely. "You got separated from your guide?"

"We didn't have a guide," Sherlock said. "Where are we?"

"You're in the Corcovado National Park."

"Anywhere near Dos Brazos?" I asked, and slapped a bug off my neck.

"Yeah, it's at the southeast end of the rain forest."

Laura opened her eyes and looked up at the man who was carefully lifting up the bandage on her shoulder. "It's all right. You just hang in there. It's not bad. But you need a hospital. What's your name?"

"I'm Laura. What's yours?"

"I'm Tom. I'm here on my honeymoon. It's a great place. Well, maybe it wasn't such a great place for you. What happened?"

"I'm a federal agent. All of us are. I got shot by some drug dealers. We've been in the rain forest for the past two days."

Tom the doctor sat back on his heels and turned to a woman who had to be close to six feet tall. "Glenis, go tell the lifeguard that we need a helicopter here fast. It's a medical emergency."

"And the police," I said.

Tom said to all of us, "The Sirena Ranger Station is just up the way a bit. It shouldn't take too long. The wound's infected, but it doesn't look too bad, considering. You guys did really well taking care of her."

"Thanks," I said.

"I want a margarita," Laura said. "With lots of lime. We'll even provide the lime."

I looked around at everyone in that circle. "I've heard of Corcovado," I said slowly. "Isn't it in Costa Rica?"

One of the women who was wearing a bright red thong bikini nodded. "Where did you think you were?"

"Maybe Colombia," I said. "Hey, I've always wanted to visit Costa Rica."

"No wonder the animals were bored with us," Sherlock said.

One of the men said, "Didn't you see anyone?"

"Just the bad guys," Sherlock said. "And some footprints that led off into the undergrowth. We couldn't take a chance of getting more lost than we already were. We've just been making our way west."

"You didn't see the tram overhead?" Tom asked. At our blank looks, he said, "Hey, we all took a ride through the rain forest on it yesterday. It was awesome. Well, I guess you must have missed it." He stuck out his hand to me. "Welcome to Playa Blanca."

31

I was staring at the man when I heard Laura wheezing and choking. I was at her side in an instant, grabbing her arms, lifting her against me. She was trembling violently. "Laura," I said.

"No!"

Tom shoved me out of the way. He peeled back her eyelids, checked her pulse, then immediately yelled for beach towels. Beach towels?

Men and women came running, their arms loaded down with colorful towels with parrots and leopards and bright suns on them. Tom covered her with a good half-dozen beach towels, wet down the end of one of them and spread it over her forehead. He sat back on his heels and said, "Bring me cold drinks, not the diet ones, the ones filled with sugar."

Someone slapped a Dr. Pepper into his hand. He peeled back the tab and said to me, "Hold up her head. We need to get this down her." I didn't think she'd take any, but she did. On some level she must have known she had to drink. "The sugar's really good for her," Tom said. "And she needs the liquid badly. Let's just keep getting it down her throat. We've got to keep her hydrated."

The beach crowd gave her some room.

"Where's that helicopter?" Tom called out as he poured more Dr. Pepper down Laura's throat.

"The lifeguard says another ten, fifteen minutes," someone yelled back.

The men and women seemed to have assigned themselves tasks. Some of them brought us drinks, others food, still others brought insect repellent and more beach towels. One woman wearing a thong bikini that was an eye-catcher dragged up a huge umbrella and positioned it so that Laura was well protected from the sun.

It seemed like an eternity had passed when — no more fluttering eyelids, no moans, no twitches — Laura just opened her eyes and looked straight up at me. She was dead white but her eyes were focused. She was back again. She smiled at me.

Tom gave her more Dr. Pepper.

"You're doing great, Laura," he said. "Just hang in there. Breathe slowly and lightly. Yes, that's it. Don't let yourself go under again. Okay?"

"Okay." It was her voice, frail and paper thin, but she was back.

"I can hear the helicopter," I said. "Don't leave me now, Laura. No more going back into the ether. It would really piss me off. I think Tom would freak out. Just smile at me every couple of minutes while you concentrate on breathing. I need reassurance. Okay?"

"I'm all right," she whispered. "It just hurts really bad, Mac, but I can deal with this. How's this for a smile?"

"It's the most beautiful smile I've ever seen. I'm sorry, but I don't have any more pain pills. Just squeeze my hand when it gets really bad."

When the helicopter landed some twenty yards away from us down the beach, I was nearly a basket case. Two men, each with a gurney slung over his back, and one woman carrying a black bag ran to us. For the first time, I began to really believe that Laura would make it. I wanted to cry with relief.

When the helicopter lifted off, I was

holding Laura's hand and one of the medics was sticking an IV into her arm, saying as he did so, his English beautifully deep and soothing, "It's just sugar and salt water. Nothing to worry about. The doctor said she's been drinking soda. This is even better."

"She's dehydrated," another medic said, a young woman wearing a Mets baseball cap backward on her head. She fit a plastic oxygen mask over Laura's nose and mouth. "Is she allergic to anything?"

I shook my head. "I don't know."

The woman said nothing, just nodded. "I'm going to give her an intravenous antibiotic called cefotetan. It's very rare that anyone's allergic to it." She added, slanting a look at me, "She your wife?"

"Not yet," I said. Another of the medics was checking Sherlock. The helicopter rose well above the treetops and we got a panoramic view of the rain forest. Dense, forbidding, so green you felt like you were growing mold just looking at it. Low, thick fog was hanging over parts of it, like a wispy gray veil. It looked mysterious, otherworldly. It didn't look like a place where human beings belonged. Far off to the southeast must have been where we ran into it to escape the helicopters shooting at us. The town of Dos Brazos was over there, I guessed, somewhere, and a few miles southwest was the compound and Molinas, the bastard, and his men who had balls but no discipline.

We'd survived. Odd to think that trams ran tourists through the rain forest, all snug and safe, hands holding cameras and soft drinks.

It was too difficult to be heard over all the noise of the rotors, so we just sat there, looking down at the huge stretch of rain forest that had been both prison and haven.

The woman paramedic lightly touched her hand to my shoulder. I leaned close. "We're going directly to San José," she said. "The *señorita* needs the best facility."

"How much longer?"

She shrugged. "Maybe an hour."

I took Laura's hand. She was still mumbling, still out of it. It was a very long hour.

I'd always wanted to visit Costa Rica, but not like this. Another five minutes and the helicopter set down in the parking lot of the Hospital San Juan de Dios.

There were medics with a gurney waiting. The last I saw of Laura was her long hair hanging off the side of the gurney

— tangled and damp from the cold wet towels they'd kept on her forehead — beautiful hair, I thought. Hell, I was in love. She could have been bald and I'd have admired the shine.

The woman medic turned, smiled, and said, "Go to the third floor as soon as they've checked you all out. She'll be in surgery there."

Sherlock took my arm and led me toward the emergency room. "We made it," she whispered. "Don't worry, Mac. Laura will be fine."

An hour later we'd been examined, cleaned up somewhat, but Savich and I still looked like wild men, with stubble on our faces, filthy, torn fatigues, and swollen insect bites covering our necks and the backs of our hands. As for Sherlock, she looked like Little Orphan Annie before she hit the big time, her red hair a wild nimbus around her head, her face pale where it wasn't covered with dirt, her clothes stiff with dried mud. I leaned down and kissed her cheek. She tasted like insect repellent.

But at least we looked human again, barely, and that was a good start.

I called Laura's boss, Richard Atherton, of the DEA. Savich set up a conference call with his boss, Jimmy Maitland, and

Carl Bardolino, my chief. We went over every detail of what had happened. It took at least an hour, some of it peppered with curses from Atherton. We agreed they would fill in our embassy and contact the local authorities to get us protection. They all wanted to come and bring agents with them. Bottom line, no one was going to take four federal agents and haul them off to another country and get away with it. They were arranging for an assault on the compound with the Costa Rican military. Edgerton was already covered with agents, searching for us, questioning everyone, turning the town upside down. I thought of my sister. I was worried and scared for her.

I listened as Sherlock and Savich called his parents and talked baby talk to their son.

Dr. Manual Salinas came to us in the waiting room and said in only slightly accented English, "You did very well. Two days in the rain forest with a bullet through her shoulder, I will tell you that I am surprised Ms. Bellamy survived. You took very good care of her. We went in and cleaned the wound. There was not any deep infection, which is a big relief. We were able to stitch the wound. She will be all right. She is still under the effects of the medication. You can see her in another hour or so." He shook my hand. "You did an excellent job, all of you. I would like her to remain here for another two days to be sure there are no complications. Then you may fly back to the United States."

I wanted to kiss him.

After assuring myself that Laura was going to be all right, I left with Sherlock and Savich to buy new clothes. Since we had no wallets, no ID, and not even a dollar bill among the three of us, we asked Dr. Salinas to lend us money. Once Savich and I had shaved and no longer looked like desperadoes, they let us into the stores. When we got back to the hospital, we all showered and changed in the doctors' locker room. Then we ate, wearing our new duds, and waited. Local police authorities arrived to question us and to provide protection, which made us all feel better, given the tenacity of Molinas's soldiers. They agreed to wait until representatives from the DEA and the FBI arrived. They seemed concerned and cooperative. One police lieutenant told us that he'd heard about an old army compound near Dos Brazos. He was surprised someone would try to use it for the drug trade into his country. They wouldn't get away with anything like that in Costa Rica.

The day seemed to last forever. Laura awoke briefly, but mostly slept. We all elected to stay at the hospital that night, at the urging of the six police officers there to protect us.

The next morning we were seated in Laura's room, speaking quietly since she was sleeping. I heard a man's voice but didn't look up. Then the hospital room door opened and Savich roared to his feet. "Good God, sir, am I glad to see you!"

Assistant Director Jimmy Maitland, Savich's boss, came into the hospital room like a tackle bursting through the line, grinning from ear to ear when he saw Sherlock and Savich.

"S and S, good to see you guys on your feet! I don't mind telling you though that I'm glad this sort of thing is mostly behind me." He hugged Sherlock tightly and shook hands with Savich.

Behind him was my own boss, Big Carl Bardolino. He was a man I'd walk over coals to work for, a man who was ferocious in his loyalty to his people, just as Jimmy Maitland was to his. Big Carl came in at just under six feet five inches and weighed a lithe two hundred pounds. I'd never yet seen an agent who could take him in the gym. "Sir," I said. "Welcome to Costa Rica."

"Good to see you in one piece this time, Mac."

Another man I'd never seen before walked over to Laura's bed. I knew he wasn't FBI. Funny, but I knew that immediately. I also knew that I wasn't going to like him.

"We met this fellow at the airport," Jimmy Maitland said. "He's DEA. We let him come with us because he's Laura Bellamy's boss, at least that's what he says. His name's Richard Atherton."

I looked him over. He was tall, thin, too well dressed for a Fed, very blond, and looked supercilious. He was wearing loafers with little tassels on them. I said to him, "I was not in Edgerton on assignment for the FBI. I was there on a personal matter, to help my sister. You were dead wrong."

"That's what you told me on the phone," Atherton said, looking at Big Carl. He ignored all of us and looked down at Laura a moment, then said to Savich, "I suppose you were there just to visit with him." He nodded in my direction.

"That's right. As I'm sure he told you,

someone tried to kill him. Sherlock and I don't like it when folks try to kill our friends."

A too-blond brow arched up. "You're Sherlock? You're the agent who took down the String Killer?" There was stark admiration in his voice, and Savich frowned.

Sherlock flinched and I knew she was remembering the drug-induced nightmares filled with Marlin Jones. Ignoring him, she addressed Big Carl and Maitland. "The local cops want to take out that compound as much as we do. Shall I tell them that you're here and ready to go?"

"It's okay, Sherlock," Maitland said. "We've already set things up."

"This is DEA business," Atherton said. "It's not in FBI jurisdiction. Anything you have to say, you say it to me first, not these guys."

"Are you always an asshole?" I asked him.

Atherton took a step toward me, looked uncertain, then stopped. I wanted him to take a shot at me, I really did, and so I added, "Laura said you were ambitious, but she didn't say you were an asshole. Surely that isn't a requirement for supervisors in the DEA?"

I heard Maitland cough behind his hand.

Atherton took a step toward me.

Savich took his forearm. "Don't do it," he said to him quietly, very close to his left ear. "Trust me on this, Atherton. It wouldn't be smart. We're both pretty pissed at your attitude. I suggest if you want to keep your nice capped teeth intact, you sit yourself down and listen. It's time for full cooperation. This isn't some sort of game. Look at Laura. She nearly died."

"Yeah, because she disobeyed my direct orders."

And that, I knew, was the truth. I said, "Yes, she did. As a matter of fact, we were all hot dogs, but believe me, we paid for it."

"You wrecked my operation."

"That remains to be seen," Maitland said. "We've got about a dozen FBI agents in Edgerton as we speak, turning over every rock."

"We were about to holler for help," Sherlock said. "We just didn't have time. They got us that very first night."

Maitland said, raising his huge hands, "What's done is done. Carl and I are used to S and S playing things too loose. We'll deal with that later. As for Mac, he wasn't there on the job but on personal business. We're all in Edgerton now tearing the

459

place down to the ground. If there's still anything there to tie Tarcher and Paul Bartlett to this drug operation, we'll find it."

Atherton stepped back from me, looked hard at Maitland, and sighed. "Well, hell. If there's a chance we can get anything on Del Cabrizo, I want to be there with you to find it. But I think they must have hit you guys so quickly to give themselves time to close down shop, to destroy evidence."

Maitland, always a diplomat, said, "If you can nail Del Cabrizo it would be quite a feather in the DEA's cap. We can use all the help we can get."

"As of right now," Big Carl said, "this is an interagency operation. All right with you, Atherton?"

Atherton nodded. He was looking at Laura, oxygen in her nose, an IV in her arm, lying there pale and silent. He walked over to her and lightly touched her shoulder. Maybe he really gave a damn about her.

Laura, her voice a thread of sound, said from the bed, "Please get Molinas. He tried to make us think he was so noble, trying to make his daughter well, but he isn't. He would have done anything to us. He wouldn't have cared if we died or just went crazy. He's as bad as Del Cabrizo." She blinked, closed her eyes, and turned her cheek into the hospital pillow.

Maitland stood up. "It's time for the FBI and the DEA to mount a joint operation. We'll all go down to this compound to see what's going on."

32

"Out with it, Mac. What happened?"

"Molinas is dead," I said to Laura. "It wasn't our side who killed him. Del Cabrizo's people arrived before we did and executed him."

"He was afraid of Del Cabrizo."

"He was right to be. Unfortunately, we didn't find Molinas's daughter. By the time we and the Costa Rican people got to the compound, it was deserted. The police burned it to the ground to prevent any possibility that it could ever be used again as a halfway point. They're going to patrol the airspace, too."

"Any word yet from Edgerton?"

"They searched the Tarcher house from top to bottom, and they're going through his business records. Nothing yet, no financial records to indicate anything concerning drugs.

"Paul's gone, everything in his house including his computer, gone as well. Tarcher says he doesn't have any idea what all this is about. They can't hold him, at least not yet. They're still looking for Jilly, too. But as of two hours ago, we've got nothing on anybody."

I helped Laura move herself higher on the pillow. "There, that's better. Now, what about Charlie Duck and the traces of the drug the M.E. found?"

"Tarcher said he hadn't any idea how Charlie Duck had gotten ahold of Paul's drug. Maybe Paul killed him, Tarcher said." I lightly kissed Laura's hand. Her skin was smooth and soft. Her fingers clasped mine. Her grip was stronger. "As you can imagine, the local sheriff, Maggie Sheffield, isn't a happy camper. She and Atherton are going at each other like two cocks after the same hen."

Laura laughed.

"Well, two dogs after the same bone. You get the idea. Since I got this from Atherton, he didn't quite phrase it like that, just complained that this cop in Edgerton was a pain in the butt."

"What are we going to do, Mac?"

I kissed her mouth and the tip of her

nose. I got her earlobe on the third kiss. "We're going to stay right here until you're well enough to travel. Then" — I drew a deep breath — "I've got to go back to Edgerton. I've got to find Jilly."

"Give me a couple more days, Mac. We'll go together."

Four days later, all four of us landed in Portland, Oregon. Sherlock and Savich wouldn't let us go alone.

Savich rented a Toyota Cressida and I rented a Ford Explorer at the airport. They remembered us from last time and gave us a distrustful look, but our original rental cars had been returned to the rental company, the repair bills paid, everything right and tight.

I laid back behind Savich's car, bright red and in-your-face, on the road to Edgerton. We pulled into Paul's driveway on Liverpool Street a little over an hour later. It was two o'clock in the afternoon, a Thursday, in early May. A thick wet fog hung over the coastline. Since Paul and Jilly's house wasn't even fifty feet from the ocean, the fog was thick, so thick I could barely see Savich's red car right in front of me. I ached all over in the dampness, a lingering present from my injuries in Tunisia,

I guessed. I wondered if this bone-deep damp made Laura's shoulder ache and pull.

There was no one around to see me pop the lock on the front door.

"It's not really breaking and entering," Savich said, providing me some cover as I broke in. "This is your sister's house, after all."

The house felt as cold and hollow as ever.

And empty. If Paul had left any notes or journals or equipment, the cops had taken it. I imagined that he'd taken everything.

"We might as well look," Laura said beside my elbow. "You never know."

Sherlock, humming, went off to the back of the house. I stood there quietly in the living room, wondering just where Paul would have hidden something he hadn't taken.

I turned slowly, taking in the modern art, the glass and furnishings, all cold whites and blacks that filled the long room. I still hated it.

Thirty minutes later I joined Savich upstairs in Paul's laboratory. Savich was looking through an empty closet, singing a country-and-western song under his breath.

I smiled as I carefully scanned the long

narrow room, looking, I suppose, for anything that might be out of place, or something that wasn't quite in the right place, like a seam in the wall. Anything that felt even slightly unusual to me.

Nothing.

Savich was singing about *Tommy breaking out of that hot, dark Mexican jail* . . .

He stuck his head out of the closet. "I even tapped around the walls. Nothing."

He rose, wiped his hands on his pants, and said, "Well, I say we go over to the Tarcher house and see how glad they are to see us."

I said, "This is probably off the wall, but once Maggie told me that Jilly was sleeping with Rob Morrison. Let's just go see if he knows anything."

Morrison's cottage was deserted, not even a car parked in front. No fresh tire tracks. The place looked like it had been empty for a good number of days.

Savich tried the front door. It was locked. Savich looked at me and said, "This is personal, Mac." He pulled out his small pick set and went to work. He couldn't get it open. "Interesting," he said.

"It is," Sherlock said, crowding in on him. "Why would you have a Fort Knox lock on a shack?"

"Good question."

I walked around the cottage to the large glass window behind the sink in the kitchen. I whistled as I gently broke the glass. Now this was breaking and entering, for sure.

I managed not to cut myself as I pulled myself in over the sink and jumped to the linoleum floor. The lock on the front door was elaborate, state of the art. It took a minute to figure out. Finally, I flipped three switches and opened the door for Savich and Sherlock.

"A guy lives here?" Sherlock said, looking around. "Alone? This place is as neat as ours, Dillon, just after Julie our housekeeper's been there."

"Morrison's got a housekeeper too, a retired Alaskan fisherman named Mr. Thorne. I've never met him, but he sure does good work."

We got to it. Twenty minutes later, we gathered in the living room, not a whit wiser than twenty minutes before. We'd found a file drawer that held his insurance papers, medical records, car repairs from three different mechanics, and a few odd letters from relatives, nothing interesting or informative. There were a few framed photos around, but the only one that made me stop cold was one of Jilly, set in a gold frame, facedown on the bedside table. She was standing on a cliff, smiling big, wearing a sundress and big sunglasses.

"The shed beside the house," Savich said. "I want to take a look in there."

The shed looked as old as the dirt it sat on, the wood rotting and smelling of damp, the door rickety. It was locked. Savich gave it a solid thump with his fist. The door shuddered off its hinges and fell inward. An ungodly odor slammed out at us.

"What is it, Dillon?" Sherlock was crowding him.

"Jesus," Savich said, turning slowly and taking her arms. "Stay back."

We hadn't found Jilly.

We'd found Rob Morrison.

33

I looked on as Maggie watched them put her lover into a body bag. Two men heaved the body bag up into the coroner's van and slammed the doors. She just stood there, watching the van disappear around a curve about half a mile away from Rob Morrison's cottage.

She'd looked only once at his body, her hand covering her nose and mouth, then walked away and said nothing to any of us for at least ten minutes. Then we'd waited for nearly an hour before the Salem coroner's office and forensic guy showed up, Detective Minton Castanga in charge. Until now, he'd said nothing at all to Maggie, done nothing more than greeted us.

It had started raining just as the coroner's van pulled away. Castanga motioned all of us into the house.

"Talk to me," he said, and sat down on Rob Morrison's sofa.

We told him everything, except we told him we broke into the house after finding the body.

Castanga scratched his chin with his pen and said, "Now, let me get this exactly straight. You federal people have been all over this town for nearly a week now, then you four came here expecting to find Mac's sister, Jilly. Or because Morrison might know where she is?"

"That's right," I said. Laura sat beside me, listing slightly to the left, against my shoulder.

"Do you have any idea who killed Rob Morrison?" He lifted a beautifully polished red apple from the full bowl on top of the coffee table, rubbed it on his jacket arm, and took a big bite.

"None of us know who killed Rob Morrison," I said. "None of us know anything about this. His murder must somehow be connected to the drug operation that's being investigated, but we have no direct knowledge of that. We were just looking around, saw the shed door hanging open, and checked it out. There was Morrison, dead." So the door hadn't been exactly open. I didn't think Castanga needed to know we were searching Morrison's property.

"Two gunshots in the middle of the back," Castanga said. "Someone wanted him gone and took care of it efficiently. It appears he's been dead for at least four days." Castanga put down the apple core on the polished coffee table, frowned, then gently set it atop the other apples. "Don't want to stain the wood," he said.

"You never cared about staining wood when we were married," Maggie Sheffield said.

"I was young and foolish then."

"Yeah, no more than thirty-five." Maggie stood.

Castanga said gently, "Maggie, I understand that you were seeing Rob Morrison. Hadn't you wondered where he was?"

She shrugged. The pain in her eyes was there for all to see. "He's not known for fidelity. When he didn't call me, I tried to get him a couple of times. Then I just stopped."

"We're really sorry, Maggie," Sherlock said.

"I am, too," I said. "He saved Jilly's life."

Maggie's chin went up. "Thanks. Now, I'm going to start interviewing to see what I can find out."

Castanga looked as if he'd object, then he just shrugged. "Go easy, Maggie, and be careful. I'm not being overprotective. People are in the habit of dying around here."

Maggie said, "Shit, I should have stayed in Eugene."

Castanga turned to Laura, who was still leaning against my shoulder. "Take care of her," he said to all of us. "She should be in bed."

Castanga closed his small notebook and shoved it inside his jacket. He rose, wiping his hands on his slacks. "Oh, yeah, not a clue as to who drugged you two. As you probably know, the DEA also slammed the lid down on our investigation. It wasn't going anywhere, anyway."

We had lunch at Grace's Deli on Fifth Avenue. I think Grace was the only person in Edgerton who was actually pleased to see us. She took one look at Laura, started patting her, and led her to a chair.

While she made us sandwiches, she talked nonstop about all the trouble. "Must have been thirty federal officers. They blanketed Edgerton, even tucked in the corners. No one could get in or out. They were everywhere, talking to everyone.

You know what?"

She handed Laura her tuna salad sandwich and answered her own question.

"No, of course you don't know anything. You poor people were down in a drug dealer's camp, being tortured."

"How did you know about that?" I asked and, unable to wait, took a big bite of my corned beef sandwich on rye.

"Everybody knows everything. There was a meeting of the BITEASS and we all talked about it. Isn't it something about that drug that Dr. Bartlett invented? And Rob Morrison, murdered because he knew about it and was going to turn those dealers in, whoever they are. Poor boy. Of course, Cotter Tarcher was telling everybody it was all ridiculous, that the drug just gave you great sex, and what was wrong with that?"

"Great sex," I said, shaking my head.

"I wonder," Laura said, "if there has been an increase in rape reports around here lately."

When we pulled into the Tarcher driveway, it was like an alarm went off. Laura straightened up, blinked, and insisted she felt wonderful and renewed after her tuna fish sandwich and nap.

"A five-minute nap."

"I'm a woman. I can do more on less."

Sherlock and Savich pulled up behind us in the driveway.

My knock brought an immediate response.

"Jesus, not you clowns again. What do you want?"

I smiled at Cotter Tarcher, who was blocking the front door, dressed like a thug in black jeans and a white T-shirt. He was even wearing black boots. He looked as dark as a night in hell, spoiling for a fight.

"Hi, Cotter," I said. "You remember Savich and Sherlock, don't you? And Ms. Scott? Sure you do. Savich and you caused a little ruckus."

He stepped back to slam the front door in my face. "I don't think so," I said. I slammed the door open, sending him onto his back, skidding across the black-and-white Italian marble floor.

"Control yourself, Cotter. We're here to speak to your parents. It's time for you to show some manners." I walked into the house, with Laura, Savich, and Sherlock right behind me. "You've really got to change that bad-boy image."

He started to get to his feet so he could come at me, but a woman's voice stopped him.

"No, Cotter, don't waste your energy on the federal agents. There are four of them and just one of you, although the women probably aren't that tough. I'm sure you could deal with the one wearing the sling. Don't forget, too, that they can always arrest you."

She turned to us. "I see you've come into my house without invitation. Since I do have some manners, quite good manners, you may stay for a while. You said that you wanted to speak to me?" At my nod, she waved her hand. "I suppose you will come into the living room. Goodness knows, we've had more federal agents trooping through the house, tearing everything apart, making huge messes and not bothering to clean them up."

Elaine Tarcher looked elegant in a pair of tight white jeans and a loose pale peach cashmere sweater. Her rich brown hair was tousled around her face, and she wore cream-colored ballet slippers on her feet. She led the way, not looking back to see whether or not we followed her.

"Poor Maggie," she said as she gracefully displayed herself on an elegant wing chair that looked at least two hundred years old. "Is she dreadfully distraught over Rob's death?"

"How did you find out so fast?" Sherlock asked, uncrossing her legs and sitting forward.

Elaine shrugged elegantly. "One hears things so quickly in Edgerton. Perhaps it was our postman who told our housekeeper who told me, just minutes ago. I can't be expected to remember everything."

"He didn't just die," I said. "Someone murdered him. Two shots in the back. They threw him in the shed and left him there. We found him by accident."

"Yes, I know. Rob wasn't at all faithful to Maggie, you know. It wasn't Maggie's fault. Actually, I've never known Rob to be faithful to any woman for longer than perhaps two and a half weeks, maximum."

I leaned back in my chair, a match to hers, my elbows resting on my thighs, hands clasped between my knees. "He was only faithful to you that long, Elaine?"

"I suppose there'll be an investigation," she said, giving me a sad smile. "It was two and a half weeks exactly. I'll tell you, I was very surprised when he patted my cheek one evening after we'd made love and told me he was moving on. He was speaking metaphorically, of course, since we were at his cottage and so I was the one who had to leave. It was always so clean, that precious little house, what with Mr. Thorne taking such good care of it. I never even questioned if the sheets were fresh. I knew they were." She sighed and dabbed a very pretty swatch of white handkerchief to her eyes. "Rob was such a lovely young man. I could be with him for hours, not saying anything, content to touch his beautiful body." She actually sighed again. "Such endurance he had. And he just got more and more devoted as time went on." She looked over at me through her lashes. "In matters of the flesh, I mean."

"Who did he move on to?" Savich asked. He'd remained standing behind Sherlock, who was sitting on a low blue brocade love seat, his hand lightly resting on her shoulder.

"To Maggie. I tried to tell her that he was a Teflon kind of guy, but she just laughed and said just because I was rich didn't mean Rob would stay with me."

"Mother, get rid of these creeps. Tell them to get out. They don't have a warrant. They have no power to make us do anything."

"Now, Cotter, there's no call to be rude," Elaine said. She looked at him like she really loved him, but she also let him see her parental disappointment. "You did learn manners and good breeding when you were growing up, remember? I don't know what happened to them though."

"You can take the boy out of the loony bin," Sherlock said, giving Cotter a small salute, "but you can't take the loony bin out of the boy."

I thought Cotter would leap on Sherlock, but then he saw Savich's face.

"I'm not crazy."

"No, of course you're not, dear. You're just high-strung, like I was when I was your age. I want you to keep yourself calm. Our guests are nearly ready to leave."

"Do you know anything about Rob Morrison's murder?" I asked him.

"Not a damned thing," Cotter said, his voice savage. "But no big loss. The bastard's dead. No one wants the prick now."

Savich said in that deep, calm voice of his, "I'm tired of your foul mouth, Cotter. You're an undisciplined boy in a man's body. You're offending me."

Cotter just stared at Savich for a long moment, then he took a step back.

"I can say whatever I want to, you fuckhead."

"That's quite enough," Elaine Tarcher

said, rising gracefully to her feet to face the man who was her son, and who was also certifiable. "You're not off in the woods with them somewhere, Cotter, you're here in the living room of my house."

To my wonder and relief, Cotter said in a calm, controlled voice, "I'm sorry, Mother. I don't want to make a mess in the living room. You have so many nice things in here." He'd made the right choice.

"Yes, dear. It's kind of you to remember. Go find your father now."

Cotter walked out through the elegant arch of the living room doorway. He turned and said, "Rob Morrison was a fool. He only wanted you for two and a half weeks, Mother. Was he blind? You're so beautiful the bastard should have been crawling to you. Rob was fucked up, crazy." Then he was gone.

"I apologize," Elaine said with a charming smile to all of us. "Cotter gets overstimulated sometimes. My mother was exactly the same way. I believe it's drinking too much coffee. He doesn't mean any harm. Now, are you all ready to leave? It's time, you know. I do have a lot to accomplish this afternoon."

Sherlock shuddered. Laura said, "Mrs. Tarcher, your son is very seriously disturbed. He's a sociopath. He needs professional help before he hurts someone or himself. Surely you see that?"

"She's right," Savich said. "He's dangerous, ma'am, and one of these days he won't back down."

"I'll deal with it if and when that day comes," she said. "He doesn't need a shrink. That's absurd. Actually, I believe he got himself involved with that terrible drug of Paul's. As soon as some time passes, I'm sure he will be all right again.

"I'd like you all to leave now. I've been very cooperative, but enough is enough. Why are you staring at me, Agent Savich?"

"You said your son was taking Paul's drug," Savich said, his hand still on Sherlock's shoulder.

"Yes, I'm afraid so. I'm not sure what it was, but he's seemed more aggressive, not always in control of himself."

"What we gave Cotter, my dear, was a simple tranquilizer that Paul recommended, nothing more." Alyssum Tarcher had entered the room speaking these words. He stood tall and imposing in tailored Italian slacks and a white shirt open at his throat. How much had he heard his wife spill?

He continued, "Well, if it isn't more fed-

480

eral agents, in my living room, threatening my wife and bullying my son. Poor Cotter is in a state. Now, I've had it with all of you. If you don't have a warrant, I want you out of here."

"Sir," I said to Alyssum Tarcher, "we came to ask you about Jilly. She's still missing. I'm very worried about her. Have you seen her? Do you know where she is?"

"We haven't seen Jilly since before her accident," he said.

"Do you think Jilly was taking Paul's drug?" Savich asked. "Do you think she was taking too much of it? That it made her mentally unstable and that's why she drove off the cliff?"

"I don't know what you're talking about. You are upsetting my wife."

Laura was hurting, I could tell, but she was controlling it well. She said, "Did you know that John Molinas was murdered in Costa Rica at a drug compound run by Del Cabrizo?"

"It was on the national news," Alyssum said slowly, one eye on his wife. She was sitting very still, her eyes on her ballet slippers. "Neither Elaine nor I have seen John in a very long time. We were saddened to hear of his death."

"Unfortunately, your niece is missing," Sherlock said.

"My brother loved his daughter very much," Elaine said, rising slowly to stand by her husband. "He wasn't a bad man."

"I want you to leave now," Alyssum Tarcher said. "I am innocent of any drug-trafficking charges, these horrible murders that you and your sister, Mr. MacDougal, seem to have brought to us. There is nothing for you here. I don't plan to fall apart and confess because there is nothing to confess. Get out now."

We were nearly to the front door when he said from behind us, "I'll be sending you a bill for the repairs I had to have done on Seagull Cottage. You left it in a mess."

He had wonderful gall.

"That was a good touch," Savich said as we left. "That man's something."

I turned to look back at the house. I saw Cotter staring at us through one of the upstairs windows. When he saw me looking up at him, the curtain fell back over the window. I knew exactly what the drug had done to him. But he'd probably loved it. Had his father taken the drug as well? His mother? I didn't think so. As for Cal, I'd probably never be certain one way or the other.

I felt empty. Coming here had been a waste of time. Jilly was gone and I had no idea now where to look.

"Let's spend the night in Salem at my condo," Laura said. "I want to see Grubster and Nolan. When I called the super from San José, he said they were eating well, but not happy that I was gone. It was very nice of Maggie to take them back home."

"Will they sleep with us?"

"It's a queen-size bed," Laura said. "There'll be room enough for all of us. Oh, yes, I've got a nice guest room for Sherlock and Savich."

I called Maggie Sheffield and told her where we'd be if anything happened to turn up, which I strongly doubted. So did she, but she was nice enough not to say so.

I fell asleep in Laura's very comfortable bed, at arm's length from Laura because Grubster had decided to purr the night away snuggled against her side.

I dreamed I saw headlights, bright and sharp, piercing through a dense fog that seemed to cover everything in a thick veil of white. But I could clearly see the road ahead. It was coming at me quickly, too quickly. I wanted to yell and smash down on the brakes, but I couldn't. If there were brakes, I didn't know where to find them. I wanted to get away from that highway that was moving so quickly, but I was helpless. I was trapped.

I couldn't draw a breath I was so afraid. Suddenly, I heard a soft keening sound from beside me. It was a woman moaning as if she hadn't anything left, as if there was nothing more for her and she knew it and accepted it.

I wanted us both to stop, but the road kept coming up through those bright headlights, faster and faster. I tried to tell her I was here with her, that I would help if I could. But she couldn't hear me.

I heard her speaking now, quietly. She was praying. I was nearly part of her in those moments when she prayed for forgiveness.

The road disappeared. I was thrown forward hard, but then everything seemed to fade away. We were flying out into the fog, sailing high, then dropping toward the water.

I was aware of immense pain slamming through me, a tremendous pressure against my chest that didn't really hurt but was just there. Then it too was gone. There was just an eerie sense of calm, of finality. So easy, I thought, it was so very easy. I smiled at the gentleness of it, smiled even as everything simply went black, and I felt nothing at all.

The four of us stood together on the cliff, looking out over the water. It didn't take long. A man in scuba gear split the surface of the water and yelled, "She's down here!"

I'd known Jilly would be.

Another man came up beside him. He called out, "There are two cars down there, next to each other. There's a white Porsche and the one she's in looks like a rental car."

Epilogue

Washington, D.C.
Three Months Later

"Squawk."

"Keep your feathers on, Nolan." I dumped a pile of sunflower seeds in my palm and reached inside his cage.

"Squawk."

"Here you go."

Grubster rubbed against my bare leg. "Yep, you're next, fella."

You'd look at Grubster and believe he'd eat anything that didn't move out of his path he was so big, but it wasn't true. Grubster ate only gourmet cat food. That had started the day we'd all moved into a new town house in Georgetown.

"He thinks he's upscale now," Laura had said. "It's his statement of self-worth."

I put a slice of bread into the toaster and got out the can opener. I forked out an entire can of salmon and rice into Grubster's big white bowl, with a smiling cat face on the bottom, petted his back, rubbed his ears, and listened to him purr as he chowed down.

"Squawk."

I waved a hot slice of toast until it cooled and broke off small pieces for Nolan.

"Everyone happy now?"

There was blessed silence.

It was Saturday morning, already warm and promising to be hot by noon, and Laura was still asleep. I was about to go back to bed to kiss her awake when the doorbell rang.

"Just a minute," I called out and went into the bedroom to pull on a pair of jeans.

"A registered letter. Are you Mr. MacDougal?"

I nodded. "Who is it from?"

"It's from Oregon, that's all I know."

I don't know what I expected, but this wasn't it. It was a short note from a lawyer in Salem, Oregon, telling me only that my sister wished this to be mailed to me exactly three months after her death had been confirmed.

My hand shook as I smoothed out the pages.

My dearest Ford:

I wonder if you will be with me tonight. If so, you will know what it is I have done. I am so sorry to cause you this pain, but I will be grateful if you are there with me.

How can I begin? At the beginning, I suppose. Paul and I had such great hopes for my brainchild. I managed to bond a neurotransmitter involved with memory to an opiate, and was surprised when the compound proved stable. We thought we would accomplish so much with it when it seemed not to be toxic and had such pro-found effects in our laboratory. We thought we'd found a key to how memory works, and maybe sexual drive, too. But no matter what we tried, we couldn't control it or pre-dict its effects well enough, and the bastards at VioTech pulled the plug on us.

Actually, Ford, they pulled the plug be-cause both Paul and I had tried the drug ourselves, and they found out about it. It was the stupidest thing I've ever done. It was so wonderful at first. The sex was simply incredible. By the time we left VioTech, I was badly hooked. Paul was al-ways afraid of it, even though he loved what it did to his sex drive, and so he kept his doses in check, and it saved him.

But we had to be able to make more of it

by then, and I wanted to keep trying to alter the drug, or control it better. We approached Cotter Tarcher in Edgerton, whom Paul knew well enough to think he'd be interested. After Cotter tried the drug, he was willing to help talk his parents into supporting us. Cotter thought he would get rich beyond his dreams. We didn't know his uncle, John Molinas, was a drug distributor, and that Cotter'd tell him about us. Nor did we know that he'd bring that big drug lord in on it — Del Cabrizo.

We didn't make any progress, and I got worse. The drug just took over. It still has control. I'm not proud of what I've done in the last six months, Ford, the men I've been with, including Del Cabrizo. When Del Cabrizo had Molinas tell us Laura was DEA, it turned me completely psychotic. She was inside my head, tormenting me, and I couldn't stand it. I tried to kill myself so that I would be killing her, too.

And then you arrived. You were such a comfort to me. I left the hospital because Cotter called to warn me that Del Cabrizo knew that you'd found Laura, and he was threatening to kill both of you. I don't know how he found out, but he did. I was so afraid for you. There was nothing else I could do, so I left the hospital and went into hiding. I stayed with Rob Morrison for a little while, another man I'm not proud to say was my lover. Because Rob crossed them by hiding me for just that first night, they killed him.

Del Cabrizo needed me to make progress on the drug, you see, and it became a sort of standoff. I told them I'd keep working on the drug if they didn't kill you. But I couldn't stop them from taking you. They promised not to kill you if I helped them clear out all the evidence and move the operation to a cabin outside Spokane. They wanted me to get back to work once we moved everything to Spokane out of sight.

They also killed Charlie Duck, an old man who just dug and dug once he suspected what was going on. I told Molinas I was afraid of what he'd found out and that he'd talk. With those words, I signed his death warrant. Del Cabrizo sent some goons to his house to search for anything he'd written down about what he'd found out. Paul told me that they'd forced a lot of the drug down him, then killed him when he tried to break away.

I'm so sorry about what they did to you, Ford. Please forgive me. I heard about your escape. Good for you. My brother the cop, *you were always my hero.*

I've been responsible for so much death and pain. It's all my fault.

As you know, I got away from them. But they've still got Paul. I know you can track him down if you want to, but they will kill him in a heartbeat if you do. Let him live. He can't help them. He just doesn't know enough. Please, let him live.

I wanted you to know what happened so you could put me away, maybe tuck me in the back of your mind as at least a bitter-sweet memory. No matter what I was, what I became, I loved you, Ford.

By the way, you should get together with Laura. She's perfect for you.

Good-bye, my dearest. Jilly

I slowly folded the pages and eased them back into the envelope. I lit a fire in the fireplace. When it was going strong, I gently placed the envelope on top of the flames.

I sat on my haunches and watched as it burned. I didn't move until it was completely gone.

"Mac? It's got to be ninety degrees in here. You lit a fire?"

I rose slowly and walked to my wife. I hugged her tightly against me. "Would you believe that I found an old photo of me hugging a girlfriend just like this and I burned it before you saw it and got jealous?"

"Squawk."

"Nolan believes me."

"Sure, Mac," she said. I knew she didn't understand, but she was willing to accept that I didn't want to explain.

I hugged her for a very long time.

The employees of Thorndike Press hope you have enjoyed this Large Print book. All our Large Print titles are designed for easy reading, and all our books are made to last. Other Thorndike Press Large Print books are available at your library, through selected bookstores, or directly from us.

For information about titles, please call:

(800) 257-5157

To share your comments, please write:

Publisher
Thorndike Press
P.O. Box 159
Thorndike, Maine 04986